He pressed a kiss to her ear, circling the shell with his tongue, following it with a breath.

All over, her skin tightened. He murmured encouragement and lifted her wrists to his mouth. On first one and then the other, he kissed the spot where the pulse throbbed. "The heart of my beloved beats here. It is a precious spot."

He kissed between her breasts, kissed her stomach, her thighs, the arch of her foot. Turning her over, he kissed the delicate skin behind her knee, the curve of each buttock, the base of her spine. "The heart of my beloved beats here. It is a precious spot."

In each place, she found it was true.

CHRISTINA DODD

Treasure Of The Sun

AVON

An Imprint of HarperCollinsPublishers

This is a work of fiction. Names, characters, places, and incidents are products of the author's imagination or are used fictitiously and are not to be construed as real. Any resemblance to actual events, locales, organizations, or persons, living or dead, is entirely coincidental.

AVON BOOKS
An Imprint of HarperCollins*Publishers*
10 East 53rd Street
New York, New York 10022-5299

Copyright © 1991 by Christina Dodd
ISBN 978-0-06-104062-7
www.avonromance.com

First Avon Books paperback printing: December 2010
First HarperPaperbacks printing: September 1991

Avon Trademark Reg. U.S. Pat. Off. and in Other Countries,
Marca Registrada, Hecho en U.S.A.
HarperCollins® is a registered trademark of HarperCollins Publishers.

Printed in the U.S.A.

10 9 8 7 6 5 4

For my mother
Who taught me everything about bravery and perseverance,
and blessed me with more self-confidence
than any one person deserves.
Thank you.

AUTHOR'S NOTE

There was never at any time an attempt by the missionaries in California to settle the interior. The mission and the treasure are the author's inventions.

19 May, in the year of our Lord, 1777

We were not able to defend ourselves, and the mission, rich though it was, has fallen to the Indians. Every day we pray and tremble, every night we move a little closer to Mission san Antonio de Padua and the coast of California. I fear the Indians know our whereabouts with some certainty, and that we will not be able to evade them much longer. Therefore, I dip pen in ink to leave a record for my brothers in Christ, to tell them of the history of the gold.

—from the diary of Fray Juan Estévan de Bautista

Chapter 1

California 1846

Frozen in battle, the bull and the man eyed each other.

"Toro, toro." Borne on the wind, the sound of the man's voice wafted to Katherine, as sweet as if he called a lover, deep, low and coaxing.

Against the twelve-hundred pounds of belligerence, Damian de la Sola stood armed with a red cape: velvet, with fine embroidery and a shredded hem. The whipcord strength of his shoulders strained against the seams of his smudged white shirt. He stood, one tanned hand on his hip, as if the bull were insignificant, not worthy of his consideration. Katherine noted the hand, dark, capable. She noted the hip, and heat brought a flush to her cheek.

He was well formed—beautifully formed.

He cracked the cape held tightly in the other hand.

She jumped; the lack of reality wrapped her round. The drama in the corral possessed her. She stood as silent and as intense as any who sat in the stands. The sun of midday almost blinded her. The restless California wind stirred the dust in the corral, and the scent drifted to her nostrils. It mingled with the stronger smell of the bull, crafty, aware, almost too clever for the man who faced death—taunted death.

The cape cracked again. The bull exploded from standstill to a full gallop. He flew at Damian, who barely moved to let the animal by. The bull passed beneath his arm with inches to spare. As if she stood inside the corral, Katherine felt the brush of death on the sensitive skin of her arm. She felt the pounding of the earth beneath her feet.

The combatants froze, evaluating each other with new appreciation.

Katherine loosened the top button of her dress. Despite the mild March temperature, sweat trickled down her back and tickled her forehead; dust devils swirled, but not a creature moved. She didn't understand what made her so warm.

It couldn't be anxiety. She was Katherine Chamberlain Maxwell of Boston, and she was a sensible woman. She understood that when a man chose such a hazardous pursuit, the consequences were his own responsibility. So it couldn't be anxiety that made her clutch the wooden rail so tightly splinters dug into her palm.

In the stands, the señoras' fans drifted to and fro as they tried to cool their faces and their excitement. The rustle of their fans blended with the snap of the cape, but Damian paid them no heed; nor did Katherine. She focused all her attention on the beast and the warrior.

She had seen this bull before, many times. He was a prize stud. The warm, rich brown of his coat reminded Katherine of cocoa, of the thick sweet mud of springtime between her toes. His nose looked velvety. His eyelashes made a pretty fringed arc on his face.

She had seen Damian before, many times. The beauty of his pure, classical bone structure reminded her of a Greek god. His high forehead was swept clear by the wind that caressed him. Below the ridge of his brow, his eyes were set deep, lending him a scholarly thoughtfulness. His nose was long and noble. Well-defined cheekbones revealed sensitivity; his square jaw revealed determination. His was the face of civilization, of poetry, of philosophy.

But it was an illusion. It was all an illusion.

The bull was a competitor, a fighter by instinct and a gladiator by chance.

The man was a conqueror, intent on proving his superiority in primitive conflict.

The crowd sighed, and Katherine heard a first hushed call. _"Olé, torero. Olé!"_ It sounded like encouragement of the brutal sport, but she couldn't tear her eyes from the corral to frown her disapproval. Staring fixedly at Damian, she saw him stomp his foot. She heard the small sound of provocation, saw the little puff of dust it raised and how it spooked the beast.

"Olé! Show us your colors, my son!"

That did make her glance aside. Damian's father held a fist to the sky, proud as the devil, proud of his son.

"Stupid," she said, disgusted with Don Lucian, with the bullfight, with the whole barbaric display. Her comment was whisked away on the wind.

As if Don Lucian's encouragement released them from restraint, everyone erupted in the blast of cheering. The women came to their feet, the men surged forward, and from every throat roared, _"Olé. Olé, torero!"_

The bull responded with arrogance. His ears pointed skyward. His head swayed to the rhythm of the cheers as he studied Damian and the tattered cape. Walking in a circle, the bull acknowledged the crowd, then came to a stop facing his opponent. His eyes fixed on the gold metal gleaming around Damian's neck. His head lowered.

The razor-sharp horns reached for Damian, for his stomach, his chest, but Damian never retreated. With flicks of the cape, he lured the beast in. He evaded him by a hairbreadth. The bull made a swift running turn and raced back.

Damian stood there, prepared, disdainful. His passes were precise. He stayed tuned to the moods of the beast, not hearing the screams of the crowd, moving the cape with the sweeping sensuous dance of the bull.

The game was horrible and graceful and free. Katherine could see the beauty, but more than that, she could smell danger. Watching Damian's straight back, his small, confident smile as he turned his head, she wanted to leap into the corral and stop the nonsense.

The bull leaped and whirled, coming straight at Damian and not at the distraction he waved. Damian laughed, tossed the cape aside, and waited.

Katherine wanted to cover her face with her hands, but she couldn't move. All was silent; no fans fluttered. Damian reached over with his hands. Slowly, yet in a blur of speed, he grasped the horns. The bull lifted his head. Damian tucked and somersaulted over the broad back. Landing on his feet beside the astonished animal, he raised his hands high and bowed.

The air exploded into pandemonium. Women screamed, men bellowed. Four vaqueros vaulted over the fence and dashed toward the bull. Confused by the disappearance of his prime target, he charged at them zealously. The cowboys darted around, working in teams until the beast entered the gate and dashed down the chute to the pasture.

An auxiliary part of Katherine's mind sighed with relief. She just couldn't loosen the grip of apprehension from her body. Her breath still caught, her fingers still clutched; all her concentration riveted on Damian. She looked, feeding eagerly on the beauty that underlay his brown skin, the hint of black beard on his chin, the mustache that defined his upper lip.

Then he swung that face on her.

He observed her attention, her admiration, her surprise.

Echoing the moment when the bull had rushed at him and he'd tossed the cape away, he laughed, softly at first, with personal satisfaction. Then flinging his head back, he laughed out loud.

She wanted to glance around, see if any of the Californios noticed. She couldn't. She couldn't tear her eyes from the exultant man.

Like the brightness of the sun and the endless wind, his pleasure made her uncomfortable. He measured her. Measured her responsiveness, measured the life that returned to her in a rush.

It had been almost a year since she'd been aware: of her body, her surroundings, her self. A numbness had protected her from the vicissitudes she couldn't face. Now life rushed into her mind, and it hurt. It hurt like blood rushing into frozen limbs.

Someone jolted her, and she jerked from Damian's spell. She glared at the boy who had smacked her from behind, but he climbed through the fence. All about, humanity moved and cheered. Men leaped the rails, women stood on the benches. Children danced, heedless of the dust that rose at their feet. Everyone called Damian's name.

She looked for Damian, but men surrounded him in the corral, clapping and whistling, making clear their approbation of his magnificent feat. Then he rose on their shoulders, teetering as all hands sought to carry him. He laughed again, but it was a pleased and public laugh. They carried him around the ring, and without a glance, he passed the spot where she stood.

An odd mood possessed her, as if she'd stepped into a timeless world for a moment. Now she'd returned, and she was out of place.

That wasn't unusual, though. She was always out of place.

The tingling in her hand demanded her attention. It still clutched the rough wood railing with all its strength, and it required a moment of willpower to loosen her grip. The palm and the pads of her fingers shone white. One by one, she straightened her fingers, and a thousand needles pricked at her from beneath her skin. Blood oozed around one large splinter at the base of her thumb.

"What did you think of that, Doña Katerina?"

She lifted her gaze from her hand and stared at Damian's father. She had no time to dissemble, to gather her composure and be the steady, reliable pragmatist she knew herself to be.

When her voice projected normally, she was pleased. "Quite unusual. Is that the way all bullfights proceed?"

Don Lucian de la Sola smiled. "Never. Never have I seen a torero who fought with such courage." Taking her cramped hand in his, he massaged it and watched as the cheering crowd passed Damian a boda bag filled with wine. "Of course, he is my son."

"The guests seem to agree that he fought bravely." Katherine smiled at the elderly gentleman who had guided her through this foreign society and taught her its ways.

"The bull is very dangerous, even more than you can imagine."

"I found I could imagine quite a lot," she said with exasperation.

"A woman's fantasy." He chuckled and patted her hand. "I should have known. You're a sensitive woman."

"I am?" Astonished by such a misreading of her character, she covered her annoyance. "The word is sensible."

"Of course. Of course. I thought you were concerned about the fate of my son."

"Yes, I was concerned. He's been my employer for almost a year," she said primly.

"Quite so." His fingers pressed on the splinter and when she started, he looked at her palm. He squinted and patted his coat. "I don't have my reading glasses with me." He carried her palm as far away from his face as he could and focused. "Tsk, tsk. You mustn't let this fester."

"I'll take it out," she assured him. "I have a medical kit in my room."

"And where did you get that?"

She smiled at his astonishment. "I brought it from Boston. I had no idea what I'd find here in the wilds of California."

He snorted in disparagement. "Is it as wild as you suspected?"

She looked out over the seething corral. "In some ways."

"That's not what you were supposed to say," he reproved

with mock seriousness. "You were supposed to reassure me that my Rancho Donoso is the equal of your Boston, and that you love it here."

A smile broke across her face at his droll reproof. "I do love it here, and California isn't the equal of Boston, it's better. It's clean and bright and new. When the United States annexes this land, it will be the best country they've ever acquired."

"Don't tell Damian that," he commanded.

"Why? Doesn't he want the United States to annex California? As a sovereign, Mexico has done it no good."

"Damian would have agreed with you once." With old-world courtesy, he tucked her good hand into his arm and strolled with her toward the hacienda.

The previous four days of fiesta had furthered Katherine's acquaintance with the Californios. Seeking the cool of the shade trees, everyone would assemble on the grass eventually. Only the few who sought to escape the stifling crowd at the corral already clustered on the benches. The others would trickle back, demanding refreshment.

In a thoughtful voice, Don Lucian remembered, "Two years ago, he urged annexation on Señor Larkin."

Her mind elsewhere, Katherine asked, "Who?"

"The American consul. Damian urged annexation on anyone who would listen to him. Now an American threatens to take Damian's land when it comes under the jurisdiction of the United States, and Damian fears for the rights of Californios under the new law."

She chewed her lip and frowned. "My uncle is a lawyer, my father was a lawyer, and I know a bit about the law. Land title transfers from one jurisdiction to another can be awkward, but I believe the United States will be fair in its decisions."

"Explain that to Mr. Emerson Smith. He's a vulture, waiting to pluck the heritage of my son from his grasp."

"Mr. Smith? Isn't he that tall man with the face like a gravestone?"

Don Lucian nodded. "The one who looks like he escaped from the circus."

The lack of kindness in the remark and the snap in his voice startled her. "Why is he here at this fiesta if Don Damian dislikes him?"

"We welcome everyone. It is our way."

"Yes," she said, stopping and facing him. "I've noticed, and I'm indebted."

"I wasn't speaking of you." His face mellowed and his eyes warmed. "You're family."

"Thank you again." The words seemed inadequate, superficial, yet she didn't know how to express the gratitude she felt. In Boston, she'd been taught she was a burden, a responsibility to be endured. These people, these Californios, had no sense of place and rank, taking friends and strangers to their bosom indiscriminately. And for her, the regard had been warmer, sweeter, gentler. Stumbling to express herself, afraid she would offend, she said in a low voice, "You've behaved as if I were the prodigal daughter, returned from my travels."

Don Lucian moved closer and put his arm around her shoulders. "You are the daughter I've never had."

She looked up at him. "No one seems to realize I'm only the housekeeper. The other servants aid me with respect. The guests insist on treating me as if I were an honored friend."

"Then we're happy." He paused just inside the edge of shade, close to the trunk of the tree. "Let me take you to Doña Xaviera Medina. She'll surely have the implements to take care of your splinter, and you'll not have to leave the fiesta."

"I couldn't."

"Nonsense." She stepped back, but he turned to the matron who sat on a bench and fanned herself so negligently. "Doña Xaviera, could you help our little friend?"

The lady was dressed in a large black tent designed to conceal her ample contours and let the air cool her. She ruled the fiesta like a queen, or like the unofficial hostess, which she seemed to be. She took the hand Don Lucian thrust at her and examined it. In a smooth, languid move, she pulled a two-inch hat pin from behind her ear and flicked it beneath the skin of Katherine's palm. The splinter disappeared with only a bit of pain, but the blood welled up and Katherine sat beside Doña Xaviera in a sudden display of weak knees.

"Our little friend is not as brave as she'd like you to think," Doña Xaviera observed, grasping Katherine's neck and shoving it down.

"It would seem not."

Don Lucian moved to block the view of her weakness from the other ladies, and Katherine concentrated on controlling her queasiness, turning her face sideways, gulping great breaths of air. She let her hands dangle beside her feet. The wind helped, and the massage of Doña Xaviera's beefy hand on her shoulders. When she felt well enough to sit up, she pushed against the hand and it fell away. She leaned back against the tree trunk with a sigh, and her hair tumbled around her arms. "Ah, Señora Medina," she complained. "Not you, too."

"You bind your hair so tightly, it must rob you of your circulation," the señora said in simulated reproof. "You should leave it down. It draws the eye like a river of gold."

Katherine tried not to show her exasperation. These dark-haired aristocrats were fascinated with her blond hair. No matter how diligently she pinned it, no matter how expansive the headgear that covered it, when she encountered a group of men or women, her hair always ended up around her arms and her pins disappeared onto the floor.

It had become a game, she suspected, one that began when her hair slipped loose and ended when she blushed. They'd found she blushed easily. They'd found that she was unused to compliments. They'd found it a combination too irresistible to ignore.

The women observed benevolently while the men complimented her on her eyes. The green of the sea at sunrise, one said. The still serenity of a mountain pool, said another.

They complimented her on her skin. Like the golden kiss of the sun, said one. Warmed by the sweet sprinkle of freckles, agreed another.

And everyone, men, women and children, commented with admiration on her figure. Of little more than average height in Boston, here she stood out among the shorter, plumper Spanish women. They made her feel as if her long arms and coltish legs were fluid as a ballet dancer's. It astonished her to find how avidly she had begun to listen to the plaudits—and how much she wanted to believe them. Yet she found herself at a loss to deal with their informality. She couldn't understand how they could dismantle her coiffure and stroke it with their fingers while maintaining a civilized demeanor.

"Why don't you wear the lace mantilla I gave you?" Doña Xaviera asked. "It's black, but it's romantic and feminine."

In stern reproof, Katherine replied, "That's why I never wear it."

Her response brought nothing but a husky laugh and a kind pat on the cheek. "The time will come when you wish to flirt, to smile, to put off the worn black dresses. Your year of mourning is almost over."

"I'm aware of that, señora," Katherine agreed stiffly.

"The gentlemen who so admire your beauty will soon be released from the constraint of propriety and flock to your side." Señora Medina passed her fan in front of her face with lazy assurance. "Your creamy skin will glow from beneath the black lace. Keep the mantilla."

"Yes, señora." Katherine didn't trust herself to move, to reach up and bind her hair without another fainting spell, so she looked at Doña Xaviera without turning her head. "Thank you for helping me," she said. "I can't stand the sight of blood."

"Poor child." Doña Xaviera touched her arm. "No wonder."

Wanting to change the subject, not wanting to dwell on the

memory of her grief, Katherine offered, "I have never seen any-thing like this before."

"This?"

"This fiesta. I would think half of California has come."

"The other half sent their regrets," Doña Xaviera agreed.

"In Boston," Katherine waved an arm, "we have nothing to compare to this."

"How boring you Americans are," Doña Xaviera said with indulgent humor.

Katherine gave it some thought. A melange of parties and feasts, games and displays, the fiesta celebrated Damian's feast day. The tradition of celebrating the eldest son's feast day was a custom brought from the old world. The feeling of tradition, of an unbroken chain that reached back into the mists of time thrilled her, and she agreed, "Yes, I suppose we are dull. At my uncle's table, there were only Americans. Here there are the Spaniards whose families settled California seventy-five years ago. There are Americans, who come to California to trade. There are Russians, Germans, and Englishmen."

With a calm authority, Doña Xaviera claimed, "You like it here."

"Very much."

"Good. That will make your life so much easier."

Doña Xaviera chuckled, a deep, soft sound, and Katherine raised an eyebrow. She hadn't meant to amuse, yet her inbred reserve made it impossible for her to question such a venerable lady. Instead, she asked, "All the other men who fought bulls did so on horseback. Why did Don Damian dismount?"

Don Lucian shook his head. "To give this old man some grey hairs."

Señora Medina protested, "Not you, Lucian. Your hair is a distinguished silver."

He smiled at her but spoke to Katherine. "In Spain and Mex-ico, they fight the bull on foot, and in the end, when the bull is wise—"

"Wise?" Katherine raised the other eyebrow.

"The bull improved. Couldn't you tell?"

"I thought so, but how could a stupid animal know?"

Appalled, Don Lucian raised a finger to stop her. "Bulls are not stupid. They're powerful and wily and courageous, an opponent worthy of a man. A bull is only fought once. Only once, for they realize the cape is illusion and they never make the mistake of attacking it again. In Spain, in Mexico, when this happens the torero takes a sword and kills the bull. Here in California, we're not so foolish. Our cattle are our lives, our most precious resource. We fight the bull on horseback, to give our men some small advantage against the dynamic, clever beast."

Doña Xaviera sighed. "Your son had to make a show."

"His woman was watching." Startled, Katherine looked around, expecting to see this woman, but Don Lucian continued, "He acts like a peacock faced with a chance to display himself."

"Where did he learn to jump the bull?" the older woman asked. "I tell you, Lucian, my heart stopped when he stood while the bull rushed him."

"I taught him." Lucian shrugged at her horrified moue. "My family has practiced it time out of mind. But only in the dark of night, for fear our wives would catch us."

Xaviera nodded with serene amusement.

"And with heifers. God knows, they're tricky enough. When he faced that bull and I realized . . ." He shoved his hands in the pockets of his short jacket. "I hope he lives through the courting."

"Ah, he will." The lady opened her fan and began a languid waving before her face. "I believe he has his dear one's attention at last."

"Absolutely. I'll be interested to observe the courtship ritual. It promises to be unusual."

Katherine felt rather like a china doll: on display but easily ignored. She took the time to look around, to see if she could discover this woman Damian courted with such intensity.

Only one señorita was a stranger. A tall girl, young and shy, hovered behind Doña Xaviera, and Katherine felt sure this must be the candidate for Damian's hand. Masses of blue-black hair streamed down her back, seeming to be too great a weight for the delicate neck. Her shoulders were rounded, like the shoulders of a girl who'd outgrown her contemporaries and slumped to make up the difference. Her pale skin was untouched by the blazing California sun. Her eyelids quivered shyly as Katherine surveyed her with a forthright gaze, and her birdlike hands fluttered.

"Vietta." Doña Xaviera noticed her and called her forth. "How good to see you here. Are you over your illness?"

The girl Vietta limped over, listing to one side in obvious distress. Katherine felt a great compassion, and an admiration for Damian. What a noble man, to love a girl so handicapped by birth or misfortune!

"Doña Xaviera." Vietta acknowledged her greeting, and when she spoke her voice chimed like mission bells. "I'm feeling better, *gracias*, and I couldn't stay away from Damian . . . from his celebration one more day."

Doña Xaviera slid to one side of the bench in invitation, but Vietta ignored her, moving closer to Katherine. She wasn't as young as she appeared from a distance, Katherine realized. Her eyes burned with some kind of fervor, and tiny lines emphasized her frown. Her turned-down mouth gave her a pinched look of petulance, but there was, too, such an obvious intelligence that Katherine felt an immediate kinship.

Katherine waited until Doña Xaviera performed the courtesies. "Katherine, this is Vietta Gregorio, the daughter of one of our oldest and most noble families. Until her family moved to Monterey, she was a neighbor of the de la Solas. Remember, Lucian, how she used to trail around after Damian and Julio and try to do whatever they did?"

"Indeed I do," he said.

Katherine gave a little seated bow, murmuring, *"Tengo mucho gusto en conocerla."*

Doña Xaviera continued, "Vietta, this is Katherine Maxwell."

"You're in mourning," Vietta interrupted, with abrupt disrespect for her manners and the señora.

This was not what Katherine had come to expect from the Californios, with their never-ending courtesies and their kindness, but she answered mildly, "Yes, I'm a widow."

"Recent?"

"Vietta!" Doña Xaviera admonished.

"It's all right," Katherine soothed, and then replied to Vietta, "Less than a year."

"Why are you here?"

Ah, Katherine reasoned. That explains it. She's jealous, unsure of Damian, and Katherine thought to reassure her. "I'm Don Damian's housekeeper. I make sure the house is run efficiently during the time he's away, so when he comes back, he'll be comfortable."

"He's here almost all the time."

"I assure you, he isn't."

"This is his favorite hacienda."

Katherine smiled, but with restraint. "I've seen no evidence of that."

Vietta tapped her nervous fingers on her waist. "He's always here."

Katherine couldn't help the stab of hurt that came with Vietta's insistence. She'd devoted herself to making this house welcoming, prepared at all times for Damian's infrequent visits. Holding in the embarrassment, she replied, "After he settled me here, he left for his rancho in the Central Valley. He visited infrequently, and I saw him for the evening meals. During the days, he rode with his vaqueros or ordered the stocking of the barns."

"That's all?"

"He hardly wiped his boots on the veranda."

"Then why did he hire *you?*" Vietta said. "You're an outsider, an Americana, and we all know what Damian thinks of Americanos."

"Ah, child." Doña Xaviera groaned, but Don Lucian set Vietta in her place.

"He hired her for her charm." He smiled and bowed, took Katherine's hand and led her away.

"Poor girl," Katherine murmured as they walked. "How was she crippled?"

"They say she took a fall . . . let's see, last August, while resting in the mountains. In my opinion, she needs to rest her tongue."

Surprised at the anger in his voice, Katherine stopped him with her hand on his arm. "Why do you say? . . . Oh, her rudeness. Don Lucian, she spoke Spanish so rapidly, I had trouble following all she said. As to why she said it, you must pay no attention. She's young, and afraid she can't hold her man."

"Young?" He snorted. "She's older than you."

"Surely not," she said mildly. "I'm twenty-four. Quite the old woman."

"Vietta's much older than you. And she hasn't got a man, no man will have her. She's too . . . too . . ."

"Intelligent?"

"I would have said cranky, but yes, she's intelligent, too. Far too intelligent for her own good."

"That's what men always say about women who are less decorative than clever."

He raised her hand in his and pressed his lips to the back. "Lucky for you, you are both."

Amused, she smiled at him. "*Gracias.* You are ever the gentleman."

"And you are ever the sleeping beauty."

* * *

Katherine lay on the feather bed and stared at the ceiling. The night air cooled rapidly, bringing a chill temperature to the third-story attic bedroom. The wind blew the curtains, and she knew she should rise and shut the window, but she was tired with the kind of bone weariness that hard work brings.

Unfortunately, that weariness couldn't shut down her mind. The apprehensions she'd kept at bay during the day leaped about her head now, and she seemed to have no control.

Visions of Damian: vaulting the bull, raising his hands in revel. Visions of Damian: looking like a god, staring into her eyes.

He was handsome.

It had taken her this long to notice. She'd been in a state of shock for too long, and she blamed that for her lack of attention. That, and the fact that she wasn't used to seeking beauty in the swarthy complexions and dark eyes of the Spaniards. Today she'd noticed Damian, and it had been an upheaval that jarred her to her roots.

She'd regained control of herself immediately, of course. A lady of Boston never betrayed her emotions by word or deed. When she glimpsed Damian later, moving among his guests, speaking to Vietta, she'd been able to admire him as one would a statue, or any work of art.

But now, tonight, it wasn't so easy.

He'd laughed at her. Why had he laughed at her?

Two weeks ago, he'd returned to prepare for his birthday fiesta. He'd stayed at the house and she'd seen how intimately he'd been involved with his servants, his family. She admired a man who knew what he wanted and how to get it. He handled people with a finely honed instinct she valued, soothing tempers, easing mistakes, making every person an important cog in the planning and execution.

Sometimes she wondered why he never extended his charm and his skill to her, but she was an honest woman.

She was an outsider. Damian had done what was honorable

to care for her, and no more. The smile he gave to his aging, toothless nanny, he would never waste on Katherine Chamberlain Maxwell. The hugs he handed out to the Indian children, he would never extend to Katherine Anne. He treated her differently because she was different, and she'd do well to keep it in mind.

A gust of wind blew out her candle, and she jumped at the sudden darkness. A black night, the clouds raced past on the breeze and a tiny moon peeked in and out timidly. Restless, she turned on her side and tucked her hand under her cheek. With a little willpower, she could block these thoughts of Damian and his enigmatic actions and go to sleep. She'd never had trouble sleeping before last year; she was too sensible for such nonsense.

So sleep, she commanded herself, and dream of anything but Damian.

She dropped into sleep like a rock into a well, a long, dark descent.

Rain wet her face. Fog obstructed her vision. She knelt in the dirt of the street.

She could hear the roar of the ocean muted by distance. She could hear people, murmuring around her, and a woman screaming. She could really hear it. She was there.

She could smell the horse feces under her knee, but it couldn't mask that other smell. The smell of blood.

She could see him. Face up, he lay in the mud, his mouth open, his jaw cocked askew. She couldn't see his features well. They were obscured by fog and a great rhythmic spurting of blood. A woman's hands pushed against his throat, trying to hold the blood inside. The hands jerked with each stream that gushed out.

The sound of the waves seemed to be the sound of that blood, but the blood stopped, and the waves did not.

Those hands lifted away, and they were her hands. She turned them over and over, and she could feel it. All that blood, so slippery. All that blood, so sticky. She didn't want to wash it away, because it was his.

And then she couldn't wash it away. It wouldn't come off.

Blood seeped in so deep she could taste it.

21 May, in the year of our Lord, 1777

*The Indians who roam the mountains of the interior
and live in the great central valley are wild and savage.
Our mission was established to convert them to the true
Christ and bring salvation to their souls. I led the mission,
for God had planted the idea in my mind. I am a strong
man, healthy, determined, and well trained in the arts of
medicine. Among the Franciscan brothers in California, I
am considered to be the ablest curandero. The grace of
God sends healing through my fingers, and only the poorest
wretches are beyond my help. Fray Amadis speaks the
Indian's heathen language. Like our Lord Jesus, Fray
Patricio is a carpenter. Luis Miguel, Joaquin de Cordoba,
Lorenzo Infante: they all performed their special purpose.
Frail as he is, Fray Lucio begged to come, also, and Pedro
de Jesus convinced me to bring him.*

*Now only four of us remain: Amadis, Patricio, Lucio
and I.*

—from the diary of Fray Juan Estévan de Bautista

Chapter 2

Katherine groped down the stairs through the dark with her wool cape clutched tight around her. Feeling her way along the hall to the door, she knew when she'd found Damian's study; she smelled the smoky cigar scent that permeated the room. Slipping through the open door, she breathed that warm, sweet odor, and she began to relax.

She didn't like cigars; she thought they were extravagant and messy, but the smell of these particular cigars symbolized safety to her. Reaching into the darkness, she stretched until her fingertips grazed the desk. With one finger on the whorled edge, she inched along until she could see the French doors, their windows lighter than the rest of the wall. She knew that outside hung the second-story balcony. That was where she wanted to be.

In two big, careful steps she was against the doors. Her hand scrabbled for the knob; she turned it and pushed. As she expected, the wind rushed into the gap, trying to tear the door from her grasp. She eased it open and stepped out. In the moonlight, California spread out before her. Clouds scuttled across the sky, passing dark bands over the narrow, flat valley of the Salinas River.

She shut her nightmares in the house behind her and leaned her elbows on the rail. She inhaled a deep, shuddery breath. That terror, that remembrance hadn't come to her in a long time. She had hoped it would never come back again. What had happened a year ago had changed her life, destroyed her aspirations. Aunt Narcissa's prediction of disaster had been correct; how that woman would have enjoyed knowing.

From behind her she heard the click of the latch, and she whirled around. Damian shut the door behind him and came to rest his arms beside hers on the rail, a smoky scent about him. He, too, stared out at Rancho Donoso, at the Salinas River, a mere trickle of silver, and at the plain hemmed in by mountains on either side. "Can't sleep, Katherine?"

He spoke English, as he always did on those rare occasions they were alone. His voice tolled deep and kind, exactly like the controlled Damian she'd always known. No trace of the magnificent warrior of the afternoon lingered.

"How did you know?"

"I confess to sitting in my study and watching you go past."

"In the dark?" That made her uncomfortable. "What were you doing?"

"Thinking."

That made her even more uncomfortable.

"I'm grateful there've been no fights between the Valverdes and the del Reals boys. Usually I'm breaking up one fight after another the whole fiesta."

She relaxed. "Why aren't they fighting this time?"

A wry amusement colored his tone. "I'm keeping everyone thoroughly entertained. What keeps you from sleeping?" He was nothing but a voice beside her, and he sounded odd, strained. "Tell me," he coaxed.

"I dreamed about Tobias."

"Well." He coughed a little. "That puts me in my place."

He sounded so diverted, she didn't wonder what he meant. She just knew she could talk to him; he was the only other person she remembered being there in the street with her. "I dreamed about the blood."

He sobered. "Ah, my dear." His hand covered hers, and she found she had clasped both her hands together in one tight fist.

"I keep thinking if I'd been nearer to him, it wouldn't have happened."

"If you'd been nearer to him, you'd probably be dead, too."

"At least I could have seen who did it."

He stood silent. Then he asked, as someone who'd asked many times before, "You didn't see anyone?"

"It was dark and raining."

"It was night," he corrected, "but it wasn't raining. There was a moon, and enough illumination from the lights of the houses to see."

"It was raining! There was water all over."

"Tears and blood."

"I could hardly see him."

"You were hysterical. You were screaming. My God, you were screaming. I came back because of your screaming." For a moment, his calm logic gave way to horror, and he squeezed her hands tight. Mastering himself, as he always did, he continued, "I found you kneeling in the mud, trying to staunch the blood from his throat. A great crowd of people had gathered, and you cursed them. You cursed the smell, you cursed the noise, you even cursed the ocean. You said it was making the blood spurt faster."

"Then the blood stopped spurting."

"How can you remember all that and not remember who did it?"

She lifted her hands to her forehead and rubbed it as if she could polish the information out of her brain. "As you've just pointed out, what I do recall, I don't recall correctly."

His hand slashed the air. "You remember the chain of events perfectly. You left my home—"

"—after the wedding reception you gave us. It had been one week since I'd disembarked in Monterey. You and Tobias had greeted me."

"Only one week." He sighed as if he couldn't believe it.

"You arranged for us to be married in an English ceremony

right away. You stood up with us and you loaned us your home while you stayed at the Medinas' so we could be alone."

"Yes."

He sounded grim, but she ignored that, lost in memories of the happiest time of her life. "You arranged the reception for us at your house. After the guests left, you and Tobias teased me into going to the cantana for a late supper. You went on ahead to arrange the meal. I stopped to speak to Señora Medina. Tobias waited for me, but the señora told him she'd bring me when we'd finished talking, and he went on ahead."

"You're a trusting soul, you know." Standing up straight, he reached into his pocket and pulled out one of the long, thin cigars. He rolled it between his fingers and sniffed it with a connoisseur's appreciation. "You come here with me after your husband is killed with no thought to the facts. It could have been I who slashed his throat."

He sounded sharply critical, but she said, "No." She said it with complete certainty. "It wasn't you."

Placing the cigar in his mouth, he brought forth a wooden lucifer and pulled it through the abrasive paper. A shower of sparks, the noxious odor of rotten eggs, and the stick blazed. "I don't look like the attacker?"

"I didn't see the attacker," she insisted, watching his eyes in the brief glare as he ignited his cigar, then shook out the flame. "Señora Medina left me at the corner. I could see Tobias, his shiny domed head before me, crossing the street." She examined the scene in her mind and turned to him. Smoke drifted about them, the cigar clutched between his fingers. The clouds had whisked away from the moon, and a feeble light illuminated his face. With earnest candor, she put her hands on his shoulders. "I always knew I could trust you, even when I couldn't think. You weren't nearby when he was killed, and I was. You didn't know me at all." Her fingers gripped him; they trembled. "Perhaps I'm the one who slashed his throat."

She wasted her candor. His mouth turned down on one side

and he struggled to keep a straight face. "No. For several reasons, no. If you could have seen yourself that week . . . you glowed. Your hair gleamed like living sunshine, your eyes changed with your every mood. Green when you argued, blue with your happiness, a lazy gray when you were sleepy. Men were falling like fools at your feet, and you never even noticed."

"Were they?" she asked, charmed.

"How like a woman to ask!" His voice lowered, deepened. "And how unusual for you to act like a woman."

"What else have I been acting like?"

He stuck his cigar in his mouth with decision. "Like someone encased in cotton wool, unaware of events around her yet doing her duty without conscious thought."

She took her hands from him as if he burned to the touch. "You've been watching me."

Indecision chased across his face. Taking his cigar from between his teeth, he examined the glowing end as if it were quite fascinating. When he answered, his voice sounded light and indifferent. "How could I be watching you? I haven't been here."

She didn't answer. He was right, of course, but something about the way he stood made her uncomfortable again. In the past year, he'd been kind, but distant; caring, but disinterested. He'd allowed her to find her own feet, only taking time to teach her enough Spanish to communicate with his servants before leaving her alone in the house.

She had been, it must be confessed, relieved. In the shock following Tobias's death, she'd done as Damian had told her with no thought to the future. But as shock had worn off, leaving greater awareness, she'd realized Don Damian de la Sola's position.

He was not some elderly philanthropist. His age matched Tobias's. At thirty-one, Tobias had been older than she, but she'd been twenty-two on the day she'd accepted his proposal. So Damian was of an age to attract her, and that thought alone frightened her. Like a child providing a distraction, she argued, "I could have contrived his death somehow."

"You'd have had to be the finest actress God ever created. However, there's another part to slitting someone's throat. Tobias was my best friend, and he wasn't stupid. He wasn't a big man, but his hands contained a workman's strength. How could someone have gotten close enough to slit his throat?"

"What do you mean?"

"There are so many strangers moving into California. Some of them have an unsavory past. Tobias knew that. He was wary, but you don't slit a man's throat in the midst of a crowd."

She winced, awash again in the memory of blood. Panic lurked not far away, and she rubbed her hands up and down her arms in sudden chill.

Damian didn't seem to see, remembering his friend's acute mind and searching for an answer to the puzzle. "He must have believed the killer presented no danger to him—and the knife must have been very sharp."

"He was robbed!"

"His wallet was gone," he corrected. "Only his wallet. Not his watch, not his rings. Tobias wasn't a rich man. Why would the thief take his wallet when the gold of his jewelry represented so much more sure money?"

"I don't know."

"And to slit his throat. That takes skill. At the time, I thought perhaps a farm hand or a rancher was guilty. Someone with experience with the slaughter of cattle." He turned away from her, placed his elbows down on the rail again, stared out at the view.

Butchered like a steer. The comparison made her ill. Butchered like a dumb animal with no choice. A pleasant man, a decisive man, a man who loved children and puzzles and telling a good tale. A man who never met a stranger, who inspired her with enough confidence to join him on his travels and be his wife.

Who could take a man's life coldly, methodically, without concern? Who could so disguise himself that Tobias never suspected the ice in his veins? Her hand crept up to her mouth as sickness assailed her, and she couldn't repress a shudder.

Yet this pain had come to her before. She mastered it, as before. She knew, in her sensible, well-ordered soul, that such a reaction reeked of indulgence. She knew fainting at the sight of blood showed weakness, and that the dreams that haunted her should be suppressed. She had never raged or screamed or shown openly emotional signs of grief. To do so would be weakness . . . but why, after almost a year, was she still so affected?

Lost in his own futile anger, Damian didn't notice anything but her silence, and he tried to explain further. "Everyone I found who knew of such ways of death had an alibi. I've done everything I could to find his murderer, and I've found nothing."

His despair bit through the fog of misery surrounding her. Seeing his hunched shoulders, she knew a moment of kinship. He suffered, too, from the death of his *compadre*, and he suffered in a different manner than she did. He was the *patron*, the lord of his lands, of his people. He held himself accountable for the well-being of all who depended on him. Like an umbrella, that deep sense of responsibility protected his family and his friends.

Whether or not he should, he held himself liable for her heavy heart. He held himself accountable for the unavenged justice in the death of Tobias. His compassion touched her, his dejection gave her the courage to speak. With light fingers, she touched his hand. "I'm grateful."

"What?"

He sounded bewildered, and she sought to explain. "I'm grateful. I'm grateful to you for your search for Tobias's killer. I'm grateful for all you've done for me."

"Grateful?"

His voice rasped, but she plunged on, afraid to stop for fear she'd lose her nerve. "I'd be a heedless boor if I never said it. No other person would have been as kind as you've been. To take me into your home, give me a position, pay me well." As she catalogued his indulgences, her voice thickened and quavered. She lowered her head, tears trembling on her lashes. "If there's ever anything I could do to repay you in any way . . ."

"No." Flinging the cigar to the deck, he crushed it beneath his heel.

"What?"

"No. I never want to be paid back." He stood straight and proud, his shoulders stiff, his chest thrust out. He looked as he had when facing the horns of the bull, but she didn't understand why. "Everything I did, I did for Tobias. It had nothing to do with you. Nothing."

Swinging on his heel, he marched to the door and jerked it open. The wind caught it, slamming it back against the hacienda with a crash. Katherine cringed, but he never stopped to see the damage. He left in silence, and she stared after him, wondering at the outraged pride of the man.

The riders thundered down the track, controlling their glowing palomino horses with verve and skill. Katherine sat alone on the top step of the porch and hugged her knees, thrilled in spite of herself. The hidalgos were centurions all, bred to the saddle from birth. Their minds and bodies were dedicated to racing. The señoras screamed with excitement, breaking their fans on the shaded benches as the men streaked past. They called the names of their husbands, their sons, their friends, as their flashing eyes and exuberant gestures displayed their pleasure.

There was a great deal of laughter when Don Julio de Casillas beat Damian by a nose, and Katherine smiled tentatively towards Don Lucian as he mounted the stairs to join her. "I don't understand what's so funny."

Don Lucian seated himself on the end of a bench and lit one of his cigars. "Damian claimed he lost because he was a good host and let Julio win."

"Oh." She stared at the shouting crowd around the riders, avoiding his eyes. "That's not correct?"

"Neither Julio nor Damian ever consider manners when given a chance to surpass the other," he assured her. "Did you enjoy the races?"

"Yes. They were . . . exciting, in an odd sort of way."

"We'll make a Californio of you yet."

"It's a unique experience for me. In Boston, women are never allowed to attend such an entertainment. In Boston, the men have all the fun." She bestowed on him a prissy smile.

"There you are, Doña Katherina." He touched her cheek. "I thought you must be angry with me. You refused to look at me."

She should have realized that he would notice. Normally she wasn't such a coward. Normally, she looked everyone right in the eye, but she felt a constraint today. A constraint that had its origins this morning, when the servants had cleaned up the broken pane of glass on Damian's patio. Not a word had been spoken, and she'd wondered at the lack of questions and comments. What could she say to Don Lucian? A social lie won out, and she said, "I broke a window last night."

He puffed on his cigar. "Yes, I heard you . . . break it."

From inside the cradle of her arms, she asked, "Who else heard?"

"The hacienda's grapevine is swift and sure," he said obliquely.

"Everyone knows?" She'd wondered if there were ever any secrets in such a large house, and she'd wondered how many of the guests knew Damian had spoken harshly to his house-keeper.

Don Lucian patted her shoulder. "Don't distress yourself. It's not sensible."

Was he mocking her? Her head snapped up and she examined his face, but he was watching the events below. "Look!" He gave a shout of mirth and stood up. "Damian's trying to fight Julio."

Distracted, she stood also, squinting through the afternoon

sunlight. Two figures danced around each other, one dressed all in black, one a rainbow of brilliant colors. "Why, Don Damian's trying to smash that man's face in."

"You seem so shocked. Didn't you think Damian was a man?"

He sounded so superior, so amused, she lifted her chin. Ignoring that inner voice that reminded her she'd noticed exactly how much of a man Damian was, just yesterday, she sniffed. "Indeed? Is that how you judge a man? By his abilities with his fists?"

"I judge my son to be a man because he uses his fists only on those capable of defending themselves. He only displays his talents for those capable of appreciating them, and he only courts the woman he loves."

With stiff dignity, she said, "The fighting gentlemen seem to have been separated by their friends. What are those stable hands doing now?" She indicated the boys running out to the track, one lugging a cage full of roosters, the other holding a shovel.

Don Lucian accepted the change of subject without a qualm. "A rooster is buried up to its neck in sand in the middle of the race track. Young caballeros race past and snatch the rooster out of the ground by its head."

Katherine winced. The rooster soon looked somewhat the worse for wear. Another rooster was shoved into a hole, another youth charged at it, leaning so far out of his saddle he rode the side of his horse. She covered her eyes and over the fervent cheering, she said, "Perhaps you won't make a Californian out of me." She heard a shout, a thump, and a groan so loud it shook the air.

"You'll excuse me." Dropping his cigar onto the step, Don Lucian ground it out with his heel. "Young Guillermo just broke his arm."

Katherine rose with him. "You'll excuse me. I'll send for the *curandero* and prepare a bed."

Don Lucian waved an acknowledgement and leapt off the porch with a vitality that belied his age.

The servants, prepared for just such an emergency, assumed responsibility with hardly a nod to Katherine's authority, and she was secretly grateful to be relieved of the chore. As she left the patient's bedroom, she heard Guillermo's uncle tell the father, "Your little boy is gone forever. He is a grown man, now."

"How brave," gushed the beribboned girl who kept vigil in the hall.

Katherine didn't think Guillermo was brave, she thought he was stupid. This break wouldn't heal well, and he would be pained with it for the rest of his life. Rheumatism would settle in it, and every cold day he would remember the time he fell off his horse and hit the ground so hard his bone snapped.

Out loud she said, "See, Don Lucian? I'll never be a Californio."

"*Perdón*, Señora Maxwell?" A serving girl looked around the hallway for the person to whom Katherine spoke. Her puzzlement at seeing no one made Katherine acutely uncomfortable.

"Nothing, *nada*," she said.

The girl shrugged, used to the peculiarities of her mistress. "Leocadia says that all the wine chosen before the fiesta has been finished, and you must speak to Don Damian. He needs to select more, and you carry the keys."

"Now?" Katherine asked, horrified.

"*Si*. With all the excitement, the guests are thirsty. They drink to the return of spring, they drink to Guillermo, they drink to . . . to anything. We need the wine now."

"Of course, I'll get it." In a moment, she thought, as she hurried away. First she needed to brace herself for the impact of Damian. Stepping out onto the porch, she took several deep breaths. She couldn't see him, and she was glad. She should want to get the job done at once, but her own mortification kept her cringing on the porch. If she were daring, she'd search him out. If she were daring, she'd face a scene like the one last night with aplomb. If she were daring, she'd demand an explanation for his extraordinary behavior.

She wasn't daring. She hated scenes. She was a coward.

She watched the crowd until she spied Cabeza Medina and hailed him. The sixteen-year-old came running to stand on the step below her, a grin on his handsome face. "You want me, Señora Maxwell?" He flirted with his eyes, giving his question unsuitable connotations.

Starting at the tips of his deerskin boots and ending on the fringe of his gold-trimmed sombrero, she surveyed the young man. Her survey failed to dent his conceit, and he posed for her. She scowled at him. "I need a favor, if you please."

"My heart is in your hands." He placed his hand in the starched ruffles of his shirt and bowed slightly.

His slurred speech, his open flirtation engendered in her a suspicion. "Have you been drinking wine?" She stepped aside, avoiding his hand as he snatched at her black cap.

"*Si*, señora. Don't you approve of drinking wine, either?" Her maneuver was unsuccessful; he snatched the mob cap and stuck it in his pocket.

"Not in such a young man," she said. "What do you mean, 'either'?"

He swayed close to her, and the sweet smell of the grape fanned her face. "*Madre* says you don't approve of any of us."

Slapping at his fingers as they went pursuing her hair pins, she complained, "I don't know what you mean."

Cabeza leaned back on the step and almost overbalanced. Katherine grabbed him by the lapel and stood him upright. The boy didn't seem to notice, preferring to explain, "You never come out to dance with us. You don't wear the lace mantilla my mother gave you. You frown at us all the time." He peered at her. "Like now."

"I certainly do not! Ladies never frown." She frowned harder. "I like you all very much. I do not believe in making friendships that must be broken when I leave here."

"Leave here?" Distracted, the young man stared at her in astonishment. "This is your home."

"No, strictly speaking, my home is in Boston, in the United States of America. I'm a stranger here. I speak your language with an accent."

"No, no, no." He sighed.

"I have different customs, different ways."

"Charming and old-fashioned."

"I must leave here," she concluded.

"Leave?" He seemed to be stuck on the word. "You can't leave."

"I assure you I can leave when I choose."

"Haven't we made you welcome? Haven't we become your family?"

Cabeza seemed insulted, and she hastened to affirm, "Indeed, everyone has been most generous, most kind. But you must admit I'm out of place here. I'm like a blackbird in a nest of cardinals and finches." And chattering magpies, she added to herself, but she wouldn't for the world hurt Cabeza's feelings by saying so.

He crooned, "Your golden hair alone, señora, earns you a place among the most beautiful birds in the world. We call you Sunrise." He peered at her slyly. "Didn't you know?"

"What nonsense," she said with brisk decision. "I know what I am. I own a mirror."

"I suspect, señora, that your mirror is distorted." He sounded sure of himself, rather amused by her bluntness. "One day soon you'll learn the right of it."

Katherine controlled her annoyance at being chided by such a young man. "I've been saving the generous salary Don Damian has paid me this last year. I've almost earned enough to support myself for an extended period of time. I'll be gone soon."

"Does Don Damian know about this?"

"We've never spoken of it, no, but I'm sure he realizes I can't stay here in his hacienda forever," she answered. More than that, she realized he wanted her gone. He wanted her gone, and she had worked to that end. "But this is of no moment. I wish you to take a message to him. I need to see him at once. I'll wait for him in the library. Can you tell him that?"

"For you, señora, I can do anything." He bowed deeply and staggered. He walked backwards, eyeing her with the masculine eye of a young roué, and mumbled, "You've been saving for passage home. This explains why you hide that magnificent figure behind those old mourning clothes."

Katherine whirled on her heel. Her hair tumbled down, her pins scattered on the tile floor by Cabeza's inquisitive fingers. Slipping into the dim room they called the library, she sat on the fainting couch, and pulled her hair over her shoulder. With her fingers she combed and braided it. Prepared for the inevitable loss of her pins, she pulled a ribbon out of her apron and secured the ends.

It made her uncomfortable to realize there had been speculation about the way she dressed. It distressed her to realize there was motivation to the gift of clothing she had received. She wished Tobias were here; he'd tell her how to handle this situation. Reaching into the pocket at her side, she pulled out the massive watch that had been Tobias's. She smoothed her hand over the gold and silver decorations on the cover. It was a work of art and her dearest remembrance of her husband.

Tobias had been a watchmaker, a hardheaded Swiss who had come first to Massachusetts to ply his trade. Restless, he'd moved on to California, drawn by the lure of new lands, new legends, new explorations. That had been one of the things that had drawn her to him—that mix of total practicality and impossible visions.

Sometimes, before Tobias had died, she had dreamed impossible things. A dream had drawn her to California. A dream had grown with her wedding, blossomed during the short week of her marriage. And all the dreams had withered in the blood in the street.

It was time to go away, to leave her friends in this warm, golden land and find a new place. The dream was dead.

She popped the catch on the watch and the cover sprang open. Music filled the air, and she smiled. Such an unusual song for her pragmatic Swiss to build into his watch. "Bonnie Barbara Allen," with its tragedy of lost love and the tune that brought tears to her eyes. In her pure voice she sang softly,

> He was laid to rest in the lower chancel,
> Barbara Allen all in the higher;
> There grew up a rose from Barbara Allen's breast,
> And from his a briar.
>
> And they grew and they grew to the very church-top,
> Until they could grow no higher,
> And twisted and twined in a true-lover's knot. . . .

A prickle on the back of her neck brought her to her feet. She swept the room with an anxious look and saw only the dark drapes, the heavy furniture, the small dim branch of candles. She looked again, and saw him.

His black coat and trousers blended with the curtains, his face was a dark blur. Like last night, they were alone, but this was different. Today his eyes glittered, alive in a way she'd never seen before, and the upward slant of his eyebrows seemed pronounced and demonic.

"Don Damian," she stammered, uncomfortably aware that he'd been observing her as she braided her hair and sang. She tucked the watch in her pocket. "I didn't hear you come in."

He took the step forward that brought him to her side.

Too close. She stammered, wishing he looked less like an apparition of night, wishing he would remove his mesmerizing gaze from her face.

Hurriedly, she said, "I asked for you to say—"

He picked up her hand and put it to his mouth. "Say nothing, Catriona," he whispered. "We will speak our words in other ways."

The warmth of his lips shocked her. His gesture shocked her. And the small nip of his teeth against the pad of her thumb made her jump, made her tug at her hand.

Catriona? Who was Catriona? "Oh, Don Damian. You've made a mistake."

His other hand reached out to her mouth and he covered it. They stood like matching statues: hand to mouth, mouth to hand. "Catriona, it's you who've made a mistake."

Chapter 3

There was no doubt; anger held Damian in its grip. He repeated, "Say nothing." His mouth slid up to her wrist, and he pressed his lips there against the thundering pulse. She felt his breath as he murmured, "Or I'll find another way to seal your lips."

She stood frozen to the floor. He slid his mouth up her arm to her elbow, and she cursed the open sleeves she wore.

His mustache brushed the tender skin at the inside of her elbow, his tongue tasted her, and that was too much. She objected, "Don Damian! I must tell you—"

He'd been waiting for her words. His hand encircled her shoulder; he pulled at her, wanting her against him.

She planted her feet, determined to resist, but for the first time she discovered how Damian towered over her. She discovered he could jerk her up on her toes with one hand at her waist; she discovered when his fingers cupped the back of her head she couldn't move it.

She discovered his muscles in the press of his body from her chest to her knees.

She didn't like this.

She didn't like the way he overwhelmed her good sense with pure intimidation. She didn't like the scent of him, of tobacco and brandy and mint, or the strength of his body emphasized next to the vulnerability of hers, or the sight of his face so close against hers.

She didn't like the patience he exhibited as she looked and clutched, or the way the frozen parts of her body tingled at the thought of tasting him.

She didn't know what to do. She'd never dared to dream of such an experience. His lips were too close; only a fool would open her mouth to remonstrate. Yet the patience she noted still lurked there, a faint smile, then the whisper, "Catriona."

She forgot her wisdom. "I'm not—"

He swooped on her, as she'd known he would.

He tasted as smoky as she suspected. He wielded his tongue like a weapon in a siege while she fought him. She decided, unemotionally, to go limp.

He bent her over his arm, tucked her head in his shoulder, and kissed her until she kissed him back. The world became a place of total darkness, untouched by any color, yet whirling all her senses into a pool of pleasure. It worked like a drug, changed her from plain Katherine Anne to a creature of the senses.

Her hands lifted to his hair and clutched at it. It slid silky between her fingers, and she twisted it like a rope to hold his head close to hers. She liked the texture of it; she wanted to massage it with the flat of her palm, but she feared to release her hold. She feared he'd remove his mouth.

Craving flowed from his mouth to hers, a craving that tightened the muscles of her stomach. Then solace came, a teasing morsel for her appetite. Then craving again, stronger this time, building on her previous desire, carrying her up, bringing her body to rigid attention.

This time he didn't feed her. He left her wanting, tearing his mouth from hers. With his thumb on her jaw, he tilted her head back. His lips pressed against the hollow of her neck; she struggled and cried out. She was sensitive there. No one ever touched her there. This man used his tongue and his intoxicating breath, and the sensation wasn't ticklish. It wasn't laughter she felt, but a surge of pure heat to her body.

How could such a kiss radiate from her face, her neck, extend down her limbs? How could it seek and find the center of her body? A sound struggled to escape her, a release of emotion such as she'd never imagined she'd desire.

She suppressed it, but he seemed to know. She could feel his emotion vibrating in his arms. She could feel it lifting her off her toes. Then her body was laid on the fainting couch.

A crafty movement, done by a master. Done slowly enough that she wasn't alarmed by the perception of falling, yet quickly enough that she knew what was happening and was alarmed—alarmed by the message he transmitted.

With a sigh, she lifted her heavy eyelids and gazed on him. His thin face revealed harsh satisfaction. "Catriona, do you understand what this means?"

She said nothing, mute with emotions she'd never imagined.

"Do you understand?" he insisted. "You'll never go away from me now. I've been biding my time, waiting for you. Listen. Do you hear what I'm saying?"

Oh, she heard. She was his, to do with as he liked. She couldn't move unless he allowed it; she couldn't call out or it earned her a kiss. She couldn't refuse his passion, for his passion reduced her intelligence to less than a whisper.

Never taking his eyes from hers, he lifted his knee and pushed it between her thighs.

"Do you understand?" he whispered.

It was too much. For her body, chaste too long; for her dignity, tattered as her dress.

"Understand this!" She jerked back, then forward, bashing him under the chin with her head. Her blow didn't land as it should, for he'd been watching her too closely and read her intentions. But it gave her a chance.

He cursed and caught at her.

The wiry child she'd been had learned her lessons well. In her fights with her cousins, she'd been defeated many times, but only when all four of the boys and both girls had jumped her at once. This fight against one man was almost even when he couldn't wield his most potent weapon—her own sensuality.

One of her fists tapped his Adam's apple before he leapt back. One fist twisted in his shirt collar. If his knee hadn't been so firmly tucked between her legs, she would have had the use of her whole body. The knee held her skirt; the skirt held her waist. She dragged herself to one side, then the other.

He captured one flailing wrist. "Catriona. Hellcat! How many times I have called you that in my mind!"

He captured the other hand; she lifted herself in one giant convulsive effort, one huge bid for freedom. She heard the rip and gasped in dismay.

He heard the rip and smiled a slow and wicked smile. "A new dress, my Catriona. You must have a new dress now."

Bound by a torn dress that would tear more if she moved, secured by her hands in his hands, she cried, "Don Damian! You must listen!"

His white teeth flashed. "Tomorrow I can listen."

"Listen," she urged again, and he lifted his head.

"Don Damian!" The call came from outside the patio door. "Don Damian, you must come. We've run out of wine."

"Only two more days to go." Katherine comforted the servants as she helped them carry the platters of fruit, cheese, and empanadas out of the kitchen and toward the empty banquet tables under the trees.

"Two more days and we can start cleaning up," Leocadia said with a pucker of her lips. "That will take days and days and days and days." And to the others, "Space those plates evenly, you fools!"

Katherine grinned at the lady who'd been housekeeper before her. "I can always trust you to view the bright side."

Leocadia's Indian blood kept all expression from her features; her Spanish blood sang in her articulate voice. "Three gigantic meals a day, plus the little tidbits they eat all the time. Don

Damian replaced me because he thought I couldn't handle it any longer. I carry fifty-three years on my shoulders, and he thinks one fiesta is going to crush me."

With a thump, Katherine placed her platter on the tablecloth and put her arm around Leocadia. "You know he just moved you aside to give me a place where I could stay. You know he just fed a sop to my pride."

Not a muscle moved in her face, but Leocadia's brown eyes slid sideways to examine Katherine. "I knew. I didn't realize you did."

"I didn't know for sure until just now, when you said so." She smiled at Leocadia's grimace, the woman's acknowledgement that she'd been trapped by Katherine's cleverness. Consoling her, Katherine said, "Why else would he replace a trusted servant? You're healthy, the hacienda is so organized it runs itself, and the *patron* is not a man who would remove a faithful servant for no reason, so. . . ." She shrugged.

Leocadia plucked a grape from the bunch on the plate and offered it to Katherine. "Eat. You need something to fuel that too-gifted brain of yours." She shooed the half dozen maids. "Move, move. The evening meal is finished, the evening snacks are on the table. Now we must clean and prepare for breakfast in the morning."

Groans of gigantic proportion swept them, and Katherine turned to go back to the kitchen. Leocadia stopped her. "Stay. As you've said, we don't really need you. You can mingle with guests, visit a bit. Perhaps you can find Don Damian and discuss your position as housekeeper."

"No!" Katherine erupted in instinctive rejection. Calming herself, assuring herself that no one knew of the unfortunate incident in the little library, she repeated, "No. Don Damian's too busy with his guests to waste time with me."

Leocadia didn't smile, but Katherine suspected amusement lurked beneath her impassive surface. "Don Damian always has time for me. Surely I'm of less importance than the woman privileged in his company. But if you'll not converse with him, perhaps you can find an American and have a chance to speak your own language."

"I doubt it. There aren't many Americans here."

"There are too many Americans here." Her mouth puckered. "They hover like giant moths, waiting to settle and devour the cloth of our world."

"I don't want to talk to a moth."

"But you're the flame that draws them." Leocadia nodded over Katherine's shoulder, then melted into the evening.

"Miz Maxwell."

Katherine clenched her teeth and pivoted. "Mr. Smith. Is there something I can get for you?"

"The pleasure of your company."

The man towered over her. He was too much of everything. Too tall, too thin, too pleasant, too hearty. He gave a little bow. His long torso seemed ready to topple over, but he never spilled a drop of his beer.

He smiled at her from his immense height, displaying bad teeth. "These Spanish señoritas are all so short I feel like I could squash them beneath my heel. It's good to see a woman who is tall enough to speak to." His gaze roved over her as if the compliment wiped out the insolence of his gaze.

She smiled, a stiff, tiny movement of her lips. His flattery was nothing more than an unjust disparagement of the people she found so attractive, and she was offended. "Señorita Vietta is much taller than I. Perhaps you'll enjoy your friendship with her."

"Don't know who she is."

Startled, she raised her brows. "I saw you speaking with her."

"Not me," he insisted.

"No doubt you didn't realize who she was."

"I haven't talked to no Vietta."

He leaned closer to her, and she stepped back from the wave of beer fumes. Suppressing the desire to wave her hand in front of her face, she agreed, "As you say. Try the empanadas, they're still hot from the oven." To her relief, his eyes lit with greed and he moved aside to survey the food.

"Well, thank you, ma'am. What a good idea." He put his glass down on the white cloth that covered the trestle table. His large hand hovered over the plate, touched first one turnover, then another, swooped on the largest and carried it to his waiting mouth. Watching her from the corner of his eye, he said, "I'm a big man, and these morsels hardly dent my appetite."

"I'm sorry," Katherine apologized with not an ounce of true remorse. "I'm responsible for the food. I'll speak with the cook and have something special made up for you."

He choked on the flaky crust and coughed. She handed him his glass of beer. He drained it, eyes watering. "I didn't mean that. You do a wonderful job, making all these foreigners happy. I know you gotta feed them what they want. But it's a far cry from real American food."

"Real American food," she said thoughtfully. "For me, real American food means baked beans with brown bread. Would you like me to fix some?"

"Well, I don't know." He floundered, seeking the correct tone of conciliatory humor. "I don't rightly know if I've had them."

"Yet the Pilgrims at Plymouth ate baked beans and brown bread almost from the first winter."

"The Pilgrims didn't land down by where I live." He smiled with wholesome good humor.

"I see." She couldn't place his accent, and asked with real curiosity, "Where are you from?"

"From Washington, D.C.," he said with pride. "The pulse of the nation. I was born there. I was raised there. I love that great city, and I know as much about the capital as any man alive. If you have any questions about our government, you just ask me. I'd be glad to explain it to you."

"Whatever made you come west, sir?"

"Oh, the urge to travel just struck me." He shrugged uncomfortably, burped loudly. "Not bad manners, just good beer." He brayed with laughter and she watched, fascinated, as his long arms flapped in merriment. "These folks sure do serve up the fixin's, don't they?"

He'd avoided her question. She wondered what crime he'd committed, and against whom. In California, it wasn't uncommon to find that the man who worked as a trapper or store manager or farmhand had left a warrant behind for his arrest. It amused her to ask, but she wouldn't push.

After all, the warrant could be for murder.

"Yes, the Spanish are very hospitable," she acknowledged.

"It's almost a shame we're gonna run them out." He sounded reflective, but not a bit sad.

" 'Run them out'?"

"Well, sure. You didn't think we'd let them keep this bit of land, did you? If we don't take it, sure as hell—excuse me, ma'am—sure as heck the English'll grab it."

Remembering what Don Lucian had told her, she challenged, "Don't you think the Spanish will have a word to say about that?"

"Nope. Why, look at them!" He waved a hand at the chatting groups of gaily dressed folk. "Lazy as bedamn. Won't fight for anything. Every time they have a battle about one thing or another, they never fire a shot. They solve everything with their proclamations and their endless talk."

"Some people would find their insistence on peace admirable."

"Sign of spinelessness. Don't even know how to fire a gun."

"Not at another human being." She heard the snap in her voice, and modulated her tone. "Yet the bears walk warily."

"That's another thing. They're always tying a bear to a bull and watching them tear each other to pieces. Savages!"

"Ah." Katherine leaned forward, her eyes gleaming. "They're savages if they watch animals kill each other, but they're spineless if they refuse to kill each other."

"Yes." He beamed at her. "You do understand."

She settled back with a sigh. If there was anything worse than a rude and ignorant man, it was a rude and ignorant man who didn't realize he'd been bested in an argument. "Most of the Spanish—"

"They aren't Spanish, they're Mexican."

"Mexico holds California, that's true," she conceded. "I understand they've held California as a province for over twenty years, but many of these families came directly from Spain. The Mexican government has done little in the way of administration."

"They're nothing more than a joke," he agreed.

"All of our hosts consider themselves to be not Mexican, nor Spanish, but Californios. This is their home, settled by their fathers and grandfathers."

"They don't farm the land like Americans do. They have ranchos, with cattle and sheep. They raise horses and ride them so their Californio feet don't touch the ground. They don't plant cash crops because they don't want to get their hands dirty." Taking three empanadas, he bit his way through the crust, cursing as the hot meat juices dribbled down his chin. "Look at them! Lazy, wanting only to sing and drink and lie around in the shade while their vaqueros work for them."

Katherine looked, but she didn't see what Mr. Smith did. She saw a group of people happy to be reunited after a long year of work on their ranchos. They were singing, yes, and drinking, yes, and lying in the shade. The young men and women were dancing and flirting. The men were gossiping about horses. The women discussed their babies. The children dashed from one spot to another, playing games and comparing toys.

Mr. Smith's jeers interrupted her musing. "These people take the easy way, raising cattle and slaughtering them for their hides and tallow. A bunch of greasers."

She'd never heard the term before, but she recognized an insult when she heard one. Her distaste for Mr. Smith grew and solidified into a block of dislike. She arranged her face in an expression of polite interest. "Our host, Don Damian, farms the land."

"Yes." The word hissed from his mouth.

She studied him as she would any reptile—repulsed, yet fascinated.

"Yes, Don Damian does indeed farm the land. The de la Solas are sitting on one of the richest areas of California. They've managed it very well."

"And you want it?" she asked.

"I'm going to have it. Look at this place. Look at that house. Lily-white, tall and wide, with a fountain in the courtyard and those balconies hanging all over. Inside it's all polished wood floors and expensive rugs to walk on. Gold teapots and thin china and fine furniture from the U.S. of A. It's a fine place."

His avarice annoyed her, but a note didn't ring true. "The de la Solas built this home for comfort, not flamboyance. There are many haciendas that are much more impressive. Why this place?"

"Everybody likes to come here. Everybody likes this place. When I have it, I'll throw parties like this. Everybody'll be proud to come."

She could believe that respectability had eluded him. He wanted it so badly he imagined he could purchase it. She almost felt sorry for him, but he hadn't finished with his disclosure. Lowering his voice like a conspirator, he said, "There are riches here. If I were free to tell you, I could tell you about riches beyond your wildest imaginings."

The man thought she was too feebleminded to realize that this fertile and mellow climate could one day produce the crops to feed the world. "You want the land for its riches only? Is there perhaps a shade of rivalry in your resolve to snatch de la Sola land?"

"You bet. I'm gonna show that uppity Mexican just who's in charge. He knows it, too. Look at him." He jerked his head toward the spot where Damian chatted with his guests. "He talks so pretty and moves so slick. He wears those black clothes with that silver trimming, strolling among these colorful peacocks who call themselves men—he sticks out like a sore thumb. All the women think they want him. They won't want him so much when he's penniless."

"He'll still be handsome." She said it quietly, gauging her voice just low enough that he had to strain to overhear. When he jerked, she knew she'd scored a direct hit to his vanity. Louder, she asked, "How would he lose his lands? I'm just a woman. I'm afraid I don't understand."

"There's a lot of things women just can't understand." He tried to put his hand over hers, but she stepped aside to arrange the bowls of fruit and platters of cheese. "Like I said, I'm from Washington, D.C., and if you need to know anything, I'll be glad to help you."

"Tell me how he could lose his land."

She fixed her big green eyes on him, and he melted. Against his better judgment, he expounded, "It's the right of the United States, more than that, the *duty* of the United States to own and manage all of the land stretching from the Atlantic to the Pacific. Those damned Englishmen are trying to get in here and take this land, like they've taken half the world. The Russians would like it, too, and the French. But they can't. It's ours."

"Ours by whose definition?"

"By God's definition."

Katherine smothered a startled exclamation. "Did someone talk to Him?"

"President James K. Polk." He nodded in awe. "I left Washington, D.C. just six months ago, and they're using a new term to describe what's happening in the U.S. of A. They call it Manifest Destiny."

"Do they? What does that mean?"

"It means this whole land, from sea to sea, must be in our hands." He lowered his voice conspiratorially. "President Polk has a plan for California, and if the law must be bent to ensure its success, we'll bend the law."

"I see."

"And the Americans that get here first'll have best pickin's."

"Is that why you're here? For the best 'pickin's'?"

"Yes, ma'am." With a wealth of meaning, he said, "Why, you should find yourself an American man to take care of you. When the dust settles, you'd be a rich woman."

A small, genuine smile lit her face. "Why should I attach myself to a man? You've made it clear that any American living in California can eventually confiscate the lands."

He frowned, puzzled. "That's right."

"I don't need a man to steal land. My uncle is Rutherford Carr Chamberlain. Are you familiar with his name?"

"Why . . . yes, ma'am. He does business in Washington, D. C."

"Yes, indeed. He could hardly stay away from that corrupt city. In fact, he works for the wealthy all down the eastern seaboard, helping them steal from the poor."

Her confidence bewildered him. "Ma'am?"

"I worked as his unpaid legal clerk for years."

"A woman?" Mr. Smith snickered.

"To become a lawyer, it isn't necessary to attend a college. Most lawyers apprentice themselves to another lawyer until they absorb the knowledge they need. If I hadn't been a woman, my uncle would have sponsored me until I could pass the bar exam for his firm. Instead, he found it useful to hang a debt of gratitude over my head."

"I'm sorry. I don't understand."

"My father, Uncle Rutherford's brother, was a lawyer. He was the kind of lawyer who believed in an honest deal for every man, woman, and child in the United States. We never had much money. When Daddy died, my mother and I went to live with Uncle Rutherford Carr Chamberlain and his wife Narcissa."

"Oh! So you knew how to read books a little bit."

"My father taught me to read English, Latin, Greek, and German," she corrected.

"My golly."

He sounded so awed, her suspicion firmed. This man couldn't read. She felt a spasm of sympathy, instantly dispelled by his next comment.

"Didn't your father know book learning can injure a woman?"

She snapped, "It didn't injure this one."

"No, it sure didn't." His eyes skimmed her figure again. "Your Uncle Rutherford let you do some work for him to repay him for his charity, huh?"

"You understand. He 'let' me do all the legal research, all the background searches, write all his briefs. After I came on, he turned one of his hardworking, underpaid clerks out on the street. After I went to work for him, his business increased immeasurably."

"Why?"

"I don't like to brag—" it was a lie, she loved to brag "—but I was the brains behind my uncle's current success."

She could almost see Mr. Smith's mind working furiously. "If that's the gospel, you could go to work for another lawyer out here and do real well."

"That's true."

"You didn't really mind paying your uncle back for his kindness."

"What kindness?"

"Taking you and your mama in, giving you room and board, welcoming you into his family."

His words activated the memories of humiliation. How well she remembered her uncle's sneers, her aunt's attempts to banish her to the kitchen. She remembered how her mother, never strong, had suffered in the tiny, hot, stuffy storage room that served as their bedroom. In her mind, she saw her mother's anxious face, urging the fifteen-year-old rebel to mind her manners, to do what she was told. She heard Uncle Rutherford insinuate that he would put them out on the streets if Katherine didn't cooperate and do his dirty work. His teeth had shone sharp and white beneath his black beard when he realized his young niece would do anything, *anything* to protect her mother. Again she tasted the bitter bile she had sampled as she used her mind and her legal knowledge to help her uncle destroy rival careers, blacken rival reputations. And she could never forget the smiling face she presented to her dying mother every night as she assured her she enjoyed her work.

Her mother's death had broken Katherine. Broken her because of the loss of the one person in the world who loved her. Broken her because of the hidden relief she felt. No longer would she be bound by anyone.

The healing had taken a long time. She didn't know whether it was complete even yet.

"Hey, Miz Maxwell." Emerson Smith waved a hand in her face. "You slip off there?"

Drawn back from the old pain, she stared at the grinning, bobbing face, and answered his original question. "No, Mr. Smith, I didn't really mind working for my uncle, but not for gratitude. When I worked for Uncle Rutherford, Aunt Narcissa couldn't use me as a scullery maid and my cousins couldn't use me for a whipping boy."

Like a hound after a bone, he dug down to the fact he wanted to investigate. "But . . . didn't you like the law?"

"Yes, it sharpened my mind."

That cheered him, she could see. Leaning over the table, he ignored the bunches of grapes to scoop another empanada from the platter. He dismissed her success as boasting, her claims of cleverness as nothing but feminine nonsense. "Any woman would be proud to help support her husband, when her husband does so much for her."

"I don't have a husband."

"Play your cards right—"

"I have no need of a husband. Thank you for your advice. It's been so helpful."

"You're welcome." He melted under her approval, but his bewilderment shone through. "Advice?"

"You've made me realize that with my legal knowledge, my American citizenship, the length of my residency in California, I can lay claim to this very land, the land I stand on—" she stamped her foot in the grass "—and it will be mine."

His empanada crumbled in his fingers. "What?"

In an efficient flurry, she fetched him a napkin. "I'll be a very good landowner. Perhaps I'll even hire Don Damian as my majordomo."

His big-knuckled fingers closed over hers, and she winced as he mashed the beef filling into her palm. "That's just not possible, little lady. I know there's a lot of talk here and there about how men shouldn't have so much power over their wives. I tell you the truth, that's a lot of nonsense."

"That's the truth?"

He nodded solemnly, intent on quashing such unsuitable thoughts before they took root. "I blame the western expansion. Those folks move out West and stake a claim. Then the man of the family dies. His wife takes over and raises the crops and her children and manages to hang on to the claim. The fact of the matter is, that just ain't attractive."

She lifted her eyes from their well-sauced, entwined fingers. "Not attractive?"

"Women aren't meant to think for themselves. Men are just smarter than women. Any woman should be glad to work for her man. Now, in Washington, D.C., there's actually talk—I know it's wild, I don't want you to laugh too much—there's actually talk that in some places women should be allowed to vote. Only in the West, you understand, where there's not much population and they need every vote. Every woman would vote just like her husband told her."

"What about the widows and spinsters?"

"That's just it! You really do have a good mind for a woman! That's what the problem is. Can you imagine what a state this country would be in if women just jumped willy-nilly into the voting booth and picked whoever their little pea brains thought was best?"

"Dear heavens. Peace would run rampant, education would be open to all, and the poor would be gainfully employed! Whatever—" she jerked her hands out of his and wiped them, one by one, on his coat "—would America do if all her social problems were solved by a bunch of pea-brained women?" She stepped back and smiled at his dumbfounded face. "You've convinced me, Mr. Smith. Someday women will have the vote. We can't continue to let the country be run solely by males, ignorant of law and literature."

"Why, you—" He snatched at her and grabbed her by the sleeves. "You're a shrew."

The sound of tearing, the release as worn material gave way and the touch of cool air on her shoulder wiped the smile from her face. "Perhaps not a shrew, but I know I'll get the vote, and I know I'll own this land someday." Her fist flashed up and smacked him in the Adam's apple. She put the full force of her arm behind the blow, as she hadn't with Damian, and Mr. Smith's painful gag resounded across the now-quiet yard. His hands fell away and she stepped back.

The man striding across the yard halted in his tracks.

Leaning over Mr. Smith, whose head bent over his knees and whose fingers clutched his throat, Katherine said, "I know all these things. You see . . . it's manifest destiny."

Chapter 4

She laughed, although it wavered, and stalked away. As Mr. Smith cast an embarrassed glance at his audience and staggered towards the creek where the beer barrel cooled, Don Lucian loosened his restraining grip on Damian's arm. "You haven't the right to interfere, Damian," Don Lucian reproved. "I wonder where she learned such an effective blow."

His son shook his head, rubbing his own Adam's apple in remembrance.

"She'll make you a fine wife," Don Lucian said. "Better than Vietta."

"There was never a question of Vietta."

"Her family hoped—"

Damian never took his eyes from Katherine as she strode toward the house. "Her family hoped I'd rescue them from their own stupidity."

"Luis Gregorio is a poor excuse for a rancher," Don Lucian acknowledged, "and an even poorer excuse for a neighbor."

"He lost their lands because of his laziness, but Vietta never expected me to marry her as an obligation."

Don Lucian's voice revealed his distaste for the woman. "No, she expected you to marry her because she loved you."

Damian glanced at his father and spread his hands helplessly. "A youthful fancy. I did nothing to encourage her, I assure you. I didn't even know until I heard the rumors of our impending nuptials."

"Of course you didn't know. It's not as if she were an innocent child you led astray."

"Come, admit it. You don't like Vietta."

"I don't like her, but what's worse, I didn't even like her as a child." Don Lucian's mouth puckered as if he'd bitten into a green persimmon. "She was a sly thing who clung to you like a parasite. I was glad when the Gregorios moved to Monterey to live in genteel poverty."

"She's my friend," Damian answered.

"You are too loyal. What of her renewed affection for you?"

"You have noticed? Her devotion seems to have returned in the past year. I'd hoped it was my imagination." Damian shrugged. "She's a spinster and prone to strange fantasies. I thought for a few months she loved Tobias. Her eyes burned when she watched him, but he detested her."

"Tobias called her a vampire," Don Lucian said without emotion.

"The only quarrel Tobias and I ever had, we had about Vietta. She clung to me as if Tobias were a rival. When Tobias suggested he and I travel the countryside seeking out the old Indian and Spanish legends, we returned to find her sitting on the step of the townhouse, demanding an accounting of our trip."

"She's an odd young woman," Don Lucian stated with emphasis.

"Then Katherine stepped off the ship. Vietta refused to meet Katherine. When I gave the reception for their wedding, Vietta refused to come."

"Jealous of every bit of your attention that isn't hers."

"Surely this, too, will pass."

"Perhaps you're right." If Don Lucian had his doubts, he disguised them beneath a paternal smile. "Vietta has time before your wedding to accustom herself to the thought. Before you can announce your engagement, a month remains in Doña Katherina's mourning."

The smile disguised concern, and Damian wondered if his father knew in some omniscient, parental fashion, about the scene in the study the previous day. "I can't wait any longer."

Don Lucian frowned. "To urge a woman to abandon the rightful grieving for her husband is the act of a scoundrel."

"I can't wait any longer," Damian repeated.

"Tobias was your friend."

"Tobias was more than my friend. He was the brother I never had. I never met a man I liked more than Tobias. I never met a man I understood better than Tobias, or who understood me."

"Everyone could see how you two spoke without words." Don Lucian shook his head. "A landowner from California and a watchmaker from Switzerland. How could you have more in common with him than with the people you knew from your birth?"

Damian shrugged.

"So why do you now begrudge Tobias the mourning she owes him?"

With unconscious fingers, Damian stroked his mustache. "I begrudge him nothing. I rejoiced with Tobias when he sent for Katherine. I rejoiced when her ship docked in Monterey harbor. But when I saw her, Papa—she's beautiful, is she not?"

"Very attractive."

"So stately, with an inbred dignity that makes me long to shake it loose."

"If you destroy the dignity, my boy, you'll destroy the woman."

"No, you misunderstand me. I don't want to destroy her dignity, nor rein it in. I want her to realize that with me, she can abandon her dignity, and I'll still recognize her as the finest of women."

Don Lucian chuckled, an echo reminiscent of his son. "So your mother was with me."

"*Madre?*" Damian remembered the kind, generous, formal

woman who had been his mother. "*Madre* lost her dignity with you?"

"Not lost. Never lost." Now he laughed out loud. "She always found it again . . . eventually. I remember when we first moved here, and we'd had a drought. . . ." He noticed how his son's mouth hung open. "I don't know if you're old enough to hear this story."

"Papa, I'm thirty-one."

"Probably not old enough to hear this story." He shook his head at his son. "After all, she was your mother. But I'll tell you anyway. During the first year we were married, a drought parched the land. Lord, it was awful. So hot. No water for the cattle. Only well water for us to drink, and that warm and full of sludge. Finally, it was too much. Teresa and I fought. Shouted at each other, raged at each other. She went tearing out to her horse, I went after her. I chased her for miles."

"You couldn't catch her?"

"She was a hell of a horsewoman." Don Lucian lifted his glass in remembered tribute. "Perhaps I didn't want to catch her. Perhaps I knew it was best not to. We rode out to the middle of nothing, out over the plain and to the foot of the Sierra de Gavilán. There we stopped. We dismounted and raged at each other until, boom! The heavens opened up to douse our anger. It was the grandfather of storms. Your mother and I, we stripped to the skin and danced in the rain."

"Naked? Outdoors?"

"*Sí*. And do you know what your mother's saddlebags contained? Soap. Dry blankets. Food. Leocadia was your mother's maid, and that woman listens to the earth. We found a cave—that mountain is riddled with them—and we didn't go home for two days."

"*Madre de Dios.*"

"You were conceived on that mountain."

Unwillingly amused, Damian asked, "So you found the treasure of the padres?"

"*Si*, we found it. It was not gold."

Surprising a blush on Don Lucian's face, Damian refrained from laughing.

"I'm sure you and Doña Katherina will be more sedate than that."

"God forbid. The first time I saw Katherine, I realized Tobias and I had too much in common. I recognized her with my heart, my soul."

Don Lucian nodded. "Just so I recognized your mother."

"Yes, but I suffered. She barely glanced at me. All her attention centered on Tobias. It gave me time to collect myself, and when my friend introduced me to my love I was cold, distant."

"The best response," his father approved.

"Yes, but she would have none of it. She was so happy. She threw her arms around me and I . . . suffered. My heart didn't know whether to leap for joy or die for the pain."

Don Lucian winced in sympathy.

"I've kept her safe, never let her know how I feel. The time of grief is coming to an end, and I was willing to wake her slowly."

"What changed your mind?"

With a suppressed fury, Damian said, "She's saving the money I pay her to return. Return to Boston, to the family who despises her. Young Cabeza told me and assured me he heard the words himself."

Staggering back as if he were stunned, Don Lucian asked, "Why?"

"I've thought about it. I believe she has decided it's her duty. I know my Catriona. Her will of iron was tempered by the fires of duty, and she'll go unless she's bound hand and foot by a greater duty here."

Don Lucian thought, too. Clapping his son on the shoulder, he urged, "*Vaya con tu corazon.* Go with your heart."

With a vicious jerk, Katherine pulled her sleeve loose from its stitching, and clutched it in her fist. She had made a scene. She hated scenes. She hated that defiant demon inside that never let her back down. She hated the sick feeling that roiled in her stomach afterwards.

She didn't handle men well. She never had. She loved an argument, and her father had taught her to think, to debate, to succeed. He hadn't taught her that men took losing an argument poorly, that their response was violence. When she thought of Emerson Smith's twisted face towering over hers, she wanted to crumple up and cry, but the control her mother had taught her was too rigid for that. She'd turn her attention to other matters and gradually, she knew, the distress would fade.

Until the next argument.

She stepped in front of the full-length mirror and glared at her own reflection. She owned two dresses in plain serviceable black muslin, both of them torn. She could baste this sleeve back into the bodice, but the other dress required major repairs.

How she would love to astonish the guests with a flattering costume!

The woman in the mirror looked startled, then disapproving. Where had that errant thought come from?

Removing her mourning clothes would be her final good-bye to Tobias. She didn't wish to discard the memory of her marriage, or the safety it represented. She smoothed the black cotton of her skirt.

Still, seeing the pretty señoritas in their gay outfits had whetted her appetite for something new. Something befitting her station as housekeeper and widow, perhaps in mauve. Never in her life had she been allowed to wear anything attractive. Even Uncle Rutherford had complained about her depressing attire, but Aunt Narcissa had been adamant. With two girls of her own to outfit, she'd seen fit to clothe her niece by marriage in castoffs. Katherine smoothed her skirt again and turned away from the mirror.

She fetched her sewing box to the table that stood close to the straight-back chair. Undoing the buttons that held her bodice, she stripped it down and stepped out. She took her seat near the dormer window, where the sun could light her work, yet she wasn't visible to the crowd below. She should sew, dress again, and go down to work. For a moment, though, she sat with her hands at rest in her lap and studied her bedroom with affectionate eyes.

It was one-third of the huge attic that ran atop the U-shaped house. When Don Lucian first led her up the tiny stairs to the room under the roof, she'd wondered, for a brief, despairing moment, whether this was his way of saying he didn't want her here. It had been dull and dusty; it echoed the pain in her soul. But Don Lucian knew what he was about. The servants cleaned and when next she saw the room it sparkled. The wooden floors had been polished until they gleamed, the walls had been white-washed. The room was too big for one person, yet she'd felt an immediate sense of belonging, a sense of spaciousness and light that appealed to her.

Behind a door in the other part of the attic was all the furniture discarded from the hacienda. She'd been given carte blanche, and she had furnished her room as she wished. A frayed rug covered part of the floor. A large carved wooden table held her quilting. Chairs of wood and leather were scattered about. Another small table beside the bed held a mismatched porcelain pitcher and bowl and a candlestick. Behind a folding screen that divided the room into living space and sleeping space, wooden dowels had been fixed in the wall for her clothing.

An immense bed with carved headboard and footboard dominated one corner of the room. She had sewn the quilt in Boston and transported it in her marriage trunk. A free-standing mirror stood beside it, and a comfortable chair sat against the opposite wall in the shadows. In the beginning of her sojourn here, she'd spent many hours curled in that chair, wrapped in a blanket and staring at the wall. Her need for solitude and security had faded, and now the chair stood alone.

She'd never found a place where she felt more at home. With a sigh for passing time, she threaded her needle with sturdy black thread and plunged it into the sleeve.

Laughter below attracted her attention, and she twisted in her seat. From up here she could see them all. The Berretos, the Rios, the Alavarados sang the bawdy kind of song that brought forth those bursts of laughter. The Garcias swayed together in a circle, their arms wrapped around each others' shoulders. Mariano Vallejo of Sonoma was here, passing through on his way home from Monterey. He formed the center of a serious group of men who discussed California politics and tried to decide California's fate.

The Valverdes weren't laughing. They were there en masse, glaring across the room at the del Reals, and Katherine wondered when the fight would erupt. They'd been snarling since the day they arrived, and no one seemed to think it out of the ordinary. The guests seemed to think it more extraordinary that they hadn't been fighting. What had Don Damian said? He'd been keeping them so entertained they hadn't done battle.

Weakly she heard the call, "Don Damian!" and an irresistible curiosity pushed her forward to peer below.

"Don Damian! Don Damian!"

Damian cursed to himself. He didn't want to speak to anyone right now. Anger still raced through his veins and coiled in his belly. He wanted, very badly, to take Mr. Smith out and beat him bloody. To restrain himself—and as host, restrain himself he must—he wanted to leave this fiesta and all of his nosy, well-meaning friends. He wanted to saddle his wildest, most bad-tempered stallion and ride until both of them were exhausted.

"Don Damian!"

He ignored her, hoping to gain refuge in the stables. At least in the stables, his friends confined their comments on his love life to a few whinnies and neighs.

"Don Damian!"

What a fool he was to think Vietta would ever give up. She was like a bulldog with jaws that clamped tight and never released. Whatever she set her mind to, she would attain. Schooling himself to patience, he turned. Seeing Vietta's eager face as she hurried, her painful limp as she struggled towards him, he reproached himself. What manner of beast could be so cruel as to ignore Vietta? After her accident last year, she'd been reduced to waiting for life to come to her. How could he forget their friendship in the pain of love?

The thought of his new love sent his mind veering back into fury. How dare Katherine try to leave him? How dare she suggest she'd be better off in Boston than in his arms? Didn't she know, even yet, that he would move heaven and earth to keep her at his side?

Vietta's hand shyly touched his sleeve, then tugged at it, and he started when he realized she had caught up with him. "Aren't you glad to see me?" she asked in pouting bewilderment. "You're frowning."

He rearranged his lips into a smile. "Vietta." He patted her hand. "I'm sorry. I was thinking of something else. How's my dear friend?"

She giggled like a silly girl, which she wasn't. She was his elder by six months, past the thirty-second birthday that loomed before him.

"Damian, I've hardly had a chance to speak to you this whole fiesta." One of her hazel eyes winked in a parody of flirtation, and his pained gaze roamed over the milling crowd. How could she tease him? Didn't she know what was obvious to everyone else?

Vietta wasn't pretty, he supposed, but she wasn't as ill-favored as some of the women who were her age, and married. She spoke in a deep, rich voice. One of his friends said she sounded as if she were the madam of a bordello and knew every trick in the book. Everyone had laughed, but it was true. Her voice, by itself, inspired fantasies of lust. Unfortunately, the voice was only an extension of her height.

She had grown too tall, looking many of his friends in the eye.

Her lips were every man's dream. Lush, moist and pouting, they made a man think of long, slow kisses on a hot, summer night. But her black hair made a man think of a hot summer day. It clung to her head when she perspired, and she seemed to perspire all the time.

Her complexion was the most marvelous alabaster, pure and transparent as a baby's skin. But she sunburned whenever she set foot out of the house, and so she stayed within. To read, she said, but the horse-worshiping Californios didn't understand that. She'd acquired a stoop from the books she devoured, and the books had given her knowledge and a vast conceit to go with it.

So she'd never had a real suitor.

Vietta's tug at his arm was stronger this time, a sharp pinch, and he brought his attention once more to her. "I'm sorry, I . . . thought I heard one of the servants call to me."

"Your housekeeper?" she asked tartly.

Ah. She did know. Life hadn't been easy for Vietta. She was a poor, landless spinster. If bitterness tinged her attitude from time to time, he was man enough to ignore it.

"Your leg is better?"

"So much better. I have little pain, except when I try to run." She winced, and guilt ripped through him. He put his arm around her waist and led her towards the laughing group of men and women who congregated around the benches under the trees. "I don't want to go there," she objected, tweaking his arm. "I only want to be with you."

He gently insisted. "You can sit and rest your leg, and we can talk to our friends."

"*Your* friends," she murmured.

The truth of it struck him; why didn't any of his friends like her? He pretended he hadn't heard, knowing they would welcome her for his sake.

The women made a place for Vietta on the bench, voicing their concern for her injury but with no regard for her replies. All their attention strained to hear the men as they closed on Damian.

Damian's turbulence faded as he looked around at the smirking faces of his friends. How they loved to see him squirm in the agony of love. How they enjoyed teasing him. Like interrogators facing a stubborn criminal, they thrust a long-legged stool beneath his knees and knocked his feet out from beneath him. They leaned forward in anticipation and Damian relaxed. He needed his wits about him. He would sharpen them on Alejandro and Rico and Hadrian and Julio, and any of the rest who dared ruffle his feathers.

Especially Julio de Casillas. His gaze shifted to the sharp restless face of his dearest friend, his greatest rival, his most fearsome enemy. Julio hung back, examining his fingernails as if he hadn't the slightest interest in seeing Damian roasted slowly over the coals of mockery. That, Damian knew, was untrue. Since the day when they toddled about in dresses, Damian and Julio had competed in every way possible. Sometimes Damian had won, sometimes Julio, but always they struggled.

For all their unholy delight at his predicament, he knew he could trust his friends. Never by word or deed had they displayed to Katherine their knowledge of his love. They treated her with affection and sought to know her because they understood, even if she didn't, that soon she'd be one of their group.

He deflected their arrows once more, saved his own hide once more, provided entertainment once more. In a flash, he realized Vietta wasn't a member of the group, and he stood to look for her.

· Over the heads of the men, he saw her sitting on the bench where he'd left her. She'd said nothing as they'd joked. She hadn't joined them. Yet there was nothing pathetic about her loneliness. Her back was ramrod straight, her fingers intertwined. Her gaze traveled over each member of the society that ignored her, and he thought she noted them with a kind of satisfaction.

From beyond the crowd, Mariano Vallejo hailed him. "Damian, look who's come to visit."

Damian craned his neck and saw the dapper Mariano accompanying a stout blond man. Damian gave a shout. "Gundersheimer! *Mi amigo*, what are you doing here? Mariano, where did you find this fellow?"

"I was out at the stables and there he was." Mariano's broad face beamed, the whiskers that grew across his cheeks bristling. "I invited him out when I met him in Monterey, so I've been watching for him."

"Good for you, Mariano. Gundersheimer, let's get you a drink and a seat." Circling the group, Damian embraced the dusty fellow.

"Thank you." Gundersheimer sank down on the proffered seat and accepted the water pressed on him. With hearty goodwill, he drained the gourd and wiped his hand across his mouth. "Very good." A glass of beer found its way into his hand. Settling down, he grinned at Damian. "Now I can talk."

"How are things in Nueva Helvetia, and how's my old friend, Captain Sutter?"

"He is well and sends his greetings. I traveled to Monterey to oversee the unloading of our goods off a Yankee ship." He nodded pleasantly. "Now I return. When will we see you back in the Sacramento Valley?"

"After I settle my affairs here."

Damian's words brought groans and laughter from his guests, and he bit his lip when he realized how his unthinking comment had been interpreted. His rude and explicit gesture did nothing but bring more merriment.

Gundersheimer watched with bright eyes, and Damian said, "I shouldn't introduce these tactless folks to you, but for your own ease, I offer them. This is Godart Gundersheimer," Damian told them as they one by one accepted Gundersheimer's handshake, "a legal adviser for Captain Sutter. He's a neighbor of mine at my rancho in the Sacramento Valley."

"Can't you convince this fool to move back to civilization?" Julio drawled. "He's spending all his time in the interior, up by the mountains, and depriving us of his company. It's not safe, with the wild Indians who kill for the pleasure of it."

"No," Gundersheimer said. "I come to tell him to return."

"Why?" Damian asked with alarm. "Is there a problem?"

Gundersheimer scratched his ear. "That American is back."

"Which American?" Bewildered, Damian stared at the uncomfortable German.

"That . . . that bullyboy. That Frémont."

Damian's brows twitched together. "He's back?"

"Yah, in December."

"Oh, Frémont," Mariano said, disgust rife in his voice. "Now there's a character."

Gundersheimer took a swallow of his beer as if it would wash the bad taste out of his mouth. "I'll tell you. Captain Sutter wasn't there. Frémont gave Bidwell a list of supplies he wanted, just like the Fort was a storehouse. It wasn't cheap stuff, either—sixteen mules he wanted! Packsaddles and flour, too. Things have been tight at the Fort, and when Bidwell couldn't fill Frémont's order, he threw a tantrum. Well, Bidwell buckled under and Frémont got almost all he wanted. Food. Fourteen mules we could ill afford to lose, and we shod them for him."

Mariano said, "That's generous of you."

"That's not all. He left for a month and when he came back, Captain Sutter was there to welcome him. Frémont was much more pleasant to the Captain." The man nodded vigorously. "Much more pleasant to the Captain than to the peons."

Mariano asked, "Where is he now?"

"He took Captain Sutter's schooner down the Sacramento River. Went to Yerba Buena, went to Monterey, visited with all the officials and gave them some cock-and-bull story about how his trip was in the interests of science and commerce. About how he was surveying the nearest route from the United States to the Pacific Ocean." He sniffed in disdain. "If they believe that, they're dunces of the first water."

"I know the officials in Monterey." Mariano smiled, drawing on his knowledge of area politics. "General José Castro, the *comandante* , can be quick to temper. I didn't always agree with Alvarado's dictates when he was governor. But it would be ill advised to assume they are dunces. What is Señor John Frémont doing that you doubt his word?"

"He's got—" Gundersheimer squinted towards the westering sun as he tried to figure "—sixty men in his party. They're all trappers and shooters."

"Shooters?" Damian said.

"Yah. Just to show off, one of them shot a vulture out of the sky by breaking one wing. You know—shooters."

"Marksmen." Damian looked thoughtful. "Do the officials believe Frémont came for science?"

Alejandro elbowed his way forward. "No one believes anything this Frémont says. His men insulted the family of Don Angel Castro. They insisted their daughter drink with them. They are drunkards and thieves. They don't act like guests in a foreign country. They act like they own the country."

"Thieves, yes. Did you hear what Frémont did to Don José Dolores Pacheco?" Rico asked.

Mariano's face grew stern. "Tell us."

"There was a complaint lodged with Don José's office. He's the *alcalde* of San José, you know." The heads around him nodded. "Don Sebastian Peralta discovered that one of the horses in Frémont's camp was his—was stolen. So he sought to retrieve it, and Frémont insulted him. Insulted him about the return of his own horse. As if there aren't horses to be had in California. They mock our hospitality with their rudeness."

"What about Don José?" Hadrian stood snapping his fingers.

Rico answered, "He wrote a letter to Frémont, a very nice letter, broaching the problem. Frémont insulted him, too. He wrote a letter back calling Don Sebastian a vagabond."

An angry murmur followed the general groan.

"Where is Frémont now?" Damian demanded.

Everyone turned to Gundersheimer. "Making trouble somewhere, no doubt."

"What does Governor Pio Pico say about this?" A relative of Pico's, Rico felt honor bound to query, but he knew he'd asked the wrong question when Alejandro rounded on him.

"What does Pico ever have to say? He's hiding in his headquarters in Los Angeles, demanding all the money from the treasury in Monterey. The question is, what does General Castro say about this?"

"I know the answer to that." Gundersheimer grinned as the faces turned on him. "He's not happy. You should return to the valley, Don Damian. You need to protect your interests."

"Oh, why?" Alejandro said in disgust. "Damian works until he has callouses on his hands like a vaquero. What could possibly be there worth going back for?"

The blunt German stuck out his neck. "You are the fool if you think you have anything here. This is a well-kept ranch, true, but in the Sacramento Valley we have everything. The elk stand up to their knees in waving grass. We have flowers and trees in abundance, and sweet soil that welcomes the grape. The rivers, they flow crystal clear, so clear you can pluck the salmon out with your bare hands."

Julio drawled, "Ah, yes. In the valley, the land is tough with turf. You must come miles to bring your hides to market, and go miles back with your supplies. The company is few and far between, and there are no women with which to ease your hunger."

"Julio!" His wife joggled his arm. "That's not a subject for the daylight."

Julio turned to Maria Ygnacia, a tiny woman with a snow-white streak in her hair. She blushed beneath his scrutiny and took a step back. "Of course, my dear." He bowed courteously. "I forget myself."

Godart Gundersheimer hadn't forgotten himself. Belligerent in defense of his chosen home, he said, "There are getting to be too many people in the valley."

"Americans," Damian sneered.

"You're judging all Americans by the actions of one hothead," Mariano chided. "They're a young, energetic race, with all the brash rudeness of a child. Yet when I was *comandante general* of California, I warned Mexico to take action if it wished to retain this province. They ignored me. With the continued uninterest of Mexico, who better to turn to than the United States?"

Damian rounded on him fiercely. "Perhaps there's none better, but I don't have to like it. You make excuses for Frémont, but in my opinion, he's an example of what we can expect from these people."

Putting his arm around Damian's shoulders, Mariano said, "We'll do the best we can, Damian. California is a tasty morsel, and the wolves of the world salivate over us. If we're not careful, there'll be armies marching over our soil and destroying everything we've built."

"Couldn't we govern ourselves?" Hadrian wondered.

Both Mariano and Damian laughed, amused in varying degrees.

"We can't even do that with the occasional interference of Mexican officials. Southern California struggles to wrest control from Monterey, and no one knows who's in charge." Mariano shook his head. "No, I don't hold out hope for that."

"So the Americans will take California, and I will go live in the Sacramento Valley." Damian turned back to Gundersheimer. "But the Americans are taking over there, too?"

"Yes, there are Americans," Gundersheimer admitted. "But not long ago, one of the men found a lone Californio working to build a house. He had papers from the governor saying the land was his. So you see, company is coming, and only the early claimants will get the best lands." His voice rose. "Ducks and geese by the thousands, figs heavy on the trees, a paradise on earth."

Putting his hand under Gundersheimer's elbow, Damian assisted him to his feet. "You're tired." He lifted his finger, and Leocadia materialized before them. "Find Señor Gundersheimer a bed. He can join us later."

"Yes, I'll do that, with gratitude. I'm not the horseman you are, Don Damian, and my back aches from the ride."

"He's a fanatic," Julio said with cool distaste as the man strode away. "He talks too much."

Alejandro insisted, "There's nothing in the Sacramento Valley to keep you there."

"I like it," Damian answered plainly. "This is my father's land and my home. But my rancho in the valley is my own and I will return."

"Every man should have the thrill of conquering his own land and taming his own woman." Mariano bowed. "Ladies and gentlemen, I must leave you now and prepare to return home."

Damian grasped his arm. "Must you, Mariano?"

"You know I must. My wife awaits me in Sonoma, and I'm gone too much with this nonsense in the government. As usual, your hospitality was warm."

"Next time, bring the family," Damian ordered.

"I will." Mariano walked away, looked back and grinned. "The Vallejos will come to dance at your wedding. We wouldn't miss that."

A raucous burst of laughter followed him away.

Damian glanced up as new guests rode up the road towards the stables. "I, too, must leave you." He held up his hands against the sighs and complaints. "Guests are arriving for the fandango, and I must prepare our musicians to play. Until then, find someone else to distress with your teasing." He reached out and touched Maria Ygnacia's cheek with his finger. She had been the only woman he'd ever worshiped in his youth, and he retained a fondness for her.

She smiled at him, then glanced at Julio.

Damian found Julio watching them with a cynical gaze.

She folded her hands and lowered her eyes, and Damian wanted to groan in distress. The increasing animosity between his two friends distressed him, but what could he do? Neither of them would thank him for his interference.

As he drew abreast of Julio, the man took his arm. Damian jumped, almost guiltily, but Julio had other matters on his mind. "Look, _compadre_," he said into Damian's ear.

Following Julio's eye, he saw her.

His Katherine.

Carrying a dusty carpetbag that bumped against her knee, she followed Leocadia and Gundersheimer to the house. She was discussing something with the man, Damian was distressed to note—perhaps shipping schedules. And she was smiling at Gundersheimer until he reeled beneath the attention.

She'd sewn the seam on one of her unattractive black dresses. She'd tucked her hair beneath a voluminous black cap so that not one strand shone in the sun. She looked hot, struggling to fulfill everyone's needs. She looked flustered and harried, working too hard and sleeping too little.

She looked wonderful.

All his anger, his fear, his delight rushed back at him as if they'd never been banished. He had eyes only for her. Only for Katherine.

Beside him, he heard Julio laugh sharply. "Perhaps you don't like the Americans, Damian, but I bet you're going to annex that piece of the country soon yourself, hey?"

22 May, in the year of our Lord, 1777

My brothers and I knew the danger. We were not fearful, putting our trust in Christ. The very soldiers sent to protect us started the trouble. What imbeciles they were, to believe the Indians would accept such insults. Their chief's wife raped, his son dragged behind a horse to his death! The soldiers died in agony, without last rites. The mission burned like a torch in the night and too many of my brethren remained within. Yet they died in a state of grace, so surely their souls will be received directly into Heaven, and they'll stand beside the martyrs and saints exalted by Holy Mother Church.

In that belief is my comfort.

—*from the diary of Fray Juan Estévan de Bautista*

Chapter 5

"Doña Katherina, we have new guests."

Don Lucian's voice stopped her as she stepped onto the shaded veranda. She broke off her eager discussion of the Sacramento Valley's virtues with Mr. Gundersheimer. Temporarily sun blind, she blinked and struggled with her dismay. More guests! Already the hacienda strained at the seams. Now four more men stood silhouetted against the setting sun, their faces in shadow. One she recognized as Don Lucian. One wore the sombrero of a Spanish hidalgo. One had whipped off his hat at her appearance and one—one smelled like a skunk. She blinked at his pungent smell, but offered a cordial welcome in Spanish. "Of course, it's a pleasure."

Mr. Gundersheimer touched his hat to the strangers and stomped into the house without a word, his boots heavy on the floorboards. Puzzled, she stared after him as she handed the carpet bag to Leocadia and waved her inside. Turning back to the guests, she said, "If you gentlemen would take a seat, I'll send someone with refreshments while I prepare a room."

"Thank you, but I brought these gentlemen over for the day, only."

The pure British accent identified him, and she said in English, "Mr. Hartnell. Forgive me, I couldn't see you." She took the proffered hand of the courtly gentleman, the owner of one of the largest ranchos along the Salinas River. "Where is Señora Hartnell? Didn't you bring her?"

"As if I could keep Maria Teresa away," he scoffed. "We brought three of our daughters and seven of our sons. Twelve of our grandchildren trailed along, too. They're mingling with the ladies." He nodded out toward the lawn. "They want to whip up some enthusiasm for a dance tonight."

Familiar with his twenty children and his uncounted grandchildren who lived and visited at will, Katherine wasn't surprised by his wry humor. "They'll not have a struggle, I'm sure. There's been a *danza* every night of fiesta."

Smiling, she turned at the new sound of boots on the stair behind her, but her smile faded when a too-familiar voice agreed, "The mariachis are warming up already."

The sun blindness had faded, she realized, for Damian looked only too clear to her. One flashing glance from his fiery eyes, and she turned away to find the two strangers studying her.

They were Americans. One held his hat in his hand. He was tall and blond, tanned and windblown and attractive. The other . . . was dirty. A mountain man, clearly, dressed in the same kind of buckskins as his companion. Where his companion had taken advantage of civilization to wash, this man obviously considered cleanliness optional.

"Don Damian, you're looking well." William Hartnell stepped forward with the hearty good humor that had earned him his place as one of the most popular foreigners to settle in California. "I was here for that ridiculous display of bravery before the bull. You've started a whole new trouble for me. All my grandsons have decided they, too, should challenge the bull in such a manner."

"Lo siento." Damian grinned.

"Sorry, indeed," Señor Hartnell grumbled. "You're not sorry. You enjoy stirring the pot. But I have here someone who puts your exploit into the realm of mere braggadocio. Let me introduce my guests. Señora Katherine Maxwell, this is a great explorer from your country. John Charles Frémont, Señora Maxwell."

"John Frémont!" Katherine exclaimed, startled out of good manners. "John Charles Frémont, the explorer of the West?"

The blond man smiled in modest acknowledgement. "You've heard of me?"

"Heard of you?" Katherine held out her hand. "When I left Boston last year, all of the city was reading of your exploits. The pamphlet you published had been passed through many hands, and your courage was standard drawing room conversation."

He dropped his head and shrugged, but not before taking her hand. "I'm doing no more than any good man should do for his country."

"When I read 'The Report of the Exploring Expedition to the Rocky Mountains and to Oregon and Northern California,' it gave me the courage to proceed with my plans to board my vessel," she said, sincerity ringing in her voice. "If it weren't for you, Mr. Frémont—"

"Call me John Charles."

Startled, she disengaged her hand. "Thank you. I couldn't be so unceremonious."

"We're countrymen in a strange land. It's not familiarity, it's just friendship." He smiled with engaging candor. "You call me John Charles. I'll call you Katherine."

He made it sound so reasonable, and she was so thrilled by the request from a man she admired, she almost capitulated. After all, she argued to herself, many of the Californios called her Doña Katerina. Surely it was the same, and she could slip from her formality just once.

Then she looked at John Charles Frémont, and she knew it wasn't the same. The Californios used "Doña" as a title, an indication of respect. The use of her first name by an American wouldn't mean the same thing, and Frémont displayed a shallow familiarity by suggesting it. Firmly, she refused. "Thank you, Mr. Frémont, but I'm not used to being so disrespectful to a hero."

He wavered, wanting to press, to encourage intimacy. Yet he seemed to recognize her resolve. "A hero. You exaggerate."

"No, not at all." Instinctively, she identified his weak point and utilized it, flattering him with the truth. "If it weren't for you, I would still be languishing in Boston."

He twisted his hat and smiled modestly. "Well, if it weren't for Kit Carson, here, I would have never made it over the Sierras during that dreadful winter crossing."

"Of course. I should have guessed you were Kit Carson." Courtesy reasserted itself, and she shook his hand. His body odor discouraged any prolonged contact, and she stepped back. "To meet two such famous men is an honor."

"An honor." Damian agreed from above her left shoulder.

She glanced up, but he wasn't looking at his guests, as he should be. He watched her, and the fire of his displeasure scorched her. She glanced away and then back. She must have imagined it, for nothing on his smooth countenance revealed anything but polite welcome for his guests.

"An honor for all of us. I met you on your last trip into California, Señor Frémont," he said. "It is indeed wonderful that your writings brought us to the attention of the United States."

"Of course, of course!" Frémont said. He shook Damian's hand. "A pleasure to see you again, Don Damian. You and I spoke of California's annexation by my government."

"So we did." Damian's smile was nothing more than a cool curve of the lips. "That was when I believed the Californios would be allowed a say in their fate."

"The United States government has a policy of fair treatment of all its citizens, rich or poor."

"A pleasant fairy tale. If the United States were interested in anything but its own welfare, it wouldn't be hovering over California like a bird of prey over a dying man."

"England is hovering, too," Frémont reminded him. "Last

time I was here, we discussed the advantages of administration by the United States."

"Please, not on an empty stomach," Damian protested.

Bewildered by the change in Damian, Frémont lifted one hand and dropped it. Don Lucian and Mr. Hartnell, too, seemed paralyzed with shock.

Only Damian remained in control. "I'm told you have a large armed force with you."

Promptly, Frémont assured him, "Only sixty men. I left them at Mr. Hartnell's rancho. They're not a threat to you."

"General Castro doesn't agree, does he, Señor Frémont?"

The ingratiating smile on Frémont's face disappeared as if it had never been. "General Castro is nothing but a churlish windbag, a braggart. If he thinks he can command me with a letter—"

"A letter?" Damian leaned back on his heels. His shot in the dark had found an unexpected mark, and he pressed for information. "What does General Castro write?"

Mr. Hartnell sighed. "Lieutenant José Antonio Chavez arrived with a letter from General Castro, ordering Frémont and his men to pack their rifles and get out of Mexican territory at once."

"That Chavez spoke rudely to me!" Frémont quivered with the insult. "I told him I wouldn't obey such an order."

"Did you tell Castro?" Damian asked.

"I told Chavez to inform him of my displeasure."

"You didn't even have the courtesy to take pen in hand and reply yourself?" Don Lucian sounded scandalized.

Damian snapped, "Have you no respect for the *comandante* of your host country?"

Buffeted by conflicting emotions, Katherine stammered, "Why would General Castro order such a thing? Where is the Californio hospitality?"

In deference to her femininity and her nationality, Hartnell answered only, "Mr. Frémont ignored the General's specific order to stay away from the major coastal towns of Alta California. General Castro considers Frémont a threat to the continued peace of the area."

With sincere assurance, Frémont said, "I assure you, Miss Katherine, my men carry guns for their own protection."

He looked young and earnest, and Katherine didn't notice his use of her first name. "You have accomplished so much," she complimented him sincerely. "What a fantastic life you've led."

"Why, thank you, Miss Katherine."

This time she noticed. She stiffened, fingering her watch chain, but before she could chide him, Damian interrupted.

"Extraordinary, indeed," he agreed, a sarcastic edge in his voice, "to so betray his hosts."

Frémont shook his hair back from his forehead and struck a pose. "I have betrayed no one."

Rounding on Damian, Katherine declared, "Mr. Frémont would never cheat anyone. He's a national hero."

"Not of my nation." Damian drew himself up and looked down his aristocratic nose at her. "Not of my nation."

She stepped back, stricken.

"Now, see here, sir," Frémont objected, his southern accent ringing out.

"Damian," Don Lucian expostulated.

Recovering herself, Katherine lifted her chin. "No. Don Damian is right. I'm grateful for his reminder." Lifting her skirts, she strode into the hacienda, bumping the door frame in her rush to be away.

John Charles Frémont mashed his hat onto his head. "Sir, I'm a man, big enough to ignore the threats and lies of a bully, but you have been cruel to one of the flowers of womanhood. You, Don Damian, are no gentleman."

"Why do you look one way and steer another?" Don Lucian pitched his voice below the wild rhythm of the guitar, but he questioned his son with fierce exasperation. "She admires this

Frémont, and rather than let her discover for herself what a braggart he is, you drive her into his corner. She went storming off one way, he went storming off another. Everyone's mad at you."

Damian crossed his arms over his chest like a man who knew he'd done wrong, but would maintain his actions to the end. "She defended him."

"She's an American. He's an American. Why shouldn't she defend him?" Don Lucian's voice rose, and Damian shushed him. "What, you don't want our guests to know you're angry at Katherine? You think they haven't noticed how you stand and glower while they dance? You think your attitude hasn't soured the mariachis? It's the last _danza_ of this fiesta, and you act like a mule with a stone in its hoof."

"She thought he was attractive."

Don Lucian shook his head, turned on his heel, shook his head again. "Do you think that she'll never look at another attractive man as long as she lives? It is possible to admire your neighbor's apples without stealing any from his tree."

"She's a woman. Women are modest, shy, retiring. They wait until a man chooses them and accept with gratitude."

"Bachelors know much more about women than married men." Damian glared. "They must. If they didn't, they would be married, too."

"Well, she shouldn't think men are attractive."

Don Lucian shouted with laughter. "You mean she shouldn't think any man but you are attractive."

"She hasn't even noticed men for a year."

"Did you think this state of blessed blindness would last?" Don Lucian stepped back as one of the dance couples whirled off the cleared area and disappeared into the trees. "You worked hard to break through her isolation. Be glad that at last she's behaving as a normal woman should."

"I break through her isolation so every man can catch her eye? That wasn't my intent."

"No, I suppose it wasn't." Rubbing his forehead with his fingers, Don Lucian said, "Love is a temporary derangement, I suppose. Perhaps your courtship will proceed more smoothly when the fiesta is over and our guests leave. Meanwhile, why don't you find a woman and dance?"

"Who would I ask?" Damian queried.

"Ask Doña Maria Ygnacia. She's got enough problems, she'll hardly laugh at yours."

"Why?" Damian looked around him with observant eyes for the first time.

"Julio's neglecting her for the punch bowl again."

"Oh, God." Damian pushed away from the tree trunk where he rested his back. "What's the matter with that damned Julio?"

"That's what they're saying about you," he heard his father murmur, but Damian ignored him as he strode to the circle of chairs where the ladies rested between dances.

Maria Ygnacia sat there, talking with the elderly matrons, the widows, the women who had no one to dance with them. She wore flowers in her chignon, accenting the distinctive white streak in her black hair. Her dress, a crisp dimity, hung with lace at the collar and sleeves. Her lips smiled, her toe tapped, she fluttered her fan and gossiped madly. She gave every appearance of having a marvelous time, and Damian knew how miserable the quiet lady must be to put on such a performance.

Straightening his cuffs, he bowed before the group of women, then before Maria Ygnacia. "Dance with me," he commanded.

The wind off her fan dusted his face. "Thank you, Don Damian, but—"

He pulled her to her feet. "I'm honored." His arm around her waist, he led her away and whispered in her ear, "Misery loves company."

An unwilling laugh puffed from her lips. "Really, Don Damian, that may be true, but I swear this is not a good idea."

"Leave the swearing until I step on your toes," he advised. "They're playing a *jarabe*. You know how bad I am at those."

A smile played at the corners of her mouth as they took their places on the floor. "I remember."

"You would." His droll disappointment brought forth a genuine laugh.

She curtsied and he bowed. "As usual, the fiesta has been marvelous. This dancing in the meadow is a wonderful idea."

"To dance beneath the stars is always memorable," he agreed, "and I got to use my lanterns."

"They are pretty. Indeed, the ladies exclaimed over them, but we never suspected they were your idea, Damian." She took his hand and followed him through the intricate steps.

"I enjoy the Indian art work, you know that. I had the Indians take bits of colored glass and set them in wood, like the stained glass in the missions, and encase a candle holder in them." All around them, the trees hung with the glowing lights, adding a gracious fillip.

"They're like a flickering rainbow. I suppose you've just set the newest fashion among us." Old habits took over, and she looked at him with warmth and interest. "You always made me laugh."

"Looks," he said severely, "aren't everything."

She gurgled with merriment, and the sound caught at his throat. So had the young Maria Ygnacia laughed when the self-important Damian came courting. She'd been the loveliest thing in Alta California. It had been too long since he'd listened to her joy. "You were the only girl I ever asked to marry me."

"So many years ago," she retorted.

"You were the only girl I ever wanted to marry."

Her smile was still genuine, but a wisp of sadness stilled her sparkle. "Until last year, when a certain Americana—"

"Named Katherine. Yes, I know, but if I'd been married to you I would have never even seen her."

"Ah, we'll never know that." She spun in the dance. "Perhaps we'd have been so dedicated to each other you'd have never seen her—and perhaps you would have been stricken, as you are, yet trapped in a marriage with me."

"We'd have been so busy, I'd have never seen her. Our children—"

She stumbled. He cursed the tactlessness of his remark, first to himself, then, when he saw the tears hovering on her lashes, loudly. "I stepped on you. *Perdón, perdón.* Please, let me help you." He stood between her and the other dancers.

"Don't concern yourself," she said, playing along with him, holding an ankle he'd never come close to.

"I'm so clumsy. Let me take you to the house."

"I just need to sit."

"No, I insist." With a firm hold on her waist, he drew her away from the dancing and into the darkened walk between the party and the hacienda.

She struggled in earnest as they swerved into the trees, but he ignored her, dragging her along behind him. He stopped where they could still hear the murmur of voices and music, and see in the faint light from the lanterns. To go farther abroad would cause talk—talk he already risked. This chance he felt compelled to take, however. Angry with her unhappiness, he demanded, "*Madre de Dios,* Nacia, what made you take Julio over me? At least I'd have made you happy."

"I love him. Now will you stop tugging on me as if I were a dog?"

Letting her go, he turned to her. "You love him. Does he love you?"

She hesitated. "I think so. Yes."

He couldn't see her face in the dark, but he felt her distress. "Nacia," he began and stopped. He didn't know what to say.

"You want to know why there are so many rumors about us? Why they say Julio doesn't stay home? Why he drinks when we go out in public? Why he treats me as he does?" Her voice rose as she recited the litany of their woes. "Well, I don't know why he's doing those things. I don't know why he—" her voice broke "—why he treats me as if I've betrayed him. I haven't betrayed him, not ever. Not even with you. I never even teased him with you. I could have, for you were so dedicated and everyone knows what rivals you are. But the first time I saw Julio I knew I wanted him, and he wanted me. I didn't care that his father never married his mother, or that his mother was so poor they had to depend on the charity of others. Everyone said he was below me, but I had enough money for us both, and I thought it was forever."

"Now?"

"Now I don't know."

Hearing the tears she fought, he kept compassion from his tone. "Tell me what he's been doing."

"He leaves. For days, for weeks. I don't know where he's going. In the mountains, somewhere, or into the wilderness. He comes back with dirt under his fingernails and blisters on his hands."

"Julio?" he said, startled. "Julio would never . . . He adores the town. He adores civilization and all its trappings."

"I know, I know."

"Do you ask?"

"Not anymore. He won't tell me. But he likes it when I tend his hands and hover over him. He treats me with affection when we're home. It's better than the way—"

She stopped so abruptly he knew what she wouldn't say. "I hoped you didn't know."

"How could I not know? He fornicated with every whore in Monterey, the widows, the Indian women, the servant women." Humiliation sounded clear in her tone. "As if I wouldn't be slapped in the face with it every day."

"He's stopped that," he offered.

"Oh, my, yes."

Sarcasm and hurt, he diagnosed. "Julio's not an easy man to understand. I've known him all my life, and I still don't understand him. When we were young, the other boys called him 'bastard' and beat him. I leaped in to help him, and we both got our teeth knocked out." He chuckled a little. "Lucky they were loose, hmm?"

She didn't move, didn't react to his humor.

He sighed. "When he staggered to his feet, he kicked me for trying to help him. Then he helped me up. There are dark undercurrents in the man, but at the same time, if I had to trust my life to anyone, it would be to my father, or to Julio."

"But what is he doing, to get dirt under his fingernails and blisters on his palms?" she whispered. "What if it's illegal? Those dark currents you speak of—they worry me. What is he *doing*?"

"I don't know."

She began to cry, and he pulled her against his chest. "I don't know. I wish I could lie to you, but we've known each other too long for that. I don't know." She cried harder, and Damian wished, with all his heart, he was elsewhere. No matter how much he adored Nacia, no matter how badly she needed this emotional release, her tears still made him squirm.

She seemed to realize it, for as soon as she could, she controlled herself and stepped away. Her voice hoarse with grief, she said, "You always did what was necessary for my good, even if I didn't want you to."

Relieved, he stepped back. "Aren't I always right?"

"Yes, and aren't you a monster for pointing that out? But then—" her voice sharpened "—you're the same monster to all your friends."

"Are you calling me a busybody?" he asked, surprised by the notion.

"A dreadful busybody. I wonder, who does what is best for you?"

With the assurance of a strong and opinionated man, he replied, "I do."

"Well, in the opinion of your friend Nacia, what is best for you is also what's best for Doña Katherina. Perhaps you should think on that."

"My friend Nacia could hardly tell what's best for me or Doña Katherina in the space of one fiesta."

"The same could be said about my friend Damian."

Her rejoinder silenced him, and with astonishment, he wondered if she could be correct. Was he making hasty judgments about Nacia and Julio? Was he treading where no man should go? Most important, were Katherine's good and his own identical? Tucking it all away to bring up and examine later, he said, "_Arriba los corazones!_ Keep heart. You're a good woman, Nacia. The best woman for Julio, and he'll realize it soon."

"You're a good man." She touched his cheek. "When next I see you, I expect to be dancing at your wedding. Remember, a woman like Katherine will never—"

A male voice spoke close to them. "A touching scene. A farewell kiss between lovers, perhaps?"

Nacia quickly stepped away from Damian, and what had been a friendly talk now appeared furtive.

"Julio," Nacia faltered.

"The promise of another assignation, perhaps?"

"Julio, don't be an idiot," Damian ordered.

"An idiot?" Julio's voice grew louder. "Yes, I am an idiot. Thinking any woman could honor her vows. Thinking years of friendship mean anything."

Trying to hush him, Damian moved closer and observed, in the dim light, the swaying and disheveled figure of his friend. "We've been talking."

"Talking! A pleasant euphemism, that. Perhaps the wronged husband should take himself away." The darkened figure took a step forward. "Perhaps I should leave you two to your kissing."

The thick smell of liquor in the air washed over Damian, and he almost groaned. The punch bowl had too obviously been Julio's refuge this evening. Nevertheless, Damian had to try to defuse the situation, and he kept his tone low and reasonable. "No one has been kissing. Doña Maria Ygnacia would never—"

"*Doña* Maria Ygnacia? Just a moment ago, she was Nacia."

The loud, slurred words sounded like an accusation, and Damian cursed the caution that had brought him to a halt so close to the dance floor. At least if they stood farther away, the heads wouldn't be turning at the sound of a fight. "We are old friends, and your wife has never even allowed me to kiss the hem of her dress."

"My wife," he sneered. "My wife."

"Please, Julio." Nacia stepped forward to grasp Julio's arm. "Please. Please don't be angry. It was nothing."

"Nothing?" Julio shook her off, his voice raising to a shout. "Nothing? Is that what you call infidelity? Nothing?" Like a pronouncement of an elder, he roared, "You're a whore."

Damian caught Julio's fist as it lifted above Nacia. "Are you crazy, man? You don't want to hit her."

Julio paused and swayed, peering up at his captor. With the impaired faculties of a drunkard, he decided, "You're right. I don't want to hit her, but I want to *kill* you." His other fist came up in a roundhouse that caught Damian unprepared and knocked him to the ground.

Nacia screamed and Damian cursed, more at the noise she made than in pain. Julio leaped at him, but he rolled away. Julio smacked a tree trunk with his head. It would have put another man under, but the liquor had numbed Julio. He came up shaking his head and shouting, "*Idiota!* I'm going to murder you."

The music faltered as the dancers stopped, drawn by the peal of rage ringing out of the trees. Lanterns flickered their way, held by men running to the scene.

Damian tried to leap to his feet, but Julio met him halfway. They fell, pummeling each other, breaking their fists on each other's faces. Men and women surrounded them as they rolled on the grass.

A punch to his stomach doubled Damian over. Julio pushed

him down and yelled, "How dare you touch my Nacia? How dare—"

Fury burst in Damian. With a clip to the jaw, he knocked Julio off and seized him by the throat. Sitting on his ribs, Damian roared, "Only yesterday you knew I didn't want your wife. Stop being so stupid."

He felt a pounding on his shoulders and glanced up to see Nacia crying, "Stop, oh stop."

In a flash, he saw the lanterns around, the staring faces, and knew he stared social disaster in the face. Nothing could save them now, but he prayed for a miracle. Released, Julio's fist plowed a furrow in Damian's ribs. The wind erupted from Damian in a rush. He heard the blood explode in his head. There was a sudden silence.

The tinkle of glass drew his attention, and he realized the explosion he heard was not in his head, but a gunshot.

Chapter 6

A gunshot? The candle Katherine held dipped and almost went out as she jumped off the veranda and skidded to a stop. She could see the dance floor across the yard, and a circle of lanterns in the trees. She could see the shattered lamp above the mariachis, see the guitarist shaking glass, wood, and wax out of his hair. She could see the people who stood looking past her, past the hacienda. She turned with a sensation of dread.

Lumped together on the lane, a large group of rough-looking men were mounted on horses, leading mules, and carrying rifles. They watched the dying festivities in a grim, satisfied silence. One of them spat on the ground. Then a horse neighed restlessly, but the stillness conveyed a threat that no words could express.

In the middle and in front of the gang, John Charles Frémont sat astride a cream-colored horse. His hat was cocked over one eye, a little smile lit his face. He posed with arrogance, looking down his nose at the assembled Californios.

Before the peril implied by the Americans, the Spanish men had no defense. They carried no guns to a dance. Their women and children were assembled with them.

In the trees, she saw Julio reach down and pull Damian to his feet. Damian stood alone as Julio put an arm around Maria Ygnacia.

One by one, the children sought the protection of their parents. Their wives moved to their sides, motioning the children behind. The men stepped in front of their families, offering the feeble defense of their bodies.

Then, on Frémont's command gesture, the intruders rode away.

The Californios watched until the sounds had died. Before Katherine's appalled gaze, they moved toward the hacienda. Señora Medina came by, leaning on her son's arm. Alejandro led his pregnant wife, slow under the burden of his child. Rico had his children organized into a line, and he counted them as they entered the hacienda. His face bruised, Julio led Maria Ygnacia as if she were more precious than gold. Don Lucian came last, helping the stragglers carry their children. Passing her where she stood at the base of the porch steps, all of them mounted the steps with polite nods.

They said nothing, she realized, out of respect for her and the other Americans mixed in their number. What they wished to say about their contempt for Frémont's band would be said in the privacy of their chambers.

Tears pricked at her eyes, and she restrained the impulse to apologize. The Californios would only point out that she wasn't responsible for the actions of her countrymen. It would be true. Yet, in another sense, she carried the burden of that discourtesy on her shoulders.

As the last of the families moved into the house, the servants came out. In a giant sweeping motion, they removed the food, cleaned the broken glass, picked up the dropped handkerchiefs. Dazed at the rapid dissolution of the fiesta, Katherine still stood, candle flickering in her hand.

As the servants tugged the extra chairs toward the storage shed, Damian strolled out of the trees. He tucked one hand in his waistband. He gazed around, shook his head, and began to extinguish the lanterns. He pulled the branches down so he could douse the candle with a pinch of his fingers. Around the circle he went, and lights went out one by one.

He stood out there, in the darkness.

Katherine stood in the light of the porch lamps. An ache filled her, an ache she didn't understand. Walking through the grass to the edge of the porch, she leaned against the corner post and watched him return to his home. He didn't seem to notice her as he checked the hacienda's facade.

Disdaining the use of the stairs, he leaped the rail at the far corner, and extinguished the lamp. He walked to the steps and doused the lanterns that hung from the posts on either side. Only the candle above her head and the one in her hand still flickered. As his boots rang against the boards she was assailed with shyness. She turned away to compose herself, and turned back to find him watching.

Standing with uplifted face, she understood he'd always been aware of her.

Concern, pride, and anger warred in him; his puffed and bloody mouth expressed his rage.

Without real comprehension, she held out her hand, palm up. She didn't understand her emotions; she didn't understand his, but she felt the need to offer something, if only her friendship. Leaning over the rail, he ran his two fingers over her cheek, hesitated, caressed her lips. Giving her a rueful smile, he put out the candle over her head and went into the house.

She stood alone, holding the only light in the yard, her hand against her mouth.

"What are you doing?"

Mr. Smith jumped as if Katherine's words were a warning shot.

"Nothing! I . . . wanted some clean paper to write . . . my wife back in Washington, D. C."

She moved farther into the library and stared at the scattered documents on Damian's desk. She saw the splintered wood of the locked drawer. "Mr. Smith, you're getting a little confused. Two days ago you proposed to me."

"I never!" His indignation was a palpable thing. "Your own

conceit made you think I was proposing. I wouldn't propose to a plain thing like you."

"Yes, I can't imagine your 'wife' would appreciate it," she agreed, quite unmoved by his insult. "The other guests are leaving. Perhaps you should have asked for paper sooner."

He spread his hands in an innocent gesture. "Shucks, the company was just so good, I forgot to ask. Then you and that don of yours were busy with leavetakings. I thought, 'Why bother them?' and came in here by myself."

"Shucks," she answered back, her voice laden with scorn. Taking a breath, she controlled herself. "It occurs to me you may have left the States because someone took exception when you went through his desk."

"A man needs to find some peace and quiet where he can write his mother, doesn't he?"

"Your mother?"

"I mean, my wife."

"Mr. Smith. Far be it for me to make accusations without justification, but in light of your recent confessions, I find myself suspicious of your presence here."

"Ma'am?"

With the precise pronunciation of a Boston lady, she spelled it out. "Perhaps you're nothing but a common thief."

Mr. Smith took one giant step and loomed over her. "Little lady, that's a mighty big accusation. I don't like the way you're talking to me. Now I'm sure you want to apologize for that comment, and for hitting me the other day."

Her gaze traveled a long, long way up to the man's muddy eyes.

She was a lady. Hidden in the far reaches of her mind, she heard her mother's soft voice chiding her, urging restraint.

But he was trying to intimidate her, and she responded as if he were her Uncle Rutherford. Politely, emphatically, she spoke the truth. "A man who displays bravery only when confronted with a lone woman is not a man to be admired. What were you doing in Don Damian's desk?"

He snatched her wrist in his hand. "I don't think that's any of your business. I want an apology."

"Or what? You'll break my arm? You'll beat me?" Sarcasm sharpened her voice, and she could hear the challenge. "Better men than you have tried."

The pressure on her wrist increased; he bent it back. She glared, too angry to show pain as the bones ground together.

"Apologize," he demanded.

The ache expanded and became agony. Mr. Smith seemed to grow before her eyes.

A hand reached from behind her and grabbed Smith's elbow. She barely noticed it in her haze of pain, but Smith yelped and dropped her wrist.

"I believe you are making a mistake, Mr. Smith."

Cradling her arm, Katherine knew it was Damian, yet his voice was so clipped and his English so precise she hardly recognized him.

"You will please leave now. Your horse, such as it is, is saddled and waiting for you."

Smith's hand dangled off the end of his arm as if he were disabled. If Katherine hadn't been hurt, she would have wondered what Damian had done. Instead, she watched with fevered eyes as Smith leaped out the door.

That same hand that had disabled Smith now took her shoulder and turned her around. Damian clutched her and shook her. "You, my dearest Katherine, will do me the favor of not attacking like a bantam rooster after a fox."

The blood in her veins froze in resentment. Who did he think he was? In a few short days, he'd stared at her as if he considered her his property, been angry with her, kissed her. She was in no condition to consider safety or propriety. "I am not," she pronounced in her clear, crisp tones, "your dearest Katherine."

"Perhaps not, but you are a lady." He spoke English, but his accent strengthened. "I never expected to hear you speaking so, using such manners. What would your family say?"

Without realizing, he struck deep into her soul, and her self-possession shattered as it hadn't with Mr. Smith.

"You mean, 'what would your mother say?' Or perhaps, 'your mother didn't teach you very well.' " The bitter lessons of her Aunt Narcissa echoed in her tone.

Katherine sagged against his desk, and offered a tentative excuse and a tentative smile. "My Aunt Narcissa would tell you it's that streak of rebellious ingratitude that blemishes my character. No doubt she's right. I have found that being used brings out the worst in me."

He failed to respond with empathy or expression. "In the future, you will behave with a trifle more sense while under my roof."

The smile was wiped from her lips. "Would you have me let him rifle your desk? The man is convinced he'll receive your lands if—when!—the Americans welcome California into the fold. And what right have you to comment on my pugnacious tendencies, when your eyes are blacked and your lip's split?" His face darkened as she called attention to his injuries. She waved a hand at the chaos of papers Smith had created. "Did you believe I did this?"

"American ways are beyond my understanding."

At first, she could scarcely comprehend him. As the significance of his words found their mark, she found herself standing straighter, taller, with lifted chin and accusing eyes. "Do you believe I would search your private papers?" She walked behind the desk and jerked out the drawer with the broken lock. "Do you believe I would do this?"

"You misunderstand me. American ways are beyond my understanding, for should a California woman come upon a thief in my desk, she would run for help." He watched her with compelling demand. "She wouldn't attack the thief."

"I am not yours to command, nor am I subject to your whims."

"My whims?" His voice deepened, and she observed his eyebrows. They didn't curve across his brow as most eyebrows did, but slanted straight up. They added a devilish fillip to his countenance, and accentuated the impatience in his eyes. "You consider it a whim that I'm concerned about your well-being? That I wish you to avoid the broken bones and brutality that come with belittling a much larger opponent?"

Logic. How she hated its use in an argument. How like a man to interject it. "I think—" she drew a breath "—that you are concerning yourself with my well-being more than is allowed between employer and employee."

"I'm responsible for you in a way that has nothing to do with employment."

She ignored that. "This might be a good time to tell you my plans."

"Your plans?"

"My plans to leave here."

"Ah."

All expression smoothed from his countenance, and he looked so bland she stumbled as she spoke. "I realize, I appreciate, your efforts on my behalf. I do not know if I would have survived this last year without the help and goodwill of your family, your servants, and you."

"I?"

"Of course, you." Irritation shuddered up in her, but she subdued it. "You were my savior, as I tried to explain to you just two nights ago on the balcony. But I also know you created the position of housekeeper for me, dislodging the qualified Leocadia from her work so I would have something to focus on until I was capable of functioning in society. That time has come." She was, she realized, rambling on like a lawyer. She hated it, but she sprang from a family of lawyers. When she was nervous, the pomposity she detested in her uncle sprang forth from her own tongue. "I also know that this is your favorite house. Yet since my arrival you've avoided this hacienda. I believe that if I were gone, you would feel comfortable once more with your family."

He turned away from her and picked up the statue created for him by the Indian artisans on his rancho. It was a female, naked except for her hair, which trailed down her back and over her shoulders. Her hands worked busily to braid one side; her face was tender and thoughtful. "My rancho in the Central Valley has represented a freedom to me this past year. I needed a place to grieve for my friend. I'm sorry if you mistook my desire to be alone for the desire to be away from you."

His hands roved over the dark wood, and her gaze followed, fascinated. Katherine had admired the work when it had been presented to him at Christmas. It was art at its purest, and she'd seen nothing wrong with the unclothed state of the woman. But now an odd feeling possessed her as he examined the rounded hollows and belled hips with his fingers. He seemed to be taking an almost sensuous pleasure in the smooth grain; she felt as if she were intruding on a personal moment.

He caught her gaze. "I hope you will change your mind and remain with us. I promise you I will spend more time at this hacienda."

Something in those dark eyes reminded her of the bullfight, and she answered with care. "I don't believe that is the best solution. I can't stay here under your roof. No matter how ill-founded, the rumors would begin."

"My father makes an admirable *duenna*."

"I don't believe he will serve," she said austerely.

"No, I suppose not." Not a crinkle of amusement disturbed his face. "It's too late, anyway. The rumors have already swept Alta California."

"Oh, no." Her dismay was automatic. "A rumor like that could follow me."

"All the way to Boston," he agreed.

But she wasn't going to Boston. It hovered on the tip of her tongue, but some sense of self-preservation kept her from uttering it. Her plans were her own, she decided. She would remain in California, seek a position in Los Angeles, and send a letter to Don Lucian when she was well settled. Very well settled. "I must go at once."

"As you say." He smiled amiably, without emotion, and placed the statue on the desk once more. "I will have to find another way to convince you to stay. Now I must go say goodbye to my guests. Will you come out?"

"Right away." For the first time, she realized how worried she'd been about Damian's reaction. As he left, a swell of relief swept her. He hadn't been angry or upset that she would leave his home. He really hadn't been upset.

He hadn't been upset at all. Katherine chewed her lip as she opened the door to her bedroom. She closed it behind her, resting her head on the wooden panel. Her stomach had ached so much she hadn't eaten dinner. Uselessly, her hands clenched on thin air.

Leocadia had seen no reason to continue the pretense of letting her do the housekeeping, so Katherine had been reduced to a figurehead. She directed the servants in the cleaning and stowing of the party equipment, yet never dirtied her hands. It left a lot of time for thinking.

Damian hadn't been upset at all. Her relief had changed, twisted, become anxiety. Another scene with Emerson Smith. Another scene with Damian. Two such unpleasant clashes should have sent her into a black depression. Instead she worried and struggled with the inconsistencies.

Why had Damian been so untouched by her announcement? He should have been surprised. He should have protested and exhorted. Instead, he had been indifferent. That was out of character for a hidalgo whose courtesy extended to the lowest of his servants. He had made her uncomfortable with the confirmation of the rumors she feared. He had said he would have to find another way to convince her to stay. That almost sounded like a threat.

She shrugged uneasily. Surely not.

Untying her crumpled apron, she tossed it on a chair. She unpinned the broach that held her white collar and winced. Her wrist was still tender, and she muttered, "He was right. I have to stop attacking ten-foot-tall bullies." Now that she no longer faced Damian, she admitted his reproof was justified. More than justified, deserved. A broken wrist healed poorly, if at all, and her unthinking anger was a poor excuse for seeking one.

Someone had lit the candle on her bedside table. Leocadia, she supposed. Her dressing screen protected the flame from the window's breeze, and the glow turned the polished wood of the bed and the floor amber. It pleased her eye and drew her gaze to the corner. Collar in hand, she came farther into the room.

There, spread out on her bed, was a dress. She closed her eyes, and opened them again. Yes, it was definitely a dress. A pretty dress.

The wishes of the previous day rose up to haunt her. She took a fold between two fingers and rubbed it; the texture was fine-grained and smooth. It was a cotton muslin of green stripes alternating with tiny flowers. She picked it up by the shoulders. The neck was plain cut and a kerchief of white lace fluttered to the floor. The sleeves were puffed; tiny buttons shaped like flowers ran up the back. The skirt flared in yards of material.

Holding the gown against herself, she stepped in front of the gilded mirror. In a spasm of pleasure, she exclaimed, "It's beautiful." She twirled with it once, hugged it, laid it back on the bed. Keeping her eye on it as if it could disappear, she unhooked Tobias's watch from her waistband. Tenderly, she put it in the drawer of her bedside table. She stripped her black garment off so quickly she never noticed the pain in her wrist. The flowered dress slipped over her head and she fussed with the sleeves to set them correctly. With her hands at her back, she held the bodice tight around the waist.

"Such an attractive woman," she said aloud. Her eyes sparkled in the candlelight. Her hair—she reached up and ripped off her cap. The pins went flying. Her thick hair reflected the candlelight in glints of gold. The low neck of the dress combined with her hands-in-back pose brought her bosom up over the top of the bodice. The kerchief would be needed.

The Spanish señoritas would find Katherine Chamberlain Maxwell a competitor when next they met. She would buy a fan. Ivory, with green ribbons threaded in it. She imitated a señorita's flirtatious pose with the imaginary fan. She lifted her skirt to display her shapely ankle. She fluttered the fan before her face, batted her eyes and murmured, "*Por favor, querido.*"

She looked ridiculous.

She dropped her hands, stopped her posturing. The face in the mirror looked embarrassed, and she lifted her chin. She was a sensible American woman, out of touch with the fiery-tempered Californios. "Well, that's that," she said bracingly, lifting the dress off. She hung it with care on a dowel, her hands lingering on the kerchief. Her petticoats followed. Her shoes required patience, for the strapping laced around her ankle had knotted. She worked it until her leather slippers rested side by side against the wall. With a sigh, she went to stand back in front of the mirror for ruthless self-examination.

Plain yellow hair with no curl. Plain green eyes. Freckles marching across the bridge of her nose, down her chin, across her chest. A plain body, with a medium-sized bust, a small waist made smaller by her plain white corset, and medium-sized hips. Legs that were too long for her body. Even the wide lace at the bottom of her pantalettes couldn't disguise that. Plain Katherine Anne trying to act the coquette was as laughable as an old mare pining for a young stallion. Her eyes wandered to the hook where the fine dress hung. "I can't keep it," she said aloud. "I'll give it back to him."

"He won't take it."

She jumped and screamed. The deep voice came from the shadows by the wall. She strained her eyes, and a lucifer flared. Damian sat in her cushiony chair, a cigar between his fingers, his dark gaze fixed on her. He rested on his spine, his legs stretched out straight. He should have looked relaxed, but his heels were braced against the floor. Braced, to keep him from flying at her. He lit the cigar and shook out the light.

Putting her hand on her chest to still her thumping heart, she quavered, "What are you doing here? Are you mad? Today you tell me there is gossip about us. Tonight you're in my room?" Her voice gained strength. "What are you doing here?"

"So many questions," he chided.

"And what do you mean, 'he won't take it'? Your father understands I can't accept charity."

"My father didn't give you that dress. I did. My father's not the one who tore your widow's weeds." He drew on the cigar and the tip glowed brightly. "Remember, my Catriona?"

She leaped towards her wrapper, still hanging on the wall, and his hands closed on her shoulders before she had taken two steps.

"You enjoyed it." His breath was smoky; his voice a deep growl.

She tried to jerk around, but he wouldn't allow it. He kept one hand firm on her arm, the other tangled in the strings of her corset.

"No, my Catriona. I've already made the acquaintance of your fist. I heartily approve of its use on a certain Señor Smith, but my throat is still tender from your caress."

She stomped back with her heel, but he leaped up and avoided her.

Chuckling, he said, "Yes, you're lethal from the back as well as the front. No doubt about it." He let her go.

Swinging on him, she drew herself up with steely dignity. She glared as fiercely as she could, imitating her aunt's haughty expression.

She wished that he were just a little shorter. A little shorter, not quite so broad of shoulder, and not so like her dream of the devil and temptation. His white shirt was open, all the studs that held it gone, and his carved mahogany chest shone in shadow and light. His cuffs were rolled above his elbow. The muscles of his arms revealed his inclination for hard work. He wore no stockings, no boots, and it bespoke an intimacy she feared. "You are in my bedroom. You have no right in my bedroom."

"Sometimes a man takes his rights." He stepped back to his thin cigar, smoldering on the tin pan that had never been in her room before, and lifted it to his lips. He studied her defiant posture. His gaze lingered on the swells of her breasts, and his eyes, when he raised them, held amusement and appreciation. "You've woken up at last. Haven't you?"

Rage and fright faded beneath his inviting smile, but she replied to only the words, not the meaning. "I wasn't asleep."

"Weren't you?"

She understood his message, and she held herself stiffly erect to combat the croon of his voice.

"You're awake now, aren't you, *mi querida*? Completely awake. You've been a butterfly, hidden away in a cocoon, protected from the winds of life. Now the time has come. You're crawling out and spreading your wings. All your nerves are exposed. You don't know if you're ready to face the world." He stepped forward. His hand rose and stroked her cheek. "Yet beauty isn't meant to be hidden, and you're so beautiful."

She wanted to laugh his words to scorn, but how could she? The woman she saw in the mirror didn't seem to be the same woman reflected in his dark eyes. Sincerity and admiration shadowed the tender curl of his mouth. He practiced seduction with his smooth Spanish-accented English, with the smoky scent of his breath, with the unveiled appreciation of his countenance—and she, like any credulous girl, believed him.

She sighed deeply, and the corset that held her in its tight clasp slipped. Startled, she grabbed at it, looked down and wondered why the garment had failed her.

His chuckle caught her off her guard.

She peeked at him, and remembered his nimble fingers caught in her laces. Pride brought her chin back up. "Is that my function, then, to provide you with diversion?"

"You're diverting in your innocence." His words were meant to soothe, but the white flash of his grin told another story.

"Innocence, indeed, if I thought you rescued me from my distress for sweet friendship's sake. Is this the payment I make to you for your kindness?" She nodded towards the big bed. "Do I reimburse you in the traditional way?"

His smile vanished, but not his understanding. "I told you before, gratitude has no place between us. Everything I've done, I've done for Tobias. Everything I do tonight has nothing to do with Tobias. This is between you and me. Between the woman who wants to leave and the man who would keep her here. If there is obligation involved, it will be my obligation."

"I beg your pardon?" Astonished, she glared with a lady's indignation.

"Such dignity," he admired. The smile tugged at his mouth again. "I expect to find pleasure in that bed tonight. I expect to give you even more pleasure than I receive. That is obligation, is it not?"

"You conceited—do you think I'm tamely going to take you to my bed?"

"Tamely? No, there will be nothing tame about it." He ground the cigar out in the tin plate, stalked toward her like a big cat on the prowl.

23 May, in the year of our Lord, 1777

Fray Patricio and I risked our lives in the burning chapel, rescuing the holy vessels we had fashioned from the gold the Indians gave us. We put the vessels in a chest and ran with it to the river. There we met Fray Amadis and Fray Lucio, and together we hid in the reeds. Constantly wet and hungry, we followed the river west. Our prayers availed us, and that river joined a much larger river flowing north. From there we could see the mountains, and we fled over the plains to the foothills.

It was then that the Indians spotted us. They have bedeviled us ever since. We live in fear of the unknown, buoyed only by our determination to carry the gold back to the mission. There it will be received as proof of our success.

—from the diary of Fray Juan Estévan de Bautista

Chapter 7

She stumbled back, but he reached out to her and lifted her protective hands away.

Pain shot through her wrist, and she muffled a groan. He dropped her hands as if they burned him. "Did I hurt you?"

His concern was so sincere, his distress so obvious, she assured him, "No, it's only a twinge." Then she cursed herself. If she were a clever woman, she would have moaned and complained until he left her from guilt or disgust.

His gleaming eyes noted her bravery and her mistake. With care he gathered her fingers in his and brought her hand close to his face. "Ah." He sighed. "The injury of a valiant woman." He probed the swelling. "It will heal, but I'll be careful."

"What are your injuries?" With a jerk of her chin, she indicated the bruising of his face. "Are they the injuries of a valiant man?"

An ironic smile curved his lips. "Not at all. They were the results of stupidity, pure and simple."

As he spoke, her other hand crept up surreptitiously. Seeking protection, she hitched the corset up, but he noticed and ordered, "Let it go. That thing won't protect you. It will only get in our way."

" 'That thing' is a corset," she replied fiercely. "True ladies sleep in them to protect their bell figure."

"Then you're not a true lady."

She repeated the phrase as if it were a prayer. "I beg your pardon?"

"When you first came to Rancho Donoso, I guarded your door every night. Every night, you cried out in your sleep. I would check on you. Your corset was always on the chair, and when the nights grew warm, you discarded your nightgown, also." Embarrassed by his revelations, exposed by his memory, grateful for his care, she looked up. Right above her, his face was noble and sure and possessive. He let go of her wrists, reached around her as if he had every right, and loosened her corset strings until the traitorous garment could slide down. He tugged, and she let him push it to the floor. "Step out," he demanded.

Picking it up off the floor, he set it on a chair. "The rest is up to you."

She took a breath, the kind of deep breath her corset forbade her. "Do you think I'm going to disrobe for you?"

Stepping up against her again, he said, "Not without persuasion." He swung her up on the high mattress. She wiggled back, and he let her go until she found the middle of the bed. Then he vaulted onto the mattress and wrapped his arms around her.

She protested, "Hey!" but he held her close against his chest. Just held her, accustoming her to the feel of him.

It wasn't what she expected. She expected fire and struggle, not such a feeling of solid inevitability. His bare chest tickled her cheek. His heartbeat thumped in her ear. Involuntarily, her body relaxed. Sternly, she brought it back to attention. "Why are you doing this?"

"Because you seek to leave me." His reply took her breath with its simplicity and candor.

"I don't understand. There's never been anything between us. Only friendship, and I have many friends who never expect to bed me."

"You are an unobservant woman. Your male friends would love to find heaven in your arms, but your own lack of interest stopped them. Most men need encouragement to seek out a woman."

"You've already seen how poorly I encourage." She burned with humiliation as she remembered her performance before the mirror.

She couldn't see his face, but she heard no laughter in his voice as he agreed. "No, the light flirtation is not for you. Your dignity doesn't encourage it."

"What is it about you that needs no encouragement?"

"A man doesn't choose to be struck by lightning." He sounded wry and resigned. "But he thanks God when he is."

She pushed at him and he sat up obediently. She didn't expect that, and she lay there, staring at him, until his gaze wandered down her form. Then she scrambled to her knees. There was a readiness about him that discouraged flight, yet she was aware of her dishevelment. The neck of her chemise drooped, her pantalettes rode up over her knees. She ought to look around for a way of escape, but it seemed smarter to keep Damian under observation.

"You stare at me so warily, Catriona." His lids drooped over his eyes. "What do you expect me to do?"

"I don't know." She pushed her hair from her eyes. "What are your plans?"

She watched in horror as his hand cupped her breast. Shock hit her like a dash of cold water. Why did he touch her there?

Why did the contact bring her pleasure?

She didn't move as his fingers moved over the cotton to find her nipple. Only when he began a slow circling did she come alive, dashing his hand from her. "How dare you?"

Scrabbling away, she kicked at him when he grabbed her ankle, but he held her firm and demanded, "Why the alarm? Why now?"

"You stroked me." Her breath came in little gasps.

"It's necessary," he reminded her.

"Not there."

"No, not necessarily there, but I promised to bring you joy." Observing her until she tucked her trembling hands beneath her knees, he suggested, "That's a good way to fulfill my promise."

Emphatically, she shook her head, pushed to an admission she didn't want to make. "Pleasure is something men find in bed."

He released her ankle and she pulled it under her hip. She curled up now, a ball of defensive inhibitions. He considered her. "Are you saying that no one has ever touched your breasts?"

She blushed to hear him say the word, but she replied with bravado. "My cousins used to try until I taught them better."

"Good God." He sighed. "Tobias never. . . ." He waved an expressive hand.

She made a sound of dissent.

"It's not my intention to pry into your married life, but didn't he even attempt to—?"

"No."

"So you've never—"

He hesitated, and she prodded, "Never what?"

With deliberate care, he pulled his shirt from his waistband. "A virgin."

She shook her head.

"Perhaps not in the literal sense, but . . . what did you feel when I kissed you in the library?"

She covered her hot cheeks with her hands. "Please."

He laughed softly. "Thank God I didn't mistake that reaction." He slid the cloth down his arms and pushed it off onto the floor. "Do you like to look at me?"

Her gaze skittered across his shoulders. "Yes."

"Why?"

"You remind me of a statue my father kept on his desk. Except for—"

"Except for—?"

"The statue didn't have a head or arms."

He wasn't provoked; indeed, he seemed to find delight in her sharp retort. "I have all the necessary parts."

"No doubt." She checked him once, quickly. "The parts are damaged."

"These, you mean?" He indicated the bruising across his ribs. "More evident stupidity. If you're worried about buying mangled goods, I assure you they will fade."

Her little nose tilted into the air. "I'm not interested in buying at all."

"So you'll give yourself to me if I hurry and get it over with."

His phrasing offended her, and her discomfort with the subject produced her prim response. "I do not give myself to anyone. I was momentarily tempted to comply with your wishes for the feeling of closeness such union provides."

"Ah. Have you changed your mind?"

Irrepressible sarcasm bubbled up. "Am I allowed to change my mind?"

"No." He drawled as if he thought about it as he spoke. "But you are allowed to imitate me. Take off your chemise, so I may enjoy the liberties your eyes pursue."

"You are quite mad."

"Am I?" With deliberate movements, he unbuttoned his breeches.

"What are you doing?" A stupid question, she supposed, but it appeared he was taking off his pants.

"Watch and find out." In a smooth, fluid movement, he slipped them over his hips and tossed them on the floor.

She was petrified. Not with fright, but with an overwhelming disturbance. She'd never seen a naked man before. Tobias certainly hadn't found it necessary to remove all his clothes at any time in their brief marriage. Damian, on the other hand, seemed to consider it an obligation. He stretched out on his side. One hand cupped his chin, the other rested on the bed near her knee. Unbidden, her gaze ran down his body, then jerked up to his face. "Do you never wear undergarments?"

Ignoring both the ice of her tone and the tremble in her voice, he answered, "I believe I'll have no need of them." He smiled at her with warmth and invitation. "You can look all you like."

For the first time since she'd discovered him in her room, he was relaxed. There was no menace in him, no amusement at her expense. He seemed to have all the time in the world. In some strange way, he made her feel restricted. Where before she felt distinctly unclothed, sitting there in her chemise and pantalettes, now she noticed she was overdressed. She wondered how he could so distort her perceptions.

When she said nothing and stared fixedly into his eyes, he waved his hand down his body in an encompassing gesture.

She looked. She couldn't help it. Her gaze lingered. She couldn't help that, either.

"As you can see, men make their desire obvious. It makes them vulnerable."

"What?"

"Vulnerable. A man cannot deny his attraction, yet a woman can hide hers beneath a cloak of lies and innuendo."

"There's nothing to hide," she snapped.

"Ah, then you'll take off your top."

He was clever. Diabolically clever. If he kept talking, he'd have her convinced of his truth. Yet, if she didn't keep him talking—

"We've got all night."

Could he read her mind?

"Did you know there's a difference between men and women?"

She snorted.

"For instance, men tend to find their satisfaction very quickly. Women, on the other hand, take longer. But with preparation, a woman can become—" his voice became a breathy whisper "—aroused."

She crossed her arms, one elbow over the other, on her stomach. His blatant appreciation made her glance down and realize her protective gesture had carried her bosom up. She rearranged herself.

"When a woman becomes aroused, she becomes soft, pliant. There's a way for a man to bring her to that state." He shifted closer, wrapping himself around her tightly held knees, enclosing her in his warmth. He tugged on the string at the top of her chemise, untying it. She grabbed for his wrist, but he took her hand, tucked it back in her lap, patted it. "You were willing to take me, if I didn't drag it out."

His fingers caught at her lacing again. She put her nails into his hand and said, "No!"

"Why would you give yourself without a fight?" He stared into her eyes, demanding truth. "I expected to be covered with bruises by now, ripped with your nails." He pulled his hand away and showed the four crescents of blood. "Yet I have only this. Why would you give yourself so easily?"

Impatient with his curiosity, unwilling to share her unorthodox ethics, she felt driven to revelation. "Must everyone believe fornication brings such a tremendous adjustment? I found it changed nothing. The morning after our wedding, Tobias was the same. I was the same. We spoke of the same matters. He told me about the legends in California. I told him about the quilt I worked on. We went for a walk. It was nothing."

"Madre de Dios." He flung himself onto his back, his arms outstretched.

His whole, beautiful body lay before her, and the vaguest tingle disturbed her nerves. She ignored it, charging on. "I have long held doubts about my sense of propriety. Most ladies swoon at the mere thought of their wedding night. I approached it as a sensible woman, and I was neither frightened nor disappointed." He groaned, and she looked to see if he were in pain, or making noises of dissatisfaction. She couldn't tell.

She noted a definite difference in body color that began at his waist. He was lighter below, darker above, with the exception of his calves. They, too, were tanned. She puzzled for a moment, deciding that it was the result of working without a shirt. With very little effort—really, very little effort—she dismissed his body from her thoughts. "I admit, the thought of carrying your baby when I leave is distressing. Nevertheless, in my understanding, conception is unlikely at this time."

"What a disappointment." He sounded reflective.

"What do you mean?"

"You dear, sweet, innocent *niña*. I mean our child will be welcome at any time."

She was alarmed again, shaken from her conviction she could expound and convince.

Clearly he read the message of her body. "Our child would be an extension of ourselves and our dedication to each other."

"You are quite insane. We mean nothing to each other. If my body found this pleasure you seem convinced you could give me, then I could find the same pleasure with another man of your skills."

"What?"

He sat up, and she nodded at him. "Of course. If there is more to this man-woman thing than I'd experienced before, it's a matter of skill and practice. I already know that Tobias had had little practice, so it stands to reason—"

"Good God, woman!" he said. "You reduce the most wonderful mystery in the world, the mystery of attraction and passion and love, to a tangle of reason and pedantic words." Under her nose, he slapped the back of his hand into his palm. "Who am I?"

Jumping beneath his emphatic stress, she stuttered, "Why, you're Don Damian de la Sola."

"Yes, but *who* am I?"

She didn't understand what he searched for with such intensity. "You're the Spanish son of a landowner here in California."

"Yes," he answered, pleased. "Who else am I?"

"You're a good friend, and a responsible master. You smoke. You dress quietly." A cloud drifted over his features, grew stormier when she stammered, "You have the respect of your vaqueros, so you ride well, work the cows well, breed good horses. You have a rancho in the Central Valley. You like it there."

He rubbed his hands wildly in his hair. It stood on end, and its ruffled state displayed the white that salted it above the ears.

"You have some grey hairs," she added, trying to repair his distress.

"No, no. That's not what I mean at all," he said in despair. "When you look at me, you see only things. You see my possessions. You see my friends, my horses. You see skin over muscles and bones. You see legs and arms and a masculine part that makes my voice deeper than yours and puts this hair on my chest. But I'm more than that." Leaning over her, he stared into her eyes as if he would tell her something without words. "I'm the man who waited for you before I knew who you were. I'm the man who recognized my mate from the moment you stepped off the ship. I'm the man who has foresworn women, all women, since the day I saw you."

She shook her head against his intensity, and he tried again.

"Mine is the soul that reaches for yours. Mine is the soul that sings to yours without words. Mine is the soul that lifts yours through the empty places where you must walk."

She could hear him, but she couldn't comprehend him. She wouldn't comprehend him.

One winged eyebrow rose in cynical disdain. "Bah, you're too immature to know. Let me know when you can see me. Let me know when you know me. Call me by my name when you want me."

He rolled off the bed and stalked to the window, and tears rose in her eyes. She didn't know this Damian. She didn't know him at all.

When her eyes opened, a grey light permeated the room, yet it wasn't early. Dawn had slipped by, masked by the clouds and a slow, steady drip of rain. As if he'd never moved all the night long, Damian stood leaning against the window sill, looking out over his land. A curl of smoke drifted in on the wind, and she knew a lighted cigar rested between two fingers.

He was naked.

His dark hair lay ragged against his shoulders. His back tapered down to a . . . a hinderpart that was so muscled the sides of his cheeks were concave. His legs were the legs of a rider. She blushed and closed her eyes at the comparison.

After all, she was a sensible woman. Looking at him solved nothing and most certainly wasn't the act of a lady.

On the other hand, she would probably never look on another naked man, and if she did, he couldn't be as pleasant to the eye as Damian. She preferred to think of herself as sensible; logical was another adjective she applied. Temptation, she realized glumly, was something she'd never encountered before.

Opening her eyes, she got the full frontal view.

She didn't blink. He leaned against the wall, his cigar in his hand, watching her with the same possessive challenge he would a fractious horse.

She looked him over. In for a penny, in for a pound, her father always said. After all, he'd come to her last night. He'd never left the room. She'd been asleep, curled into a little ball of misery when he lay down, yet she'd known he rested there. He'd pulled her quilt over him, keeping the blanket between their bodies, and she'd snuggled tight to his shoulder. She wouldn't speak of his tenderness in the daylight, yet the dark would always bring the memory.

"Why did you guard my chamber every night?" she asked,

picking up the conversation just as if they were seated in a parlor and she'd interrupted him to serve him tea.

He raised his cigar to his lips and took a long pull. His eyes half closed with the pleasure, and he relaxed as he let out the smoke in a steady stream. "Because I didn't know if your life was in danger. It was a possibility, although I'd taken every precaution to ensure that no one, except the servants, knew where you were."

A thrill at his protectiveness flustered her, and she willed it away. "Did you think the murderer was interested in me?"

"Probably not, but since there was no obvious motivation for the killing of Tobias, I had to ensure your safety. You were in no condition to ensure it for yourself. My vaqueros patrolled every night; my servants watched over you. When nothing happened we released the information of your whereabouts and I left, making a great noise, for the Sacramento Valley."

"Why?" she asked, startled.

"To bait the trap. It was as guarded as I could make it, yet we had to draw out the murderer, if he were interested in you."

"I can't believe you would abandon the hacienda when—"

"I did not." He smiled grimly. "I lived with the vaqueros."

Knowing the rough conditions of the cowboys, she objected, "Why would you live such a life, when comfort was so close?"

"It gave me something to distract me."

"From what?" she asked, unthinking.

His steady gaze answered the question before he said, "From the death of my best friend. From the thought of his wife, sleeping in my house and bedeviled with nightmares."

She found herself looking at the walls, the bedposts, the chair, the pitcher. Anything was better than looking at him. She didn't want to contemplate what she'd learned about his passions last night. Not yet; she wasn't ready.

Turning to lean on his shoulder, he stared out the window. "No one came after you, though. Eventually, I really did go to the Sacramento Valley. My rancho needed attention, and I'd been neglecting it. Still, you didn't see me every time I came back to check on you."

"Oh."

"You've depended on me for a long time."

"So it would appear." She didn't like his insinuation, and she sat up, tucking the sheet beneath her armpits briskly. That air of efficiency was one of her best-loved and most effective masks; she wore it now with determination. "Well, it's not necessary any longer." Holding her hand up when he would protest, she said, "I assure you, I've been taking responsibility for my own safety and my own actions for many years."

"You don't have to do that anymore. I'll take care of you." He watched her intently.

"A pleasant euphemism for an unpleasant thing. My uncle said the same thing to the chambermaid, and within a year she was thrown into the streets swollen with his bastard."

He looked disgusted. "A disagreeable term for an innocent baby."

His biting reproof made her feel ashamed. Defensive, she retorted, "The poor girl was bewildered, lost, starving. I'd sneak out with food, but she finally sold her body until she swelled so big no man would buy it. But men aren't finicky, she discovered. She'd made enough to support herself until the babe was born."

"What happened?" he asked.

"The baby, she left in a church. She'd hang around the alleyway outside Uncle Rutherford's, and I'd talk to her." She grinned in lopsided amusement. "Maura was pretty, you understand. That's what attracted dear Uncle Rutherford, of course. She was none too intelligent, either, and that kept her on the streets. But she knew despair when she saw it. She offered me money."

"For what reason?"

"Because I had none. Because I had less than the lowest servant." With the same twisted smile, she looked him straight in the eye. "Because she felt sorry for me."

He didn't smile back or indicate in any way he'd heard or understood what she'd told him. "Did you tell your uncle about the child?"

"When it was born, do you mean?" He nodded and her smile vanished. "When I told Uncle Rutherford he had a son, he never even raised his head. He asked, 'So?' "

"What did you say?"

"I threatened—" her voice cracked, her eyes swam with tears, and she lowered her head to hide them "—I threatened to tell Aunt Narcissa. He asked me how long I thought my mother would survive in the streets like Maura."

His hands clamped onto the sheet on either side of her hips, and she jerked her head up. How had he gotten across the room so quickly? The blaze of fury that ignited his face was answer enough.

"Do you compare me to your Uncle Rutherford?"

"No," she stammered. "That's not what I meant at all. I meant—" She remembered what she'd said and she knew why he roiled with anger. "I didn't mean it that way. I simply meant you can't 'take care of me.' I realize you'd never turn me out onto the streets. I know you'd take care of our children. But even though I'm not one of your Spanish doñas, I still have my pride."

His grip on the sheet loosened and he tried to interrupt, but she waved him to silence.

"When I lived with my aunt and uncle, I would sometimes be informed, mostly by the men who were shocked my uncle used my legal services, that Cinderella and I had much in common." She grinned, a gamine grin that astonished him, and allowed him his first glimpse of the young troublemaker she had once been. "I found I lacked the gentle resignation that made Cinderella such a popular heroine. When Tobias came to dinner—well, he wasn't the perfect prince, but I knew I could make myself happy with him." Her smile grew wider and her eyes danced. "He was a foreigner, a craftsman who worked with his hands.

Uncle Rutherford and Aunt Narcissa looked down their noble noses at him. They cited their exalted ancestry. They talked about how it ran in an unbroken line back to the Pilgrims of the Mayflower and they reminded me, grudgingly, that my ancestry was theirs."

"Who are these Pilgrims?"

Her smile faded as she realized the gap between them. "They were the beginning of my nation. They were the aristocracy of the English colonies, just as you are the aristocracy of California. It means nothing to you, but regardless of my penniless state, I come from people who are moral and proud. I can't be your mistress. It's demeaning. I couldn't live like that."

"To sleep with me once, then casually turn your back on me —that's less demeaning?"

She blushed. "I didn't sleep with you, not like you mean."

"To all in Alta California, you did just that." He made a place for himself beside her, and he sat so close the warmth of his hip seemed to melt the sheet. She wanted to look down, but she found the courage that allowed her to gaze on his body evaporated with his proximity. Keeping her gaze firmly attached to his, she concentrated on his words.

"Catriona, I've never asked you to be my mistress. English isn't my first language, and this . . . this 'taking care of' has more than one meaning. I wish to provide you shelter, food, give you children, fight your battles for you." Lifting his hand to her cheek, he stroked it until she was hypnotized. "I want you to be my wife."

28 May, in the year of our Lord, 1777

Fray Amadis found the journey into the mountains too strenuous. He has passed on to glory. We laid him to rest in the dirt of these California mountains with many prayers and the proper rites.

I fear the lack of food and chill of the nights are taking their toll on Fray Lucio, also. He is old and weary. He droops as we walk and moans in his sleep. God grant him strength. If he should go to his reward, there would be only Fray Patricio and me. Fray Patricio stands as tall and as broad as the oak trees of the interior, with a hearty attitude and a cheerful belief in our mission, but the chest we carry weighs greatly. We must find somewhere to hide this gold until we can return for it.

—from the diary of Fray Juan Estévan de Bautista

Chapter 8

"Your wife?" Katherine skittered out of the sheet, over the pillow. She stopped only when she felt the headboard against her spine, then she molded each vertebra flat against the wood. Her chemise and pantalettes provided inadequate cover, but she used her hands to conceal what she could.

"Yes." Damian's voice was gentle. "My wife."

"Your wife?"

This time he said nothing.

A choking indignation filled her, and an unnamed fear. Marriage—indeed, any kind of attachment to this man—would never be the easy relationship she'd shared with Tobias. Damian would demand everything she had to give. He'd hold her in the kind of love that took prisoners and never let them go. "Are you mad?"

Lifting his knee, he perched his elbow atop. One of his fingers stroked his mustache, and he sighed. "Not to my knowledge."

His equanimity calmed her, until he added, "You have no choice."

She jerked the pillow over her chest. Her motions revealed her agitation, she realized, but his composure rattled her. "I admit it. I've needed someone. Now I can't wait to stand on my own two feet again."

"That's fine. As long as you do it in my bed." His mouth quirked. "And keeping your feet while in my bed is unlikely and possibly dangerous."

She wrapped the pillow around her like a suit of armor. "You want me to come to you impoverished, with nothing of value except a mouth that needs feeding and a body that needs shelter. You're not mad. You think I am."

He stared coldly down his nose. "Perhaps that's how an American man considers his wife, but a Californio sees more than a hungry mouth and a demanding body."

"I've had experience with this situation and its disadvantages. I never want to be the poor relative again."

"Perhaps for an American man."

"For you, there is the obstacle of my nationality."

"Pardon?"

She put her face at eye level with his. "I'm an American. An American, descended from the English settlers two hundred years ago."

She glared right in his eyes, and he glared back. "Do you perceive a problem?"

"You're a pure Castilian Spaniard. Proud as the devil, bragging about your lineage, telling the world about your Moorish ancestors and ignoring any others. Do you want an American to be the mother of your children?"

"Why not?"

"Because my nationality would be a stain on your pure blood line. Do you deny it?"

He opened his mouth, but no words came out. She waited, but he could say nothing, and for the first time she realized how much she'd wanted him to refute her accusation. "In my country, the Irish immigrants are despised, as you despise Americans. Some of them are scoundrels, but most are just people seeking a better life."

"Americans seek a better life at the expense of the Californios."

"Americans are as proud of themselves as you are. Our ways are different. Individually, we're governed by land hunger. As a nation, we're governed by a sense of destiny." She coaxed him with a smile. "Surely you, with your Moorish background, can understand destiny."

He wouldn't be coaxed. "American destiny will destroy a way of life I love."

"So the Spanish destroyed the Indians."

He was impatient with such foolishness. "In my heart, I believe the United States should annex California. The United States is a young, vigorous country. Mexico has no organization. The English lick their lips when they gaze on us, but we've already seen how the Old World treats the New. It's the people of America that stick in my craw. Brash, rude, impatient. Thieves and prostitutes." He stopped when she winced.

"My Maura's an Irishwoman. There are those who told me she came to prostitution through the natural corruption of the Irish."

"I would never accuse you of prostitution."

"I would have given you my body with little struggle. Even this morning, you stare out the window and wonder why."

He sat back, his face awash with red, his nostrils flared with the white of distaste.

Never pausing to wonder how she could read him so well, she continued, "You wonder if I'd be as easy for any man. If you were my husband, every time you left me, you'd wonder who was sleeping in my bed." She stabbed at herself unmercifully, feeling the pain but unwilling to cease until all the words had been spoken. "We have different customs, different backgrounds. I'm not even a typical American woman. I've studied with Margaret Fuller. She was a friend of my father's."

By not a blink of an eyelash did he betray his bewilderment, and for that she gave him full credit. "Margaret Fuller, like myself, was plagued with financial difficulties when her father died, but she went out into the world and made a living. She taught at Bronson Alcott's Temple School in Boston and later conducted classes for women."

"This excites you?"

He sounded not a bit impressed, but she paid him no heed. "I wish I could have done something so wonderful."

"Is teaching so unusual a vocation for an American woman?"

"No, but she taught at an innovative school." She clasped her hands together. Although she didn't realize it, her expression betrayed her enthusiasm. "I used to sneak away from my uncle's house, to listen and participate."

"What restrained you from teaching, if this was your desire?"

"I didn't want to teach," she said impatiently. "I wanted to be independent. When my father died, I had my mother to care for."

"At fifteen, you cared for your mother?"

His smooth sympathy lured her into confession. "Mama wasn't well. But even if I could have supported her, she wouldn't have permitted it. Mama was a lady, and she raised me to be one also." She mimicked her mother with a fond smile. " 'Ladies don't work.' "

"So you had to live with your uncle?"

Her smile faded. "Yes."

"Did you resent your mother?" he asked.

"I adored my mother." Defiantly, she glared at him. "Until the day she died, she was the stick with which the Chamberlain family drove me."

"Ah." He comprehended more than she said, perhaps more than she comprehended about herself. "Your mother didn't approve of this Margaret Fuller?"

"I didn't tell her about Margaret Fuller. She understood that my life with my uncle was less than ideal, and I shielded her as best I could. I presented her the image of a satisfied daughter."

"Did she believe your image?"

"As time went on and her illness progressed, she wanted to believe it. She needed to believe it." Her sigh wavered with remembered grief. "I stopped going to see Margaret Fuller."

"What does this woman teach that you feared to continue your lessons?"

"Margaret Fuller believes that women deserve enrichment, deserve the education that men have. They deserve dignity for their place in society."

"Of course," he agreed. "What has this to do with us?"

She suspected him of sarcasm, but he displayed none of the signs. The respect with which he'd always treated her, had always treated all women, nudged at her consciousness. "I can't stay," she faltered. "When our children came, with their fair skin and freckles, you'd look at them—" She stopped and sniffed. "What's that smell?"

He sniffed, too, and rose with a curse. "My cigar." It smoldered on the window sill, burning a slow path along the polished wood.

Katherine pinched her nose against the acrid odor. "I hate cigars." She noticed her own petulance, but her world had been tossed askew.

"Do you?" Gingerly, he pinched the brown stub between his nails and tossed it out the window into the dripping rain.

"They stink. They make me want to sneeze. They make my eyes water." It must be the cigar that made her eyes water, she thought wretchedly.

He picked up the silver cigar case and ran his fingertips over the raised pattern. "Is this the truth?"

"Why would I lie?" Clutching the pillow, she slid back under the sheet.

"At this moment, I can think of several reasons."

She wasn't such a fool as to ask what the reasons he imagined. "Tobacco is nothing but an evil weed." She shuddered as she stared at the offending case.

He nodded slowly. "Very well." Opening the case, he pulled out every one of the long, fragrant cigars. He weighed them in his hand; he lifted them to his nose and inhaled. His eyes closed in enjoyment, then he flung the whole handful out into the rain.

Her jaw dropped.

He leaned out the window. "They're in the mud."

It took two breaths, but she brought in enough oxygen to say, "Why did you do that?" Only she didn't speak, she shouted.

"You're noticing me again," he warned.

"Noticing you?" She gestured wildly and grabbed for the sliding sheet. "I don't even understand you. Those cigars are expensive."

"Too true," he agreed pensively.

"And you love them."

"Love them?" He snapped the case shut. "I don't love them. I like them. I enjoy them."

"Every man smokes in California. You can't just throw your cigars out the window."

"How scandalized you are. Is it the waste of money?"

"Yes," she said with wholehearted agreement.

"I can afford it. Is it the message behind my action?"

She blinked. That wasn't a question she could answer. At least, not now. "If it is your plan to refrain from tobacco, you should have given the cigars to your father."

He noted her evasiveness with a chuckle, and the answer he gave replied to more than she'd said. "Ah, but if they were mine I'd crave them . . . as I crave you. If there's a choice between you and the cigars—" He waggled his fingers out the window.

"I'm going away," she insisted, although she was beginning to lose sight of her reasons why.

"What of last night?" he asked. "What of the gifts we have to give each other?"

She had no reply to that; she didn't want to look into his dark eyes anymore, nor at his amber body.

He strolled across the room. She scooted backwards, but he flashed her a grin and leaned down beside the bed. He came up with his shirt in his hand.

He pulled it on with such a slow, unmistakable sensuality she couldn't help but think about removing it again. Of course he knew it; she didn't like the way he kept anticipating her reactions.

Buttoning the shirt from the bottom to the top, he rolled the sleeves up over his elbows. "Better?"

"Yes." But it wasn't. Somehow the sight of his muscled legs beneath the long tails of the shirt made her wish to see it all, even if she no longer dared to peek.

"What of your family? What of this uncle and aunt? Once you're back in the bosom of your family, you'll again be at their mercy."

She shook her head at him. "As I've said before, I can take care of myself."

"As *I've* said before—" a knock rattled the door, and he moved to open it "—that's no longer necessary."

Katherine wilted down into the feather mattress as Leocadia walked in. She wanted to pull the covers over her head. Why didn't Damian just lean out the window and shout that he'd graced her bed with his presence? How could he ignore his own half-clothed state? How could he ignore the implications of his presence in her room? He seemed not at all embarrassed as Leocadia handed him a paper and said, "Your father insisted I give you this right away."

Glancing at it, he frowned. Glancing up at the housekeeper, he frowned more.

With a graceful gesture, she waved toward the door. "I bring a bath for Doña Katherina."

Damian read the scrawl on the note and stiffened. "Damn him to hell."

"Don Damian?" Leocadia questioned.

"What?" He looked up at her. She indicated the servants, the bathtub, the steaming water. "Bring it in."

"Don Damian," Katherine protested. "I don't want everyone in my bedroom."

He looked at the maids filing in. "Oh, that's not everyone," he said absently, his mind elsewhere.

"Close enough," Katherine choked. He paid her no attention. "What's happened?"

He tapped the paper with his hand. "This is an announcement from General Castro. It would seem your band of adventurers has done more than shoot out a lantern at my fiesta."

"Frémont?"

"Oh, yes. Your beloved Frémont has managed to make Castro so angry he's calling out every citizen to—" he raised the paper and read "—*lance the ulcer which would destroy our liberties and independence. . . .*"

"But that's a declaration of—"

"War."

Clearly, Damian was in a fury, and clearly, this was the moment to explain to him—

He pointed a finger at her. "If you tell me that this is an indication of our national differences, I'll demonstrate to you the real differences between us."

"Don Damian, this really is—"

"That's it!" Flinging the paper aside, he marched to the bed and picked her up by the shoulders. "Our differences are male and female, man and woman, not this political nonsense with which you seek to separate us."

"Don Damian, be reasonable." This time she would use logic, she resolved, even though he could have intimidated a lesser woman. "Your reaction to Mr. Frémont is an indication of your deep revulsion for Americans." His mouth smothered her protest. She fought him until logic fled, until she responded to his fever with a fever of her own. When he dropped her back on the bed, she tingled from head to toe and clutched at him.

Grasping her chin in his hand, he stared into her eyes. "Be here when I get back. Don't you dare try to get away from me. We have too much to prove to each other."

She closed her eyes. When she opened them again, he was gone. Seven of the house maids stood and stared at her, laden with steaming buckets and bent beneath the weight of the high-backed tub. Leocadia tapped her toe and shook her head at the foolishness.

Katherine's thoughts righted themselves, and she pulled the sheet around her in belated decency. "Don Damian might be wounded!"

Leocadia shrugged. "Not likely. Our battles in California involve much clashing of swords and swearing, and little bloodshed."

"But this time—"

Picking up the paper from the floor where he'd flung it, Leocadia handed it to Katherine. "See what it says."

She scanned the note. "It sounds serious enough to me."

"Don Lucian knows all about it. He talked to the messenger. Those ruffians have encamped in the Gavilán Mountains not far from here. They built a fort and raised the flag of your United States."

"No." Katherine groaned, pressing the heels of her hands against her eyes.

"I believe that's what Don Lucian said."

"I'm not doubting you, I simply cannot believe they would be so foolish. Don Damian will be frothing."

"For more than one reason. Your Frémont—"

Katherine sat up with a jerk. "He's not *my* Frémont." The maids giggled and she blushed.

"*Señor* Frémont," Leocadia emphasized his title, "has pulled Don Damian from the bed of his lady, and he'll not be in charity with the man."

There wasn't the slightest hint of disapproval in her tone. When Katherine gathered her nerve and examined the maids, they all smiled and curtsied as if she were nobility. It wasn't something she cared to encourage, but how could she prevent them?

"Are you ready for your bath, Doña Katherina?" Leocadia asked.

As if she had a choice. As if she could say no, and send everyone plodding back downstairs with their burdens. "Yes, thank you. You may put it down there."

The girls filled the tub while Katherine twisted the sheets between her fingers and considered excuses. Perhaps innocence would work best. *Don Damian came to my room last night to talk and accidently fell asleep on my bed.*

No. Perhaps not.

Perhaps boldness would provide the best defense. *Don Damian never accomplished what he came in here to do.*

Ugh. Perhaps—perhaps she'd be better off if she didn't say a word and let everyone assume what they'd assume anyway.

The housekeeper tested the water with her hand, then walked to the bed. Before Katherine suspected, Leocadia ripped the cover from her hands. "Change the sheets," she ordered over her shoulder. "Bring more warm water."

Katherine fled across the room and plunged into the tub. The water covered only her hips, wet her pantalettes and the fringe of her chemise, but that symbolized her bewilderment. Leocadia and everyone under her seemed to assume that Katherine deserved to be waited on, as if she were their mistress. She didn't see the smile that the housekeeper hid, or the bar of soap Leocadia unwrapped. Yet she knew by the hustle of bare feet that the commands were being obeyed.

"It'll be good to have a new mistress to direct the doings of the hacienda." Leocadia tugged at Katherine's chemise until Katherine let her pull it off. Plunging her hand into the extra water left in a bucket, Leocadia soaped a washcloth.

"No." Katherine shook her head. "I'm going away."

Shoving Katherine's long blond hair aside, Leocadia scrubbed her back and chuckled. "Of course you are."

"I am," Katherine insisted. "I'm going away."

"Don Lucian." Katherine swept into the cozy room like a winter storm. "I need transportation to Monterey."

Don Lucian swiveled around in his easy chair and stared. "My, my. What a pretty girl."

The chill that insulated her melted beneath the mellow,

beaming gaze of the older man, and self-consciousness returned in a rush. She smoothed the skirt of her new gown, then wished she hadn't given in to that revealing gesture. She folded her hands at her waist and tried, with limited success, to meet his eye. "Leocadia burned my mourning clothes."

"It's the girl that's pretty, although the dress enhances her beauty. Come sit by the fire. It's pleasant on a rainy day like this, although the sun is already peeking out."

A fresh realization of his kindness swept her. When he rose and indicated a seat across the hearth, she took the chair and waited for him to speak. He fumbled in his coat pockets. "Where have I put my reading glasses? Why can't someone invent some way for me to find my spectacles when I don't have them on?"

"I'll suggest it when I arrive in . . . Boston."

His eyebrows flew up. He squinted at her, his head thrust forward. "Here, here. What's this? You can't go now."

She didn't say anything, just handed him his reading glasses off the table at his elbow.

Taking hold of the silver Franklin frames, he settled the nosepiece and hooked them behind his ears. He took one look at her face and pursed his lips in a silent whistle. "I don't often say the wrong thing, so apologizing is good training for me. I didn't mean to offend you. You're free to do as you like, of course, but . . . I was serious when I said you were like a daughter to me."

Sudden tears hovered on her eyelashes, and she couldn't seem to call them back.

Stricken with consternation, he roared, "My son didn't hurt you, did he?"

"Oh, no, no," she denied immediately, and was glad she did. Don Lucian looked ready to thrash Damian. "I don't want you to think that."

The color faded from his face, and he shook his head. "You don't owe me an explanation, but I wish you would tell me why you would leave us. You were happy here until last night, so I can't help but blame Damian."

"I stood at my window and watched him ride out," she said, her mind on the stern shake of the finger Damian had aimed at her as he'd left the yard.

"He'll puff and snort with all the other young bucks," he confirmed. "He was ornery as a buck in mating season, too, stomping around here." Light dawned on his face. "That's what upset you, isn't it? That he's gone to fight one of your heroes."

"Not at all. John Charles Frémont is acting like a spoiled child."

He pursed his lips. "If you called him 'John Charles' in that tone of voice, I can imagine why Damian was raging."

"What tone of voice?" she asked, bewildered.

"As if you were his fond mother. Frémont is not a boy."

"No, of course not, but he's acting arrogantly in a host country."

"What is it about some men that brings out the protectress in women?" he wondered.

"I'm not protecting him," she protested, but faltered under Don Lucian's quizzical gaze.

"Does Damian know you're going?"

Her eyes flashed at him. "He told me not to leave."

"Then I can't think of a better reason to abandon Rancho Donoso as soon as his back's turned," he said wryly.

She couldn't accept his accusation of cowardice. She'd planned this for months. Damian's absence was nothing more than coincidence. "You're trying to make me feel guilty, and I won't have it. I won't be a kept woman."

He sputtered as if he'd swallowed wrong. "If my son refused to do what is honorable, I'd be glad to act as your father would and put a gun in his back." He waved her objection aside and rose to pace before her. "A woman is not something you try out to see if she's to your satisfaction, then abandon if she is not. Young people don't understand the value of patience. If intimacy isn't ecstasy the first time, it can be developed between a man and his wife over the years."

"He asked me to marry him," she interrupted in desperation.

Rubbing his brow as if his head hurt, he murmured, "I will never understand women." Aloud, he said, "Then what is the problem?" She didn't answer, and he sighed. "Perhaps you are the one who needs to be told about intimacy."

"No!" she flared. "We did nothing." He indicated disbelief in the tilt of his head, the amusement in his eyes. "Almost nothing," she amended.

He sank back into his chair as if he were confused, and stretched his hands towards the fire. "Young girls these days sometimes expect to love their husbands before the wedding, so I'm told. Perhaps—"

"No. I'm too sensible for that." She looked at the older man. How could she be speaking about such a carnal matter with him? Yet she owed him an explanation, and with averted eyes, she said, "I'm a sensible woman. I've always been sensible. I can't live like this, always thinking of one thing, always enslaved by some emotion I don't understand."

"This emotion is the emotion you feel in the bedroom?" he asked softly.

She spread her hands, palms out. "It's too powerful. Don't you see? I have to leave. I can't stay."

"You are running from something most women would give anything to have," he marveled.

"What is that?"

"If I have to tell you, I suppose you may as well go. I'll arrange everything." He stood and kissed her forehead. "Everything."

Damian leaned against his saddle horn and glared at the makeshift fort atop Gavilán Peak. "I'm sick of this waiting."

Alejandro scratched his stubbled chin. "_Sí._ I could use a shave. So could you."

Running a hand over his bristles, Damian shrugged.

"Don't worry, Damian," Ricky said. "Katherine will love you anyway."

Damian shifted his glare from the flagrant American flag to his impudent friend. Ricky laughed protestingly and lifted his hands in the sign of the cross to ward off evil. "Hey, I was just joking."

"Maybe all's not well with love's sweet blossom," Hadrian suggested.

Damian ignored them. The wind whipped his hair, the sun warmed his shoulders, the smell of the morning coffee drifted to his nostrils. Behind him, soldiers' voices called out with authority.

None of the normal pleasures dented Damian's dissatisfaction. Not even the early morning gallop on Confite had eased his tension. That man, that Frémont should be horsewhipped for creating this kind of tension-ridden situation when Damian needed to be home, reinforcing his claim on a woman too proud of her mind to be aware of her body.

Three days he'd been here close by Mission San Juan Bautista under the command of General Castro. The first afternoon, the sun had come out and the landowners had arrived, their bedrolls strapped onto their horses. They'd stood about in clumps, growling about the arrogance of this Frémont. They'd admired the three pieces of artillery that would blast those fools off the mountain. They'd bragged about their fighting prowess.

The cavalrymen from Monterey rode up in their brightly colored uniforms. General Castro and his men marched up and down, creating a great display. Indians joined them, persuaded by liquor and free meals. Everyone had camped on the flats of the Salinas Valley. The congeniality reminded Damian more of a friendly bear hunt than a war.

The second day had been more of the same. Steaks cooked over a fire. Coarse jokes and sweet reminiscing. Friendships renewed and forged. The only excitement in the whole day had occurred when the wind whipped up and blew the defiant flagpole over. The Californios had cheered; the Americans hadn't put the flag back up.

This morning the novelty had palled. The early morning sun still shone, the wind still blew. On a dare, Damian had put Confite through his paces, showing off the intelligence of his prized stallion. Alejandro had tried to buy Confite; Ricky had offered to gamble for the horse. When Damian wisely refused, his friends teased him about his love affair. Damian wanted to spur his horse and ride where his whim took him.

Back to the rancho.

Nothing could hold his thoughts here. He thought about Katherine every moment.

Stirring uncomfortably, he remembered her objections to his proposal of marriage. She used pragmatism to avoid love and some surprisingly clever insights to hold him off. How had she known about his feelings of Spanish pride? How had she known it amounted to a virtual prejudice against her bloodlines? He hadn't even realized it himself.

It wouldn't affect their union. He fidgeted with the reins. He knew it wouldn't. Katherine would become a Spanish Señora: plying a fan with ease, bearing his children, becoming a devoted Catholic. Of course, he couldn't imagine her without that drive and efficiency . . .

She wielded that efficiency like a weapon, and she presumed it kept him at bay. If only she could have seen herself the morning he left her, sitting there on the bed, her soft shoulders emerging from the sheets, her hair tousled with sleep, her eyes languorous and her mouth marked from his kisses. Irresistibly, a smile crept up on him. How could he not smile? She played the part of the pragmatic housekeeper with vigor. Because she didn't realize her own frailty, she sailed through life coercing and convincing people to do as she ordered. Only he saw the gentleness in her. Only he knew her desires.

Only he understood that if she should decide to board a ship and sail away from him, she'd leave without a backward glance.

He drummed his fingers on the saddle, then stilled his horse's restless response. They didn't need him here, he argued to himself. There was the tempestuous General Castro for rhetoric. There were soldiers to oust the invaders. There were his friends to avenge the scene at his fiesta.

"Damian, stop daydreaming. Pay attention." The urgency of Hadrian's words penetrated his reverie. Lifting his head, Damian listened.

"They're gone!" A soldier came galloping down the peak, shouting with glee. "They're gone. They snuck out in the middle of the night."

"That worm Frémont ran away?" Damian grinned with cruel enjoyment. "It's too good to be true."

The soldier flew past to the general's tent, and the four friends followed at a sedate pace. They joined the throng around the *comandante*. "Castro's your relative," Damian said to Alejandro. "Find out what's happened."

Alejandro dismounted with a grimace and fought his way in.

"I never thought he'd do it," Damian commented. "He must be curious."

"Or he's feeling guilty because he teased you so much," Ricky suggested.

A long look passed between the three friends.

"He's curious," Hadrian said and the others nodded.

Alejandro returned with a holler. "The Americanos slunk away in the night like the thieves they are."

"Where are they now?" Damian demanded.

"About three miles from here," Alejandro replied.

Groaning, Damian sank his head into his hand, and Alejandro patted him with mock sympathy. "You can return to your lady love. General Castro isn't going to pursue them."

Damian raised his head. "Do you swear?"

"That's what he says."

Without waiting to hear more, Damian turned his horse and galloped through the camp, avoiding men on foot, jumping campfires, waving jubilantly. Clods of earth flew up from Confite's hooves and Damian coaxed him ever faster along the road to the rancho. Be there, he urged Katherine in his mind, be there. A lone rider on the road ahead caught his attention, a rider coming toward him. He eased up, preparing to shout the news and proceed, but he knew the horseman. In silence, he reined Confite in.

"Well met, Julio," he greeted him, awkward from their last meeting.

Julio glanced around as if he couldn't bear to look at him. "You're alone?"

"You've come too late. Frémont and his gang have fled from our superior marching ability."

Julio smirked, as Damian meant him to. "No shots fired?"

"None."

"I'll go and check in anyway. Just to show my interest."

"What kept you?" Damian did his best to keep accusation from his tone, but censure crept in and Julio stiffened.

"I was away. I didn't hear the news about this robber until I saw Nacia again."

"*Madre de Dios*, where have you been?" Damian asked, startled. "The whole of Alta California knows what has passed here."

Julio shrugged, uncomfortable, and Damian recalled Nacia's confession. He left, she'd said, for days, for weeks, and she didn't know where he went. Damian glanced at Julio's hands, and there were the telltale signs. Dirt ground into the nail beds, scabs on the knuckles. Damian opened his mouth to ask. Something in Julio's sunburnt face forbade it, so he blurted, "I've never kissed your wife."

Rejecting him, Julio sat straight in the saddle, his features cold with pride.

"Julio." Damian held out his hand, but Julio ignored it.

"I must go now."

Julio trotted off to the encampment, and Damian called after him, "Tell Nacia—"

Julio pulled his horse around to face him, fury twisted in his face.

"Tell Nacia I took her advice about Doña Katherina."

Relaxing, Julio tipped his hat, then turned back to the camp.

Distressed by his friend, puzzled by the mystery surrounding him, Damian set Confite in motion again. The miles fell away, and he rode into the yard as the sun reached its zenith. The stable hands ran to his assistance, asking for news, and he told them what he knew as he searched the grounds for sight of her. "Is she still here?" he demanded.

They waved him toward the hacienda. He ran, and his father met him at the door. In a glance at his face, Damian knew she had fled. "Damn it." He threw his hat to the ground. "Did she escape at night?"

Don Lucian put his arm around his son. "Come in and have lunch."

Damian shrugged him off. "Did you search for her? Has she been gone long?"

"Not a word until you eat," Don Lucian insisted.

"Eat?"

"She's safe," Don Lucian soothed. "Come and have some *caldo habla.* "

Frustrated, Damian strode into the dining room and pulled out his chair. Immediately, the dish of serrano ham and chorizo appeared before him, and the fragrance of spices convinced him it would be rude to ignore the soup. "Where is she?" Dipping his spoon in, he took a long, grateful sip. He was hungry. Damn, he was hungry and his woman had escaped him. He could feed the hunger, but God knew when he'd find Katherine. He glared at his father, who pantomimed eating. Reluctantly obedient, Damian took a big mouthful, in a hurry to end the meal.

"She's in Monterey."

Dropping his spoon, Damian choked until his father

pounded his back. Through the napkin in front of his mouth, he gasped, "Monterey?" Getting his breath back, he said louder, "Monterey? Are you mad? She could sail at any moment."

"No, no." Don Lucian punched Damian's arm. "I knew about the sailing vessels before I sent her, and I took the precaution of bribing the only captain likely to sail away with our Katherina."

"Well, at least you checked—you sent her?" Damian felt like a fish, all pop-eyed and gaping.

"Sí." Don Lucian pulled his watch from his pocket and checked it. "She's been there almost twenty hours. It took us one whole day to pack for her. Even then we told her we'd have to send Tobias's trunk on later."

"Later?"

"There's no use dragging it all the way to Monterey just to drag it back. That trunk's full of rocks, papers, tools. It's heavy. Besides, if you'd finished up that business with Frémont sooner, you would have been back to stop her." He glared at Damian as if the delay were his fault. "She threatened to go without help, so I kissed her good-bye yesterday morning. She'll be staying at the boarding house of that American woman—what's her name?"

"Mrs. Zollman."

"That's right. Mrs. Zollman's boardinghouse. After your lunch, your shave, your bath—" he sniffed significantly "—you can be on your way."

"I'll be there by—"

"Tonight." Don Lucian smiled with satisfaction. "Late tonight."

29 May, in the year of our Lord, 1777

*A hearty mountain rain brings us unending misery,
dripping on us by day and flooding us by night. We're lost,
unable to guide by sun or the stars. Our clothes are wet.
We have no food and no way to make a fire. Last night,
Fray Lucio shivered until I believed his old bones would
rattle, but Fray Patricio speaks stoutly of our return to the
coast. God works in mysterious ways, and for the first time
I, too, have hopes our prayers will be answered. The
sound of the Indians' pursuit has faded and I fail to see
how they would trace us through this unending mud.*

—from the diary of Fray Juan Estévan de Bautista

Chapter 9

"Oh, Don Lucian." Katherine sat on her heels before one of her overstuffed carpetbags and dashed an unwelcome tear from her lashes. "How sweet you are." Lifting the bag, she dumped her clothes out onto the floor and jerked the feather pillow from the bottom where it had been hidden.

Her pillow. Her pillow from the rancho.

If she weren't tired, she wouldn't be so tearful. So pleased. She hid her face in the pillow and breathed in the scent of hacienda.

So homesick.

She corrected herself. She wasn't homesick. She couldn't be homesick for a place that wasn't her home. Still, she would miss her friends there. And Don Lucian. And . . . well, everybody.

The pillow would help her sleep. Her fingers lingered on the embroidered edge of the pillowcase. Standing, she checked the room. The heavy wooden door was secured, latched with a leather thong that connected to the frame with a large bolt. She'd slipped a hole at the other end of the leather over a protruding bolt, like a buttonhole over a button. It held the door closed, afforded her privacy, and the open windows provided her with air. She leaned against the wall and stared at the bed which seemed so far away. Gathering her willpower, she staggered across the room and flung Don Lucian's gift. She followed it with a weary shrug.

Tonight, with the help of her pillow, she would sleep.

Of course, she'd thought the same thing yesterday. The trip to Monterey had taken a long time. Too long, she suspected. The servants seemed unwilling to go to Monterey and too willing to ride back. They'd taken her to a boardinghouse run by the elderly American woman. They'd left her on Mrs. Zollman's porch with her bags around her. They'd waved good-bye as if her departure meant nothing to them.

She had ignored the hurt their attitude caused as she lugged the bags to her room. She'd been amazed at how weighty they were and recalled briefly the pleasure of having servants to do the heavy work. It spoiled a woman.

She'd better get used to doing without.

She straightened the soft cotton of her nightgown. It bothered her to sleep in a bed so narrow she couldn't turn without complicated convolutions. It tangled the nightgown around her legs and made her feel as if she were strangling.

It was a feeling she'd better get used to.

She hoped she didn't fall out. The bed was hard, but not so hard as the floor. Just as the servants and the bed had spoiled her, so had the large, open space of her attic at the hacienda. The walls of this bedroom, so close, so dark, made her feel as if there wasn't enough air to breathe. She could have stayed with any of the prominent families in Monterey, but instead she'd spent her first full day unsuccessfully dodging her Spanish friends. She'd seen Doña Xaviera and Cabeza, seen Vietta Gregorio and her mousy mother, seen the entire Valverde clan strolling en masse through the presidio, had even seen Julio de Casillas. He'd nodded to her curtly without a word, and she'd nodded back, relieved to be ignored for once.

Not that she didn't wish to tell them all farewell, but explanations of her unchaperoned presence were complicated. Mrs. Larkin hadn't understood Katherine's feeble excuses. Katherine suspected she'd offended the wife of the American consul, but after all, she was leaving. It didn't matter. Did it?

Monterey was a pretty town. Built around a square, the presidio was nothing more than a few cannons housed in one-story buildings. The adobe homes with their red tile roofs were scattered like pearls and rubies in the grass, unrestrained by organized streets. The Santa Lucia Mountains served as Monterey's backdrop, the Pacific Ocean as its admirer. Yet for her, the town held a combination of memories. Memories of marriage, of happiness, of friendship. Memories of death, of blood, of grief. She felt confused here. Wanting to stay, wanting to go. She wanted to go. She did want to go. She couldn't wait for her ship to sail. The Yankee captain she'd contacted had agreed to transport her down the coast to Los Angeles. He'd promised they would leave as soon as he had finished conducting his business. When that would be, she didn't know. He'd been too vague for her satisfaction.

She yawned again and collapsed against the pillow. She really was tired, the previous nights contributing to her fatigue. Since the hours she'd spent with Damian, she'd never slept; she'd only dozed. Half her attention seemed always tuned to his return—whether in anticipation or anxiety, she didn't care to define.

When she did nod off, she imagined he was there. She'd feel his hands in her hair: braiding it, combing it, raising it to his lips. She'd smell the smoky odor of him. She'd hear him whisper how he adored her . . . and she'd wake up alone.

In the dark, when one was exhausted, she'd discovered, it was harder to ignore the disappointment and the yearning.

But tonight the small bedroom no longer seemed so strange to her, she had her pillow. She lay there and smiled, comforted by the familiarity of it, and she slept, realizing it only when she came awake in a rush.

Danger lay in wait, cloaked by the night. Somehow she knew it; somehow she was afraid. Every muscle in her body clenched; her eyes strained to stay closed. This wasn't a nightmare, nor was it the return of Damian. There was someone in the room with her and that someone made her afraid.

She didn't know why or who, but she was in danger.

The sound of light, quick breathing came to her ear. Was it close? Too close. The scent of medicine tickled her nose. Was it the intruder? Or what he held?

Her eyes flew open and strained to see in the dim light. She gathered herself to leap off the bed. She heard a small shuffling noise beside her. A giant, masked figure leaned over her. She gasped. The figure laughed. A sweet smell clogged her nostrils and stole her mind away.

The bed rocked beneath Katherine. The movement made her nauseous.

Why did she feel so strange? Why was she afraid to open her eyes?

She couldn't remember. She couldn't remember, and right now it seemed more important to follow her instincts than to battle for courage.

Did she rest on land or sea? The bed was rocking, yet she couldn't hear the slapping noise of the waves, nor smell the sour brine-soaked wood. So she was on land, and the nausea-inducing movement was all in her head.

Good. Better fuzzy thinking than a return to a ship.

No, wait. She wanted to be on a ship. She was fleeing Damian, his proposal and his insistence on passion.

That wasn't right, either. She wasn't fleeing him, she was taking the logical, correct step to correct their situation.

Sickness hit her like a wall of water, and a tiny groan escaped her.

"Are you waking up?"

The voice was deep and muffled, and she didn't have to struggle to remain still. Like an animal sensing danger, she lay quiet. She heard the footsteps shuffle across the floor boards, knew whoever it was stood above her.

"Too much chloroform," the voice lamented.

A palm cupped Katherine's chin, fingers pinched Katherine's cheeks, and her head was shaken back and forth.

"Hurry and wake," the voice urged.

The footsteps shuffled away.

Shoeless, Katherine deducted. Tall, and strong, to have pressed that cloth over her face until . . . in a rush, the remembrance of fear came to her. Someone had come into her room. Someone had attacked her.

Oh, God, where was she?

The scent of the hacienda wafted to her nostrils. So her head still lay on her own pillow, her body rested on the bed in the boarding house. She fought to recover her self-possession. It was both easier and harder than she expected, for some of her perceptions were sensitized, others dulled.

Through her closed eyelids, she could see a light. Not a bright light like the sun, it flickered, tickling her blindness with little flares and wavers.

A candle. The night still pressed around her, wrapping her tight in its coils, imprisoning her movements.

No. She traced feeling to her fingertips and wiggled them. Shooting pains stabbed her hands, and she bit down hard on her lip.

Ropes imprisoned her. A cord bound her wrists behind her back and all her weight rested on them. Her shoulders ached, the skin of her arms tingled. Not even the feather mattress could ease the agony.

Her feet were bound, too. Was she tied to the bed?

The noises of the intruder distracted her. Grunts, soft curses in elaborate Spanish, the sound of cloth ripping.

She wanted to look. She wanted to open her eyes and see where she was, see how she could escape . . . see her captor. She knew she shouldn't open her eyes, yet she wanted to, so badly. Her palms sweated with her desire; she couldn't control her breathing. She concentrated, wanting, needing, to make her breaths slow and deep and even.

What did it mean? Why had someone stalked her? Why had this person gone through such elaborate preparations to hurt her?

God, how she hated Monterey.

A tear of fear and grief crept from her lids and down her cheek, and she grimaced to hold back the flood that threatened to overwhelm her.

"Whore!"

Water slapped Katherine with the force of anger behind it. She gasped, sputtered and opened her eyes. Like a fool, she opened her eyes.

Her captor stood beside her bed, in her boardinghouse room, and said in Spanish, "I knew you'd try to deceive me."

The great flood of water, Katherine saw, was nothing more than the contents of a tin cup, clasped in one big hand and dripping the last of its contents on the floor. She blinked the moisture from her face and squinted against the illumination of the candle. Set on the floor among her bags, it drew her gaze.

As she flinched from the light, her captor callously commented, "Your eyes aren't such a pretty green now."

"What?"

"They're red."

Katherine stared as the intruder placed the cup on the table, making sure the metal didn't clatter against the wood. Clearing her throat, she said, "My eyes are red from the drug. How did I deceive you?"

"You deceived me by faking sleep, but I knew you were awake. I'm craftier than you are." The bizarre figure leaned over her.

"I can't disagree." Katherine peered into the glittering eyes, trying to decipher the twisted features shadowed by the wide-brimmed hat. The skin of the forehead and cheeks looked shiny and hard. The mouth had no lips, no tongue, only an ebony gash set deep in dark skin. A line ran from ear to ear across the hump of a nose. Was she hallucinating?

No, she decided. A master with scarves and masks, this villain obscured the features that would betray identity. That would explain the muffled voice, the indistinct words. Was any of that mutilated face real? She couldn't tell.

Was the brawn encased in the black shirt authentic? Were the lumps that widened the waist of the breeches actual rolls of fat? Did a wizard of masquerade stand before her? Certainly the eerie form seemed to have no fear that she would penetrate this camouflage, asking scornfully, "Why do you look at me like that?"

The tension in her coiled tighter. From a pocket in the dark breeches, the intruder pulled a silver chain. From one end of the chain dangled a familiar silver watch. She clenched her hands in a useless fist. "That's not worth much." The watch moved closer to her face, and she stared at it with hypnotic fervor, as if she could whisk it away with her fear for its safety. As it swung before her nose, she whispered, "It's only valuable to me."

"Such a pretty little toy—your remembrance of your husband."

The hushed voice and odd phrasing brought her gaze to her tormentor's face. "How did you know that?"

"I'm no common thief."

The eyes behind the mask burned with relish.

Frantic to soothe the beast, she agreed, "I can see that. But please don't take my watch."

"Take it? No, no. You misunderstand." With gentle stealth, the watch was laid on the table beside the cup. "I'm going to open it."

"Push the button on the side."

Her advice earned her a withering glare. "I'm opening the back." A thin file appeared in one black-gloved hand and slid into the groove that circled the silver watch. A twist of the wrist and the back fell off with a *ting*. The intruder twirled the back, then lifted the exposed works and examined them. They ticked loudly, undisturbed by this baring of their secrets. The intruder cursed and carried it towards the candle. Katherine raised her head, staring at the retreating back. The intruder probed the works with one finger; she heard a disgusted mumbling. Like an accompaniment called forth by impatience, the love song clicked on and the music tinkled.

"There grew up a rose from Barbara Allen's breast—" Katherine blinked. She sang the words before she'd even thought, and the room spun on its axis as she fought the drug's effects.

"Bastardo." The music clicked off, the watch was tossed onto one of the carpet bags. "There's nothing there."

A protest tore from Katherine. "It's delicate."

"I ought to smash it—" a grotesque smile advanced on her "—but my own kindness forbids it."

Katherine didn't believe that, and an absurd confidence stirred her dazed mind. The lady of the house slept down the hall. This intruder didn't dare make a noise. If she screamed, help would arrive. "What did you expect to find? Why are you doing this? I have nothing in my bags to interest you."

"Don't you?"

"Of course not. I'm a poor American widow."

"The widow of Tobias." The voice of her captor thinned; the mask couldn't disguise the avarice and the threat.

"Tobias . . ." She faltered. Was this the one who'd killed Tobias? She shifted to test the strength of the bonds that held her.

"You'll never get free," the intruder observed with pleasure.

"I'm not trying to free myself," Katherine lied. "The ropes hurt me. Why are you interested in Tobias's widow?"

"Tobias was a very smart man. Too smart, in some ways. Too innocent in others. He found something I want."

Staring in fascination as the wrapped mouth spoke, Katherine almost missed her cue. "What is it you want?"

"As if you don't know. As if that sly man from Switzerland wouldn't have told you."

Even the scarf across the mouth couldn't constrict the flow of malice.

Katherine answered, "We were only married a week, and mysteries weren't a topic of conversation."

"That would be too bad for you," the intruder said casually, "even if I believed you."

Katherine glanced around the room and saw the jumbled mass of her belongings torn from her bags. "Oh, no, why did you—" She tried to sit up, but pain shot through her wrist; she jerked and groaned. Twisting, she managed to scoot onto her side and relieve the worst of the pressure on her hand.

"Do you think all this nonsense is going to make me pity you?" the intruder asked in amazement.

"Not at all." Katherine wiggled her toes, trying to encourage circulation. "I'm doing it for my own edification. Why did you destroy my clothing?"

"I didn't destroy much."

The trace of defensiveness encouraged Katherine, and she asked, "What was so important that Tobias would tell me about it on our wedding night?"

"The treasure occupied Tobias's mind as much as it occupies mine, and he trusted you. He trusted you and I know it. He told me so often enough."

Staggered by the information thrown at her in such casual disregard, Katherine sputtered, "Treasure?"

"The treasure of the padres. The gold of legend, waiting for me to rescue it from obscurity."

"Gold?" Katherine gaped at the absurd face before her.

"So much gold. So much influence and freedom can be bought with gold." The palms in the black gloves rubbed together. "I will be all I have dreamed of being with the gold."

"Gold?"

"Tobias had the key." The intruder leaned over her, giving Katherine a clear view of the mask and scarf that created such an effective disguise. "Where's the key?"

"Key? A real key?"

"You play innocent. You fool everyone, except me."

"I don't have the key."

"Then you have the treasure. You're fleeing Rancho Donoso. You're in Monterey, avoiding people who call themselves your friends. You're seeking the first ship out."

Guilt spread over Katherine's face. "There are reasons."

"Why else would the de la Solas send a message to the captain that you must be delayed?"

"What?" Katherine struggled, her discomfort forgotten. "That deceiver of innocent women—"

"Who? Damian?" The intruder flicked one forefinger into the air in disdain. "It's treasure he seeks. He's always been fascinated by the treasure."

Katherine froze, hurt at being dismissed so casually, hurt by the assurance with which the intruder spoke. "Don Damian protected me. When I first went to the hacienda, he kept my presence a secret."

"I knew where you were," the intruder said with scorn. "I didn't choose to risk my life at the hacienda for you."

"He guarded me."

"Would he do any less for the least of his servants?"

Stricken, Katherine collapsed onto her back, and the pain reintroduced rationality. Who was this person who knew Damian so well? Who was this person who understood Tobias and the desires of his soul? Again she examined the tormenting figure, trying to see beyond the camouflage. Disgusted with the relentless masquerade, seeking to draw out the facts, she taunted, "Couldn't you find this key on your own?"

"I thought I could," the intruder admitted.

"I don't know what the key is. I don't know where the treasure is. I've never even heard of this treasure. How are you going to find the key if I don't tell you?"

A knife appeared in the intruder's fingers. The handle was dull black; the blade was obsidian and shone in glints like broken glass. It looked uncivilized, barbaric, like a knife used to sacrifice virgins in the rites of old. As Katherine stared, it flipped and twirled with a life of its own. Then it settled into the gloved palm, and touched her throat. "I'm going to kill you if you don't tell me."

Such plain words. Such an expressionless tone. Such a bloody image.

Red specks began a slow promenade before Katherine's eyes. "You don't understand."

"I can take all night to slice you up." That voice warmed with pleasure. "I can make shallow cuts all over, just barely slicing the skin. You'll bleed, but you won't die for a long time. When you do, your corpse will be mutilated."

Katherine pulled in a deep breath to scream but the point pressed against her skin at her windpipe and she exhaled slowly and carefully. A buzzing started in her ears and increased to a rhythmic pounding.

"The gold."

That voice spoke right beside her on the pillow, and the threat beat at her like nails being hammered into her coffin. Katherine whispered, "I'm telling you—" Pressure increased; the point was so sharp, she wasn't sure if it penetrated. "Please . . ."

It penetrated. Deliberately, the thin point of pain slid around her throat. She felt the blood trickle down her neck. Her stomach heaved. She cried out, a piteous scream of appeal.

The bed rocked beneath Katherine. She'd never felt so ill. If she opened her eyes, she would vomit. If she kept them closed, the world might disappear.

Her eyes sprang open to see a giant brown blob descending on her.

She screamed, and the blob was snatched away. It resolved itself into a washrag, held in two narrow, veined hands. They hovered over her forehead, and a thin feminine voice said in

English, "Poor gal, she's hysterical. I can't blame her. To think that such a thing should happen. And in my boardinghouse, under my very nose."

A face inserted itself into Katherine's field of vision. "Catriona? You're awake?"

The sight of Damian's face sent a jolt through Katherine's tattered system. Here was the man she'd feared, wanted, longed for. The deep timbre of his tone, the quirk of his eyebrows portrayed concern. His hands held hers close to his chest and chafed them.

"Of course," she answered. The pain surprised her; the act of speech hurt her neck. She swallowed carefully; that hurt, too. Her hands explored the linen bandage wrapped all the way around her neck. It confirmed the violence she thought she'd dreamed. She fought the nausea, but the lacerated skin protested. She relaxed; that helped the pain and in turn the sickness.

"How do you feel?"

She could see the rope marks on her wrists. She twisted them from side to side, experiencing the pain of compressed bones and raw skin. Surely that would dispel the weakness of wanting to fling herself onto Damian's chest.

Sidelong, she examined Damian. Probably he'd torn his coat off, for his shirt was untucked and the collar had popped half off. Two of his buttons dangled by a thread, another two were gone. His dark hair looked windblown, and she asked, "Where did you come from?"

"I just rode in from the hacienda. I would have been here sooner, but my horse cast a shoe and I had to borrow an ill-broken stallion. I arrived in time to hear you scream my name."

"I didn't scream your name." She whispered, but whispering didn't seem to help. Nothing seemed to help. The throbbing in her throat grew as she struggled to subdue it.

"Yes, you did, Mrs. Maxwell," the woman inserted. "Woke me clear in my bedroom."

Katherine looked at him, and he nodded in soothing agreement. "How do you feel?" he repeated.

If he'd been angry, pointing out the folly of her flight and its bleak conclusion, she'd have dissolved into tears. Instead, his sympathy caused a contrary reaction in her. Her spine stiffened and she brushed away his compassion. "I'm fine."

"Fine!" The landlady settled the cool rag on Katherine's forehead. "As if a gently bred woman could be fine after such an ordeal. Her room is broken into, her clothing ravaged, she's bound with rope so tightly her hands and feet are blue, her throat is almost cut in two—"

Damian's eyes rested on Katherine's face when he suggested to Mrs. Zollman, "You might want to wait outside for the *alcalde* to arrive."

"This poor girl needs a woman's care. Look at how pale she is. Why, she looks as if she could faint this minute. Probably just the realization of how close she came to having her throat sliced from ear to ear—"

He looked up at Mrs. Zollman. "*Alcalde* Diaz will need to hear every detail you can remember."

"That's true." Mrs. Zollman clucked. "He'll want to hear about all that blood, dripping onto the pillow—"

His hand grasped Mrs. Zollman's wrist and turned her toward the door. "Yes, he'll want the story from someone who was here at the time."

"Don Damian, if you'd arrived only a few minutes later, it would have been too late. Of course, I still can't approve of you kicking in the door."

Ushering the gregarious woman through the gaping door, he assured her, "It's only the leather latch that's torn. I'll have it fixed in the morning. For tonight I'll prop it closed so Doña Katherina can have her rest."

Mrs. Zollman halted abruptly. "I can't leave Mrs. Maxwell here. It's not proper to leave a lady alone with such a handsome devil." She grinned, displaying a few teeth among the red gums. "Not at this time of the night."

"She needs my care. My very special care." He smiled with such tender meaning, he put such a loving eloquence into the words, Mrs. Zollman couldn't help but understand.

"Oh! It's that way, is it?" Like a cow with a cud, Mrs. Zollman chewed with open mouth. Nothing was there. Katherine could see nothing was there, yet the old lady chewed until she pronounced, "I heard rumors that that's the way it is. Well, it's your business, but I think you ought to marry the gal. Keep her safe, you know?" Mrs. Zollman winked, an exaggerated drop of the eye and wiggle of the brow.

Elbowing Damian, she shuffled down the hall, leaving him with a half smile and Katherine well enough to sputter, "What a nosy old bat."

"She's a smart woman. You should listen to her." He tossed her a persuasive glance and went to work on the door. Swinging on loosened hinges, the dark heavy wood was tattered where the leather latch had been. "If Señora Zollman used better hardware, you'd be dead right now."

Her hands beside her hips, Katherine pulled herself up. The room did one quick rotation, then settled back to normal. Her nausea, she noted with relief, had subsided. "You don't want Mrs. Zollman to frighten me, but you don't mind doing it yourself?"

His white teeth flashed in his dark face. "Exactly."

As he tinkered with the torn leather, she saw that his hands shook, that he frowned. He looked like a man vacillating between two powerful emotions, between anger and fear. She'd never doubted he would be angry when he discovered she had fled; nor could she doubt his deep apprehension for her life. In his way, he cared for her. She knew it, and even if she feared the emotion, she could appreciate it, too.

He scooted two of her empty carpetbags to block the door.

"That won't keep anyone out," she observed.

"No one will disturb us. Señora Zollman will tell them you are devastated, and the officials will leave us in peace."

"What about any—" her voice rose as she spoke and deliberately she lowered it "—intruders?"

His big strides brought him to the bedside. "I will protect you."

"I know."

He towered over her, but she refused to say anything else. Instead she fussed with the pillow, turning it so the spill of blood was hidden, pulling it behind her and plumping it to support her back. She made a show of relaxing against it, until one roughened hand tapped her cheek. She turned her face around to his.

"You know?"

"Yes, I know you'll protect me." She refused to give in to the tenderness she saw hovering behind his concern, preferring to pull up the sheet, arranging it to cover her shoulders.

"How does this feel?" His fingers stroked her throat and she leaped away. "Tender, I see."

"It aches," she admitted. She couldn't seem to keep her hands away from it; it confirmed the violence she thought she'd dreamed.

"Tell me what happened."

"I woke up, and there was someone in here with me in the dark."

"Did you yell?"

"No."

"Why not?"

Offended by both the query and his censorious tone, she said, "I'm not one of those women who screams at every little thing."

"Of course. What a foolish question on my part. Tell me—"

He was going to be sarcastic, she could tell.

"Tell me, just what do you consider enough of an emergency that you'll open those rosy lips and scream?"

"If I had realized the seriousness of this situation—"

"Never mind." He waved her to silence. His hands clasped behind his back, he paced away and paced back. "How did this intruder get in?"

"I . . . through the window, I suppose." She waited for the inevitable pointed comment, but he visibly restrained himself. Relief eased the tension of her limbs, and that made her impatient. Why should she care about Damian's opinion of her mental powers? He meant nothing to her.

"What did he look like?"

She rubbed her hands over her ears. Something wasn't right, something niggled at her mind. What did she want to say about her intruder?

Damian insisted, "Don't tell me you can't remember this, either."

"Either?" she asked, startled.

"You don't remember who slashed Tobias's throat, but you have to remember what this man looked like."

"You make me sound like an idiot."

"An idiot? For running away from people who care for you, for running away from safety and straight into danger?"

His eyes flashed with fury, and her indignation rose to meet his. "I wouldn't still be here to have my throat slashed if you hadn't bribed the captain of my vessel to keep me here."

"I didn't even know you had left the hacienda. How could I? I was off risking my life against a braggart from your country who threatens war and then sneaks off. Sneaks off like another American I could mention."

"I did not sneak."

He lifted a brow; she snapped her mouth closed. How could she utter such a falsehood when he stood amid the result of her sneaking?

Scornfully, he said, "You did what you thought best. Isn't that the trait you admire? I've certainly heard you use that phrase to excuse every imprudent escapade you've embarked on."

"I do not have escapades. I am not imprudent."

"Oh, no. You don't even close your windows in the very town where your husband was killed."

His index finger shook before her face as his censure bit deep into her pride. "Should I stifle myself in an airless room when you assured me that I was safe? You said I'd been the unwitting bait in a trap to catch the killer of Tobias, and as bait I'd been ignored."

"In my home," he reminded her. "You were bait in my home. There's a vast difference in being protected by the vaqueros and being a helpless victim in a boardinghouse where no one can protect you."

"I thought I was doing the right thing. I thought I was being sensible."

"For a woman who worships at the altar of logic, you do incredibly stupid things."

She opened her mouth, but nothing came out.

One look at her shocked, indignant face called forth a bark of his laughter.

She burned with humiliation. "You dare to call me stupid? You—a man who worships at the altar of passionate commitment, yet lets an imaginary boundary between countries decide your loyalties?"

"You're right. I have been stupid."

His quiet admission took the wind from her sails; she glanced at him, and his indignation had vanished. He brushed his mustache with his fingers in the gesture she'd come to recognize as thoughtfulness and stared into the distance.

"It was stupid of me not to possess you when I had created the occasion." He stripped his shirt off and grimaced at its condition. Wadding it into a ball, he tossed it into the corner. "I should have known that you would create an impenetrable defense."

"I did nothing. I simply pointed out—"

"You pointed out so many things so logically, I found I didn't have the stomach for such cold-blooded loving." He sat on the bed and wrestled his boots off. "It took this attack for me to realize my mistake."

Dazed by his implacability, she asked, "What mistake?"

"You'll have to have my passion and loyalty proved to you, over and over. You won't believe it until the body of evidence has grown so large there is no other argument you can make." He looked at her, and in his calm amusement she found reason for alarm. "We'll prove it in trial, hmm?"

"I really don't think that having my throat cut has put me in the mood for any experiments."

"Trials," he reminded her. "Trials, not experiments. You're a lawyer, not a scientist."

She tried to lift her chin and found she could not afford such defiance. The skin pulled, and she clutched her neck.

"See what happens when you try to argue with me?" He placed his hands on her shoulders and nuzzled the top of her head with his chin. "*Dios*, but I came too close to losing you. I would perform one of these trials, but tonight you're hurt and tired. Tonight you'll sleep with me."

"Sleep?" She struggled against him and he caught her before she fell off the mattress. "Really sleep?"

"Yes." He lifted the covers, and slid in. His body, all skin, no cloth, pressed against her. With one hand, he carefully lifted her head and put his arm under it. "Really sleep."

She was determined to ignore the diabolical man. She *would* ignore him, pretend she was asleep, even though she knew she could never sleep after the night she'd been through. She'd pretend to sleep. Pretend to sleep.

She dropped like a rock into a well: a long, dark descent.

Rain wet her face. Fog obstructed her vision. She knelt in the dirt of the street.

She could hear the roar of the ocean muted by distance. She could hear people murmuring around her, and a woman screaming. She could really hear it. She was there.

She could smell the horse feces under her knee, but it couldn't mask that other smell. The smell of blood.

Someone lay in the mud, mouth open, jaw cocked askew. She couldn't see his features well. They were obscured by fog and a rhythmic spurting of blood. What she could see was a woman's hands on his throat, trying to hold the blood inside. The hands jerked with each stream that gushed out.

The sound of the waves seemed to be the sound of that blood, but the blood stopped, and the waves did not.

Those hands lifted away, and they were her hands. She turned them over and over, and she could feel it. All that blood, so slippery. All that blood, so sticky. She looked down at the body, and it wasn't him.

It was a woman. A woman with blond hair bound tightly about her head and staring green eyes.

It was her.

Chapter 10

She came up fighting, trying to scream.

Awake at once, Damian grabbed her, but she slapped at him.

"*Mi vida* , stop." Afraid she would fall from the bed, he tried to catch her shoulders. "Ah, please, *niña*, stop this." One wild hand clawed across his face and he jerked back. He caught the hand. "You're hurting yourself. Open your eyes. Catriona, open your eyes." He lay on her, using his body to curb her, and her eyes sprang open. There was no recognition in them. They were solid black disks, dilated with fear and terror. "Catriona." Trying her English name, he pleaded, "Katherine Anne, come back."

In a snap, she woke. She whispered, "Don Damian." Her tears surged from her. She sobbed, a loud and ugly sound. She made no effort to restrain herself; she pushed against him like a kitten seeking the warmth of its mother.

Clumsy with sympathy, he wrapped her up in his arms, trying to rub her back, pat her head, kiss her cheek, do anything that would cure her of despair. He murmured meaningless words, rocked her back and forth, performing by instinct his own mother's rituals of comfort. It seemed like forever before the hysterical note disappeared from her crying, even longer before she could say, in a hiccupy voice, "Please, I need to wipe my nose."

He looked around frantically, but there was nothing close and he wouldn't let her go. "Use your sleeve," he ordered.

Her little sigh almost sounded like a chuckle, but she obeyed as if any other effort cost too much.

He murmured, "I was afraid you'd dream about Tobias."

She looked at her nightgown as if it were repugnant to her now.

"Damn," he said in disgust. He unbuttoned the sleeves, unbuttoned the front. "This is no time to worry about handkerchiefs."

"I didn't dream about Tobias." Docilely, she let him strip the nightgown away from her. "It was me."

Her hands were trembling, so were her lips. He pushed the skirt of the gown into her hands. "Use this," he said gruffly.

She buried her head in the soft cotton, the quaver of her voice muffled by the material. "I was dead. Someone killed me. Killed me with a black knife that dripped red. I sprawled in the street like a broken puppet. My eyes bled. My hair mixed with the mud and dripped with rain."

"Stop." He shook her wrist. "For God's sake, stop. This has been too much for you. You like to think you're invincible, but you are a sweet maiden who should be sheltered."

"Oh, Don Damian."

"Don't interrupt." Her crying slacked off and she peered at him from bloodshot eyes. "In the future, you'll stay close by me. I can't stand this kind of worry. I can't stand to live in crippling fear. Whether or not we like it, there seems to be a reason behind Tobias's death, and we need to discuss it."

Her hand reached out and touched his chest.

He froze. First her fingers, then her palm smoothed his pectoral, following the line of the muscle. Intently, she watched her hand, fixated by the motion and his involuntary contraction.

Pushing her hand back toward her, he said, "What kind of man would love a woman who'd just had the experiences you've had?" His breath caught. She held her nightgown wadded in her hands, and her body lay exposed. Her braid rested on her shoulder, her arms hid her breasts, the sheet—God knew where the sheet was. It wasn't doing what it should, of that he was positive.

When he jerked his gaze from her anatomy and wrestled it back to her face, he saw the way she looked at him. Wistful, sad. "No," he said. The hoarseness of his denial worried him, and he tried again. "No, Catriona, you're too weak."

She picked up his hand and kissed it.

"You've had a horrible experience. Look at the nightmare you just had."

Her tears still swept her cheeks. She whispered, "Make the nightmares go away."

"I can't."

She leaned forward and kissed the curve of his shoulder, ran her tongue along the ridge of his collar bone. Her tears wet him, trickling down his breast bone.

"*Querida*, you can't." He put his hand against her cheek and wiped away the moisture. "We can't."

She bit him lightly on the neck.

"*Madre de Dios.*" His surrender was quiet as a breath, but she recognized it, and laid her head against him with a sigh. He cupped her head and placed her against the pillows. His voice broke as he said, "You are so fragile, and I almost lost you. You are so beautiful." He never thought of her blotchy face, her red eyes. He only thought of his Catriona, stretched beneath his hands, needing comfort and giving comfort by her very acquiescence.

"Let me touch you here. . . ." His palm stroked the moisture from her cheeks. "And here . . ." He stroked down each arm, lifting her hands and kissing her fingers in a multitude of tiny pressures.

The tears halted under the influence of his adoration, and she kept her gaze fixed on his face as if he were the provider of all life. His eyes, dark with passion. His nose, strong and beaked. His chin, jutting with determination.

His palms skimmed her skin, trailing tiny sparks of sensation behind him. Pain, terror had no place between them. There was no room for anything but Damian and Katherine. He brushed away horror as he massaged her. A slow transformation led her from wide-open stares and shudders to the brief sighs of yearning. How did he do it? How could one man's calloused hands be so comforting, so erotic?

He whispered things, things one could shout on the street and no one would be shocked. But in his husky voice, rumbling with pleasure, they became a chant of worship.

When his palms molded her breasts, his eyes drifted closed, as if the combination of sight and touch were too much. He kept them closed as he leaned closer to nuzzle her lips, and his breath was as warm and sweet as the flutter of an evening breeze. His lips touched her eyelashes, her nose; they skimmed up her cheekbones and back down her chin. He caressed her lips, not kissing, but exploring the shape and texture. He moved to her neck, and her relaxation was so complete she let him touch it with his mouth. When he came up over her face again, his eyes were open and a faint smile brought the laugh lines around his eyes and mouth to life.

"I adore your body," he whispered with relish. "So relaxed, so sensual. Soft and feminine as I had never imagined. So accepting, yet giving me what I want. You trust me, don't you?"

Reveling in the luxury of his pampering, she rubbed her head against his hand. "I trust you. I told you I did." It was a pledge, a token that said far more than she realized. She saw the slash of his grin, and wondered belatedly if she should have prevaricated, but she couldn't work up the energy for alarm.

This was Damian. She *did* trust him, with her emotions, her body, her life if necessary.

The effort of holding her eyelids up became too much. Lazily she let them drop and considered the way he had encouraged her.

No longer did she jump in shock when he touched her.

She wasn't doing anything.

She wasn't embarrassed or wondering what to do. She didn't feel constrained to give back what he gave her. With Damian, it was all right—more than all right, it was wonderful—to accept his gifts. He seemed to relish her acceptance of him, her acceptance of anything he chose to do.

She opened her eyes. His smile displayed his satisfaction, but she'd allow him that.

He had just performed a miracle.

He pressed a kiss to her ear, circling the shell with his tongue, following it with a breath. All over, her skin tightened. He murmured encouragement and lifted her wrists to his mouth. On first one and then the other, he kissed the spot where the pulse throbbed. "The heart of my beloved beats here. It's a precious spot." Holding her arms cradled in his, he kissed the inside of her elbow. "The heart of my beloved beats here. It's a precious spot." Moving up to her neck, he kissed the bandage and repeated the formula. He kissed between her breasts, kissed her stomach, her thighs, the arch of her foot. Turning her over, he kissed the delicate skin behind her knee, the curve of each buttock, the base of her spine. "The heart of my beloved beats here. It's a precious spot." In each place, she found it was true. Her heart beat there, accelerating, warming her, bringing every nerve to life. A string of kisses up her back, and he rolled her over again. Putting his forehead against hers, he looked into her eyes and vowed, "The heart of my beloved, the body of my beloved is precious. But the soul of my beloved resides here, inside her head, and that is most precious of all. When time has gone and we are no longer, still the soul of Katherine will be precious to the soul of Damian."

Her chest tightened; she couldn't breathe beneath the weight of his vow.

"Knowing that, you'll let me love you?"

She sighed; it meant yes.

He understood perfectly and his eyes widened. She was the one who didn't understand until he pressed closer in a slow dance of titillation. The roughness of his feet tangled with hers. The warmth of his legs covered hers. His thighs slid inside her thighs; one knee came up and pushed for a brief moment.

Her toes curled.

In deliberate tardiness, he lowered his groin against her stomach. Unnoticed by Katherine, a spiral of heat had already begun, ignited by his indulgence, his words. Now it grew, nourished by the proof that she excited him. He rocked against her, the length of him rubbing where his knee had been previously.

His arms held him up, and he assessed the reflection of her emotions as a master jeweler assessed the facets of an emerald. What he saw must have satisfied him, for he lowered his chest so the frost of his hair tickled her nipples. The weight of him compressed her. Briefly, she wondered why he had cut her off from the comfort of his hands and mouth; then the wave of response hit her. All of her skin against his, all of her self against his. All that exquisite stimuli, contained in the bone and sinew of one Damian de la Sola.

Had she ever felt stifled in the act of love? Now she felt covered, protected.

"Kiss me. Let me taste you."

His voice was an audible extension of himself, and as such excited her, intoxicated her. Her parted lips met his straight on. Their noses clashed. She tilted her head and their mouths settled together. His tongue touched her lips, wet them, dabbed at her teeth. They reminded her of the delicious kisses he had administered before—before she knew she liked them. She knew now, and she touched the tip of his tongue with hers. She felt the surge of his excitement. It was evident in his gasp, in the stir of his legs, in the growth of his manhood. Surprised by the reaction, she experimented with the stroke of her hand against his hip. He groaned and followed her tongue into her mouth.

The heat in her expanded, pushing out her relaxation, her sense of comfort. She let them go reluctantly, for the replacement was something she didn't recognize. It came from within, and that surprised her. Where had this coil of feeling been hidden? Cautiously, she explored it. It grew with the touch of his hands on her. It grew with the touch of her hands on him. It fed on tactile sensation. It fed on the sight of his face and body. It fed on his pleasured sounds. It fed on the scent of his hair, on the nip of his teeth on her nipple and the slow apology of his tongue on the tingling place.

"Don Damian?" She blinked, bewildered by the fright in her voice.

He understood. "It's normal, love. As inevitable as the tides, as pure as a mountain stream."

"I don't think—" His fingers entered her; the heel of his hand massaged her. A spasm struck her, blinding her, pushing her towards some danger in the dark.

"You're fighting it." He removed his hand; she opened her eyes in relief and protest. "Stop fighting it. I won't let you go alone." He swept a kiss back up her body, his face intent, monitoring her every respiration and reaction.

With an effort, she groped for his wrist and squeezed it. "There's something happening in me. This won't work."

He listened as if she told him a profound truth, serious, encouraging. "This is like laughter or tears or a good sneeze. It's physical, natural." Wetting his thumb in his mouth, he rubbed it across her lips. "You said you trusted me. Trust me now."

She searched his face, seeking reassurance and finding it. "All right. But hurry. I don't like this anticipation."

Chuckling in a kind of choked pleasure, he lay between her legs again. "I don't have to hurry." With his hand, he rubbed himself against her. The touch of him brought her knees convulsively tight against his hips. His eyelids drooped as he entered her, stretching her.

She must have made a sound, for he halted and considered her. She stared at him in appeal; he nodded in encouragement and said, "You're hurrying to me. Keep coming, beloved. Only a little farther."

Slowly, he thrust inside, driving a spur in her flesh. The pressure of his groin against hers made it worse, or better. His withdrawal tempted her to cry out; his return brought the cry to her lips.

She didn't know what this was, but he said it was natural. He said to trust him. He said . . . oh, God, what had he said? She couldn't remember, only knew his body carried a madness. She clutched at his back with slippery hands; she wrapped her heels tight against his buttocks. She wanted to push him out; she tried to keep him in. The spiral of heat became a conflagration.

Damian incited it. Damian comprised it. Damian.

The spasm took her, and this time there was no resisting. Her body took over, performing a ritual both sacred and spontaneous. She clenched her teeth, clenched her hands. She pushed her heels against the mattress, pushed herself against him. Breathlessly, she sought the heat and found it in Damian.

She heard him groan her name, felt his body strain and shudder in response to hers. Felt a moment of panic—or was it excitement?—as her body lifted again, produced a brief convulsion and relaxed into an almost oblivious stupor. Almost oblivious, except for the surprise that burst like a bubble in her mind. "Why didn't somebody tell me?" she murmured.

"This bed is too small," she pronounced without opening her eyes.

He grinned. It had taken her an hour of recovery to form the words, an hour in which she'd remained close and unprotesting. "I like it. I may buy it and take it back to the hacienda for us to sleep in."

She didn't respond in any way. That didn't surprise him. She'd succumbed to more than he'd hoped for this night. Later, he promised himself, she'd give him all; for the moment, he'd let her rest. With stirring guilt, he worried about her. After all, she'd just been attacked by someone with a knife, then attacked again, by himself. Different intentions, yet possibly too much for such a delicate woman. In his own actions, the element of self-indulgence niggled at his conscience. His hands on her hips, he eased her down towards the middle of the bed. "Scoot a little bit, _querida,_ so I can rest on the pillow and take the weight off of you."

She wiggled cooperatively, and he sighed with renewed delight. He shifted until they were as comfortable as the tiny mattress would allow. A wisp of her hair straggled over her forehead, and he brushed it back. "You're so beautiful."

As if she were exhausted, she closed her eyes again. As if the sight of him recalled too much. As if she weren't ready to face him. Yet her voice teased as she complained, "You're so heavy."

Reluctantly, he separated them, his hands lingering, and he squeezed beside her. "Perhaps I won't take this bed home with me," he conceded. "Are you all right?"

"I'm all right."

She said it quickly, defensively, and he winced. "I should never have taken you with such—"

"Vigor?"

"Vigor may be the word," he admitted, pulling the sheet over them. "I have only one excuse I can offer."

"I don't want any excuses," she protested.

He wanted to give his excuse while she was spent, while that ingenious brain of hers was at rest, and so he ignored her. "All the emotions I've lived through today have unbalanced me. First I was furious with you for running away from me. I rode like hell. It rained on me. I had to walk miles when Confite threw a shoe. I left him at the Estradas' with their promise to send him on, and they outfitted me with one of their pathetic parcels of horseflesh. I arrived in Monterey, and when I pounded on your door, I heard you scream. I broke in and saw some bizarre person escaping out the window. You were bleeding from the throat and I thought you'd been killed. By the time I'd stopped the bleeding and could go after that man, he'd disappeared."

"I didn't run away from you," she said flatly.

Leaning up on one elbow, he looked down at the face on the pillow. The serenity had disappeared and been supplanted by aloofness. It made him angry, to see her withdraw behind such a bland facade after an hour such as they'd spent. He taunted, "Is that all you can say? I tell you my tale of woe, and all you do is deny that you were afraid of me?"

Her eyes sprang open, as he'd hoped they would, and she said, "I'm not afraid of you."

"You're afraid of something."

"I'm the bravest woman I know." She looked startled when the words left her mouth, but she insisted, "Well, I am."

"I didn't argue with you."

"I held my own in a law firm made up of immoral predators. I buried my father and held my mother in my arms as she died. Without the support of my family and with barely enough money, I sailed around Cape Horn to California. I didn't even have a guarantee that Tobias would still be here or that he would marry me, but I came. I buried Tobias, too, and lived through the sorrow. And tonight, I talked to that thing in the room with me. I questioned him. I found out what he wanted. I didn't panic until—"

Her eyes grew big; her skin blanched. On her face was etched the memory of death. Snatching her close, murmuring meaningless sounds of comfort, he rocked her. She burrowed into his chest. She shivered and clutched at him; she thrust a knee between his and he wrapped her in his legs. She sought comfort, oblivious to anything but his warmth, and he responded as if she were a frightened child.

"I was so afraid," she murmured. "My head was so thick and fuzzy, I couldn't think. I was afraid, and I wasn't in control. When that . . . that monster pulled that knife on me, all I could see was Tobias and the blood. I thought I was going to be slaughtered, and all I could feel was regret."

"Regret?" he rumbled.

"Regret that I hadn't . . ." She struggled, tiny movements of protest, as if she didn't want to say the things buried in her soul. "Regret that we didn't . . ."

Soothing her with the stroke of his fingers in her hair, he whispered, "*Querida*, I don't understand what you mean."

"I just regretted that I hadn't given you what you wanted."

"And learned what I could teach you," he reminded.

She shook her head fretfully, but he ignored it. A crisis had shown her what all the words in the world couldn't express. He said a prayer of thankfulness: that his Catriona had been saved for him, that his prize had come from this evening's outrage.

In tiny increments, the shivering eased and her limbs relaxed.

"You can't sleep yet," he murmured, his lips by her ear. "You must tell me about him."

"Who?" she mumbled.

"Your attacker."

That she remained slack proved a tribute to his lovemaking, yet he feared she was already too deep in slumber to respond, and his restlessness demanded that he get his answers tonight. "Catriona. Tell me. Was he tall?"

"Mmm. Medium."

"Spanish? American? Indian?"

She tried to roll away from his interrogation, but the tiny bed offered nowhere to go. "Sounded Spanish. Sounded hoarse. Sounded rich."

That startled him. "How does someone sound rich?"

"Oh, please, Don Damian." Opening her unfocused eyes, she flung her arm out and smacked him in the chest. "Do we have to do this now?"

"I can't sleep. Humor me."

"After all that, you can't sleep? Does this activity energize you? Because if it does—"

"No, no. Normally, I'm the same as any other man." Humor crept into his voice. "I make love, I roll away, I sleep."

"And tonight?"

"Tonight I want a cigar. I always have a cigar after."

"Then have one."

Irritation slammed into him, and to restrain himself from shouting at her took a Herculean effort. He'd sacrificed one of the pleasures of his life for her, and it frightened her. Even now, even after this night, she refused to acknowledge his dedication to her. He kept his refusal to a clipped, "No."

She said nothing, but she was awake, he was awake, and they lay together, pretending repose. He felt her resistance collapse, and she murmured, "Don Damian? What did you want to ask?"

"Only a few questions," he soothed. "How does one sound rich?"

"Educated," she said glumly.

"What did he look like?"

"Like he wore a mask and a scarf and a hat pulled low over his hair."

"Did he give you any clue as to his identity?"

She said nothing for a long, telling moment, and he held himself in patience. "This person knows you very well."

His first reaction was distaste and denial. "Me?"

"He knows me, too, but it was you he spoke of, you he was intimate with. Or so it seems."

"What did he say?"

"He's known you for years. He's familiar with your habit of protecting your servants." Her voice didn't quiver when she said that, but he wondered what was masked behind the simple statement. "He knows your interests."

"Was there some identifying—?"

"Don Damian, I know you think I'm stupid, but if there was anything I could tell you about this person, don't you know I would?"

She sounded exasperated, but he ignored that to say, "In time of great fear, it's hard to remember things you see or hear. My questions could unlock impressions you didn't even know you'd received. If you think of anything you could tell me, any clue—"

"You'll be the first to know."

She turned on her side away from him, and he knew she was irritated. He'd implied she was incompetent; surely the cardinal sin for his sensible darling. Snuggling tight against her back, he pulled her close and held her as she drifted off to sleep.

He was happy it had turned out this way. The night in her room at the hacienda, he'd been positive, he'd known he could sweep her off her feet and into his arms.

He'd failed. She was too proud and stubborn and, he realized now, too distrustful of her emotions to give herself to him. Tonight had been different. Tonight they'd felt emotions that were undeniable.

He had misled her about her safety. He'd suspected that the man who'd murdered Tobias was nothing more than a criminal drifting through California. Perhaps an American criminal like Mr. Emerson Smith. But he'd arrived only just in time, and the villain hadn't been Emerson Smith, or an American, or any person recognizable to Katherine.

The only other reality he'd considered was that he'd frightened Tobias's killer with his vigilance. He'd believed that and insinuated to Katherine that she had no need to worry. Thanks to his wishful thinking, she'd been terrorized and her throat cut. Reproaching her for stupidity was nothing more than his own guilt lashing out at the nearest object. Lashing out at the person he most wanted to protect.

He'd never be so careless with her again. In fact, he chuckled, he'd probably never let her out of his sight again.

"What's so funny?" she asked, her voice slurred.

"I was just thinking," he lied, "that only a fool would think you could miss the clues. And I'm no fool."

The body against his softened, melted into his.

He was forgiven.

May God have mercy on his soul.

Fray Patricio has died, unshriven and in agony.

For the first time in days, we saw the sun. It broke through the clouds at sunset, and we crawled into our miserable beds in the underbrush. We slept, but Fray Patricio woke us. He'd heard slight noises which we identified as trackers. We rose and climbed a dark, narrow path that was lit only with our prayers and the feeble stars.

The ground beneath our feet gave way. Fray Lucio clung to a rock; I slipped and my cassock caught on a bush, suspending me in midair.

Fray Patricio fell a long distance. We could hear him scream as he landed. For the remainder of that black night, his moans rent the night air. Fray Lucio could do no more than pray. I feared to move, believing that any activity on my part would separate the roots of the bush from the already unstable dirt. My soul writhed in agony as I realized my healing powers couldn't help Fray Patricio, as I realized the depth of my own cowardice. Morning dawned, and the sounds from beneath me ceased. I saw the body of my brother far below. He was beyond human help.

I carefully crept from my perch. Fray Lucio was devastated, trembling, weak. I forced him to participate in prayers for the dead, and I will continue to seek rest for Fray Patricio's soul.

Miraculously, Fray Patricio had dropped the chest of gold within easy reach.

—from the diary of Fray Juan Estévan de Bautista

Chapter 11

Without moving her head, she ran her gaze over the room
washed with the early morning light. It looked different. It
smelled different. The bed seemed narrower, less stable, yet
safer. The contours of the room seemed altered, skewed from
their previous dimensions. The world—she shut her eyes—the
world no longer spun in the tight circle she'd known before. It
wobbled on its axis, and she could perceive its every twitch. She
knew what had happened; her body told her, with its muscles
aching in new places. But she understood with her mind.

Like the wind, Damian had overwhelmed her, moved her
where he wished, taken her places she'd never been before and
never wished to be. As he'd implied, he'd changed her perception of the world. She opened her eyes again and frowned.

Was that a good thing? She'd been quite pleased with her
perception of the world before. Indeed, some less sure companions had called her smug, but she considered her complacence
more of a clarity of goals and an understanding of propriety.
And this was not propriety.

Even now, Damian's form warmed her back. It counteracted
the cool of a morning on the coast, and brought her chilly feet
seeking his legs. He grunted when ten icy toes made contact, but
his light snoring never broke rhythm. That surprised her, for
the man rose as early as a farmer, declaring that morning was
the best time of the day. Perhaps he'd stayed awake the night

before. Heaven knows he'd been inquisitive long after she'd been prepared to sleep.

Taking care not to disturb him, she eased out of bed. The privy lay close outside her door, and she reached among the jumble of her bags to find her robe. She lifted it, examined it. The brown homespun looked exactly as it had, and she experienced a ridiculous thrill. The intruder hadn't harmed her robe, but . . . her gaze fell on the carpetbag she had brought from Boston. The lining had been turned inside out, cut up, ripped wide. Dropping to her knees, she searched until she found her watch. It still ticked, its works open to her gaze.

With fingers that trembled, she searched for and found the discarded back. It snapped into place. The watch was whole again, miraculously untouched by the ordeal of the night. She touched it tenderly and returned to her labors. Picking up one garment after another, folding them, she noted that all the linings had been rent. Her shoes had been cut. Yet she felt nothing but gratitude that this destructiveness had barely touched her.

A slit throat, she thought humorously, does wonders to restore a sense of balance.

That balance was ruined when she found her new dress.

At the bottom of the pile, Damian's gift had been reduced to fragments with the knife. Tears in the bodice cut across the darts. The skirt had been slashed. If this was the intruder's way of terrifying her, he'd succeeded. She felt violated, dirty, personally threatened.

She dropped it and fled the room. She gulped in the cool air of the outdoors; it revived her. The dew on the grass wet her toes and recalled her to her errand. When she finished, she returned to her room without a glance at the clothes in the corner.

That left her only one place to go. At the rumpled bedside, she gazed at Damian. She'd never seen him asleep before. A thrill, almost maternal in nature, quivered up her spine. How beautiful he was. Again she was stricken by his resemblance to the Greek gods, immortalized in marble for all eternity. Except for the eyebrows, he looked like the mature Apollo, all noble angles and seductive sensuality.

She traced one eyebrow on its upward sweep. Her hand drifted down to the sharp line of his lips against his face. It marked the contrast between the tanned, stubbled skin of his cheek and his smooth, pliant mouth. Compulsively, her hand moved to his short mustache, to his lips. His head turned under her hand. A kiss pressed into her palm, another onto her wrist.

He looked up at her, and the thrill this time was not at all maternal. Something solid, some kind of communication passed between them. She understood him without words, and an uneasy intuition squeezed her insides. He lifted the covers and pulled her back onto the bed beside him. Sliding his head along the pillow, he brought his mouth close enough to tempt her, and she hastily asked, "What's the treasure of the padres?" That halted the kiss, the early morning lovemaking, the murmur of sweet words and the tender aftermath.

"What's the treasure of the padres?" he parroted.

It pleased her to note that she'd distracted him from that kiss, and all of its marvelous repercussions. It signaled her successful retreat into rationality.

"Why do you ask about the treasure of the padres?"

"That person wants it and thinks I have it."

"That person?" Looking as dumbfounded as it was possible for Apollo to look, he said, "You mean, the fiend who slit your neck spoke of the treasure of the padres? You didn't tell me last night?"

"I'm telling you now. Last night you had other things on your mind." What a wicked pleasure she experienced, seeing him rendered speechless.

"Why would you know anything about the treasure of the padres? You didn't grow up in California."

"He thought Tobias knew about the treasure."

"Madre de Dios. This killer couldn't be serious. The treasure is nothing but a legend," he protested.

The pleasure of seeing him rattled faded, and she sobered. "That knife felt very serious against my neck."

"Let me see that wound," he ordered, sitting up. "I need to change the bandage."

Of course he didn't need to change the bandage, but she turned obediently under his hands and offered her throat. He needed to reassure himself about her health. He needed to see that the cut was healing, touch the bruised skin around it. "Tell me about this treasure," she coaxed.

"It's just silliness." He unwound the linen from her neck. "Just an old tale. Nothing of importance." She waited. "You're not convinced."

She shook her head.

"When I was young, we boys would go out to help round up the cattle. At night, the vaqueros would tell tales around the campfire. Scared us boys spitless, of course, and that delighted the cowboys. These myths fascinated Tobias, and his fascination reawakened my curiosity. It had been a long time since I'd felt the surge of excitement a treasure hunt brings."

"I can't imagine."

"Can't you? As a child, didn't you ever pretend you were a conquistador, traveling through uncharted territory, braving dangers to follow the trail of treasure?" His eyes glowed when she shook her head. "No? It was one of my favorite games. The thrill comes at the thought of gold and jewels, unseen by human eyes for a hundred years, yet waiting for me."

"That's interesting." She drummed her fingers on the covers, feeling he was trying to distract her, feeling he might succeed. "I can't imagine Tobias pretending such a thing."

"Perhaps not, but the man loved to travel and the legend was an excuse." Fixed with blood, the linen bandage stuck tight against her neck. He slipped from the bed and tripped over his breeches, wadded into a ball on the floor. With a careless disregard for her hungry eyes, he pulled them on. "The missions were secularized in the thirties. The Indians were freed, poor souls, kicked off the lands without money or guidance by the rancheros who confiscated the mission lands. Still, a few Franciscans, a few Indians cling to the old ways, and some of the rancheros allow them to stay in the mission buildings—no great favor, for they are falling into ruin. A few missions were returned to the jurisdiction of the Franciscans three years ago, stripped of the lands, of course. Tobias and I visited the ranchos and missions to hear the old folks tell their tales."

"Tobias must have loved that."

They shared a smile of reminiscence. "He did. The padres loved it, too. He was so interested, so enthused! They showed him the mission libraries and helped him seek out all the material written about the early days."

"Did you visit all the missions?"

Damian set his chin in annoyance. "Señorita, you may believe I'm a trifler, but actually I'm a very busy man. I didn't have time to visit all the missions with him. Together we went as far south as Mission San Luis Obispo."

"But did you go to all the missions with him?" she insisted.

"No," he admitted. He carried both the pitcher and bowl to the bedside, wet a rag and sat over her to drip water on her throat. "The southern missions neither of us had the time to visit. Mission San Juan Bautista was so close at hand I urged him to visit it by himself."

Startled to see his color rise, curious about the faint guilt on his face, she asked, "Why didn't you want to go there? As you say, it's so close at hand that it wouldn't have taken much of your time."

He squeezed water onto her face in a careless maneuver she suspected was a decoy for her attention. He apologized profusely and under her steady gaze conceded, "You see, I have been there so many times. Fray Pedro knows me from my childhood, and he always asks me for my confession. . . . You're just delighted to see me squirm, aren't you?"

She nodded.

He tweaked her ear, she gave him a little shove, and he almost fell off the bed. He righted himself and warned, "Careful, that floor is hard. You'd not enjoy it at all."

Pulling a skeptical face, she ignored his challenge and took the proffered towel to dab her face. "So Tobias could have found something out about a treasure?"

"Not just any treasure. The treasure of the padres."

"Haven't you tantalized me enough? Tell me what it is."

"It's just a legend. Just a story that's been told to frighten children since the days when Padre Junípero Serra walked the countryside to found the missions." He had forgotten her injury, had forgotten his self-appointed chore. "When the Spaniards came to California they expected to find gold and silver in abundance. It had been foretold by the Indians on the trip up from Mexico."

"It seems that every conquistador who roamed the New World believed every Indian who told him what he wanted to hear," she observed.

He grunted in disgust. "Too true. Of course, no one found gold in California. There's no gold in California, but there's a tale that some padres, with the permission of Fray Serra, made a move to convert the Indians of the Sacramento Valley. Pure nonsense, of course."

"Of course."

"Hell, the padres couldn't even keep up with all the converts on the coast. The interior was totally unexplored. They had no idea how far inland they would have to go, or how many mountain ranges they would have to cross. Why would they go looking for trouble?"

"I don't know. Why would they?"

He played with the end of the bandage. "The Indians on the coast, for the most part, were docile. The Indians on the interior were savages. The story says that these brave padres believed it was their duty to bring these savages the Word of Christ. One padre especially, Fray Juan Vincente—no, wait, that wasn't his name." He hung his head as he thought and produced his name in triumph. "Fray Juan Estévan traveled into the unknown to convert the Indians. In the spring of 1776, eight Franciscan brothers disappeared into the mountains with an escort of twenty soldiers."

"Why did they want to take the soldiers?" she asked, confused.

"Oh, the padres didn't want to take them. The governor ordered the soldiers to protect the brothers, but the soldiers were nothing but convicts expelled from Mexico."

"That, at least, hasn't changed," she observed acidly.

"Mexico always sends us her best." His sarcasm spoke volumes about the soldiers. "Nevertheless, the governor insisted that the padres wouldn't be safe without protection, so off they marched. The padres went from place to place, ringing their bell. When the natives gathered, the brothers would speak to them of Jesus Christ, and so their conversion was begun. The Franciscans had a hard year, but eventually a mission was built and the natives came for baptism. Crops were planted. The people were clothed. And one of the women brought a present. She brought them gold."

"Gold?" She pulled a skeptical face.

"Chunks of gold, nuggets of gold." He showed her with his hands how big the fabled gold must have been. "A pure gold, easily worked into primitive bracelets and necklaces. The natives discovered the padres liked the gold, and it meant nothing to the Indians. It was just the sun rock, plentiful in the streams of the valley."

"You sound like you believe this."

"No. . . ." He dragged his hand over his face. "Only I've heard it so many times, it's almost a history."

"That can't be all of the story," she observed, when it seemed he would say no more.

"No, that's not all. The soldiers saw the gold, and they wanted more. The padres couldn't restrain them. The soldiers behaved like savages, and the savages responded like soldiers. The Indians burned the mission and killed as many of the padres as they could find. They caught all the soldiers and roasted them over the coals of the mission until their skin bubbled and their extremities made little bonfires on their bodies."

Katherine made a noise of protest, and Damian collected himself.

"It was a horrible justice," he said solemnly. "Some of the padres escaped. One legend says five, one legend says four, but all legends say they carried with them chests loaded with gold. They fled into the mountains. The Indians chased after them. One by one the padres died there, but not before they sequestered the gold in a marked spot."

Sensitive to the inconsistencies of the tale, she insisted, "If they all died in the mountains, then who told the tale for the first time?"

"Ah, therein lies the difficulty. They say that Fray Serra welcomed the one surviving padre back to one of the missions."

"Fray Juan Estévan?"

He shrugged, his palms out flat. "The tale doesn't say, but it does say there is a record of the treasure and its hiding place."

"If that's true, then why isn't everyone combing the mission libraries for clues as to the location? Why isn't everyone tramping the mountains looking for this gold?" she demanded.

"Because men have searched for the gold down through the years. They return maimed and afraid, if they return at all."

"Tobias returned."

"You're assuming that Tobias went looking for this treasure," he pointed out.

He was right. However ludicrous the story, she believed Tobias had been interested enough to follow it to the end of the trail. "All right," she conceded. "Let's speculate that Tobias found something that told him where the gold was hidden. Where did he find this thing?"

"He went somewhere, discovered something, and returned to Monterey. He never stayed away long, so where could he have gone?" Warming to his subject, he answered his own question. "To the mission at San Juan Bautista, where I never went with him. What did he find there?"

Absorbed against her better judgment, she sat up and wrapped her arms around her knees. "It has to be something that was previously hidden. Perhaps it was a puzzle he solved, or a code he deciphered. That would interest Tobias as much as a treasure."

"That would have kept him alive, too."

She lifted her brows, startled by his somber reflection. "What do you mean?"

"No one believes in the treasure, but there are stories about its hiding place. They say there are traps set everywhere."

"If there are traps, they're only for thieves. The Franciscan brothers would know how to retrieve the treasure without injury, and so would any person who had access to the records of the rightful owners."

"Not . . . necessarily. There's another part of the tale that keeps a lot of the potential treasure hunters at bay."

"For someone who denies the truth of these tales so stoutly, you know an incredible amount about them." She smiled, entertained by the incongruity.

He didn't smile back; his pensive aspect sobered her. "I was only one of the youths who listened as the vaqueros told their ghost tales, but I alone stayed when the fire died. When the other children were asleep, when the moon had set and the cool air crept around and only red embers remained, I was there. There was one old man—dear God, he was old. No teeth, only one leg, hands crumpled with pain, but everyone treated Jaime with respect."

"Because. . . ."

"Because when he was a young man, he saw the padre who returned from the Sacramento Valley."

She blinked. "Did you believe him? I'd love to meet this Jaime."

"Unfortunately, my skeptical one, he's been dead these ten years." He crossed himself. "May he rest in peace."

"It would have been interesting to speak to him." Her eyes were thoughtful. "If nothing else, it would have been like talking to an oracle."

"Interesting is not the word I would apply. Marvelous. Terrifying. Mesmerizing. You see, he was one of an expedition of Indian renegades who slipped away from the mission and tried to retrieve the treasure."

"Chasing after a legend," she said, a bite in her voice. "What an adventure."

"An adventure that scarred his whole life, changed him from a strong young man to a cowed old one. He prayed constantly and feared death as no one should."

Puzzled, frowning, she asked, "What happened to the renegades?"

"You must understand that in those days the padres held much power. Once converted, the Indians weren't allowed to leave the missions. If they escaped they were beaten, mutilated, perhaps hanged."

"By the Franciscans?" she asked, horrified.

"Indeed. The padres believed that, if the Indians were allowed to return to their wild state, they would slip into sin once more. The punishments were a way of saving their souls." His face lost all expression as he added, "There was the profitable consideration, too. If the Indians ran away, there was no one to work the fields and the cattle. The missions were lucrative organizations."

Interested and appalled, she asked, "So this vaquero, this Jaime, risked his life by leaving to pursue the treasure?"

"In more ways than one. Misfortune dogged the expatriates from their first steps into the Sierra de Gavilán. Injuries, missteps, wrong turnings; Jaime recounted them in a most dramatic way. At night, the wind kept them cowering in their blankets. It moaned like a man in pain. By day, the scream of the panther followed them. At least, they thought it was a panther, although they never saw it. The fog froze their bones as they groped their way up the mountain. It followed on Jaime's back as he crawled down."

Beneath the spell of Damian's deep voice, the bright morning dimmed and her incredulity failed her. It seemed as if the fog entered the bedroom windows and crept around them, and she could hear noises in the house—a creaking as the floor settled, a sigh as the breeze leaked through the narrow shutters. Trying to warm herself, she hugged her waist. "What happened to his companions?"

"They all died. They found the cave, and it was just a hole in the mountain. There was room for one man at a time to wiggle through, and their leader insisted on going in first. His accomplices waited outside, but he never returned. They feared he'd found another way out, and one by one they went in. Their leader was gone, as they suspected, yet the treasure remained—gold and holy vessels from the mission. They snatched at it like boys at a stick of candy, and suffered for their greed."

"This is silly," she whispered to herself as she reached down and pulled the blankets up.

"One by one the Indians were struck down. One man was impaled, one man beheaded. Jaime was smashed, his leg caught beneath a boulder. He had to amputate his own foot to escape. To the end of his days, he remained convinced he had been spared so he could tell his story and warn off prospective treasure hunters. Such ghostly stories are nonsense, yet when night falls, nonsense becomes truth." He shook his head. "This assailant who attacked you in the night frightens me for more reasons than you can imagine."

Shaking off the spell of fear Damian had woven about her, she snapped, "I'm not pleased about it, myself."

"Do you understand what it means?" he insisted.

She could think of many things that it meant, but none, she suspected, such as he thought. She shook her head.

"It means I'm paying for my youthful fascination with the treasure. It means we'll have to seek it ourselves."

"What?" She bounced out of the blankets. "What do you mean? We don't want that treasure."

"No, but someone does. Until it's found or irrevocably proved to be a myth, our lives will be a misery."

"All the more reason for me to leave," she answered.

"Ah." Squinting one eye, he pulled a long face. "You'd abandon me here, facing a threat such as this?"

"No one would threaten *you*," she assured him. "You're a respected member in the community, and a man who ably demonstrated his physical abilities just last week during the fiesta. No one would—"

"Tobias had his throat slashed in the street."

Damian didn't add that a knife placed in his own back would be sufficiently disabling. He didn't need to.

Katherine transferred her attention out the window until his hand on her shoulder pushed her backward. She stiffened, but he only examined her bandage. Working with care, he peeled the soaked linen back and exposed the cut. "The edges have pulled together nicely. You'll hardly have a scar."

He left the bed to collect the ointment, and she watched him with helpless fascination. "Good."

He opened the jar. "When were you planning to go?"

"As soon as I had word from the captain that the ship was sailing." She glared at him and asked with poisonous sweetness, "When would that have been, Don Damian?"

Wiping the wound with a clean cloth, he murmured, "I beg your pardon?"

"How innocently you act. I know you bribed the captain to refrain from sailing until you could come to Monterey."

"Not I. That was my father. My wise—" his hand pressed firmly on her neck "—noble father who knew better than you the proper courtesy when leaving a sweetheart." Holding her hostage with his hand, he dared her to challenge his statement.

She found her courage failed her, so she folded her lips tightly together. Silent as he spread the ointment and bound it with fresh bandages, she resisted when he leaned close to kiss her.

"How can you think of leaving me?" he whispered.

She held her arm stiff against his neck, but that didn't stop his hands from kneading her shoulders or close her ears to his appeal. "I am not an exploiter of women, and together we are more than we are apart."

"This can't be love," she protested, ignoring the comfort he gave her; she concentrated only on maintaining the tension on her blocking arm.

"Perhaps not." His husky whisper seduced her. "Perhaps we're not perfect now, but we have something that deserves to be explored."

"It's nothing but trouble." But her contentiousness was weakening, as was her arm.

"You can't run away from trouble. It's not in your nature."

His eyes glowed, and she knew he felt the undertow, too. If he was brave enough to let it pull him along, who was she to be faint of heart?

"No, it's not in my nature," she agreed.

"Then you'll marry me?"

Absolutely not, she thought privately, but aloud she said, "I'll stay and see."

Chapter 12

Married!

She never should have loosened her arm and let him lie on top of her. She certainly never should have let him kiss her.

Married!

Those straight eyebrows of his were indicative of something. They were indicative of the devil's own temptation, and she would have been wise to pay attention. If she'd paid attention, she'd be much happier today.

Well, maybe not happier, but contented.

Perhaps contented wasn't the right word.

But she'd be at rest, knowing she'd done the right thing. She darted a peek at Damian, walking beside her across the square in the center of Monterey.

Married. Oh, dear Lord, she was married, and she felt as if she'd erupt from joy inside. How embarrassing. How demonstrative. How marvelous.

Unable to help herself, she slipped one hand into the crook of his arm. Putting his hand over it, he looked down and smiled. She thought the sun had burst from behind the clouds that whipped along on the wind.

She'd made someone happy today.

He put his arm around her, and she skittered away.

"A man's allowed to hug his wife," he advised. "Especially a wife who's as beautiful as a sapphire in a golden setting."

Unable to help herself, she smoothed the skirt of her new

blue dress. "It's very pretty. How fortunate that it just happened to arrive this morning from your father. How many dresses did you have made for me?"

"A man's allowed to clothe his wife."

That didn't answer the question, but when he stepped close and adjusted the silk cravat he'd knotted around her neck, she forgot why she'd asked. "This is a very attractive style," he murmured. "So concealing." Their eyes met. "I predict we'll be seeing it all over Monterey, now that the señoras know it's the rage in Boston."

"What an outrageous lie you told." She sounded severe, not hinting at the elation she felt. "I doubt Doña Xaviera believed you at all."

"No, she's too crafty for that." He smirked. "However, Vietta and her mother certainly took note. Right now, they're rummaging through their scarves and bothering Señor Gregorio to teach them how to knot them." His hands moved down her bodice to her waist, and he stepped closer. "Perhaps I can teach you more . . . knots, also."

"No." She fastened her fingers around his wrists. "We're not the only two people in the world. Isn't that right, Don Julio?"

Julio, who walked beside and a step behind, wore a puckish expression of mirth. "You could have fooled me."

Throwing him a matching expression, Damian inquired, "Are we ignoring you, *mi amigo*?"

"A man who's asked to stand up with his friends as witness to his wedding can expect nothing more," Julio assured them. "However, I didn't expect to have to fade away even before we'd left the *alcalde*'s home."

"You exaggerate," Damian accused.

"No. Actually, it's the first wedding I've ever attended where the *alcalde* was invisible to the bride and groom."

Damian cackled. "There may be some justification for what you say. I don't remember much about the ceremony."

Neither did she, Katherine mused. She did remember *Alcalde*

Diaz and his assurance to her anxious query. The civil ceremony was legal according to the laws of Mexico, he'd said, but the de la Solas would undoubtedly have a religious ceremony later. Damian, too, had been insistent that she understood the need for a Catholic ceremony.

The wedding itself was a blur of smiling faces and an elemental elation that she couldn't subdue. She remembered hearing Damian's firm responses. She couldn't remember giving any responses herself, but they were out in the afternoon sun. Somehow, she must have said the correct thing.

"You, *mi amigo*, have lost all sense of your vaunted duty," Julio said. "You haven't even asked for news from the battlefield."

Damian performed his duty with obedience, if not enthusiasm. "What news from the battlefront?"

"Castro has done his bombastic best to assure us of his victory."

"Another proclamation?"

"This one calls the Americanos highwaymen and cowards and, worst of all, poor guests."

"The ultimate insult," Damian drawled.

"What do the Americans say?" Katherine asked. She fingered her watch chain for luck. Already the issues of American and Californian, of New England propriety and Spanish warmth rose between the newlyweds. These were the issues that she'd warned Damian about; these were the issues not easily abandoned, nor cured by the rush of passion they experienced now.

Worry tugged at her happiness. Damian felt it too, for he took her hand, and played with her fingers.

Julio watched with weary eyes, but he answered only the question. "Frémont hasn't issued a proclamation. He hasn't become that much a part of California society. The word is that he, too, proclaims victory over the Californio barbarians."

Damian lifted Katherine's hand to his mouth and kissed it. A thrill started at her toes and rose straight to her heart. She forgot about Frémont; she forgot about nationalities; she forgot about everything but her longing to push the lock of hair from her husband's forehead and let her fingers linger.

A smile lit Julio's face as he bowed to them both. "*This* Californio barbarian senses he's not needed, and definitely not wanted. Congratulations on your marriage. May you live one thousand years together. May every day be a joy."

"Aren't you going to throw kernels of wheat?" Damian joked. "That ensures fertility, you know."

As if by magic, the pleasure vanished from Julio's face. "No, it doesn't. Congratulations again." He bowed once more and strode away.

Recalled to her surroundings and very much afraid they had offended Julio with their absorption, Katherine jerked her hand away from Damian's lips. "You've made it clear to everyone living in Monterey just why we've wed in such a hurry." She sounded like a scold, but the memory of her embarrassment made her wince. "When we spoke to Doña Xaviera this morning, I felt as if I traveled about the town in a gigantic bed."

"What an imagination you have. Now, perhaps Señora Gregorio and Vietta could have made you feel as if you were a scarlet woman," he admitted. "I thought they would walk past you without a word until I greeted them with the news we would wed this afternoon."

"Those women are the antithesis of Iberian courtesy," she acknowledged. "When we first met Don Julio this morning, he had a little trouble with elementary courtesy, also."

"That wasn't because he was judging us," he assured her. "During his sober moments at the fiesta, he gave me wonderful advice about catching you."

She stiffened. "You discussed me with him?"

"Never. Julio shows a most intuitive nature when confronted with affairs of the heart." He corrected himself. "Other people's affairs of the heart."

"He was surprised when you asked him to stand up with you."

That irresistible smile broke through once more. "He had to be the only man in California who was surprised to discover what our friendship means to me. I stood up for him, you know."

She shook her head.

"Maybe this will teach him to pick a fight with me." He pointed to the fading bruises on his face.

Her smile peeked at him. "I thought I had made that bruise."

Now he did hug her, picking her up and whirling her in circles.

"Put me down." She smacked at him, careful not to add to his marks.

He laughed aloud. "We are going to be the two happiest people in the whole world."

Unable to help herself, she laughed, too. He spun slower, brought her closer. Her blows weakened, her smile wavered. He brought her against his body, and she slid down until her toes touched the grass. Her head was still in the clouds, she knew, for the look in his eyes made her forget their surroundings and meet him halfway for a burning kiss.

"Katherine?"

The sound of her own name made her pull herself, slowly and painfully, from Damian's heaven.

"Katherine Chamberlain?" A spare man of medium height stepped from the shadow of the armory walls and walked hesitantly towards them.

Puzzled, she leaned back against Damian's arms and looked at the gentleman. She looked again, her attention fixed.

The ocean breeze threatened the safety of the man's tall hat, and he held his hand atop it. The strained buttons on his mustard vest showed more of the green and gold cravat than fashion called for. The wind caused his bilious green knee-length coat to beat around his legs. His trousers, gold and black striped, fit tight at the waist and billowed like a ship's sails at his ankles.

His boots were black. Katherine's eyes lingered there, resting from the assault of color that elsewhere decorated the young man. When she thought she could, she lifted her gaze and smiled with polite restraint. "Cousin." Damian tensed in her arms. "What a surprise to see you."

Looking as if he'd bitten into a worm, the man she called cousin answered, "Obviously."

That nasty sneer brought Damian's fists up. If the hidalgo hadn't been restrained by Katherine's grasp, the little peacock would have been picking his teeth off the ground. The man she called "cousin" knew it, too, by the simper he gave. The gentleman swept his top hat off to reveal a stiff wave of hair just on the top of his head; he bowed with a sweep. "Lawrence Cyril Chamberlain," he said. "At your service."

Damian nodded with cool courtesy. "Damian de la Sola." Words of courtesy stuck in his throat, but he managed, *"Mucho gusto."*

"What did he say, Katherine?"

The way he whined made Damian grind his teeth. Katherine knew it. He could see the slightest hint of a smile as she answered with fulsome untruth, "He says he's very glad to meet you."

"Doesn't he speak English?" In his desire for this to be the case, the dandy crushed the upturned brim of his hat.

"He speaks English very well, Lawrence," she informed him.

Lawrence chewed that over, his long, thin face growing longer as he considered. "I know this is California and uncivilized, yet I must ask—why is he hugging you?"

"Because I want to," Damian answered.

Lawrence jumped; clearly, he hadn't accepted Damian's ability to speak English. Lawrence spoke again to Katherine while keeping a wary eye on the Spanish character. "Katherine, where's Tobias? You told us you came out here to marry Tobias. Were you lying to us about Tobias?"

Damian watched the young man's reaction as she answered, "Tobias has died."

Joy lit Lawrence's face. He clapped his hands in one hearty smack. "He did? You mean you did marry him?"

"I did," she agreed.

"He's left you a widow already?" The glee in his tone was disgraceful.

"He did," she said impassively.

"Oh, Mother Mary McRee!" Hugging himself, he chuckled. "Wait until I tell Father! We Chamberlains knew you'd come to no good in this wilderness, but we didn't know how soon." He cocked his head. "How long ago was it?"

"He died almost a year ago."

Horror blossomed on Lawrence's face. Gaping, he said, "You've been living out here alone, destitute, without a family? How have you supported yourself?" Inevitably, the worst implications of the scene before him took hold. His eyes widened; then he averted his gaze in a parody of modesty.

Damian glared at the man, and as he watched, the wind caught the edge of Lawrence's hair and lifted it from a bare spot on the back of his head.

This man—much younger than Damian, surely younger than Katherine—this man wore a hairpiece that accented his absurdity. The hair that swept his collar was a different red than the red above. Damian supposed that Lawrence grew his lengthy whiskers to his cravat as compensation.

"If you would excuse us," Lawrence said in loud, hostile tones. "My cousin and I wish to speak alone."

"I think not," Damian answered with brisk authority.

Lawrence looked confused by the reply. His conclusions didn't include anything but the lowest expectations. He stared at Damian for several minutes before his mind made that next logical connection. Pointing a finger at first one, then the other, he sputtered, "You're her . . . her . . ."

Damian acquiesced, "I am."

Stepping forward, Lawrence tucked his thumb and forefingers in the pockets of his vest. "That may be who you are, but I am Lawrence Cyril Chamberlain, second son of the Chamberlain household. As such, I am my family's representative in California and I say you are dismissed from your position of protector."

The faint amusement Damian had felt vanished with the use of that expression. "I take care of Katherine," he said with a heavy sarcasm, but it flew right over Lawrence's head as Katherine flinched.

"Let me spell it out, my good man." Lawrence sniffed. "Your services are no longer needed."

Control failed. Grabbing the collar of the fine green coat, Damian lifted the dandy to his toes. "Let me spell it out. I stand beside Katherine." He held the young man there, nose to nose, until Lawrence wilted inside his clothes. Letting him go, Damian dusted his fingers under Lawrence's nose, adding, "My good man."

"Very well." Lawrence straightened his vest. "We need to negotiate. Is there a place where we can have privacy?" He swept his gaze around the town in disdain, but his dignity was blemished as he pulled his top hat lower. The brim rested on his large, freckled ears.

"It shouldn't blow off now," Damian commented. Lawrence looked at him sharply, and Damian gestured towards the _alcalde_'s home. "That would be the best place for us to, er, negotiate."

He put his hand under Katherine's arm and led her back to the place they'd just left, the place where they'd been married. Lawrence stalked along beside them, but well off to the side, as if contact would contaminate him.

"Where did you come from, Lawrence?" Katherine asked.

"From that ship." He pointed toward the harbor and she turned to look. The top of the mast was visible beyond the presidio, beside the mast of the vessel she would have taken back to Los Angeles.

That vessel was moving out to sea with leisurely majesty.

Her sharp pinch on Damian's arm made him yelp, and she said with keen curiosity, "When did you find time to send a message to the captain to leave?"

There wasn't a good answer, Damian knew. Not one thing he said would appease her pique, so he shrugged and told the truth. "I told Señora Zollman that the captain could set forth at his will."

She stuck out her chin. "The next ship I try to board will be captained by a man not influenced by bribes."

"The next ship you try to board—" Damian began. Lawrence's smirk stopped him. Airing their disagreements before Lawrence destroyed the appearance of a unified front, and he could see by Katherine's pained look she knew it, too. He tapped at the *alcalde*'s door and entered on the welcoming call.

The *alcalde* and his wife looked up in astonishment to see the newlyweds returning.

"If you've come for an annulment, I must tell you it's too soon," *Alcalde* Diaz joked in Spanish.

"Not an annulment, *Alcalde*," Damian said, also in Spanish. "Permission for a murder. This is one of my wife's relatives, and a troublemaker to boot."

They laughed, and Señora Diaz asked, "Have all Doña Katherine's relatives come to live with you?"

"Not yet." Damian sighed in mock relief.

Alcalde Diaz agreed, "Ah, yes, at least the rest of your in-laws are far away. You could be blessed with a large family of—"

His wife raised a hand to him.

"—lovely in-laws. My dear, what did you think I would say?"

His wife scolded and Katherine held the door of the parlor, still decorated with the flowers of her wedding. Her offended cousin, who suspected they were all laughing at him, stalked ahead of her.

"I don't know why these people can't speak English," he fussed.

"Because they're in Mexican territory?" Katherine suggested. "Because they were raised speaking Spanish? Perhaps you'll learn some of the language while you're here."

"Oh, please." He lifted a bilious green pocket handkerchief to his nose. "It's easy for you. You always spoke all those queer foreign languages anyway. I had trouble learning enough Latin to pass my law courses. I hope I won't be here long."

"Did you plan to sail back on the ship you came in on?" she queried, seating herself on one of the fragile parlor chairs.

"*We* can sail on it." He kept one eye on Damian, who had taken up a station beside the door with his arms crossed over his chest.

She waved Lawrence into another chair just beside a delicate pedestal graced by a Grecian vase. "Why would I want to return to Boston?"

"Why would you want to return to Boston?" Lawrence's voice rose as he repeated the question, making it sound like the most ludicrous one he'd ever heard. "Why would you want to stay here? This is the outpost of nowhere." He twitched a glance at her protector, but Damian refused to show expression. Lawrence spoke rapidly, hoping to confuse their impassive guard. "There's no learning here, no beauty, no civilization. It's filled with foreigners who babble rudely in some language no normal person could understand. They tell me this burg is the capital, and there aren't even paved streets. There aren't even streets. There probably aren't even lawyers."

This seemed the worst offence, yet Katherine dropped her head and chuckled.

"Oh, Katherine." Lawrence leaned forward and caught her hands. "Have you lost all sense of justice? Don't you see that if there were lawyers in this godforsaken hamlet, that hooligan over there would never have dared to lay hands on me? On *me* —Lawrence Cyril Chamberlain."

"I've never lost my sense of justice, Lawrence." She wrested her hands free. "But what the law has to do with justice, I have yet to understand." While Lawrence digested that, she asked, "Why have you come? It's a long sea voyage to undertake, and when I left Boston Uncle Rutherford and Aunt Narcissa made it clear I was never to return. Why are you here?"

"Ah. Well. That." Lawrence sat up straight, rearranged his cuffs, and recited in rapid detail. " 'The Chamberlain family cannot ignore their Christian duty, regardless of the ingratitude and deception that Katherine has visited on us. Katherine is, after all, the daughter of Father's only brother, and our ward. The Chamberlain family knows that she's undoubtedly run into trouble.' And you have, haven't you?" He beamed at her as if she'd fulfilled a marvelous prophesy, then switched back to his garbled accusations. " 'Katherine can no longer ignore the debt she owes us, and she'll return gratefully to live in our home for the rest of her days.' There!" He relaxed against the back support, put his elbows on the arms of the chair, and steepled his fingers.

Unimpressed, Katherine applauded. "A job well done, Lawrence. Who told you to say all that?"

"It was Mother, of course." He beamed at her. "She always had a way with words, even better than Father, I sometimes think."

"Oh, she did," Katherine agreed. "I'll never forget her way with words." Standing, she brushed her skirt. "You've said your piece now. Will you return to the ship?"

Leaping to his feet, relieved to find his mission so easily accomplished, Lawrence asked, "You'll gather your things, then, and come at once?"

"Not at all. I have no intention of returning with you, but if you like, I'll write a note to my uncle and aunt informing them that their little boy did his duty."

Damian stood at the ready, sure that her insolence would make Lawrence erupt into physical violence. But she knew her cousin. He huffed like a steam engine and took a turn around his chair. He came to stand in front of her, but watched Damian. "Cousin, cousin. You don't understand. You're forgiven. We'll welcome you back into the bosom of our family, just like before."

Evidently something—the expression on her face, his own memory—made him add, "Better than before. We—my sisters and brothers—discussed this. We're older now. We won't all beat you. We'll let you have your own room, on the same floor as my sisters. We're *saving* you a room. You won't have to stay in that hot little closet. Mother's anxious for you to return, so she had some new clothes made up for you." Uncertain, his gaze swept the jewel-colored dress Damian had presented as a wedding present. "Father's complaining that there's no one who borrows his books anymore. Can you believe he's actually complaining about that?" He rushed on before she could answer. "We've got enough servants now. You won't have to help in the kitchen."

"Do you have enough law clerks, so I don't have to help in the law offices any more?" she asked with asperity.

He shifted uncomfortably. "Of course you don't have to help in the law offices. But you always liked that. Remember? You always found the precedents faster than I could, recited the laws better than I could, and worked up the cases better than I could. You'd want to help in the law offices." He glanced at her incredulous smile and gulped. "Wouldn't you?"

"Never. I will never bilk another immigrant out of another hard-earned penny as long as I live. I have nightmares about the ones I've already ruined."

"Oh, that's just your father talking," he scoffed.

Pleasure brought a light to her face. "I hope so. Lawrence, this has been a valiant effort on your part, but I'm afraid it's useless. Here I am. Here I remain."

He shifted from one foot to the other. "All right. I didn't want to do it, but let's speak plainly. You have no way to support yourself. As the head of the Chamberlain family in California, I must insist that you break off the liaison with this—" he jerked his head towards Damian "—this Mexican."

"I'm afraid that's not possible."

"Not possible? What you're doing is an abomination to God and man. In polite society, you'd be scorned. Stoned! You'd be stoned." He lifted one finger into the air like a statue of righteousness. "What will happen when your looks fade? Mother always said you had a cheap kind of beauty, but she also said that blonds age early. Soon this man will drive you from his home and you'll be cast out, bearing a child, no doubt."

"Lawrence." She laid her hand on his upraised arm. "We're married."

Freezing in midflight, he stared at her with distaste. "That's impossible."

She waited for the truth to take hold.

"You can't be married. You haven't been widowed for a whole year."

She nodded at him. "I am married."

"You can't be married. What will the family say?"

"That's certainly a consideration."

"Exactly." Noticing her faint air of amusement, he chuckled nervously. "You're joking."

"Not at all. I am married."

"To him?" Pointing, he indicated Damian. Lawrence scrambled for a foothold in the shifting situation. "Well, you can't have been married for long. Could you?"

"We were married this morning," she informed him.

A vast relief made him drop back into his chair. "There's no problem, then. We'll just get it annulled."

Damian's eyes met Katherine's, and the memory of the *alcalde*'s warning brought simultaneous bursts of laughter.

"Well! Well," Lawrence sputtered.

Katherine laid a calming hand on his knee. "I'm sorry, cousin, but you can't understand."

"I understand you've had no wedding night," he said indignantly. Her hand fell away from his leg. He insisted, "Have you?"

Damian was disgusted to see Katherine drop her head and blush.

Lawrence leaped up, more upset than he'd ever been by her supposed prostitution. "Oh, that's wonderful. That makes it almost impossible to annul this marriage."

Deciding it was time to step in, Damian said, "Nobody's going to annul my marriage."

"It wasn't approved by Father. Isn't there any respect for familial duty here?" Lawrence asked.

Too much, Damian thought. If this stuffy twerp didn't return to Boston on the next ship, the laws of Californio hospitality stood firmly on his side. As a relative, Lawrence could live at the de la Sola home forever, if he desired. Damian pledged, "I will take care of your cousin to the best of my ability, always."

"Oh, that's it." Red-faced, his freckles stood out. "You've found out how rich the Chamberlain family is. You're going to ask for money. You're nothing but an adventurer."

Relaxing back against the door, Damian struggled with a grin that infuriated Lawrence.

Katherine didn't take the insult to the de la Solas with such blasé detachment. "Lawrence, you don't know what you're talking about."

"Oh, don't I?" Lawrence waggled his finger before her face. "This man's an adventurer. Why else would he want you?"

No longer amused, Damian stepped away from the door. "Watch what you say to my wife."

Caught in a full flight of fancy, Lawrence hadn't the sense to be worried. "I wouldn't be surprised, cousin, if you didn't plan this. A chance to benefit from your connection with the Chamberlain family. You would drag this . . . this parvenu back to Boston with you and blackmail us into keeping him a secret."

"Lawrence, you're treading on thin ice." Katherine clenched her fist. Her scowl would have had Mr. Smith stroking his Adam's apple.

"It's true, then," Lawrence complained. "Every dire thing that Mother ever predicted about you has come true. You've married a worthless ne'er-do-well, and look." He pointed to the scarf she'd tied around her throat. "He's already tried to strangle you. Despite Mother's best efforts to nurture you, you've sunk to the depths of your parents."

Damian caught her fist as it swung.

"You've become nothing but a brazen-faced whore."

Damian's own fist found its mark, right across the narrow lips of the man from Boston. Lawrence smacked back against the chair so hard the fragile wood split and tossed him to the floor. Grabbing his oversized lapels, Damian dragged him back to his feet. Holding him face to face, Damian said, "Stupid," and hit him again. Lawrence's hands flailed as he tripped into the pedestal. The fine Grecian vase flew into the air and crashed into the fireplace.

Shards flew across the room. Katherine cried, "Don Damian, please. You're ruining Señora Diaz's attractive parlor."

Lawrence wiped blood from his face and whined, "Is that all you can say?" He stopped and moved his lower jaw. Assured that it worked, he complained more loudly, "He's beating me up and all you can do is worry about a bunch of ugly furniture?"

"You could hit him back," Katherine advised with little sympathy. "Men do that."

Drawing himself up, he said, "Your sense of decency is dead, you hear me—dead!"

"Do you never learn?" Damian reached out again. He used more a slap than a blow, but Lawrence staggered like a drunk in a stupor and collapsed against the pedestal, which in turn collapsed under him.

The door of the parlor flew open as the wood splintered around him, and Señora Diaz screamed hysterically, "My vase!"

"I told you you shouldn't do that," Katherine advised as Damian led her away from the groaning Lawrence and into the sitting room.

Damian ignored her. "Señora, I'm so sorry to have ruined your parlor." He bowed to the señora with such charm the lady halted in midoutrage. "That cur insulted my bride. My bride, the love of my life, and he spoke to her without respect. I couldn't allow him to continue. You understand?"

She did, of course. Clasping her hands before her chest, she half swooned. "Romance."

The *alcalde* put his arm around her. "You remember?" he asked.

Damian cocked an uneasy eye at Katherine. She'd stumbled into the corner of the sitting room and held her stomach with one arm. The other hand shielded her face; her shoulders shook.

The couple stepped to the door of the parlor and the *alcalde* clicked his tongue. "Such a waste, that beautiful furniture."

"I'll pay for it, of course." Damian started towards Katherine. "In fact, señora, if you would go to my father's townhouse this afternoon and tell the housekeeper what has happened, you can pick out anything you desire."

"Is she ill?" the *alcalde* whispered, nodding at Katherine.

"I think not." An embarrassing suspicion dawned in Damian, replacing his first tremor of alarm.

"These tears," the *alcalde* said, "they are for—" He pointed with his thumb.

Damian pried her fingers away from her eyes and checked. It was as he guessed, and he could hardly wait to usher her from the Diaz home. Noncommittally, he said, "The bonds of blood are strong." He thrust her face into his shirt and hugged her against him. With careful steps, he urged her from the house. "I'll take her back to the place where she can give way to her emotions." They cleared the veranda before the strangled clamor from his chest began to leak out. "Doña Katherina is sensitive to the sight of blood."

Shocked faces peered at him from the door as her sounds, unmistakably of mirth, pealed out.

Grimly he concluded, "Although not the blood of her cousin."

31 May, in the year of our Lord, 1777

The cause of our grief caught up with us this morning.
The devout among the Indian women followed us into the
mountains. They were the noise Fray Patricio heard last
night, and the reason for his death. The three women
crept to us on their knees, obviously afraid of our wrath,
but Fray Lucio and I were too heartsick to do so much as
speak harshly to them.

They carried pouches on their backs, emptying them at
our feet. They brought us gold, huge nuggets of gold,
smooth to the touch. They brought us sacks of gold dust,
and even quartz veined with gold. Clearly, they believe we
can transform this quartz into the pure metal. In their
primitive minds, this abundance of gold will make up for
the loss of our brothers.

—from the diary of Fray Juan Estévan de Bautista

Chapter 13

"He's not a parnevu." Lawrence's pronunciation suffered from the consequences of the split lips given him by Damian. A swollen nose, acquired no doubt in his fall, contributed to his nasal Boston accent.

None of that affected his determination, and none of his determination affected Katherine as she walked around the boardinghouse bed with an armload of clothes.

"Any fool can see that Don Damian's a gentleman. If I'd taken a moment to look at his boots, I'd have realized it. I mean, he's out there right now accepting his horse from some groom or another."

"The Estrada groom?"

"I suppose so. That animal is a beautiful piece of horseflesh, even I can see that. I just lost my temper when you didn't want to return immediately. I assumed you'd see it my way. It's my father coming out in me, I suppose." He chuckled anxiously and followed her to the brand-new trunk sitting, lid up, against the wall. "You won't hold it against me, will you?"

"She's not a prostitute. Any fool can see that. She's a valued member of our family. I'm sure you understand my shock when I discovered she was widowed and remarried. Perhaps I took my responsibility a little too seriously. You won't hold it against me, will you?"

Damian tightened the girths on his saddle and ignored Lawrence.

"Perhaps my anxious concern offended you. Perhaps you're still offended, and I don't blame you. I acted like an ass. But I'm acting like a concerned relative, now. There are rumors that some murderer attacked Katherine last night."

"Doña Katherina."

Lawrence blinked at Damian. "What?"

"You may call her Doña Katherina. It's a sign of respect."

"Why, she's my cousin, and I—"

Damian lifted his cold gaze to Lawrence's face.

Lawrence gulped, his throat rising and falling with his courage. "Of course. Of course. Married women are due respect. I suppose her real name is Mrs. Sola now."

"Señora de la Sola, but as her relative you are permitted to call her Doña Katherina." Damian strapped the bags onto the back of the saddle.

"Of course. Of course. As I was saying, the rumors say that Doña Katherina—" it clearly tasted bad in Lawrence's mouth "—Doña Katherina was attacked last night. To travel the road between here and your farm—"

"Rancho."

"Huh? Oh. Your rancho as the sun sets is a foolhardy act."

"I can take care of Doña Katherina."

"I don't doubt it. I don't doubt it for a minute. I just thought that if you insist on leaving so late in the afternoon, I could ride with you and protect—"

"Do you have a horse?"

As Katherine strode up, a bag in each hand, Lawrence asked her petulantly, "Does this man ever let you finish your sentences?"

She handed Damian her new carpetbag. "Is he interrupting you, Lawrence?"

"Yes."

"Try saying something worth listening to," she advised, mounting the sidesaddle with Damian's assistance.

Damian hooked the carpetbag over his saddle horn, then vaulted onto Confite. He repeated, "Do you have a horse?"

"Well, no, but—"

"Adios, then." Tipping his hat to Lawrence, Damian gestured for Katherine to precede him. They set off down the southeastbound road out of Monterey, and Lawrence jogged along beside them.

"I could get a horse."

They increased their speed.

"It's not safe out there at night." He dropped behind. "Maybe not even in the daytime."

Katherine leaned against the neck of her horse and encouraged her to move faster.

"I can wield a gun," Lawrence shouted from behind.

Damian slowed. "Can he?" he asked Katherine.

"One time he shot a mirror, believing his reflection to be a burglar," she said definitely.

Spurring Confite, Damian kept pace with his wife, who rode as if the ghosts of her past pursued her. When they were well away, he signaled for her to slow. They swapped a grin of camaraderie, the naughty shame of two children fleeing an unpleasant duty. "He can't catch us now," he said.

"That worried me," she answered. "But it's my own soft heart I flee."

Damian suspected her dilemma and shook his head warningly. "Don't tell me—"

"I don't want to, but I feel sorry for Lawrence. Poor sap."

"He called you a whore."

"He's always been gauche, but never brave. He's the sorriest son of the sorry Chamberlain family."

"I don't want him along. If we don't get rid of him now, he'll follow us to the ends of the earth," he warned.

"You don't know how true that is. He doesn't dare go back to Boston without me. He's too afraid of his parents."

"What kind of family is this?" he asked, bewildered. "They're cruel to you. They frighten their son."

"He was sent after me because he's the most easily supplanted child of the family." She nodded at his appalled expression. "He's not good for much. His law work is sloppy. He can't hold his liquor. The girls giggle about him behind his back. His ruthlessness is not up to Chamberlain quality."

"He's been kind to you."

"Exactly. It's that occasional compassion that makes him so replaceable in his father's eyes." She glanced behind her. "If there's someone on our track, Lawrence would do us no good. He'd faint if presented with that awful countenance that attacked me last night."

Damian chuckled as they rode on, skirting the salt marshes that gave Salinas its name. They were well along the track beside the river when he asked, "Why do they want you back so badly?"

Katherine grinned. "They're running out of money."

"What?"

"I'm truly very good with the law."

Her eyes flashed a challenge, but he only murmured, "You'd be good at anything you set your mind to."

She bent her head in acknowledgement. "Thank you." She patted her horse's neck as she considered the best way to explain without bragging. "My uncle had modest success as a lawyer before I moved into his home. He was competent enough to swindle people with no lawyers of their own out of their hard-earned wages. When faced with another lawyer, however, he lacked the verbal finesse to argue his way out of a mousehole."

"You don't think much of your uncle."

"He's a bully, a master at finding someone's weakness and exploiting it. Witness his results. Witness Lawrence." The hand that patted the horse clenched in its mane. "Witness me."

"You?"

He sounded surprised, and she found him smiling at her. Encouragingly, sweetly. "Yes, me. There are some people who say I have a tendency to stick out my chin and dare someone to knock in my teeth."

"Who would say such a thing?"

"My mother. She said she couldn't understand why, but I grew belligerent at fifteen." She shook her head, watching her fingers as they loosened the knots she tangled in the horse's mane then combed them out. "Bless her, I think she believed she'd been delivered of a pixie."

"Bless her, I think she was, too."

Something in his eyes made her pay close attention to her riding. Clearing her throat, she said, "Anyway. Uncle Rutherford's fantastic success as a lawyer began when I moved into the house and started writing his legal arguments for him. I put the Chamberlain fortune on firm footing when I took over the accounting and investments. I've been gone almost eighteen months. Plenty of time for my spendthrift family to have driven themselves to the verge of bankruptcy."

He whistled.

"Of course they want me back," she added matter-of-factly.

Catching at her reins, he brought her horse close to Confite. She squawked, "Don Damian!" before she received a warning look.

"They may want you back, but I've got you. Never think you have an alternative to our marriage." He rose in his stirrups to press a kiss on her surprised lips. Turning back to the road, he set off at a gallop. As she struggled to keep up, she could hear his voice on the wind, complaining, "With such a family, you were willing to leave us to go back to Boston. A woman like you could shatter a man's pride."

She trailed along in his wake until his fit of pique wore itself out. When he dropped back to her side, she said, "I wasn't returning to Boston."

He pulled up his horse so abruptly the animal almost sat down. "What?"

"I wasn't returning to Boston," she repeated obligingly. "I was going to take the ship down to Los Angeles, find a position in one of the houses there—"

Pointing his finger right at her, he insisted, "I don't want to hear another word. When I think I would have gone all the way to your family's home . . ." He shook his head as if he couldn't stand it.

"It's all for the best," she said with bracing good humor. She pointed to the sun, dipping low on the horizon. "Where will we spend the night?"

"The Cardona hacienda is nearby. We'll stop there."

Her shoulders slumped, but she agreed.

"Don't you like the Cardonas?" he asked anxiously. "They're an older couple, I know, and dull, but they're good friends of my father's."

"It's not that." She glanced at him out of the corner of her eye. "But they'll toast our marriage. The meal will be long, and after last night—"

"You're tired. Of course, I'll tell them—"

"What? That we're newlyweds and want to retire early?"

"Ah." He stroked his mustache to conceal a grin. "I see your concern." He looked her over. "Come. I'll tell them we must rise with the chickens, else we'll not arrive home before dark."

"Before dark? We should be at de la Sola rancho by noon."

"I'll tell them you're a delicate woman who demands many rests."

"That's not much better," she pointed out.

"It will have to do."

Julio strode into Monterey's cantina. The hum of conversation halted as the drinkers surveyed the newcomer. Only four tables were occupied, and Julio returned the Spanish greetings from three of them. No one invited him to sit with them; it was a reaction he was used to. The tiny windows kept the afternoon sun from beaming in too brightly, and he stared to identify the occupant of the fourth table. Satisfied, he pulled out a chair and sat. A man hunched over the bar in the darkest corner, but he wasn't the man Julio had come to see.

Lawrence Cyril Chamberlain lifted his sulky face from a glass of brandy. "No one asked you here. What do you want?"

Julio grinned at his rudeness. He settled against the high, hard back and said in English, "I want to help you. Isn't that what you want?"

"With what?"

"With whatever you need done." He leaned close toward Lawrence's face. "This morning, you were talking about your cousin Katherine, and how you'd pay anyone to capture her and put her on the ship to Boston."

Lawrence's lip stuck out. "Yes, I did."

"Well, I'm a friend of Damian's. A good friend of Damian's."

"So?"

"I could help you."

"If you're such a friend of that Damian's, why would you help me?" Lawrence asked petulantly. "No one else would."

"Because I'm a poor friend of Damian's. Money," he rubbed his fingertips together, "is always welcome."

Lawrence's voice rose incredulously. "You'd betray your friend for money?"

"Of course. What other reason is there?" Julio asked in surprise.

"Now that's a little more like it!" Lawrence slapped his knee. He winced, lifted his knuckles and examined them. He thrust his hand toward Julio. "Can you see that? Can you see what that animal did to me? He hit me."

Julio squinted to see the injuries that made Lawrence so indignant. "You hurt your hand hitting him back?"

"No," Lawrence said, impatient with such nonsense. "I hurt my hand breaking my fall."

Julio coughed in unaccountable distress, and a few coughs shook the other tables. Julio leaned close to Lawrence again. "Maybe we'd better lower our voices."

Lawrence looked at the scroungy cantina patrons. "You mean, they speak English?"

"Perhaps. It's likely."

Lawrence glanced sideways in a parody of caution. "Let's get this clear. You think you can deliver Katherine to me before the ship sails?"

"If not this ship, then the next ship."

"The sooner the better. I want to get out of this backwater." Julio watched him with a steady gaze, and Lawrence hastily added, "Katherine will, too, once she's away."

"In return, I want money. Gold coin. Half now, half on delivery."

Squinching up his eyes, Lawrence said, "Do you think I'm a fool? You'll take the money and I'll never see you again."

"Fine." Julio rose. "Find someone else to do your dirty work."

Lawrence caught Julio's sleeve. "Just a minute. Let's talk."

When Julio left, he wore a pleasant smile and his pocket jingled. Lawrence stared at the door doubtfully.

From behind him, he heard a deep voice say, "I wonder if you'll ever see good from that money."

Rested, but not satisfied, Katherine rode into the yard of the de la Sola hacienda at noon and dismounted, handing the reins to a stableboy. Don Lucian stood on the porch, a twinkle in his eye. "So, Doña Katherina, you've decided to return to us after all."

She climbed the stairs with a twitch of her skirts and lifted her cheek for his kiss. "Si, Papa, I did."

Don Lucian's arms enveloped her in a startled hug. "Papa? Papa? You call me 'Papa?' Damian!" he yelled at his son who stood on the ground below them. "Did you marry this girl?"

"Aren't you pleased?" Damian asked with mock innocence.

"Of course I'm pleased. But the wedding! We didn't get to have a wedding. Your mother would spank you." Don Lucian kept his arm around Katherine as he moved to the bench on the porch. With his hand on her shoulder, he urged her to sit, then sat beside her. "Married. Ah, my highest hopes have been fulfilled. My son Damian finally had enough sense to hook the proud Doña Katherina." He slapped his hands on his knees. "I had despaired of the day."

"Nonsense." Katherine was brisk. "It wasn't despair that led you to bribe the ship's captain to stay in Monterey."

Don Lucian looked reproachfully down at Damian. "You didn't have to tell her that."

"I have no need to take responsibility for your sins. Mine are plentiful enough." Damian patted his pockets as though looking for something.

"Need a cigar, Don Damian?" Katherine's voice was sharp.

Ignoring her, Damian leaned against the porch rail with an expression of disdain.

Don Lucian almost grinned. He recognized a first fight when he saw it. "Best to get it out of the way," he remarked into the atmosphere. He turned to Katherine. "You aren't going to hold a message to the captain against me, are you?"

"No," she admitted with reluctance.

He exuded jocularity. "I'm your father-in-law now, soon to be the grandfather of your children."

She leaped to her feet. "So I hear."

Fleeing into the house, she left an astonished Don Lucian staring after her. "What was that about?"

Damian mounted the steps, his boots ringing out. "We stopped at the Cardonas' last night."

"So?"

"Katherine was tired, and not for the reasons you think."

His father laughed softly.

Damian stiffened. "*Madre de Dios*, Papa, don't let her hear you."

"Already you're under her thumb." Don Lucian put his hand over his mouth to stifle the sound of his mirth.

"To release her from our social obligations, I told the Cordonas we would have to leave early, that Katherine was so delicate she'd have to have frequent rests to arrive here by sunset. I forgot that they'd seen her working at the fiesta and wouldn't accept that. By the time we left this morning, it was clear they believed Katherine to be in the family way."

The sounds from behind Don Lucian's hand grew louder, and Damian eyed him with disgust.

"I tried to tell them the truth, but it just made it worse. They stopped short of sending their congratulations to the new grandfather, but only just. Katherine was furious with them."

"Did she show it?"

"Of course not."

"So she takes it out on you. Such are the tribulations of a husband."

"She's furious with me for not considering such a thing, but I never thought of it."

"Men don't, but new husbands might begin to." Don Lucian eyed him warningly. "Anyway, it's nothing but what everyone else will think, with a hasty courting and hurried wedding."

"Would you have done any different?"

"Not at all," Don Lucian denied. "Still, I think we must immediately plan a reception to introduce your bride formally to society."

"Not yet, Papa. Let me tell you all that has happened."

Surrounded by shrieking maids, Katherine stood in her attic room with her palms over her ears. When the tumult died down, she cautiously removed one hand and then the other. "If I had known you would shout at me—"

Leocadia patted her on her back. "You'll have to allow us our excitement. This is the best news we've had for many a long year."

"I'm glad you're glad. May you never have reason to regret it."

"Oh, no, Doña Katherina," one of the maids piped up, stroking a swollen stomach. "This hacienda needs a mistress to organize parties, and a woman to bring babies."

Entering the room, Damian flinched, but Katherine answered steadily, "I'll do my best to live up to your expectations. Leocadia, do you know where Tobias's trunk is stored?"

Shooing the maids out, Leocadia nodded at the door leading from Katherine's room to the storage area. "It's in the attic next to you."

"Thank you," Katherine said.

"*Gracias,*" Damian echoed.

Unable to restrain herself, Leocadia pinched his cheeks. "It's such a joy to see that little snot-nosed boy who followed me around the kitchen take a wife. Your mother would be so proud."

"Ouch." Shaking her off, he then hugged her. "You approve, *Tia*?"

"*Si.*"

"How many children do you foresee?"

Leocadia eyed Katherine. "She's older and has lost many good childbearing years. Probably not more than a dozen." She pinched his face once more. "All healthy."

"Good heavens," Katherine whispered.

Leocadia shut the door behind her, and Damian shrugged sheepishly, a red mark on either cheek. "Some would say she's presumptuous, but she was my nurse, you understand, and my mother's companion."

"You don't have to explain to me," Katherine said without heat. She took a turn about the room. "But does she predict the number and health of the children correctly?"

"I hope so." As a distraction, he asked, "Shall we go see this trunk?"

"Yes, but it seems so . . . so strange to think that Tobias would have left me a message I haven't seen yet. Almost a word from beyond the grave. I never used to be so superstitious." She squared her shoulders. "Of course, it's only a temporary aberration."

"That's my sensible girl." He opened the door to the attic which lay at right angles to hers, across a different part of the hacienda. The sun came in full through the clean, uncurtained windows. This was Leocadia's attic in Leocadia's house, and not a speck of dust dared rest on any surface.

"There it is." Katherine indicated the battered metal trunk against the wall. "It came all the way from Switzerland, then all the way around the Horn. After Tobias's death—" she took a breath "—a *while* after Tobias's death, I cleaned out his clothes. As I recall, that trunk contains nothing but some junk I didn't have the heart to throw away."

He set the paraphernalia that topped the trunk on the floor. "No letters?"

She helped him pull it out from the wall, noting there was no weight, only a rattling as the contents rolled around. "None." He stepped back as she knelt before it, ceding her the right to open it as she pleased. She loosened the straps that bound it together and flipped the corroded metal latch. A tightness in her chest held her rigid, held her in suspense. Lifting the lid as if she half expected an explosion, she gazed down at the contents for a long moment.

"There." She tossed back the cover and pointed. "See. There's his toolbox. There's the ribbon headdress, some old newspapers, a couple of rocks."

Stepping to her side, Damian suggested, "Why don't we look in Tobias's toolbox?"

"I looked in there after his death. There's nothing I didn't see or touch a hundred times."

He lifted an inquiring brow, and she said with serenity, "They were his most precious possessions, handled with loving care as he created a watch or fixed a clock. After his death, they made me feel close to him."

"Of course." He opened the metal box and peered inside, his finger mixing the tools. Setting it down, he lifted the neatly folded newspapers. "What language is this?"

"German. I've read them all. Leave them out. I'll read them again, but it's two-year-old news."

"What this?" He pointed to crude drawings of a clock face that rimmed the headline. Tobias had created human features for each one, and each clock seemed to be the embodiment of a mood. Some had smiling mouths; some had frowns and wrinkled brows. All were simple, but effective.

"I've wondered what those were for." Katherine peered at them. "I suppose he was just doodling."

"Hmm." He studied them. "Yes, I suppose."

He set the newspapers down beside the toolbox. She handed him the circular headdress, its colorful ribbons trailing over her hands. "It was his mother's. I wore it at our wedding. I mean, not *our* wedding. At my marriage to Tobias, remember?" Her words rang in her ears, and she wondered what she could say that would dispel this awkwardness between them. Damian had been Tobias's friend; she had been his wife. They both held memories of him unshared by the other; now they were making memories together, excluding him.

Regret and yearning mixed together. Damian watched her hands as she fondled the band. "Yes, I remember. You should pack it in a cedar chest. I'll order a chest made for you."

"Yes. It would be best if we pack it away," she reflected.

Briefly, he touched her hand with his fingertips. "Put it in the bedroom. We'll deal with it later."

On her return, she found him lifting the rough stones from inside the trunk. Balancing them, he looked at her in disgust, then took her two hands and placed the stones in them, wrapping her fingers around. "Hold them," he urged.

She took the weight and grunted with surprise. "This one's heavy." He nodded significantly, and she felt foolish. What had she overlooked? Lifting it to her face, she said, "That pink crystal's pretty. Is it valuable?"

"Hardly." He took her elbow and urged her to the window. "It's just quartz, but any conquistador could tell you—"

"Yes?" she prompted, when he broke off and took the stone from her. He turned it over, watching the way it caught the light.

"Any conquistador could tell you—hand me that hammer from the toolbox, would you?"

Puzzled, she did as he asked. He tapped the crystals away with the hammer. "Are you mad?" she asked, not convinced of its worthlessness. "That's not what you do with something that could be valuable."

"No? Come and see."

In the sunlight by the window, the yellow glint of ore glittered in veins between the quartz trigons, like an ornamental leaf that gilded a picture frame.

She knew what it was. She knew by the slight tremble in Damian's hand as he fingered the crystals. She knew by his smile, half appalled, half joyful. She knew because Tobias had relished a puzzle, and now he'd left her one.

Damian's thoughts ran a parallel course. "When Tobias realized what he'd found, he took precautions to ensure no enemy could discover his secret."

Her knees weakened, and she sat down on the floor in an untidy sprawl. She took the measure of his amazement when he offered her no assistance, but sat down, Indian style, beside her. Tucking her knees under her, she leaned over to stare at the stone cradled in his hand. "Are you sure that's what it is?"

"Gold?"

The word splashed over her like freezing water, shocking her with its impact. The glow in his eyes frightened her, reminding her of the morning in Monterey and his self-confessed fascination with the metal.

"Yes. It's gold. The fever of it runs in my veins as surely as in any Spaniard's blood." His fervency convinced her of its worth, and its danger.

She shuddered, caught between the fear of the gold, her terror of the murderer, and a very human rejection of Tobias's intent. "It's the padres'," she whispered.

She watched the avarice fade from Damian's face like a fire dying, leaving it wise and a little wistful. "So it is." He glanced away from her, as if he were ashamed to have her see him affected by something he could cup in his hand.

"Can't we just fling it out the window?" she asked desperately.

"You know we can't." He leaned into her, brushing the top of her nose with his lips. "I won't rest until I know you're safe, and you'll never be safe while someone believes you know the padres' secret." Taking her hand, he raised her to her feet. "Come."

"Where are we going now?"

"We have unfinished business in that bedroom." He pointed the way with a flick of his finger.

"What unfinished business?"

An indulgent smile was his only answer.

She stopped, jerking on his fingers with the weight of her body. "How can you think of something like that at a time like this?"

"We're alone. We're close to a bed." He cuffed her chin with one finger. "You're no longer angry at me. Those are not circumstances likely to occur again soon. I'm a man who takes advantage of my opportunities."

"Why, we need to . . ." She couldn't think of what they needed to do. Those damned eyebrows were tilted her way, reminding her of things she thought safely stowed. "There must be something we need to do."

"Everything can wait a few hours," he assured her.

What had happened? How had he advanced from scientific scrutiny to passionate intent so quickly?

"It's daylight," she objected without force. How could that look of his change her from bleak desperation to melting obsession?

"So it is." He unpinned her collar, taking care not to brush her neck or the scarf that bound it. Pocketing the collar, he pushed her out of the attic and shut the door on their memories.

"Someone will come in."

"Spaniards have too many manners to open a closed bedroom door." He unbuttoned the front of her new dress. "This flowered print is very attractive on you."

"Someone with good taste picked it out for me," she said.

He grinned. "I taste good, too."

"Don Damian!" She gasped, although she wasn't sure if it was because of his risqué comment, or the caress of his hands as he slid the material off her shoulders and down her arms. It caught on her breasts, on her nipples, then the bodice and chemise released in a whispery slither. It dropped to her waist. He turned her and she walked towards the bed.

And stopped.

He bumped into her, stepped on her heels, apologized, and fell silent.

There in the middle of the quilt where she had tossed it lay the ribbon headdress, the headdress that Tobias's mother had worn to her wedding, the headdress she had worn to her own wedding.

That feeling she'd experienced in the attic returned, redoubled. She couldn't name it, but it made her stiff with self-consciousness.

From over her shoulder, he asked, "Don't you think I feel guilty about you?"

He said it as if he was picking up a conversation that they'd dropped moments before. She understood him as if he replied to her stated concerns, yet they'd never spoken of this. She didn't turn. She thought it would be easier for her, for them both, if she didn't look at him. "What do you mean?"

"When Tobias was killed, I did the right thing. I helped you, I arranged your affairs, I brought you to my home and gave you the work you craved. I was glad to do it for Tobias. Yet when I got you here, all the realities eroded my sense of honor. Had I rescued you for Tobias? Or for me?"

"For you?" Appalled, afraid of what he would say, she let her gaze roam the chamber.

"Of course. My nobility didn't bear examining. When I saw you standing on the dock with your trunk beside you, I cried inside. You were for me, for *me*, and you didn't realize it."

He spoke with an eloquence that told her he'd fought this battle long before she'd had to deal with it, and that brought her some comfort. Surely if he could come to terms with it, so could she.

"You married Tobias, and I got roaring drunk on your wedding night, so I couldn't think of what was going on in my bedroom. I couldn't stand to think of you in bed with my best friend."

Horrified, she said, "So when he was killed, you were glad?"

Enfolding her in a loose embrace, he laid his cheek against her hair. "No, you know that's not true. I loved him, God knows why. It wasn't his death or my reaction that filled me with guilt, but the pleasure I felt the first night I saw you here. It was as if you'd come home. I was so happy I wanted to cry. That was the real reason I left Rancho Donoso. My land at the edge of the Sierra Nevada is beautiful, but this home is close to my family. But when you were here, I couldn't be. Not and trust myself. So I ran away."

"That's what frightens me, I think." She looked at the gaily colored headdress. "In some corner of my mind, I think I came to realize what you felt, but I didn't leave."

"How could you leave? You were as helpless as a babe stripped of its parents."

"But I made it hard for both of us. I precipitated this whole thing."

"Well, good for you."

"It's all my fault."

"Only you would have the audacity to think that."

She whipped around in indignation, but he shook his head. "Only you could expect so much of yourself."

She liked the way his face looked: he seemed at peace with himself and his decision. With her gaze fixed on his face, she groped for the headdress on the bed. Placing it on the end table, she smoothed the ribbons. "Tobias wouldn't object, would he?" It was more of a statement than a question.

"Tobias was a practical man. He wouldn't begrudge you a life apart from him. Indeed, I suspect he would have bequeathed you to me."

She frowned. "That's a dreadful thing to say. I'm not an object."

"Long before you even arrived, he told me I should cherish you, should anything ever happen to him."

"Did he know—?"

"That he would die? He knew very well the danger associated with the treasure, but he couldn't have identified my affection for a woman I'd never met. It was simply Tobias's way of securing your well-being." He held her face in his hands. "He was a good man."

"I miss him," she admitted.

"So do I." He tucked her head onto his chest. "You were the only one in all of California who refused to see that I wanted you. If you hadn't made me angry, you still might not know. But when Cabeza Medina told me you'd been saving money to leave —to go back to Boston, he told me—"

She grinned. "I let him think what he wished."

"What have I done to deserve a clever woman?" he asked the elements, but didn't wait for an answer. "When he told me you would leave, I went a little crazy. Usually I have more finesse than I displayed in the library."

Relaxing against him as her tension flowed from her, she murmured, "Really?"

"You're a sorceress." He made it sound like a compliment as he backed her against the footboard. She leaned against the cool wood, its upright a support for her back, and shut her eyes to better experience the brush of his mustache on her breast.

"Are you sure no one will come in?" she whispered.

"No one would dare." His breath nuzzled her skin as he spoke. "There is no reason good enough to bring anyone to our door before dinner."

The rap of knuckles on the bedroom door sounded loud and clear.

Damian lifted his chin and looked up at Katherine, and Katherine looked back at him. The mists of pleasure rapidly cleared, and she scolded, "Lord of your home? No one would dare?"

He nipped at her collarbone and she released a little shriek. "Little nag." He glared at the door. "No one would dare unless he had an excellent reason."

Chapter 14

Damian opened the door as Leocadia raised her hand to rap it again.

"I'm sorry, Don Damian." Wringing her hands, she glanced towards the screen where Katherine hid to button her dress. "It's ghastly news. Your father demanded I come up, and I believe it's necessary."

Taking in the distraught appearance of the usually imperturbable housekeeper, he patted her hands. "Tell me about it."

"It's the vaqueros. They say it's true, but I can't imagine. . . . Who would be stupid enough to believe they could succeed with such a plan?"

"I don't know," he humored her. "Who are they, and what have they done?"

"Those animals shot Felipe," Leocadia said.

From the foot of the stairway, his father called up in a furious tone, "They've planted themselves on my land, on Rancho Donoso. They say they are laying claim. They've taken the cover off their wagon and fashioned some kind of shelter. They're chopping wood and setting fires."

Damian stepped out on the landing. "Who is doing this, Papa?"

"The Americanos." Don Lucian waved a fist to the ceiling. "The damned Americanos."

Shutting the door behind him, Damian started down the stairs. "The Americanos," he echoed grimly. "How is Felipe?"

Following on his heels, Leocadia snapped, "Bleeding." He glanced back, and she replied to the spark in his eye. "He'll live."

"Have they no respect for the law?" Don Lucian roared.

"Let's go see if we can teach them some respect." Damian took his father's arm and asked with quiet intensity, "Where are they?"

Don Lucian glanced up towards the attic room door, realizing for the first time the need for stealth. He lowered his voice to match his son's. "On the north corner, camped on the river. Come down to the library. Prudencio was there at the river with Felipe, and he's got a level head on his shoulders. We'll have him come in for questions."

To Leocadia, Damian instructed, "Send us Prudencio, then see if you can find distraction for Doña Katherina."

Leocadia nodded, slipping away, and Prudencio joined them in the library to give up his information. "They're pigs," the vaquero told them. "They're dirty pigs."

"How many pigs are there?" Damian asked.

"Five men. Also some skinny, squeaking women and dirty children." Prudencio wrinkled his nose. "We offered to help them. We thought their wagon had broken down."

"They refused help?"

"They laughed in our faces. They said this was their land now, and we'd better get off. Felipe told them this is de la Sola land, and you know Felipe. He's a little gruff. So they shot him. When I went to him, they laughed and spit on me." He shifted from one foot to the other. "Let me shoot them."

"You must allow us our fun, also, *mi amigo,*" Don Lucian commented.

Prudencio's eyes glowed with a vengeful fire. "*Si, patron,* only put a pistol in my hand and I will show you what my practice has accomplished."

Damian shifted from one foot to the other, too, as he glanced towards the closed door of the library every few minutes. But the disaster he feared didn't occur. Katherine didn't arrive, and he thanked God and Leocadia as he unlocked the solid walnut door of the gun cabinet.

"Papa?"

"My pistols, I think, and a rifle," Don Lucian instructed. "If these Americanos are as proficient with firearms as were Frémont's, we'll need the extra shots." He accepted the horn of gunpowder and the pouches of bullets.

"I have extra shots," Damian assured him as he placed three rifles side by side on the wide desk.

Don Lucian snorted with disdain. "That revolver of yours? Are you still so proud of it?"

Prudencio grinned as he checked the barrel of each rifle. "They're clean," he told Don Lucian. Taking the powder horn, he held the long guns upright and, one by one, loaded them with gunpowder.

Don Lucian took them next and with the ramrod tamped the bullets, wrapped in a greased cloth, down onto the gunpowder.

Damian loaded his father's pistols, then brought out an elegant wooden box. Setting it on the desk, he lifted the lid and smiled down at his Colt revolver. "An Americano invention to defeat Americanos."

"Foolish nonsense," Don Lucian grumbled. "Trusting your life to a contraption such as that. When the Yankee captain sold you that, he knew he'd found himself a fool." Holding up his old-fashioned dueling pistols, he said, "These have been tried and proven. Stick with them." He tucked them into his waistband, not surprised when his son disregarded his advice.

With meticulous care, Damian loaded each chamber of the repeating pistol with ball, powder and a percussion cap. "It misfires occasionally, Papa, but mark my words, this is the gun of the future."

"Not at the price you paid for it," Don Lucian answered. To annoy his son, he rubbed his fingertips together and nodded significantly at Prudencio.

Damian ignored him, sliding his revolver into his belt. "Prudencio, take the rifles and go to the stables. Speak to the vaqueros you think we'll need, then have them mounted and ready at the oak. We'll follow."

"*Si, patron,*" Prudencio agreed. "Every vaquero on the place wishes to go, but I've selected eight to accompany us. They're good men, not given to rapid judgment." He walked out the door, then stuck his head back in to add, "And they're good shots."

He left, and Don Lucian tucked his pistols into his belt. "Where do you suppose she is?" he asked.

"Katherine? Leocadia's keeping her busy, I'm sure."

"Then why are we sneaking out of our own home?" Don Lucian trailed behind Damian as they silently slipped through the door and across the yard.

"Because de la Sola men have been wife-wary cowards for generations." Damian grinned back at his father. "Isn't that right, Papa?"

Don Lucian lifted his hands. "I've never denied it."

In the stableyard, Damian was so relieved to see Confite saddled and fitted with a rifle holster that he almost failed to see the feminine figure mounted next to Confite and waiting. Almost, but not quite. Squaring his shoulders, he strode to the mare and caught the bridle. Staring fiercely up at Katherine, he said, "I will not take you."

"As you like," she agreed. "I can arrive with you, or alone."

"It isn't safe," he pointed out.

"Not for you. Perhaps for me."

He reached up and grasped her knee. "*Querida,* a man wishes to protect his wife from the ugliness of life. In Monterey, I failed in that respect. Let me protect you now."

He relaxed as his fervent plea, the use of his expressive eyes, swayed her. But only for a moment.

She thrust out her chin. "Perhaps these Americans will listen to me. I'm trained as a lawyer. Perhaps I can make them see reason."

From behind him, Don Lucian said, "Katherina, at least change from that lovely dress into the new riding outfit I had made for you. Leocadia will help you. It will only take a minute."

She turned her clear green eyes on her father-in-law, leaving no doubt she'd seen through his ruse. "I can arrive with you, or alone," she repeated.

Wondering why he'd resisted the gentle wiles of the Spanish señoritas to marry such an obstinate woman, Damian swung into the saddle. He rode to Katherine's side, and, using the advantage his taller horse gave him, he told her, "You can go. But when the shooting starts—"

"If the shooting starts," she corrected.

He drew an exasperated breath. "When the shooting starts, you keep quiet. You get out of the way and stay out of the way. I'm serious, Katherine Anne. Your carelessness could cause someone to be hurt."

"Yes, Don Damian."

"*Madre de Dios,*" Damian muttered to his father as he spurred out of the yard. "Do you suppose she'll ever call me 'Damian'?"

A stench assaulted Katherine. Almost under the hooves of her mare, hidden in the tall green grass, a steer lay dead in the sun. Flies buzzed around its eyes and feasted on the gunshot wound in its side.

All eight vaqueros muttered as they looked down at the corpse.

"Our earmarks," Prudencio pointed out. "Our brand. They must have shot it yesterday and left it."

Katherine glanced at Damian, half frightened to see his reaction.

He stared down at the rotting corpse with a grim kind of satisfaction. "The Americanos make it easy to remove them."

She could hear an ax ringing in the distance. "I wonder what they are chopping."

Damian looked around at the flat, grassy plain, dotted sparsely with spreading oaks. "We'll find out soon enough."

Under one of the trees, close against the river, stood the American camp. They'd done no more than lift the covers off four wagons and set them on the ground. A burned patch of grass spread from their campfire. They'd let it escape, and only the wet foliage of early spring had saved them from disaster. Another butchered steer hung from a branch, its hide staked out in the sun.

Two men sat idle against a tree trunk, watching three women turn a beef-laden spit. One man chopped desultorily at an oak sapling. One stood in the wagon tossing their belongings to the ground, ducking beneath the scolding tirade of the woman who straddled the sideboard. A short distance away and off to the side, three women knelt beside the river with washboards, and every size of child ranged across the flats.

Activity ceased as the mounted party came close. Only the women at the stream didn't realize they had visitors, their hearing blocked by the running water. They continued to chat in a sort of pantomime as the others fell silent.

Damian and Don Lucian took the lead, blocking Katherine behind them with their huge stallions. In their turn, each of the vaqueros pushed her behind, until she was at the back of the group. Twisting her neck to observe, she groaned when the men resting at the tree picked up their rifles and aimed them at the approaching party. The woodcutter held his hatchet like a weapon.

Ignoring the threat and taking his time, Damian stared around the camp. "Preparing to stay?"

The fishwife jumped off the wagon and placed one hand at her waist, one hand thrust out to revile. "What business is it of yours?"

Don Lucian nodded toward the rifle barrels that stared with

such gray unseeing eyes. "That's not how we greet visitors here in California, unless we have reason for shame."

The woman's hand waved ceaselessly. "We got no reason for shame."

Don Lucian seemed to grow in the saddle, gaining dignity and stature as he communicated with the shrill woman. "You, or one of your men, shot one of my faithful servants."

"He was uppity."

"He was doing his duty. You shot him and left him to die."

"Nah." The man with the hatchet stepped forward. "I'm a better shot than that. I just aimed to maim." He laughed a little. "Aimed to maim. It rhymes. I'm a sissy-pants poet."

The other men laughed, too, but their rifles never wavered. Their rough amusement seemed to serve as a signal. The cooking women fluttered like prairie hens, swooping up small children and carrying them behind the wagons, herding the older ones in bunches into the taller grass.

"Did the other Mexican get him home?" The hatchet swung in the man's hand, and he tossed it end over end in a demonstration of competence.

Tight-lipped with anger, Prudencio took his place beside his leaders. "I'm not Mexican, I'm *Indigena*. And my friend could still die of infection."

"If he's not strong enough to stand up to a little infection, then I'm not the one who killed him." The man's gap-toothed grin leered at them until all the vaqueros moved forward in a rush. Then he seemed to realize he held only a hatchet. As a defense against vaqueros armed with pistols, lariats, and knives, it was inadequate. He stepped back.

Damian said softly, "To pick up your rifle at this moment would be an act of aggression. *Comprende?*"

For a man who didn't speak Spanish, he seemed to *comprende* very well. He grasped the hatchet until his knuckles turned white and he stood still as a rabbit in the brush.

"You clod," the spokeswoman scolded. "My man's the leader

of this expedition. Haven't I told you to let me do the talking?"
She turned back to the mounted party. "We can shoot that
mouthy Indian, 'cause we're just defending this property, 'cause
it's ours."

"By whose law is it yours, señora?" Don Lucian's courtesy
contrasted with the woman's ignorant disdain.

"By American law." She lowered her voice to make it sweet
and sarcastic. "There's this law that was passed by our Congress, an' it says we got the right to stake claim to this land, an'
we can keep it if we farm it an' improve it." She looked around
scornfully. "That shouldn't be too hard. You got nothing here
but a bunch of half-wild cows."

"We have many Americano friends who live here in California," Don Lucian told her. "They abide by our laws, but they
receive newspapers from the Yankee ships docking in Monterey.
So I have heard of your law."

"Then you know you got no right coming here with your men
an' your guns." Her voice was overloud.

Katherine saw one woman at the stream stand up, look
around, then notify her sisters. The men beneath the tree stood
up and stepped forward, and the belligerence that directed the
scene seemed in danger of exploding.

Katherine no longer saw the sense in allowing these hidalgos
to overshadow her. She'd been shoved to the back by concentrated male aggression; she was tired of seeing horses' rumps.
While all attention remained on the guns, she urged her mare
around the horses to the front. Using her businesslike voice, she
said, "I am Katherine Chamberlain Maxwell de la Sola, an
American citizen like yourself." The shrew's mouth dropped at
the sound of Katherine's Boston accent. The rifle barrels
drooped; the ax slipped.

"A woman?" One of the men by the tree smirked. "You bring
a woman to fight your battles?"

"Katherine," Damian warned.

She ignored them all. "I have some knowledge of the law, and

I'd like to bring forth some pertinent issues." Satisfied she had everyone's attention, she continued, "The law you're referring to is known as the Preemption Law, passed in 1841 by the United States Congress. Setting aside the fact that California is not under the dominion of the United States, as these gentlemen have already pointed out, there are other provisions of the law that require consideration."

One of the armed Americans said, "Lordy," and it sounded more like a prayer than an exclamation.

Katherine nodded at him. She expected no less. That was just the reaction her legalese normally caused around her uncle's dinner table. This kind of awed respect was just the discipline needed in this situation. "I must first of all point out there is a purchase price required by the Preemption Act. I can't help but wonder—who will pay the dollar and a quarter per acre required for purchase?" Her gaze swept around the poverty-stricken camp.

No one said a word.

"I would also like to point out that such claim is only applicable to what we call 'public domain,' land free of previous claim."

"You're a gal," the man with the ax accused.

"That's true." She waited, but he said no more. He only seemed to grow fatter, fed with indignation. When it seemed he would pop, she continued, "This land is not public domain and has a legal owner."

"Where's this title?" The woman recovered her voice, and her waving hand clenched into a fist. "I want to see it, but I warn you, any title I can't read ain't legal."

Damian's nostrils flared in disdain. "Can you read Spanish?"

"I knew it." The fist punched the air. "Ain't no legal title at all."

Damian urged his horse forward one step. "This is California, not the United States. We have title to this land."

"A Mexican title," the woman said derisively.

"Mexican now, Spanish before that, and always de la Sola

land. My family has been here seventy years, señora. My family will be here when yours has walked into the blue Pacific."

From the Spanish saddle holsters, the rifles slipped out to aim back at the newly lifted American guns. Like hail on a metal roof, the hammers were cocked, emphasizing the futility of their confrontation. Katherine bit off a most unladylike curse. When had the situation escalated to such a predicament? When had she lost control?

Spurring her horse between the combatants, she called, "Good people, let us not allow vengeance and ill temper to carry the day." Damian, she saw from the corner of her eye, had started towards her, but she ignored him.

The beefy woman said, "You said your last name was Delisola?"

"De la Sola," Katherine corrected. "Yes, it is."

"You're married to one of these guys?"

"Yes, and as mediator, I can help."

"That your husband?" She pointed to Damian, now at Katherine's side between them.

"Don Damian de la Sola. Yes, he's my husband. And your name is? . . ."

One of the men at the tree shouted, "Damned if I'm going to listen to preaching from some treacherous bitch who fucks Mexicans!"

Damian reached for Katherine's bridle, and in her shock she let him grab it. "Get back," he said between his teeth. "This is men's work."

"No." She resisted his fierceness, his twist of the reins. "It's only men's work if it comes to shooting, and surely sensible—"

Wading through the blackened stubble of grass, the woman waved her fist left and right, wearing the same grim expression that all in the American camp wore. "I'm a God-fearing lady, an' I know that ducks cleave to ducks, fish to fish, an' cows to cows. It's unnatural for any clean American woman to be in some greaser's bed. It's against the will of God, an' it's treason against the country."

"My good woman," Katherine said fastidiously, "cows cleave to bulls." As a retort, it sounded a bit lame, but her usual quick wit had failed her. Never in all her objections to their marriage had she thought she would be scorned as a heretic and a turncoat. She believed—she *knew*—that the common ground of language and background would smooth this encounter.

Yet when she said so, the Americans muttered and Damian urged, "Katherine, get back behind us."

He used her bridle to move her once more, and once more she resisted.

"I ain't talking to some greaser who can't even control his own wife," the man with the hatchet taunted.

Katherine stared at him, her green gaze boring holes in his bravado, and he stepped back. She was so pleased to note she hadn't lost her power of dominance that Damian placed her behind the line of vaqueros before she realized. Once started, her mare couldn't be halted; again she found herself facing horses' rumps.

A husband faced her, too, his lips tucked so tight white lines bracketed his mouth. She opened her mouth to speak, but when he leaned towards her something in his face made her stop. "Intelligent," he approved, and she bristled. Still his fury and command held her motionless. "Listen, my dear. Someone's going to get shot before the day's over. Those other women are smart enough to realize it. Even that loudmouthed *puta* knows it. Now stay out of the way, and maybe the only ones to be shot will be these squatters. Unless you want to throw your lot in with these—" he waved a dismissing hand "—these Americanos, and see our own people gunned down?"

The way he said "Americanos" shocked her, as if it were a dirty word. His insinuation shocked her more. As if she cared more for these ignorant strangers than for the people of the

Rancho Donoso. She looked aside from his blazing contempt, and he murmured, "Good."

"Don Damian?" She stared at the tree by the river where the women had been washing. "There's a strange man with a gun pointed at your father."

Damian whipped his head around; his pistol appeared in his hand. He'd squeezed off a shot before she could draw breath, but the gun only popped and flashed—a misfire. Damian flinched from the heat. The blaze of Prudencio's gun knocked the man head over heels like a puppet on a stick. Gunfire deafened Katherine; Damian took her head and thrust it ignominiously against her horse's neck. A vaquero and his horse dropped to the ground before her downcast eyes. Damian's pistol no longer misfired; it roared along with the rest.

Then there was peace.

Damian rode to the front, and Katherine cautiously raised her head. On the ground, the vaquero struggled away from the saddle, untouched by a bullet but crying with silent tears for his horse. At the river, the man lay unmoving as the water flowed over his face. One man at the tree thrashed on the ground in agony; the other stood with an ashen face. The man with the hatchet knelt, holding his arm as his hatchet quivered a few feet from Don Lucian's horse.

"You've trespassed on our land," Damian said grimly. "You've fired the first shot and gotten at least one man killed. Let's see if we can help you enough to get you on your way." He started forward into the clamorous silence, then stopped. "Unless you have any other men hidden somewhere?"

From out of the grass beyond rose a boy of about twelve, and he screamed, "Yes, we do." He jerked up a rifle too big for him and discharged it towards the crowd of Spaniards and vaqueros. Damian shouted, "No," but a rifle answered the boy's.

The shock of the American's bullet threw Prudencio off his horse and he landed, hands outflung, close to Katherine's mount.

The boy fell and disappeared, covered by the tall grass.
Prudencio.

"No," Katherine sighed, slipping from her saddle. "Oh, no,
not this. Not again." She touched him, but no breath remained
in his body, no beauty, no life. A mother's shriek from the
American camp pierced the pity she felt for the fallen warrior.

A smoking rifle identified the one who'd shot the American
boy, and he wasn't much more than a boy himself. Perhaps
fourteen, he sat in the saddle and shrugged under Don Lucian's
scolding. "If he was old enough to raise a gun in anger, he
should have been prepared to die." His voice quivered as he
added, "Besides, he killed my uncle."

"Do you have a blanket?" Katherine asked. "Don Damian?"

He looked down at her.

"Do you have a blanket?" she repeated. "We need to cover
Prudencio. The flies are already coming for the blood."

She crawled away in the grass and fainted.

Damian held Katherine firmly as they mounted the stairs to
her bedroom. She no longer had a buzzing in her ears, and her
faint, she pointed out with indignation, had been a brief one.
Still, he made sure she remained erect, his silence being more
eloquent than another man's diatribe.

His other hand, burned by the misfire of the pistol, was
wrapped in loose linen strips. The pain made him wince and,
she supposed, kept his fury at a boiling point. Certainly the
thrust of his jaw and the proud line of his back made his opinion clear.

It seemed as if he were angry at her, as if she were responsible
for the whole afternoon, filled with rancor and battle. As if she
were responsible for the evening of cleanup, of laying out dead
bodies and bandaging wounds.

Yet she reminded herself that he had reason for his outrage.
Perhaps not with her, but it was human nature to blame those
closest. As they entered her room, she plunged into apology.

"Those Americans aren't indicative of the nation." She bit her lip. It hadn't come out as contritely as she had hoped, and he only glared straight ahead. "I'm sorry about the deaths. It was good of you not to drag the squatters in to Monterey and have them incarcerated."

He looked at her with narrow assessment.

"Especially after all that woman said to you," she added, smoothing the curve of her watch. "Both before and after the violence."

Still he stared, and her conciliatory attitude soured. "Although I think you could learn a lesson from your father."

He lifted one eyebrow. "Oh?"

"Indeed." Taking a breath, she reminded herself that people respond to advice only when not accompanied by criticism. "Your father speaks first, using the voice of logic, and when you perceive failure of logic, you speak with the voice of pugnacity." In any other man, she would have called Damian's expression a snarl.

"Would you ever wonder if my father and I have assigned roles? That when logic fails, he cedes control to me?"

"Why would you do that? To act in such a manner is to admit ahead of time that logic will fail."

"Logic always fails when dealing with people who think with their emotions and not their brains." He held up his hand when she would interrupt. "Yes, Señora Hopeful, there are many who are lesser humans, as that bandage on your throat should prove. Now I don't believe we have anything else to say to each other."

"You mean we're not speaking."

"Exactly."

A band around her chest formed, and she found it difficult to breathe. "If you're looking for a way to punish me, that's the best way. For the success of our marriage, communication is the key. To speak of your anger will clear the air. You should explain to me what it is I've done that annoys you."

"Besides get in the way, almost get yourself killed, precipitate a murder?"

The injustice of his accusation jerked the band tight. "That's not fair."

He tapped his toe against the floor for one long, agonizing moment. "No, it's not. I'm sorry. You didn't precipitate the murder, at least." He turned on her like a striking rattlesnake. "But you flouted my orders. In public. You put me in a bad light with my people."

She gaped. "What?"

"You made me a laughingstock."

Her fury rose swift and sure. "Is that what this is all about? You're angry because I didn't obey you?"

"A man should control his own wife."

"I'm not your horse or your dog. I have a mind, and I do what I think best."

"What is sensible," he sneered.

"Yes."

"You wouldn't know sensible if it smacked you in the face."

"Sir, you insult me."

He took her by the arms. "Listen to me. You could have been killed today. My heart leapt in my throat when the gunfire started." She tried to interrupt, but he shook her. "Listen! I haven't waited all my life for you to have you shot for some high-minded ideal of yours. From now on, we'll live by rationality—my rationality. I ought to leave you here at Rancho Donoso and go after the gold alone."

"You wouldn't dare."

"No, I wouldn't. Because you would find a way to get in trouble no matter where you were. My father hasn't a chance against your 'sensibleness' and your willfulness. But take heed. From now on, you'll do as I say or take the consequences."

She had trouble comprehending what he meant, why his cheeks flushed with ruddy color and his hands trembled. She only heard the fury, not the frustration and fear behind it. "Are you threatening me?"

"Yes. I am. The way I feel right now, I'd take great pleasure in giving you what you deserve."

She jerked from his grasp. "Leave me alone."

He jerked her back to face him. "We have to go after that treasure. It doesn't matter how we feel right now, we have to find the source of the gold."

"I agree."

"There's danger if we don't."

"I'm not arguing."

"Very well." Taking his hands away, he looked at them with distaste. "Call for a bath. It will be the last warm water we see for a long time, and I wish to wash this blood from beneath my fingernails."

"Will you sleep here?"

"Where else would I sleep, bride of mine?"

"Your bedroom," she faltered.

"No. Perhaps we'll not finish that unfinished business of ours tonight, but we're married, and sleep together we will."

As he turned away, she whispered, "Even if we have to stay awake all night to do it."

2 June, in the year of our Lord, 1777

The great weight of the gold inhibits our speed. It's heavy, so heavy. I carry the chest filled with the worked gold of the chapel. Each of the three women carries a pouch on her back. They are bowed with the strain, for some of the nuggets are so big that they fill my hand and weigh down my arm.

In his weakness, Fray Lucio staggers like a drunken man and has slowed us almost to a crawl. The women assist him, but the narrow trails of this mountain range make walking in single file a necessity.

I fear the Indians of the interior still pursue us; I fear they pursue us even more vigorously now that their women are gone. Yet I will not abandon one bit of this gold with which God has blessed us. When I return to the mission with this great wealth, the interior will be settled with good Catholic Spaniards and the Indians' souls will be saved through continual contact.

Then will my goal of settling the interior be justified.

—from the diary of Fray Juan Estévan de Bautista

Chapter 15

The wide bed hadn't been nearly wide enough for two people intent on never touching. Damian awoke tired, snappish —and aroused. All the night through, he'd thought about Katherine. Awake, asleep, she'd been in his mind, and his body didn't understand his anger. He still wanted her.

Rolling over, he looked at her. Even in sleep, she clung to the side of the mattress with her hands, staying as far away from him as possible, and he understood why.

He knew he'd been rough and unfair last night, but when he remembered how close Katherine had come to disaster, he wavered between panic and a strong desire to lock her away. What he wouldn't do to return to the time when no one knew the whereabouts of Tobias's widow. What he wouldn't do to be able to keep her safe.

Now the newest de la Sola couple were undoubtedly the talk of Alta California. They had to leave this hacienda before a wedding celebration arrived on their doorstep—a wedding celebration with a possible murderer in its midst. Instead, they would go seek the gold, exposing themselves to that same murderer and dangers of perhaps a greater nature.

He smoothed her hair away from her lips, parted slightly with her breath. When she sighed and stirred, he lifted his hand and slid from the bed.

* * *

"Charming." Don Lucian held one of Katherine's hands out and looked her over. "Absolutely charming."

She made the effort to smile as she descended the last two steps of the porch. "Thank you for the riding habit. I assure you, I've never had anything so fine."

"The midnight blue of the jacket changes your eyes from green to the misty azure of the ocean. Don't you think so, Damian?"

Damian turned from the saddlebags he was strapping on Confite and inspected his wife. "She looks very neat," he approved, but his gaze lingered on the coat that fit tight at her waist and hugged her bosom. With a slight bite in his tone, he said, "The gold makes her look quite Californian."

The reprimand found its mark, and she looked down at the fanciful pattern of gold braid. Cleverly hidden in the folds of the skirt was a pocket for her watch, its silver chain looped up into the design to hook on securely. She fingered one of the gold buttons to hide her dismay at his indifference.

With a flourish, Don Lucian presented a hat box. "I have the finishing touch."

"You are too good to me," she protested, but she snatched the box greedily. "I can't remember the last time I had a new— oh!" She graced Don Lucian with a heart-stopping grin. "I love it."

Lifting her full skirts, she leaped up the steps into the hacienda. At the hall mirror, she pulled out the midnight blue velvet hat. Shaped like a vaquero's, its flat brim sported an intricate trim of gold braid that matched her jacket. Its box crown was wrapped with a misty gold scarf that trailed in two tails off the back. "A Californian," she muttered. "This will show him a Californian." She settled the whole fashionable, jaunty creation across her forehead. A matching scarf for her neck completed the outfit, hiding the pink scar on her throat. She saluted herself before marching out to show off.

"The perfect touch," Don Lucian hailed her. "Eh, Damian?"

There seemed to be something about the way she posed at the top of the stairs that gave Damian pain. As if flames were licking at his toes and he could hardly wait to flee, he turned to tie the saddlebag with one more knot. "We need to leave if we're to get to San Juan Bautista this afternoon. If you're ready, Doña Katherina?"

His unemotional suggestion punctured her exuberance. "Of course."

Don Lucian gave up. "What will you do if you find nothing at the mission?"

"Go to another mission," Damian said briefly. "And keep going until we find what Tobias found."

"Are you sure you have enough supplies?"

"I packed for two weeks on the road and possibly in the mountains, and covered every contingency I could think of. I've got rope, blankets, food."

"Your pistol?" Don Lucian's mouth was puckered with wry amusement.

"Yes, Papa." Damian's grim mouth eased into a smile. "I'll give it one more chance. You have to admit it performed well after that first misfire yesterday."

Don Lucian sobered. "Many times, my son, there's no chance for a second shot."

"I have my rifle and my other pistol, too," he assured him. "At least the Americanos are gone, and if they should return, you will have your own trusted pistols with you."

Don Lucian agreed. "The vaqueros patrol every inch of our land like hounds with noses to the ground. Thank God for their support."

Damian turned to Katherine. "Are you ready?"

She nodded. She didn't know what to say. She hadn't known what to say all day. She and Damian were speaking; yes, they were. So politely, so logically, they'd discussed their best plan. To the mission, first, then into the mountains. Damian would organize the supplies. She would pack the clothes they needed.

They'd smiled stiffly at each other, for all the world like passing acquaintances, then they'd separated to do their duties.

Now her mare stood waiting at the mounting block and the activities that had buffered their silence were at an end. She placed a quick, shy kiss on Don Lucian's cheek, then strode to her horse. Damian met her there and, before she could step up, put his hands on her waist. Her eyes flew to his; they stared for one awkward moment. The warmth of his palms radiated down to her skin; she blushed. Then he lifted her into the saddle.

Under Don Lucian's concerned gaze, they rode away. Eight vaqueros would accompany them, for their safety seemed precarious. Their formality affected the spirits of the men, making it a quiet three-hour ride through the warming afternoon.

The whitewashed buildings came into view and Damian broke the silence to point with his whip. "There's the mission."

"I see," she said. "It looks well kept."

"One of the best," he agreed. "It's not what it once was, but the buildings were returned to the padres three years ago, along with a portion of the land. See?" As they rode closer, he indicated a long building. Wide arches graced its whole length, and the red tile of the roof swept above like the bold brushstroke of an artist. "There's the chapel and the library. There we'll find our clue."

"We hope," she reminded him.

"We hope." At the tall entrance to the church, Damian rang the bell. "Some of you vaqueros stay close, some of you patrol the area. Keep an eye out for—" He hesitated.

"For more Americanos?" one asked.

"For anyone who shouldn't be here."

The vaqueros nodded, separating to do their duty.

A tiny old man dressed in a rough brown cowl shuffled out of the darkness behind the open doors of the tall foyer.

Damian bent with a smile. "Fray Pedro de Jesus, do you remember me?"

"Of course I do, my son." The Franciscan brother adjusted

his spectacles on his nose and squinted at the mounted man. "I haven't heard your confession since I had you weed the mission garden, saying an Ave with each weed you pulled as penance for your sins. Little Damian, isn't it?"

Katherine covered her mouth to keep in her laughter as her husband turned a dull red. The vaqueros nearby snorted and coughed.

"I should have known you would never forget me," Damian grumbled as he slipped from the saddle and reached for Katherine. "I brought you my wife."

"Your wife?" Again the glasses were adjusted, again the faded eyes squinted. "I hadn't heard you were married."

"Only a few days ago, by the *alcalde* in Monterey," Damian answered.

The bald head turned his way. "Not a Catholic wedding?"

Gently, Katherine said, "I'm not a member of your faith, Padre."

Taking her hand in his veined, spotted one, Fray Pedro told her, "That we must remedy at once. Come with me, my dear." He led her into the dim entry. "To cohabit without the blessing of God is a sin. I've worked too hard to keep Damian in a state of grace to concede defeat now."

She threw a helpless glance over her shoulder. Damian leaned against the hitching post, satisfaction on his face as he watched her disappear into the cool gloom.

Leading her down the quiet corridor, Fray Pedro gestured her into a tiny room lit by the sunlight shining through a small, high window and by the flicker of a candle. The silence of the mission made her whisper, "Is there anyone else here?"

"A few Franciscan brothers. We are few and old. You'll disturb no one with your talk, though. It's a joy to hear young voices." He smiled as the shouts of the vaqueros drifted through the open window, adjusted his glasses, and looked her over carefully. "You've married Damian in a civil ceremony. That surprises me, for young Damian's faith was deep and sure. He must

love you very much to accept you in such a temporal union."
He paused, but she had nothing to say to that. "Did you understand when you married him that you'd have to convert?"

"Yes, I know that," she admitted.

"Do you have any objections to the Catholic faith, my daughter?"

"Not at all. I'm not a very devout Protestant." She nervously
played with her watch chain. "I mean, I've never believed my
religion to be the only one."

"Just what the Americano men say when I tutor them before
their weddings." Shaking his head, the old man held the candle
up to the crowded bookshelf, then ran his nose along the spines
of the books until he found the one he wanted. He slid it toward her. "Here. You'll need to read this as soon as possible,
and I'll help you find the right way. You can read?"

"Yes, of course!"

"There is no 'of course.' Except for the boys I taught, there
are few in California who can read, and read well." He scrutinized her. "Have you had bodily commerce with Damian?"

Mortified, she nodded, wondering where her dignity had fled.
Before this elderly man's kind questions, she couldn't summon
the nerve to tell him to mind his own business. Where was
Damian during this interrogation?

"Well, well, I'll have to give you the quick course of religion.
A sort of instant state of grace." He cackled as he shuffled over
to her. "Don't repeat that, of course. The Mother Church in
Rome would never sanction such a thing, but here in the wilds
of California, we've had to seek conversion through devious
routes. Sit down, sit down."

A lack of reality, a perception of isolation tangled her emotions as she sat on the straight-backed chair he indicated.

"We'll start with—"

A tap on the door interrupted them. "Padre?" Damian stuck
his head in. "Has Katherine told you why we came?"

"To sanctify your union, I would hope," Fray Pedro answered tartly.

"Not exactly."

Katherine could almost hear Damian squirm and she relaxed. It would seem this Franciscan had the same effect on everyone that he had on her.

"Why have you come, then?" Fray Pedro conveyed disappointment and displeasure in his sharp question.

"We have a problem." Damian stepped into the room, a saddlebag flung over his shoulder.

"More than just living in sin?"

"Even more than that," Damian agreed. With care, he shut the door and leaned against it. "Do you recall the old tale about the padres and the gold?"

The shrewd eyes of Fray Pedro studied him. "The padres and the gold?" he repeated. "I'm not sure. . . ."

"Try to remember."

Something about the way Damian urged made Katherine think Damian didn't believe the friar, but Fray Pedro didn't seem insulted. "Ah, yes." Fray Pedro folded his arms across his skinny chest. "That's nothing but an old legend. Nonsense." He dismissed it with a wave.

Looking irritated, Damian tossed the saddlebag off his shoulder.

Katherine stepped in with an explanation. "We don't think it's a legend. We think it's based, at least in part, on fact. Please think about it. It's very important. There's someone who will kill to find this gold, and this person seems to think I know where it is."

Fray Pedro turned on her with a swiftness that belied his age. "Someone who would kill? You? Why you?"

"Because I'm the widow of a man who sought the gold."

"That man's name was? . . ."

"Tobias Maxwell."

Before her eyes, the friar seemed to wither. His hands disappeared into his cassock, his shoulders sank. His head drooped; he muttered unintelligible words. Alarmed, Katherine slipped her arm around his waist. "Come and sit," she urged. "You're ill."

She assisted him to her abandoned chair.

Fray Pedro asked faintly, "What happened to that nice young man? What happened to Tobias?"

"He was murdered," Damian answered, coming to squat by the old Franciscan's knees. "Murdered by this same monster who seeks to kill my wife. Please, Padre, tell us what you know."

Fray Pedro adjusted his spectacles and peered at Damian irritably. "What could I know? San Juan Bautista wasn't even built when that senile Fray Lucio came out of the mountains with his wild story." He seemed unaware of the contradiction in his denial.

"When did he come out of the hills?" Damian asked eagerly.

"In the summer of 1777, it was. I'll never understand how he made it alone, for he was ill and tired. He died within the month." Fray Pedro dropped his head as if he, too, were ill and tired. Katherine met Damian's eye.

"How old are you, Fray?" she asked, soft with his age and his sadness.

"Eighty-eight." He sighed. "I came all the way from Spain to work under Fray Junípero Serra, did you know that?"

"No, I didn't know."

"Sí. I came from Majorca, as he did. It was an honor to be touched by Fray Serra's shadow. The man was a saint."

She humored him, giving him the moments he needed to pull himself together. "Was he?"

"There's never been another like him." He shivered, drawing in on himself. "Although others have tried."

There it was. There was the thing he would prefer never to reveal. The thing, she suspected, frightened him. "Who?" she whispered.

His chuckle sounded like the rustle of old paper. "Damian, you know, don't you?"

"Fray Pedro, I don't—" Stricken by the thought, Damian said, "Fray Juan Estévan?"

"Sí. Fray Juan Estévan. The big man with the gleaming eyes. He, too, came from Majorca and was younger and healthier than Fray Serra, with a great skill for healing. Almost a godlike skill for healing. He had a charisma that blinded many to his ambition. Yet in his vanity, the man never knew about himself." Lifting one finger, he shook it in admonition of a man long dead. "Fray Juan Estévan thought that God worked through him, that his determination to convert the interior was a sign it was God's will. He would never tame his restlessness long enough to go to the chapel and ask God what His will was. I tried to speak to him about it, to explain that when God directs your actions, you feel a peace and a sureness within yourself. But Fray Juan Estévan was my elder in both years and experience."

Katherine stroked his fingers as they trembled in his lap. "What did he say when you chided him?"

"He laughed. Only—" Fray Pedro closed his eyes as if in pain. "Only when Fray Lucio came out of the mountains, he had been instructed to ask for me. I received the burden of the secret, at Fray Juan Estévan's request."

Damian poured a glass of wine. Pressing it into Fray Pedro's hand, he asked, "What did you receive?"

Fray Pedro sipped the spicy red liquid, and sighed. "A good wine. A new wine. I like new wines, don't you?"

"Fray Pedro, please." Damian knelt beside him. "We must know."

Fray Pedro studied Damian, reading his soul. "I never wanted to tell you about this. Of all the boys I taught, you were the most dependable, except when this tale was trotted around. Then your eyes glowed and you listened too intently. I feared for you." He sipped again. "Do your eyes still glow at the mention of gold?"

Damian opened one side of his saddlebag. "Let me show you." From the midst of Katherine's ruffled underwear, he drew a well-wrapped package. Unfolding it, he held the rock to the western light from the window. The gold of the setting sun brought the gold in the rock to blazing life; Fray Pedro knew what it was.

Crossing himself, blessing the gold, he murmured, "It exists. It truly exists." A smile broke across his weathered face, eroding every wrinkle to its deepest canyon. "All these years, I had wondered if I were mad, but it exists and I am not."

Caught in this topsy-turvy world of egocentric friars and hidden treasure, Katherine could only say anxiously, "Then you'll help us?"

He lifted his hand and blessed them both. "I'll seek the answer in the chapel. God is always there for anyone who seeks Him."

A little prickle ran up Katherine's spine. Fray Pedro discussed God as if He were an important friend who could be contacted and spoken to at will. It fed her sense of strangeness.

She slid her gaze to Damian, but he seemed to find nothing amiss. He leaned against the table, watching Fray Pedro as if such spirituality were ordinary, expected.

Fray Pedro, too, seemed impervious to her discomfort. "Find Fray Manuel, Doña Katherina. He'll show you to your room, where you can study the book I gave you. Damian, you can bunk with your vaqueros tonight."

Rewrapping the stone and hiding it once more in the saddlebag, Damian shrugged in resignation.

"Early in the morning, I expect to see you so we can discuss this matter." Fray Pedro looked over his glasses with a droll expression. "Our little Damian can pay attention to the sacrament of marriage. Then confession for you both, first communion for you, Doña Katherina, next the wedding ceremony. Prepare yourself."

Without a word, Damian took Katherine's elbow and directed her out into the passage. As they left the little office, they heard Fray Pedro call, "Don't eat any breakfast."

"Wonderful man, isn't he?" Damian chuckled, and she stared at him as if he were mad. "Come, I'll find Fray Manuel for you."

In the rooms ranged along the arched corridor they caught flashes of the fading sun that gleamed directly through the windows. It flashed through the open doors as they walked, catching the wood trim and transforming it to polished topaz. It faded to a glow as they left that brilliance behind, then flashed forth at another door. Katherine stared about, her eyes wearied by the rapid transitions, confused by her sense of isolation.

As Damian strode beside her, alternately sculpted in brilliance and dusted in shade, the light transformed him, too. Here, today, in this place that was so essentially Spanish and Californian, he looked different to her. Not at all like the man she'd married. Or perhaps, like the genuine man she'd married. The darkness of the corridor accentuated the austere gravity that placed him apart. The illumination revealed his somber beauty, underscored by splashes of black and accents of gold. Like a painting created with an eye for drama, he flaunted a beauty unmatched in her discreet background.

In this world of crucifix and conquistador, she was the alien.

Damian found Fray Manuel, and she heard their murmured conversation through the cushion of shock.

She was the alien. She didn't belong here.

Fray Manuel came out to escort her to her room. He blessed her before leaving. Damian set her bag beside the bed, and she turned to him, eager for friendship, for words of reassurance. Surely Damian realized how estranged she felt. Yet he said nothing. He smiled without warmth, bowed with the formality of a Spaniard, watched her with great, dark eyes as he shut the door behind him, and left her alone with one candle to lighten the gathering gloom.

She looked around the room, bare and sparse as any cell, as if she'd find an answer to the questions that overwhelmed her.

What was she doing here? Why did she ever believe she could fit into this society? What madness had made her marry a man marked by history and culture?

Sightless, she stared down at the book in her hand until she focused on it in dismay. This was the book she must learn overnight. This was her anchor to reality.

She pulled the stool up to the table, sat, and opened the book to the first page. The silence of the mission filled her ears; a silence of old prayers and new devotions. Her breathing slowed, her heart beat with a steady rhythm, and she listened intently, seeking evidence of companionship. All she heard was the deep, sweet sound of sanctity, and it touched an unacknowledged part of her.

The candle flickered, the words wavered before her eyes, and a splash of water fell on the page before she realized it. She wiped it away; wiped, too, the tears from her cheeks.

Homesick.

For the first time since she'd left Boston, she was homesick. For the first time, she wondered if she'd ever see snow again. She wondered if she'd ever wear a fur wrap again, or roast chestnuts for Christmas dressing. She wondered if her ear would ever hear the clipped, nasal speech of Massachusetts again, if she'd ever see a dockside bustling with Yankee traders or hear a cannon boom for a Fourth of July celebration. Would she ever see the men stand with heads bared as the mayor read the Declaration of Independence?

It was foolish to remember little things, to long for a muff to tuck her hands in when she lived in a land of eternal spring, but she did. It was foolish to remember only the snow, and not the slush and subzero cold, but she did. Foolish or not, nostalgia grew in the loneliness, watered by these silly tears.

In Boston, she was ordinary. When she walked down the street, no one looked at her or whispered about her ancestry and place of origin. Here she stood out. Her appearance, her speech, her habits set her apart, and she didn't know if she wanted to adjust to fit Damian's notion of a proper Spanish wife.

Changing her religion, she had assured Fray Pedro, meant little to her. There had been no succor in stern Congregationalism, and she'd seen no demonstration of kindness in the Chamberlain family's brand of Christianity.

Still, she cringed when she thought of their reaction to her conversion. They'd be horrified by her fall into "superstition," as they had discounted the comfort she'd found in the occasional Catholic mass she'd attended.

Damian's reaction, too, gave her pause. If she accepted her first communion with a compliance akin to stoicism, Damian did not. Her religion didn't matter to her; his did to him. There dwelt in him an exultation, a pleasure that made her uneasy. To him, she didn't do this as a compliance to the laws of California, nor as a nod to his beliefs. It was a gift she presented him, a jewel finer than any other: a vow of devotion to him and his way of life.

Did she dare do this? Since the death of her father, she'd sought control of her emotions, her actions, her self. She'd succeeded, too. She'd freed herself to travel, to do as she liked. She'd learned control of her reactions.

Sometimes, perhaps, that particular control had slipped. Sometimes her temper had blazed through; sometimes she slipped into the belligerence she'd learned in the Chamberlain household. But on the whole, her belief in control had been rewarded. She'd been determined to gain her independence through control, and she'd done it.

Inch by inch, Damian had undermined that determination. First she'd granted him her body, and he created a passion she couldn't control. Then she'd agreed to marriage, and he gained legal control of her person. Now she'd offered to become one with him in the only ceremony he truly recognized. What control would he take from her this time? Would she lose Miss

Katherine Anne Chamberlain Maxwell and become a stranger called Doña Katerina de la Sola?

In a flash of revelation, she realized that the Californio culture would triumph over her own, at least in the de la Sola home. The self-satisfied woman who had landed in Monterey Harbor was being transformed by forces within and without. She didn't know if she wanted to change. She knew that she could say no. If she wanted to, she could remain the person who'd set sail out of Boston.

If she wanted to.

That was what frightened her. She didn't want to. An emotion held her in its grip, an emotion she didn't dare define. It urged her to make adjustments, to make Damian happy. It urged compromise.

If she weren't careful, this emotion would flatten her into a doormat where Damian could wipe his feet.

That thought made her set her jaw.

Very well. She'd compromise on this one issue. With her whole heart, she'd become a Catholic, because it was important to Damian, because he was her husband and because she should make the best of it.

But she would not compromise any further. She was a proud American and a modern woman. Damian had better learn to accept that unpalatable fact. She nodded firmly. Yes, he'd better accept it.

Emotion would never triumph over logic. Not in Miss Katherine Anne.

She was not changing because of these stirrings in her heart.

4 June, in the year of our Lord, 1777

The Indians press us. We are lost. These mountains are rugged and unfamiliar. Fray Lucio urges that we abandon the gold. The women look hopelessly at us as we quarrel.

Why can't the fools see what I can see? That this is a gift of heaven?

—from the diary of Fray Juan Estévan de Bautista

Chapter 16

The morning light found Katherine in the study, reciting the quickly learned passages of Catholic belief for Fray Pedro. Damian looked disgruntled, combing hay from his hair with his fingers and sighing loudly as Fray Pedro de Jesus questioned her on her catechism. She wanted to smack the bad-tempered little boy, for this unfamiliar creed required all her concentration. It would be so much easier if conversion required only a working knowledge of the law.

Besides, she reminded herself righteously, she was doing all this for Damian and their marriage. The least he could do was show some gratitude.

At last Fray Pedro was satisfied. Pulling his shawl around his shoulders, he examined Damian from top to toe over steepled fingers. Under his teacher's eye, Damian squirmed like an altar boy in church. Clicking his tongue, Fray Pedro reproached, "Always so impatient. That should be part of your confession this morning."

"Yes, Padre."

"What was it you wanted to know?"

Crossing his arms across his chest, Damian slid down in the chair until his spine rested on the seat, and glared.

Fray Pedro's dry cackle sounded in the cool air. "I can't resist teasing you, little Damian." All business, he leaned forward and put his elbows on the table. "Now, God dwelt here last night, and I spoke with Him. He has passed His decision on to me. I will tell you what I know and show you what I have."

Katherine shivered as she remembered the night, heavy with silence.

With callous heartiness, Damian asked, "What did you receive from this Fray Lucio?"

"A map and a diary."

"Did you show them to Tobias Maxwell?"

"I showed him the map."

"Not the diary?" Damian insisted.

"I gave him the diary."

Katherine gasped, detesting the unbridled reaction, but she couldn't help it. Damian seemed speechless, and she stammered, "You gave it to him? Did he return it?"

Fray Pedro shook his head.

"Why did you give it to him?"

"He fixed our bell. The rope pull had broken off and we couldn't put it back together. And our clock. He fixed our clock. He stayed with us while he worked and I grew to know him." The old man tapped his fingers together. "I had a feeling about him."

She took a deep breath. "All right. What kind of feeling?"

"You know I've been the guardian of this secret for over sixty-five years. Yes, more than sixty-five years." His voice trailed off, and he moved his lips in silent computation. Triumphantly, he said, "Sixty-nine years. That's it. Sixty-nine years." The wrinkles of his face slipped and sagged. "So long. Don't you think that's a long time?"

"A very long time," she concurred.

Damian shifted, but he seemed to be familiar with Fray Pedro's quirks. "What kind of feeling did you have about Tobias?"

Fray Pedro smiled wistfully at Damian. "He was your friend. He told me about you. That gave me my first clue, the first suggestion of his purpose in my life, for I've always known your fate was somehow intertwined with the gold. I thought you were the one who would receive the map and the diary when the time was right."

"Why did you change your mind?" Damian asked. "And when was the right time?"

"Patience, my child," Fray Pedro chided. "I've been the guardian of this secret for sixty-nine years—isn't that what I said?"

Katherine nodded agreement.

"Sixty-nine years. If I died and left the information unattended, it would fall into the wrong hands. I don't know what would happen. Perhaps the treasure seekers would use the gold for ungodly pursuits. Perhaps they'd be killed. It happened once before, you know." He peeked over the top of his glasses. "Damian, you remember."

Recalling the old vaquero's story told so long ago around the campfire, Damian concurred, "Oh, yes."

"I hid that map as best I could, and still it was stolen that time. Many men died for their thievery and greed. No doubt their souls still burn in hell. The one man who survived returned the map to me, and I've been clever with it." Delighted, he rubbed his hands together. "So clever. The others who found the place did it following the trail of the first thieves. When too many men had died for the gold, the attempts lessened and stopped. So when Tobias came to me, it was the first time in many years someone had asked me about the treasure. Perhaps my thoughts wandered and I told him more than I should . . . do you think I wander, Doña Katherina?"

"Not at all," she assured him.

"You're a lovely young woman and a credit to the de la Sola family." He shifted his attention to Damian. "I had been waiting for little Damian to grow up to give him the information."

"Waiting for me to grow up?" Damian exploded. "I'm thirty-two."

"How long has it been since I've seen you?" Fray Pedro exploded in return. "How long did I wait for that avaricious part of your soul to mature? You've stayed away for no better reason than a handful of weeds."

Damian's boots hit the floor with a thud as he stood, and Katherine wondered if he would storm out. But she reassessed the measure of her husband when he strode around the table and pulled the old Franciscan up into his arms. "You're right, Padre. Forgive me."

Fray Pedro lifted his hands to Damian's face, held him and stared at him. Satisfied with what he saw there, he said, "You have matured. So. Let me show you." Tossing his shawl onto the table, he shuffled to the wall, and lifted a framed print off its nail. He handed it casually to Damian. "Here it is."

Damian stared first at the map in his hand, then at Fray Pedro. "Do you mean this is it? But this has been on your wall for as long as I remember."

"Yes. A clever hiding place, was it not?"

He shuffled back to his chair and Katherine rose from hers to peer around Damian's shoulder. Damian looked at her helplessly. She agreed, "A very clever hiding place, indeed."

Taking it into the sunlight, they examined it. "The lettering says, 'Majorca,' " Damian pointed out.

"Look closely at the landmarks and see if you recognize them," Fray Pedro instructed. He closed his eyes as if he were weary.

With his finger, Damian traced the prominent water course. "The San Benito River?" Katherine followed Damian's pointing finger as he named the mountains, the creeks, the valleys. Excitement colored his voice as he said, "I think I could get there, Padre. I really think I could."

"No doubt you could, but what will you do when you're there?" Fray Pedro opened his eyes. "The diary, with its instructions, is gone with your Tobias."

Katherine and Damian stared at one another in consternation. "Where could he have put it?" she wondered. "What did the diary look like, Padre?"

"A narrow book bound with brown leather."

"I would have noticed if Tobias had a book," she said with conviction. "Do you remember what it said, Padre?"

"I never read it. I couldn't. I tried to when I toiled at Mission San Antonio, but—" He shuddered, and Katherine went to him at once with the shawl he'd tossed on his table.

"You're cold."

"Yes."

The shadow in the friar's face gave her the courage to ask, "When did you come to San Juan Bautista?"

"I came in the year it was founded, in 1797. Previously, I had been a resident brother at Mission San Antonio de Padua, and in the halls of Mission San Antonio, I would see a ghost."

"A ghost?" She glanced at Damian, amazed.

"My tall Franciscan brother, with gleaming eyes." Fray Pedro lifted his hands to show the size. "Determination and forcefulness marked this apparition. I was young enough to be frightened. The ghost tried to lure me away from the mission. He wanted me to follow him into the hills."

Unable to help herself, Katherine stepped back from his chair.

He looked up at her and adjusted his glasses. "There's no need for alarm, my daughter. He can't come here, for he doesn't know this place."

She demanded, "Are you telling me we're dealing with a ghost?"

"He won't hurt you," Fray Pedro reassured her. "He was, after all, a Franciscan brother and one of our best *curanderos*. In the secular world, he could have been a doctor. No, for all his misplaced arrogance, he never deliberately harmed anyone. Only . . . people died because of him. He can't rest in peace until I, or my messenger, have settled the issue of the gold."

Damian sank down on a chair. "Then I had better study this."

"Take it with you," Fray Pedro urged. "Study it at your leisure. In all fairness, I must tell you—when I was ill last year, I did send for you. I wished to give you the map and the diary. That good woman Leocadia sent a message back to say you were visiting."

Damian frowned. "Why didn't she tell me you wanted me?"

"It was on my request. My sickness passed, leaving me only a little weaker. Yet when Tobias came to me, he seemed to be a messenger from God." Fray Pedro puckered his already wrinkled mouth. "We must perform our sacraments soon, before Doña Katherina faints of hunger."

Turning the map over, Damian released it from the frame and folded it along ancient creases. "Where shall I put it?"

"Use Fray Pedro's idea," Katherine advised. "Put it in your pocket."

He smiled at her, a quick flash of approval. With dismayed delight, she realized she'd missed his smiles and his pleasure in her.

"Good." Fray Pedro led them to the large, empty church.

Feeling like an interloper, Katherine stopped in the doorway. The pews along the wall gleamed with a beeswax shine. The primitive frescoes, the statue of the Virgin Mary, the flickering candles on the altar, all combined to emphasize how foreign she was. Uneasy, afraid of saying or doing the wrong thing, she stared at Damian in confusion when he lifted a mantilla from the variety of head coverings on a table and draped it over her head.

He knelt and crossed himself. She imitated him, then he urged her down the aisle. The hardwood floor amplified their footsteps, and she caught herself tiptoing to minimize the noise.

At the altar, Fray Pedro kissed each item as he dressed himself in the vestments of a priest. Turning to them, he looked different. Taller, perhaps, or happier. Infusing his every word with significance, he said, "Now it's time to concentrate on more important issues."

From the back of the chapel came a shuffle of boots, a clink of spurs. Slowly, Katherine and Damian turned. One of the vaqueros stood, his feet just outside the door, his head in the chapel. He stared and gestured; Damian looked and glared. Joaquin gestured so vigorously Fray Pedro instructed, "Find out what he wants, while I attend to our Doña Katherina's confession and her first communion." He beckoned Katherine through the arches into the confessional.

She came with dragging feet, wondering what to tell him. The candor he requested was beyond her. How could she tell another person how she feared these emotions that twisted in her? How could she confess her reluctance to release the restraints that defined her? She couldn't. She wouldn't. Despite Fray Pedro's urgings, she kept her feelings to herself and told him of the actions he considered sins.

He knew, of course. He ordered her back to the altar, never saying a word. Only his eyes were so kind and understanding that she felt like a miscreant. He performed her first communion as calmly as if they couldn't hear the neigh of horses and the rattle of tack.

The vaqueros were saddling up, preparing to ride.

She wanted to leap up, to tell the friar he must wait while she found out what was happening. Instead, she focused on the sacraments, hoping her concentration would hurry the ceremony.

As they finished and he traced a cross on her forehead, he said, "This at least will bring grace to your soul as you go on your great adventure."

Feeling like a traitor, she whispered, "Padre, I have something I must say."

Taking her hand, he helped her to her feet. "Tell me."

"You said Don Damian had matured, that you weren't afraid to send him after the gold. But when we first found the gold-veined rock, he frightened me."

He wrapped his arm around her waist and took her to a pew. "Why?"

"He looked so . . . exultant, as if he'd discovered a panacea for war or a cure for old age."

Sitting, he laced his hands in his lap. "Or discovered the lost land of El Dorado?"

Confused, she asked, "What's that?"

"It's a legend, I suppose. El Dorado is the land of the Golden Man, a place of gold and plenty. El Dorado is what all the conquistadors sought."

Struck by his description, she agreed, "That's what he looked like. A conqueror."

"My daughter, if I thought Damian would do the wrong thing, I would never have given him the map. Never. It's you who have made the difference to him. You've given a good man his final tempering, and he'll not bend to temptation. He'll never gamble with your life or your soul."

"He looked so greedy," she said urgently.

He patted her hand. "You must remember, he is a Spaniard."

Damian's boots sounded loud in the church. "Are you done, Padre?"

"With the communion." Fray Pedro adjusted his glasses. "However, I can't perform the wedding ceremony without a groom."

"It will have to wait. I must go." Damian turned to Katherine. "The vaqueros spotted a redheaded Americano watching the mission, and when they gave chase, they found a camp."

"It couldn't be Lawrence," she protested. "He's too much of a dandy to live outdoors simply for the pleasure of spying on us."

"No?" He held up what looked like a scalp.

She recognized Lawrence's hairpiece, red and plastered with glue, looking much the worst for wear.

"He can't get far. Not as poorly as he rides." Damian's sneer proclaimed his opinion of her cousin. "The vaqueros and I will find him. When we've finished with him, he'll never dare to follow us again."

She didn't know this Damian. Ruthless, scornful, wicked in his anger. Again, the wave of unreality swept over her. Faintly, then with more strength, she said, "I will go with you."

Damian looked down his noble nose at her. "No, you won't."

"I will."

He sighed with sharp impatience. "You'll hold us up. I'll return this evening, or tomorrow morning at the latest."

A wave of claustrophobia crashed over her as she looked around. She wouldn't spend another night here. She had to get out. "I'm going."

Fray Pedro argued, "Doña Katherina, you can't go with this man. You aren't married to him. It's a sin. You can't go do a man's job. It's a sin. There are too many sins in the making."

She turned on him, furious with his interference, with everyone's interference in her affairs. "That's my cousin they're chasing. If anyone's going to catch the little skunk, I am." The elderly man looked so shocked and hurt, she offered conciliation. "We'll be back as soon as I can arrange it to be married. You not only have Don Damian's word, but my own."

Lips puckered, the Franciscan peered at her, weighing her sincerity, while Damian complained, "No. You don't understand the weight of such sin."

Perhaps it was her panic, perhaps it was her determination, but something about her convinced the friar, for he interrupted to say, "Very well, Katherine. You shall go."

Damian stood, turned to stone by surprise. "What?"

"Let her go."

Looking wounded by the betrayal, Damian turned on Fray Pedro. "She's a woman. Her place isn't in the hunt. She could hurt herself or be shot."

"She's an American," Fray Pedro retorted. "Her ways aren't our ways, and you'd be wise to remember that."

He smiled at Katherine with compassion.

"I thought you wouldn't allow her to go with me until we were wed," Damian said in triumph.

"You'll come back as soon as you can. Tonight, if possible." Fray Pedro grasped Damian's arm with earnest concern. "It's better if you and Doña Katherina stay close."

Damian paced away, paced back. "I can't promise we won't break the Seventh Commandment if we're left alone."

"She wishes to go, she shall go."

Flushed with an outrage he couldn't express, Damian stared at the Franciscan brother. "Is that the Word of God?"

"No, only the word of Fray Pedro." He folded his hands inside his sleeves, waiting for Damian's decision.

With one final glare of outrage, Damian snapped, "Come on, Katherine. Make sure you don't fall behind. We won't wait for you."

"My cousin is incredibly lucky." Katherine tightened the bandages holding the splint on Joaquin's leg.

Damian's eyes met hers as the vaqueros lifted Joaquin onto the hastily made litter. "Incredibly lucky," he echoed.

"I'm sorry, *patron,*" Joaquin whispered. "I've ruined your chance to catch the redhaired man."

Damian patted the man's shoulder. "Nonsense, Joaquin. We were riding too quickly for such terrain. I should have known better, riding through the chaparral so close to the mountains. Your horse stumbled and you fell. It's just bad luck."

"Just the curse of the treasure," someone muttered.

Damian swung on the group behind him. "What did you say?"

Silence answered him.

"How did you know what we seek?"

Sullen gazes slipped away from his, and Joaquin spoke up. "We all knew what Don Tobias pursued, for he asked us to tell him the tale. We knew it would kill him, but in obedience with his wishes, we directed him to the mission. Now you go there, too." A wistfulness touched his voice. "With a mark of the knife on Doña Katherina's throat, you have no choice."

Soberly, Damian looked at Katherine, standing beneath the bright green of a valley oak. The grass rippled around her knees, the land sloped away behind her. Her hair had been torn from its braid by branches and it hung wild about her shoulders and down her back. Shining through the leaves, the sun caught the gold in bits and pieces, exposing her as the siren she really was.

The mark of the knife was covered by a scarf, but it seemed that every one of the vaqueros knew it was there.

She'd ridden so hard that at first he'd thought his threat to leave her had taken effect. As the hours had worn on, though, it had occurred to him she fled something instead, something that frightened her. Something that even now shadowed her face. He could see the anxiety in her, although no other could recognize it, and he wondered what she'd seen at the mission, what she'd heard at the mission. He wondered, too, why he feared to ask her.

Was his bright and shining bride slipping away before he'd had a chance to prove his love to her?

"Is something wrong?" she asked.

He realized he'd been staring. Shaking his head, he asked Joaquin, "Do you believe we're going to our deaths?"

"Not you, *patron.*" The vaquero spoke with assurance. "Not you, nor Doña Katherina. Your love is strong. As long as you're together, you'll protect each other." He glanced around at the other vaqueros and received some signal, for he admitted, "But we dare go no farther."

Damian stroked his mustache. "You, Joaquin, have no choice. You'll go to the de Casillas rancho and stay. The rancho is close, and Doña Maria Ygnacia will welcome us." He instructed the other vaqueros, "Put him on a litter and carry him. This fracture will heal only with the greatest care."

As they mounted, Damian told Katherine, "We'll know when we reach de Casillas land by the roses. Nacia loves roses."

As he promised, the scent of roses introduced the hacienda to Katherine. Roses climbed on a trellis, rose bushes bloomed along the drive. Roses climbed to the porch roof and blossomed in clusters of yellow, red and pink in the yard.

"How pretty," Katherine exclaimed.

"The roses remind me of Nacia," Damian said. "Sweet and pretty."

Katherine frowned as he rode ahead. She remembered meeting Señora de Casillas at the fiesta. The woman had been eager to speak, looking her over with inquisitive friendliness. Now Katherine wondered if there had been a reason for it.

Her gaze burned a hole in Damian's back. This man who called himself her husband had distanced himself from her, reproached her, confused her with his anger. Yet this Nacia elicited affection from him. Who was this paragon? Why did he compare her to a rose? Was there something Katherine should know? The intimacy implied by the tender nickname brought her hackles up. "Nacia," she muttered. "It sounds like a puppy."

Swinging out of the saddle, Damian climbed the porch steps. "Is anybody home?"

An Indian servant stuck her head out, observed him without a word, then disappeared back into the house. Silence reigned over the area, and for the first time Katherine wondered where the stableboys were, what had happened to the vaqueros and the gardeners who should be stirring in the yard. Damian frowned at her as if their unenthusiastic welcome were her fault.

She wanted to scold him. In their wild ride today, the tension of their quarrel had eased; now it tightened a clamp around her heart once more.

Damian jumped off the porch. When he heard a breathless voice behind him, he whirled around.

"Damian, forgive me. I didn't know you were here." Nacia stood in the doorway, dressed in a black skirt. She hung back, keeping her face in the shadows. "And Doña Katherina. You're traveling with Damian." A question and faint censure crept into her voice. "How good to see you."

Damian responded to Nacia's curiosity with humor. "What? Hasn't Julio returned and told you? Hasn't the news traveled Alta California like wildfire in an autumn field? Doña Katherina and I are married."

Katherine didn't see Nacia say the word, only heard the murmur, "Married?" Katherine wondered what their welcome would be now, but Nacia rushed to the edge of the porch and teetered at the top of the stairs. Her voice returned. "Married? Oh, I'm so happy for you." She clung to the post for balance and gestured to them. "Come in at once. Doña Katherina, you must be exhausted from your travel." Her sharp handclap brought the hacienda to life. Servants stuck their heads out the door; Indians peered around the edge of the hacienda.

Dismounting, Katherine smiled politely, unwilling to respond to such delight until she discovered the strategy behind it. "Thank you, Doña Maria Ygnacia. I look forward to my stay in your home."

"You must call me Nacia, as Damian does." The tiny aristocrat's words tumbled out, and her pleasure warmed Katherine in spite of herself. As Katherine mounted the steps, Nacia put her arms around her guest. "You must tell me all about it. How did this ruffian manage to convince you to marry him?"

Katherine stiffened at the fondness in Nacia's voice, but Nacia misunderstood and hastened to assure her, "I meant no disparagement of your husband. He's a wonderful man. I just never thought he'd have the good sense to do as I told him and seize you at first chance."

The distance Katherine sought to put between them lessened with Nacia's words, and the pressure of Nacia's embrace brought them face to face. The sunlight struck the white streak in her black hair, and it looked wider than it had at the fiesta. The puffy redness of her face and the pain around her eyes dealt Katherine's reservations a blow. Nacia might be the perfect Spanish señora, but the lady was unhappy. Katherine melted, responding with a squeeze of her own. "First we must make

Joaquin comfortable." She waved towards the man in the litter. "He broke his leg, and he's in dreadful pain."

"You're so good to think of your servants first." Nacia rang the bell hung on the porch. "I knew Damian would marry a wonderful woman, and he did."

Unable to believe anyone could be so sincere, Katherine looked at her sharply. No derision, no mockery, no ridicule marred her face or voice. This woman, Katherine realized, was a rare creature who meant her compliments. As the wife of one of her friends, Katherine became a comrade.

Damian supervised as the vaqueros walked Joaquin's stretcher toward the hut of the Indian doctor. "Is your *curandero* a good one?" he asked Nacia. "Joaquin is one of my most trusted vaqueros. I've already lost one good man and had another disabled."

Nacia assured him, "He'll treat the break with a poultice of ground dog bones and Joaquin will be good as new. Now sit down and have a little wine, a little food—a *merienda*. How many days will you stay?"

"Ground dog bones?" Katherine said faintly.

Laughing, Nacia waved them towards the seats on the porch. "It sounds odd, I know, but I'd trust my *curandero* over any doctor in California."

"Ground dog bones." Katherine shook her head. "Doña Maria—"

Nacia held up an imperious hand.

Katherine began again. "Nacia, pardon me, but I need to refresh myself."

"Of course, how foolish of me." Nacia patted Katherine's hand. "Let me show you to your room, and you can join us when you're ready."

The trip through the hacienda left Katherine with a confused impression of neatness and dust. Dust on the floor, dust on the tables. Each knickknack was in its place, but they needed a thorough cleaning. The hacienda suffered from neglect, and Katherine never would have suspected it of Maria Ygnacia.

The guest room, a chamber of crisp ruffles and shiny woods, held three maids cleaning with rags and brooms. They hurriedly exited, and Nacia seemed at a loss to know what to say, apologizing, "We weren't expecting guests, but we're happy to have you."

A wave of compassion caught Katherine unaware. Nacia was embarrassed. Whatever it was that brought trouble to her face also brought indifference to her surroundings, and she had let the dirt accumulate. Katherine understood why Damian compared this woman to a rose. She was dainty and too easily bruised. She made Katherine worry for her. "The room is charming. We'll be comfortable here."

Nacia gave her a timid smile as she shut the door behind her, and Katherine collapsed in a chair with a sigh. This treasure hunt wasn't going as she'd envisioned. This marriage wasn't going as she'd envisioned. She was confused.

She had committed herself to a course of action without due forethought. Now she paid the price. She was married to a man she didn't understand, a man she didn't even know if she wanted.

But if she didn't want him, her body certainly did.

More and more, she was losing sight of the Katherine she had been. Indeed, she wasn't even Katherine anymore. To Don Lucian, she was Katherina; to Damian, she was Catriona. She was losing her identity. She groped through an ever-thickening maze of manners and emotions, hoping she took the correct turns, praying she found the sunshine in the end.

Yet, one thing she did know about Katherine Anne. She knew that brooding would never assuage her desire, nor solve her problems. Standing with renewed determination, she set about making herself prim and tidy.

When she stepped onto the porch, Damian sat on a bench with Nacia, holding her hand and speaking in an urgent voice.

Nacia had her head down, shaking it. There was intimacy here, but not the kind Katherine had suspected. Too clearly, Damian had seen Nacia's red eyes and sought to alleviate her grief.

Katherine cleared her throat. Nacia's stricken gaze met hers, and Damian stood and gestured to his place beside her. "I was keeping it warm." Frustration wove an almost visible web around him, and his eyes no longer sparkled with conviviality.

Nacia waved at the food and drink spread on a low table before them. "I'm embarrassed to offer you this, Katherina, after the excellent food you served at the fiesta, but if you'd like to sample these poor morsels, I've ordered a festive dinner."

"It looks delicious," Katherine assured her.

"You flatter me untruthfully."

Damian said, "Nacia, we never had breakfast. This looks like a feast."

Katherine's stomach spoke up with an echoing growl, and Nacia chuckled, her anxiety fading. "Then I'll let you eat." As they filled their plates, she asked, "Why didn't you have breakfast?"

Damian swallowed his first bite. "Fray Pedro de Jesus wouldn't let us. Katherine had her first communion this morning."

"This morning?" Nacia cried. "Congratulations!"

"We were supposed to be married afterwards, but Katherine's scoundrel cousin was spotted nearby. We gave chase to him, so we didn't get to eat."

Nacia looked confused. "You said you already were married."

"The *alcalde* in Monterey married us."

"You haven't been married by a priest?"

Holding an empanada, Damian's hand halted halfway to his mouth. He closed his eyes as if he anticipated the worst.

Nacia rose, heading for the door. "This is dreadful. I put you both in the same bedroom. I'll just tell the servants to change your bags."

Understanding dawned, and Katherine grabbed the chance

to throw Damian's words in his face. "So much for breaking the Seventh Commandment."

From behind Katherine, a tired male voice asked, "The Seventh Commandment? Isn't that the one about adultery?"

"Julio?" Damian turned and stared. "_Madre de Dios_, Julio, I thought you were away."

Julio stepped out towards the light, shielding his eyes with his hand. "Did Nacia tell you that?"

"No, I just assumed—"

"Damian, my friend, you think you know everything. Haven't I complained of that before?" Julio grinned in wide and artificial greeting. "Never assume anything about me."

5 June, in the year of our Lord, 1777

Fray Lucio still whines about his safety, and the women will soon abandon us, I fear.

Following the advice of little Fray Pedro de Jesus, I have prayed for a solution.

God has provided one. We must seek a hiding place for the gold. As the barren mountains rise around us and thicken with the growth of trees, we will surely find this place. We must find this place, for the gold is proof that the legendary city of El Dorado truly exists.

It must be a hiding place marked by signs recognizable to the rightful owners, and the rightful owners are those people dedicated to the salvation of the Indians — the Franciscan brothers.

—from the diary of Fray Juan Estévan de Bautista

Chapter 17

"You've been drinking," Damian accused.

"So I have," Julio said agreeably.

"Julio." Damian got to his feet, but Katherine put her hand on his arm to stop him. For Nacia's sake, the game of host and guest must be played out. As Damian looked down at Katherine, his irritation faded. "Why didn't you tell Nacia we'd been married?"

With the slightest stagger, Julio strolled to the railing and leaned against it—not so much as support, but because he could walk no farther. "It slipped my mind."

Damian took a breath. "You stood up with me as witness and it slipped your mind? Julio, you're worthless."

Julio waved a dismissing hand. "You're not the only one who thinks so. All those nosy people who told Nacia she was lowering herself by marrying me have made sure to tell her, 'I told you so.' All those people who told her, 'The bastard is no good,' have been saying, 'I told you so.' All those people."

"Damn those people," Damian said inelegantly. "I'm not one of those people."

Julio's gaze fell away from Damian's. He closed his eyes as if he couldn't bear Damian's hurt. "I know you're not." He opened his eyes and smiled mockingly at Katherine. "Have we shocked you, Doña Katherina? I assure you, Damian and I have been sniping at each other for years. It never ended with more than a broken nose."

"I'm not shocked," Katherine denied, although she was. Julio's bloodshot eyes conveyed an anguish that made her ache. "I wonder what has hurt you so badly." Without giving him a chance to respond, ignoring Damian's start of surprise beside her, she continued, "You have a beautiful home, nestled in between mountains. The trees and the flowers smell of the wild."

Julio glanced over his shoulder at the peaceful scene off the porch. "*Si*, it's beautiful, but it's not mine. It's my wife's. Her family's." He smirked at her as he drove his point home. "I don't own anything. Didn't you know? I'm not just a bastard because I abuse Nacia. I'm a bastard in truth."

Katherine folded her hands in her lap and sat straight as an old maid schoolteacher. "I don't remember hearing that before."

"If you'd heard it, you'd have remembered it," Julio said. "Everyone else does."

"Perhaps they wouldn't if you didn't continually rub their noses in it," Damian interposed.

Amused, Katherine swung to Damian. "Would you care for more of Nacia's cheese-filled tortillas? They're delicious. I must get her recipe."

The bench under her rocked as Julio flung himself down beside her. In an intimate gesture, he brushed a strand of hair away from her face and pronounced, "I like you."

"Thank you." The cold in her voice would have frozen the restless ocean. "I'm honored."

His mustache drooped over his lip and his hair was rumpled, but he was handsome in the devil-may-care way that made a woman want to tame him. "You use that chilly voice and that prune face to make your point. You're not afraid to say what you think."

She heard Damian sigh, "*Dios*," but she recognized a test when she heard one.

"I know how to handle spoiled children. I lived with my cousins too long not to have learned."

"I wouldn't call your cousin Lawrence spoiled," Damian mused. "Ignorant, perhaps. Accidentally rude not purposefully offensive."

Smiling in surprise, she agreed. "A masterful description of Lawrence. And almost a description of your friend Julio."

Julio's grin widened, became sincere. "I do like you. Now I understand why Damian had the sense to snatch you from the widowhood." With a nasty grimace, he added, "Even if it put a stain on his pure Spanish bloodlines."

"Julio," Damian warned. "Such a description of my wife can only lead to your eventual anguish."

Katherine glared at Damian. Julio aimed his arrows to wound Damian, she knew, but she didn't want her husband to defend her. She could defend herself, and she discovered she disliked being described as a blot. Lifting a slice of cheese-filled tortilla roll to her lips, she said, "Your father was a foreign sailor, no doubt." Inserting it into her mouth, she chewed and swallowed.

He watched her with subdued fire. "It added to the shame of my birth."

"No doubt," she repeated. She picked up another slice of tortilla and stared, startled, as he removed it from her.

Carrying her fingers to his lips, he kissed them. "An extraordinary woman."

A choking sound turned them to the doorway. There stood Nacia, her hand pressed to her lips in unconscious imitation of Julio's gesture.

Like the court jester who performed for an appreciative court, Julio gobbled up the line of Katherine's fingers, up her palm, up her wrist. He stopped when she flicked his nose, hard. With outrageous panache, he waved Nacia to the spot beside Damian. "Isn't this cozy? Two married couples, as friendly as they can be."

Damian stood as Nacia scurried over to him. Between clenched teeth, he said, "Julio, you are a cad, and I can still beat you to a bloody pulp."

Katherine heard Nacia's inarticulate protest, and she insisted, "I can handle Julio and his stupid playacting."

"You are not required to handle him. You have a husband now." Damian's dignity was a palpable presence.

His assumption of authority annoyed Katherine more than Julio's nonsense. "I can handle him."

With wicked glee, Julio said, "Of course she can handle me, Damian. I'll help her in every way possible."

Nacia tugged at Damian's coat as he stepped forward, and Katherine eyed Julio with an unfavorable scowl.

Boyishly innocent, he shrugged. "Damian, where do you take this lovely creature in such a hurry?"

With one final hard look, Damian accepted the change of subject. "Don't you know?"

"Should I?" Obeying the command of Damian's gaze, Julio replaced Katherine's hand to her plate.

Damian sat down and stretched back in a parody of relaxation. "Everyone else knows, I fear."

"Who?" Katherine asked.

"Mi vida," Damian mocked, "even the vaqueros know where we go and what we search for. Didn't you hear what they said? It's the curse of the treasure that broke Joaquin's leg, the curse of the treasure that brought Americans camping on our river to shoot our people. From this moment forth, every tick in the vaqueros' hair or rip in their clothes will be the fault of the treasure. They'll have to be sent back to Rancho Donoso. They're no good to us if they're afraid to go on."

Julio leaned over the table and took a tortilla. "You're seeking the treasure of the padres? Such a honeymoon."

"My wife insisted," Damian answered.

Missing the humor, Nacia shook her head in reproof. "That's not a wise idea, Katherina. As the vaqueros know, there are some frightening legends attached to that treasure."

Damian ignored her as he would ignore a babbling child. "Katherine insisted on taking a relative along, too."

Nacia looked shocked. "Oh, Katherina, taking a relative on your honeymoon will put a strain on your husband."

Katherine pretended she didn't hear either of them. Not Damian with his misplaced whimsy. Not Nacia with her serious counsel.

With a deft touch, Julio wrapped frijoles in the tortilla and nibbled at the corner. "That makes it a novel honeymoon, indeed. Where is this relative?"

Damian stroked his mustache. "He prefers to follow us at a distance, when he's not running ahead like a scared rabbit. A paltry fellow, but he worries me."

Katherine put her plate down, wiping her fingers, one by one, on her napkin. "My cousin worries you?"

"If these simple Indians deduced our plans, who else has? Is your Lawrence Cyril Chamberlain watching us for that reason? That makes more sense than an unending vigil of cousinly love."

"He's not *my* Lawrence Cyril Chamberlain," she cried, stung.

"He's not *my* cousin," he retorted.

Julio stepped in with a smoothness that belied his previous mischief making. "No, some of Damian's relatives are much more annoying."

"That's rude, Julio," Nacia chided.

It seemed Julio knew his wife, for he asked, "Don't you think Damian's relatives are annoying?"

Katherine watched as Nacia struggled, torn between her manners and her honesty. "Well . . . yes. Damian's relatives can be annoying." She brightened. "But they mean well."

"Come now, my wife, you know that's not always true. When Damian's aunt and uncle moved to San Diego to be close to their offspring, you told me you wanted to congratulate Damian and commiserate with the children."

"Well, yes, but—" she stared at Julio in bright-eyed challenge "—they aren't as awful as my parents."

His smirk vanished; his wicked teasing halted. He stared at

his wife as if she'd spouted horns and a tail, then he erupted with laughter. "My marvelous, marvelous wife." He took her hand and dragged her toward him.

Her skirt bumped the table, rattling the dishes. She sputtered, "No, no," but he paid no attention.

Seating her on his knee, he snuggled his cheek close to hers. "You're a never-ending bundle of surprises."

Her face flushed, but her resistance vanished beneath his admiration. "It's true! They are awful."

Rubbing her back, hugging her waist, he betrayed the way he felt about Nacia. "I'm not arguing, but why are you complaining now?"

Nacia's gaze darted to Katherine and back to Julio. "Doña Katherina says what she wants to. Why not me?"

"Why not indeed?" Julio echoed.

Katherine's gaze met Damian's. This was the first time she'd seen the attraction that brought the unlikely pair together. The heiress and the bastard, as different as two people could be, yet they created a space around them that shimmered with *amor*. It made Katherine ashamed of the quarrel that divided Damian and her.

Damian, too, seemed to struggle with his emotions, for his eyes gleamed when he took her hand. As he leaned forward to speak, he glanced down the drive. Katherine followed his stare. Julio looked up from his contemplation of Nacia, and she turned last of all. Two identical palomino horses moved toward them, carrying a gentleman and a lady dressed in riding costumes made of identical material. The striking couple was followed by a black carriage, pulled by a horse of enormous size.

Julio spoke first. "Speak of the devil."

"No, not now," Nacia breathed.

Nose to nose with her, Julio said, "Does that mean you didn't realize they were coming?"

"I didn't know," Nacia denied. "When has my mother ever believed she wouldn't be welcome?"

Their brief accord over, she sought to rise from Julio's lap, but he jerked her back down. To the mounted couple who had halted before the porch, he yelled, "Greetings. To what do we owe this honor?"

Katherine stared. His style was coarse, his manners nonexistent. His attitude would bring hostility from a saint, but the stately lady and the noble gentleman seemed to find it no more than they expected.

The lady looked them all over with calm disdain. "Maria Ygnacia," she intoned. "Seating yourself on a man's lap is the height of vulgarity."

Desperation, immediate and complete, marred Nacia's face and bled into her voice. "Mama, he's my husband."

"All the more reason to discourage such display." The woman Nacia called "Mama" waved the hovering servant over. The stableboy jumped as if he'd had a needle stuck in him, stumbling in his haste to assist the lady. She frowned at him reprovingly. He dropped his head and scuffed his feet in the dirt before leading her mount to the step.

On her feet, she proved to be a tall, big-boned woman dressed in the height of fashion. Her husband matched her, in height, dress, and, Katherine suspected, disposition. Their expressions rivaled each other's. They looked as if they smelled something sour, and they strode up the stairs as if they were determined to find it.

The lady glanced around the veranda. "I had these servants trained when I left this hacienda. Are they all incapable of work, now?"

With an inward groan, Katherine remembered the dusty house. Trying to ease the tension, she said, "Nacia's a tremendous hostess. Uninvited, we arrived on her doorstep, and she's made us welcome."

The lady's hat had the tallest feather Katherine had ever seen. It bobbed in a maddening pattern as she examined every inch of Katherine in a scornful sweep. "Who are you?"

"This is Damian's wife Katherine." Nacia sounded so nervous Katherine could almost hear her teeth chatter.

Nacia's mother looked Katherine over again; Katherine bridled her urge to check her buttons to see if they were fastened.

Trying to divert the comment that trembled on her mother's lips, Nacia burst out, "Not really his wife. Damian and Katherine haven't been married in the Church, but they were married by *Alcalde* Diaz in Monterey and they've come all this way—" she jumped as if Julio had pinched her "—so they can visit." Guilt etched her face; guilt that she'd almost betrayed their errand to her parents. Julio let her get to her feet. "Isn't that sweet?"

"Señora." Gravely, Damian indicated the bench he had left. "Take my seat, *por favor.*"

The lady seated herself, Katherine noted, as if she were a queen gracing the rough wood with her royal body. She wouldn't, or couldn't, relax against the seat back, and that contributed to her haughty air. With no trace of motherly affection, she indicated the spot beside her and ordered Nacia, "Sit."

"I have to go . . . tell the cook you are here," Nacia said, and fled.

"In my home," the lady said into the air, "the servants make the adjustment without being informed."

"True, too true," Nacia's father grunted. He went to take his place behind his wife.

The lady addressed Katherine. "I am Señora Ygnacia Arcadia Roderiguez. My friends call me Doña Ygnacia. In your case it would be best to call me Señora Roderiguez, since I'm sure there has been some mistake."

Astonished by such rudeness from one of the dignified matrons of California, Katherine observed Nacia's mother. This intimidating woman stated the facts as she saw them, with a rare and total lack of consideration for her victim. Faced with such impervious righteousness, Katherine said the only sensible thing. "Si, Señora Roderiguez."

Benevolence settled onto the lady's face. "Very good. First, I must tell you that we do not call my daughter by that disgraceful nickname. Her name is Maria Ygnacia. She was named after José's mother and my mother, and myself. All honorable women, honoring the child and heir of both families."

Katherine wondered at the weight of so much honor on Nacia's fragile shoulders, but Señora Roderiguez didn't require an answer. Sailing on without interruption, she said, "Don Damian, this woman you claim to have married seems to be an American."

"She was born in the United States," Damian conceded.

"I am an American," Katherine added.

Señora Roderiguez shook her head in solemn distaste. "This is not acceptable. The scion of the distinguished de la Sola family cannot wed a nobody from a heathen land. It is fortunate that you had the chance to discuss this with me before the two of you were locked together by the Holy Mother Church."

"True, too true," Señor Roderiguez said. "Listen to my wife, Don Damian. She knows best."

Damian stood straight and spoke clearly. "There is no discussion. Katherine is *mi esposa*."

Señora Roderiguez sat just as straight and spoke just as clearly. "A young man's fantasy of love is nothing more than the trap of a willing female body in bed. This woman may be your wife now, but she's more suited to the duties of mistress." She pointed at Katherine, one well-manicured fingernail disapproving. "Look at her. She is blond, a magnet for our dark-complexioned men." The finger lifted, and she pointed it towards the ceiling. "But that is no reason for a commitment. Why, I do not doubt that the bizarre coloring is the reason my daughter became enamored of such an unsuitable man, also."

"Why did you allow her to marry him, if you feel so prejudiced against him?" Katherine snapped.

Taking a deep breath that raised her bosom and curled her

lip, Señora Roderiguez answered, "Maria Ygnacia eloped with him."

Julio leaned towards Katherine to whisper, "Close your mouth. It's unattractive to imitate a fish when my mother-in-law is speaking."

Snapping her jaw up, she whispered back, "Eloped?"

"There's no stopping true love." Julio sounded and looked sincere.

"See?" The magical finger waved at the two mutterers. "Their common background betrays them."

Julio laughed. "Don't compare Doña Katherina to me, I beg. She's educated, polished, and the daughter of married parents."

He didn't know that was the truth, and Katherine appreciated his faith in her heritage. Before she could speak for herself, Damian added, "She has already become a Catholic, Señora Roderiguez."

The lady didn't understand. "That's proper for any person who chooses to live in California."

"Fray Pedro de Jesus will marry us on our return to the mission."

Señora Roderiguez turned her whole body when she looked at Damian. The lady laced her corset so tight, held her neck so stiff, moved with such deliberation that she engendered an odd kind of sympathy in Katherine. How would the lady handle defeat at the hands of Damian? Defeat she would have, no matter how logical she was. Damian would never betray his wife, and in his way he was every bit as authoritarian and stubborn as Señora Roderiguez.

That was a truth Katherine had already realized.

His resolve shone in his stance and the forward jut of his chin. Something of his determination must have seeped into Señora Roderiguez's mind, but she wouldn't yield an inch. "I will speak to your father about this."

At the threat to Don Lucian's peace of mind, a half smile

curved Damian's lips. "I will inform him of your intentions, Señora."

Like a sailing ship turning its prow with ponderous deliberation, she focused her attention on her son-in-law. "Julio. We came to curtail your conspicuous fornication."

A gasp sounded from just inside the doorway, and Señor Roderiguez stepped around to see who it was. Harrumphing like a bullfrog with a cold, he said, "Maria Ygnacia, come out. Hiding from the truth is a damned poor way to live your life. Isn't that right, my dear?"

"Quite right, my dear." Señora Roderiguez peered at her daughter as Nacia stepped reluctantly onto the veranda. "We warned you against marrying this *gorrón*, this wastrel, and now you repent. It is my duty to tell you about his ways with women."

Nacia exhibited a fine, tensile strength as she drew her tiny figure up with dignity. "I have no interest in his ways with women."

"Nor I," her mother said, "except as it affects us. Every man keeps his light women, and as long as he is discreet his wife should be grateful to be relieved of the burden of ardor. But it is the duty of every good Christian to interfere when a man spreads himself so thin that his wife fails to conceive."

Nacia closed her eyes against the reminder.

Satisfied she had revealed the truth, Señora Roderiguez said, "You are our only daughter and the heir to everything we own."

"A burden I never sought," Nacia cried defiantly.

Katherine felt Julio beside her, straining to remain still, trembling with some kind of anticipation.

"Maria Ygnacia," Señor Roderiguez boomed, "you will never say such a thing again."

"It's true." Nacia stomped her foot, a smack of silken slipper against the aging boards. Julio trembled in his seat, waiting, waiting, as she continued, "All my life, I've been carrying the lands and the houses like a gigantic stone. No one's ever been able to see *me*."

"Maria Ygnacia, you will not say another word." Señora Roderiguez didn't lift her voice, but she sounded clear and cold. "This is the most thankless bit of drivel I've ever heard in my life. You will sit down, behave like a well-bred hostess and stop embarrassing your guests. I don't know where you learned such behavior." Looking hard at Katherine, she made it clear whom she suspected.

Beneath the lash of her imperious mother's tongue, Nacia wilted like a rose plucked and mishandled. One look at Julio made Katherine want to cry out, for his face was etched with the painful failure of hope.

"I didn't mean to embarrass. . . ." Nacia faded off.

Katherine wanted to shout. Nacia hadn't embarrassed her; her parents had, but nothing could convince the two omnivores of their fault. Crisply, she said, "You didn't embarrass me. I'm so ill-bred I was enjoying the scene."

The sarcasm missed Nacia and her parents. She fumbled for a stool, nodded blindly at Katherine, settled herself and groped for poise.

"Señor Roderiguez, what news from Monterey?" Damian interrupted the sad little scene without finesse. "Has there been any more trouble?"

Julio leaned close to Katherine. "He changes the subject to protect us, and I accept his guardianship gratefully." He winked, his disappointment gone as if it had never been. To his manservant, stationed in the doorway, he called "*Aguardiente* for our guests."

"Oh, Julio, I was going to serve *champurrado*." Nacia wrung her hands. "Doña Katherina will enjoy my recipe, I'm sure."

"Yes," Katherine agreed, anxious to ease Nacia's responsibility. "I love chocolate, and it will be a fitting end to the *merienda*."

Julio accepted a bottle from his manservant. "Let her try it.

Champurrado is a woman's drink, and perhaps it will sweeten their dispositions. The men will have *aguardiente*." He splashed the pungent liquor into the cups and waved the servant towards his father-in-law and Damian.

"I will drink." Damian accepted the *aguardiente*. "But I won't continue until my stomach heaves."

"A wise policy." Julio saluted him with the cup. "I'll try to follow it, also. I wouldn't want to shock our prim Doña Katherina."

"Don't let me stop you," Katherine ordered. "If you want to spend the evening on your knees in the yard, killing Nacia's roses, that's your business."

Señora Roderiguez looked momentarily amazed by her frankness, but recovered enough to suggest, "That is an ill-bred thing to say, Doña Katherina, and an even more ill-bred thing to do, Julio. Try to conform to the dictates of polite society."

"I brought it up," Damian interposed.

Señora Roderiguez smiled at him, a cold lifting of her lips. "But the difference, dear Don Damian, is that you understand the correct way to act."

Damian opened his mouth, prepared to argue, and shut it as if it were too futile. Instead he inquired, "Señor Roderiguez, what do you have to say about the events in Monterey?"

"Monterey." Señor Roderiguez cleared his throat. "Ah, Monterey is indeed a nursery of high-minded fools. That Larkin, that Yankee trader—"

"The American consul?" Damian clarified.

"That's what he calls himself," the old man said in exasperation. "That Larkin called a meeting with all the fools who have any influence, any land. He wanted to discuss California's future. As if it's any business of his."

"He does have substantial holdings in Monterey," Julio pointed out.

Ignoring such logic with grandeur, Señor Roderiguez said, "That Hartnell, that Britisher, declared England should protect

California. As if it's any business of his. Then that young puppy, Soberanes leaped to his feet and said, '*California libre, soberano, y independiente!*' And that other young puppy, Alvarado, agreed. As if those two are old enough to know anything about forming an independent, sovereign state of California." Pacing out from behind his wife, he stood against the railing and declared, "The day California left the fold of Mother Spain was a black day in history."

"What did Mariano Vallejo say?" Julio asked with wicked humor. "I heard that he was in Monterey, and he's no puppy."

Señor Roderiguez snorted. "That young—" He stopped before he called Mariano Vallejo, one of the most respected men in California, a puppy. "He dares call himself Californio. That Vallejo called for the government to detach itself from Mexico and to apply for admission to the United States."

Interested and amazed, Damian whistled. "So he said it, did he? He's said it privately for years. Did they vote on it?"

"No, they fought about it," Señor Roderiguez said irritably. "This has everyone all stirred up. That young puppy who calls himself a general—"

"José Castro?" Damian interrupted.

"Of course, José Castro." Señor Roderiguez pulled out a handkerchief and wiped at his nose with extravagant annoyance. "He's the only puppy who's calling himself a general in Monterey, although how many puppies are calling themselves generals in Los Angeles, I don't know. José Castro has called a military junta to protect us from that barbarian. Hey!" He pointed a shaking finger at Katherine. "Does this young minx know Frémont?"

Katherine refused to answer a question not asked of her. While Damian fumbled with his reply, Señor Roderiguez waved a dismissing hand. "Eh, of course she must know him. All these Americans are part of a nefarious plot to wrest California from its rightful owners."

Damian flushed a somber red, though whether from fury or

mortification, Katherine couldn't tell. "Katherine is my wife. She has no part of any plot."

"Ooh, here it comes." Julio rubbed his hands together and leaned forward. "Damian's ashamed of his American wife."

There was no challenge in Damian's voice. Only the plain, flat stating of facts. "She's not an American."

"She's not?" Julio asked. He poured himself another cup of *aguardiente*, listening with delight.

"I'm not?"

"She doesn't want to be related to such *cochinos* as those," Damian said.

Nacia blinked with complete astonishment. "Pigs? You're saying Katherine is related to a nation of pigs?"

"I beg your pardon, Don Damian." Katherine's voice rose in indignation. "What of the Americans who have married California daughters? They're your friends. They're welcome in your home. Are you calling them pigs?"

Julio made an oinking noise and sang out, "Worried about your pedigree, Damian?"

"Of course he's not," Katherine snapped. "I'm not a brood mare."

"You're not a Spaniard, either," Julio mocked, then drained his cup. "Damian's always been a conceited ass about his bloodlines. The way he feels about Americans can only compound matters."

In a low, intense tone, Damian insisted, "She became a Spaniard the day she married me."

Katherine moderated the alarm in her voice, fighting to impress him with the right level of good sense. "*Alcalde* Diaz is a very powerful deity if he can change my heritage with a simple ceremony."

Like two lights that stung in their intensity, Damian used his eyes on Katherine. "You're my wife."

Frustrated, she groped for the rationale that would make him see his folly. "Does that preclude me from being anything else? Am I not a human, a woman?"

She could see him distancing himself from her, putting his pride like a shield between them. "You're all of those things, but as my wife you must forget your previous loyalties. You must cleave only to me and mine."

She drew a deep breath, but still she felt smothered, overwhelmed in the way Mission San Juan Bautista had overwhelmed her. Like the sand pulled before a tide, it seemed her identity was slipping away from under her feet. "Is all of _me_ defined by _you?_"

With a frightening lack of humor, he said, "Now you understand, my Catriona. Now you understand."

"My mother-in-law doesn't believe in stabbing you in the back." Katherine jumped as Julio spoke from out of the shadows, his words slurred under the influence of the _aguardiente_. "I always find the hilt of the knife protruding from the center of my chest where it's easy to grasp the handle and remove it."

Katherine rubbed her forehead with her fingers, wishing she could relieve the ache that the evening's hostilities had caused, wishing Julio would go away so she could retire. "Of course," she murmured, "there is still the small matter of the wound it leaves behind."

"There is that." Leaning against the wall in the hall outside her room, he grinned with sour amusement.

"How do you stand it?" Sympathy and disgust warred in her voice. "Tell me how you can deal with being an outsider."

Resentful laughter lurched through him. "I've never been anything else. So you see, you're a lucky woman." Inch by inch, as if a powerful glue released him, he pulled his spine away from the wall. Catching the nape of her neck in his hand, he rattled her back and forth, staggering as he did. "Lucky, lucky woman. You'll fit in one day soon. Even if you fight Damian all the way, you'll fit in because you're a de la Sola."

She tottered under the weight of him when he wrapped one arm around her shoulder. "Julio, I can't hold you up." She tried to dislodge him, but he stuck like a burr and alarm shot through her. "Julio! Let go of me. This doesn't look good."

"We must look good," he sneered. "We must do what's proper. Mustn't we?" Wrapping both his arms around her, he tilted her back and mashed his closed lips to hers.

She struggled against him, but she knew it all as he kissed her: fury, hurt, pain, guilt, they tasted bitter as he passed them to her, and she suspended her own anger at his terrible retribution. A retribution not against her, but against the day, his life and the people who hurt him with no consciousness of their crime. He didn't ask for complicity; she was only a flower to shred in his violence, the kind of violence that would end in the ashes of a friendship and Julio's own bitter shame. Unwilling to participate, waiting for it to end, she stood quiet under the attack, her eyes wide open, staring down the hall.

A hard hand grasped Katherine's shoulder and wrenched her away from Julio. She found herself face to face with the blazing wrath of her husband.

Damian looked from Julio to Katherine; his hands clenched and unclenched, his shoulders thrust forward in aggression. Those demonic eyebrows formed a V, his mouth snarled beneath the mustache.

He would kill Julio, she feared. He would kill him for attacking her, for kissing her, for using her as a substitute for Nacia. Prepared to step between them, she staggered under the import of Damian's words.

"How dare you, Katherine?" he rasped. "How dare you kiss him?"

She hadn't heard him. Surely he hadn't suggested that she had encouraged this scene. He couldn't believe—

"Well?" His voice rose, questioning and accusing. "What do you have to say for yourself?"

Still she stared, and her insides began a slow churning. "You are not my father. You have no right to speak to me that way."

"Someone needs to speak to you." Katherine jerked around and there stood Nacia, her eyes aflame with the need for vengeance. "You were kissing my husband."

"I wasn't kissing your husband." Her emotions twisted in the unexpected attack. Her pity for Nacia dissolved under the attack.

Julio interrupted, "I was kissing her." He leaned against the wall again, all insolence and challenge.

"You were kissing her?" Nacia questioned. "*You* were kissing her?"

"Why not? I wanted to kiss someone who wasn't so afraid of a little shouting that she couldn't do the right thing." He pushed himself erect, yet kept one hand out to support himself. "I wanted to kiss someone with a little courage."

"You want someone who can shout?" Nacia's voice rose to a shriek. "I can shout. I can do the right thing. And I'll tell you now, Julio, if I ever catch you kissing another woman, if I ever even hear of you kissing another woman, I'll do the right thing and geld you. I'll follow you into the mountains, or wherever you hide out, take a knife—"

Damian grabbed Katherine's arm. "Look what you've done. They're fighting."

Katherine jerked away. "I've done nothing. And maybe they need to fight. Maybe they need to say a few things."

"—too afraid of your parents to tell them—"

Katherine raised her voice to be heard over Julio's bellow. "You're trying to blame me for everything. You're looking for a scapegoat and I'm not accepting the role."

"—my parents accepted you—"

"If you had stayed at the mission, none of this would have happened," Damian said with cold satisfaction.

"—just so they could rule your life like they always have. When are you going to realize—"

Katherine's fingers bunched into fists, but she trembled under Damian's attack. "I don't know why I should stay at the mission. Why should I stay to be trapped by your society and your prejudice and by you, my dear Don Damian?" She poured her scorn onto him.

"—when are you going to stop trying to prove what a hateful man you are? Can't you see what I think? Can't you see—"

"—when are you going to stop trying to prove what a respectful daughter you are? Can't you see what I think? Can't you see—"

"Trapped? Is that the way you feel?" Damian asked in outrage.

The truth spilled out of Katherine. "Just like when I was in Boston. I'm a prisoner of you and your father. A prisoner of your kindness."

Chapter 18

"Why should I care what you think?"

"Isn't what I think more important to you than what anyone else thinks?"

The words whirled and repeated in Katherine's mind until she didn't know who had said what. She only knew that they defined all that was wrong with Julio and Nacia, and in some way found a response in her.

She tucked the blanket closer around her neck, wishing she had the nerve to leap from her bed and close the window. Outside, the stars glinted in a midnight sky and a full moon bleached the mountains into stark shades of black and white. Moonbeams revealed the tumbled boulders that reached down from the heights to blend with the woods at their base. The wind pushed the oak trees and they complained, their branches creaking in sharp reproach.

The Indians blamed their bad luck on the curse of the treasure. Did the treasure's evil tentacles reach down the hill to this place? Did it affect her marriage, their friend's marriage? Did it bring disagreements and misunderstandings? This hacienda, tucked into a pocket at the base of the mountain, seemed to be the home of half-wild creatures and dreadful fantasies. All of them were visiting her now.

Where had her sensibleness fled? Was this another sign Katherine Anne had become a spineless female creature? When she had first lain down upon her ruffled bed, she'd been too angry to sleep. Over and over, she'd repeated the scene in the hall. In her mind, she'd said the right things to shame Damian. In her mind, he'd understood and apologized. In her mind, she hadn't crumpled from the pain of his accusation, hadn't whirled into her room and slammed the door. Locking it had been unnecessary, for the shouting, first between Julio and Nacia, then between Julio and Damian, had been too virulent to require more fuel. But lock it she did, with a loud, satisfying click. When Damian had knocked and sternly requested entrance she'd thrown a vase at the door. In cold blood, she'd broken one of Nacia's vases, and she couldn't even work up a sense of regret.

Now she paid for her defiance. Sleepy and frightened, still she didn't dare close her eyes. All she could do was stare at the open window, listen to the scuffling noises outside and wish her husband, her fickle, selfish husband, lay beside her. Not to fulfill her lust, although her body strummed with it, but to protect her against her own vivid imagination.

When a large, menacing shape loomed in the window, she no longer thought about a cursed treasure. She thought about knives, glinting black in the night and coming for her throat. She scrambled back in the bed, dragging the covers with her, and decided Damian was right about one thing at least. Screaming was the intelligent thing to do. Yet as the creature threw one leg over the casement and prepared to duck in, her vocal chords were paralyzed. Clearing her throat, she prepared to utter one piercing shriek, when the apparition said, "Damn it, Catriona, if you scream, I'll strangle you."

She let out her air with a whoosh. Irrationally angry, rationally angry, angry from the evening's quarrel, she snapped, "Don Damian. How dare you enter my room in such an unconventional method?"

"How else could I enter your room?" He squeezed down under the casement and hopped as he pulled his other leg in. Blocking out the moonlight with his shoulders, he put his fists on his hips. "Keep your voice down. Señora Roderiguez is guarding the hall, protecting your virtue."

"My virtue?" she mocked. "Perhaps your virtue. Or Julio's. Not mine."

"Your virtue is beyond reproach, but why were you kissing him?"

She bit off the words like a thread she snipped with her teeth. "Because I throw myself at every man I meet. Haven't you noticed?"

"After you ran away, Julio pointed out my fault to me, in most vivid language." He raked his fingers through his hair, standing it on end. "I regret I accused you."

Every word of the apology hurt him as he uttered it. She could see it in the expression on his face, an expression which mirrored her own. She glared without adding her own regrets.

He whispered savagely, "I still want to punch Julio's nose to the side of his face. You must admit it looked bad."

"I admit nothing." He put his finger to his lips, signaling quiet. She lowered her voice, if not her ferocity. "I have my defenses, but they're feeble when put up against a drunken man looking for a fight. I wouldn't use them against Julio, who wishes me no harm, unless he'd been goaded beyond all reason. A cold reception succeeds where anger would fail. But you're a *man*. You'll never have to worry about rape."

His nostrils flared, a vein beat in his forehead; he turned away as if the mere thought caused him pain.

Lashing out at him for being invulnerable, she continued, "What looks bad to me is a man who vows undying loyalty one day and displays pigheaded jealousy the next. What are you doing in my room? What do you want?"

Not saying a word, he stalked towards her. She read his body language using merely his silhouette. "Now, just a minute." She put her hand out to hold him off. "Do you think you can insult me, then come in here?"

He leaned over her, his knuckles on either side of her. "Do

you think you can humiliate me in front of the aristocrats of my country, ignore my dictates as your husband, cling to your misplaced loyalty?"

Without thinking, without using one ounce of her intellect, she copied a gesture she'd seen the vaqueros use to indicate derision. She didn't know if she'd done it right until he grabbed her wrists and roared, "Do you know what that means? Do you know?"

Her face flushed. She stuck out her chin, refusing to speak to him, but he didn't wait. "I'll show you what it means."

He imprisoned her hips with a knee on each side and his weight on her stomach. He pushed her deep into the pillow; he kissed her. He allowed no resistance. When she sought to keep her lips shut, he used his thumb to open them, and he ravaged her with his tongue. Lifting his head, he muttered, "That's what it means, only lower."

He stared at her, their faces so close their breath mixed. Her gaze fed on his lips, wet from her mouth. Her body, unaffected by her anger, his injustice, her hurt, lifted with the exaltation of passion. Primed by the wild rhythm of the ride, by her greedy scrutiny of his beauty, her mind concurred.

In her mind, there was no doubt that she would have him, would have Damian this very night. Wrestling both hands free, she grabbed his ears. Pulling him to her, she fused their lips. Like an amazon determined on her own way, she thrust her tongue into his mouth. She tasted his surprise before he responded, and she licked at him like a cat caressing its mate. When she was done, he sagged against her.

"Kiss me like that," she whispered, but it was a command.

"Are you sure this time?" His hands shook as he held her shoulders; his muscles tensed until the veins on his neck stood out. "You'll come to me with real emotion, and not just because I persuaded you with my—"

"I persuaded *you*," she asserted. "I don't know what it is I feel, but I lied to you in my attic. I lied to you in Mrs. Zollman's boardinghouse. It's you who makes me feel this way. It's not just my body speaking to me. I want to be with *you*. I want to feel you against me."

His mouth cut off the rest of her assurance. Somehow her hands left his ears and found their way to his shoulders. She massaged him with her fingertips and nails until his groan broke their kiss.

"You are—" his hands went to the long row of buttons that closed her nightgown "—a most apt pupil."

She imitated him. Together they unbuttoned each other, their hands fighting for position, tangling, reaching. "Slow down, slow down," he whispered, his fingers easing her nightgown down her shoulders.

She felt no need for the restraint he urged. Jerking at his shirt, she ripped one button off, and it landed on the floor with a pop. She heard it roll across the hardwood floor as she reached for his breeches.

The skin of his flat belly distracted her from her quest. Her hand smoothed across the warmth, the smooth ripple of muscle, the line of dark hair. Every bit of his stomach called forth an avaricious interest, and that interest led her to seek his chest. Exploring him with her fingers brought forth a desire to explore him with her mouth.

"God," he whispered as she put her tongue on his nipple, and his frame hovered at rigid attention over her. He clasped the headboard with both his hands. His knees dug into the mattress on either side of her as his whole body waited for her attention. His eyes closed over the most blissful expression of agony she'd ever seen, and she loved it. She loved the mastery she was experiencing, she loved seeing this strong male animal at her mercy. She couldn't restrain her smile of pure joy as she placed one hand on the bulge of his breeches.

But her smile faded. The power to torment faded. All that remained was the desire to explore and to reap the fruits of exploration. Her fingers weren't gentle when she pressed and molded him, and he writhed above her. She felt her own touch as if it were his. Her urgency doubled and redoubled as she unbuttoned him. When she'd freed him, when she held him in her hands and saw his fire, she could restrain herself no longer.

"Now," she urged. "Please. Now."

He opened his eyes and looked down at her. "What's my name?" he asked, his voice hoarse with his urgency.

She knew what he was doing, and it made her angry. She wanted him, she'd given him the truth, stripped herself of her defensive deception; still he wasn't content. "You bastard," she said.

"What's my name?"

His arms began to shake. A drop of sweat trickled down his breastbone right before her eyes. Reaching out with one forefinger, she traced the droplet, and took it to her lips.

It was a challenge, and he responded. Slowly he lowered himself to her. His shoes hit the floor as he pulled the sheet down. Eagerly she kicked the confining material away. His hand found her ankle, and he slid her crumpled nightgown out from under her.

"I'm going to take you tonight," he promised, "and you're going to tell me what I want to know."

"Don Damian," she answered. In despair and delight, she informed him, "Your name is Don Damian, and I need you." His triumphant grin was knocked askew when she added, "At least for tonight."

"One night at a time, then."

There was such delight at being joined—at last, being joined —that they illogically believed that they could comprehend each other's thoughts, emotions. Together, they savored the pleasure —temporary, but fulfilling at that moment—of closeness.

Trying to find the words that would bind his too-sensible dove to him, he repeated, "Just give me one night at a time, and I'll give you a lifetime of nights in heaven."

Then he set the pace, running over her constraint, trampling her rebellion. He pushed her too hard, he knew. They were joined; her thoughts were his. He knew each thrust was too much. He knew the pace was too fast. He knew that every stroke of his hands threatened to tear her from herself.

She fought him for control. She fought him, and he could feel the breathless spark of pleasure that leaped through her veins.

When she raged, "You can't do this to me," he laughed. He couldn't help it. His Catriona was open to emotion; her anger was honest and fed her passion. His laughter provoked a greater struggle, and he grasped the uprights on the headboard to use as an anchor. He used the soft feather mattress to control her fury. He liked having her toss beneath him; he knew where this would lead. The advance of pleasure in her body eased her self-control. Her eyes closed and opened; her legs clasped his hips tightly.

When the heaven he'd promised swallowed her, she screamed. She squeezed the back of her hand against her mouth, as if that would recall the sound of her joy, but he encouraged her with the pressure of his pelvis against hers and she screamed again. He crowded against her as she surged up, tightened around him, shuddered with bliss. It was such a guilty delight, to hear those cries and know that all of California would hear the echo of them soon. It was such a guilty delight, to know he'd bound her to him in ways she couldn't understand. He wanted to make her cry out again. He wanted to create another chain to bind her, but her movements, the sweet torment etched on her features, the pleasure her body gave him, they all betrayed him. The control he'd loosened in her, failed in him.

Irresistibly, his body followed the demand of hers. He gave her everything and received everything in return.

His consciousness returned, coming first in little dribbles of satisfaction. His eyes closed, he savored the comfort of her body. She cushioned him, sheathed him, barely breathed beneath him. In slow degrees, alarm replaced the sweet fulfillment that left him dazed.

Dios, had his rough handling hurt her? He struggled to lift his heavy lids, to examine the damage and do what he must to rectify it.

He saw below him a most shamefully relaxed woman. Her cupped hands dangled, palm up, off the side of the narrow bed. One foot dangled off, too, and the other had slipped down so her knee rested beside his. Her features had smoothed to a Madonna-like serenity, and he heaved a sigh of relief. However urgent he had been, he hadn't hurt her.

Loosening the grip of his hands from the headboard, he inched down to relax on her. He rested his head on the pillow next to hers. His lips touched the bright circle of her hair; his breath puffed against her ear. "Catriona," he crooned, "you say you never scream except during an emergency. Have I found the proper emergency to tap your vocal chords?"

She didn't stir.

He whispered, "You may work out your anger with me any time you like."

Her eyes flickered open, then closed. She sighed as if she would slip into sleep without regaining consciousness, without facing him or their actions.

"Catriona." He still crooned, but a sliver of warning sharpened his voice. "You seduced me."

Her hand, dangling off the edge of the bed, clumsily closed into a fist.

He watched it, understood its portent. They'd settled nothing. She still resisted becoming all the wife he demanded. He lifted up to his elbow, to wrest her from her pleasant coma and demand she behave as she ought.

The door rattled.

Damian froze. Katherine's eyes sprang open, their alertness defying her feigned sleep.

Knuckles rapped firmly on the panels. Señora Roderiguez bellowed, "Are you quite all right, Doña Katherina?"

"Heavens," Katherine whispered, trying to scramble out from underneath him.

"You'd better answer her." He spoke in his normal voice and restrained her when she kicked at him.

"Don Damian!" Katherine's whisper was fierce.

"She thinks you've been murdered. If you don't say something, she'll knock the door down." He stroked his mustache with his thumb. "She could do it, too."

"All right! You hush," she ordered. Raising her voice, she called, "I'm fine, Señora Roderiguez. I just had a bad dream."

"If that was a bad dream," he said, "the whole world would be begging for nightmares."

The pounding increased; the door rocked on its hinges. "What did you say?" Señora Roderiguez shouted in her firm, controlled speech.

Katherine hollered, "I'm fine."

The door leaped in a wild protest against her vehemence. Señora Roderiguez sniffed, so loudly they heard it through the wood. "Good. I'll be going to bed now." Her footsteps echoed on the hardwood floors.

"Now there goes a *sensible* woman." Damian's tension, his emphasis, made Katherine stare at him. "She knows I'm in here, but she wants to be in control. She wants to be in control so badly she'll not accuse us of anything, for that would be to concede she'd lost control when I stepped through your window. So she sensibly ignores the truth." Pleased with Katherine's attention, her dawning comprehension, he snapped his fingers. "She's in control. She's sensible."

She digested that, and when he seemed satisfied she understood, he came up to lean on his elbow. "It's frightening to think that once upon a time, Señora Roderiguez was a woman like you, isn't it?"

She pushed at him. "Go to bed."

"I am in bed."

"Just get out and go to bed."

She was thinking, he could see it. Dismay, frustration, and renewed anger fought for supremacy in her soul; she trembled with it. Slipping to his feet, he tossed the sheet over her and dressed to leave. He was satisfied. The memories of just how good it had been, just how brief it had been, hovered close. He knew she'd not sleep with any tranquillity tonight.

Nor would he. He wished he could sneak out and have a cigar.

"That's them, I tell you. You're letting them get away." Like a little boy in need of a privy, Lawrence Cyril Chamberlain shifted from one foot to the other and watched as the group of vaqueros rode away. "Look, there's that silly hat of Don Damian's and my cousin's cape."

Emerson Smith hardly lifted his head from inspecting his pistol to glance at the passing horsemen. "It's a decoy, Larry."

Lawrence had already decided he didn't like Smith, didn't like his uncouth manner or his casual dismissal of Lawrence's importance. "I told you not to call me 'Larry.' My name is Lawrence Cyril Chamberlain. You may call me 'Mr. Chamberlain,' or, if you must be familiar, Lawrence. Now, how do you know it's a decoy?"

Smith looked up at Lawrence, and Lawrence shuddered. Those deep-set brown eyes surrounded by bony sockets reminded Lawrence of a cadaver. Smith's fixed gaze observed the reaction and he bared his decayed teeth. "It's a decoy. De la Sola is such a noble gent, he'd never force his sniveling vaqueros to go into those mountains against their will. I'll be lucky if the men I hired keep their position until I return, as frightened as they are by dead papists."

"Will they stay?"

"I think so. I made 'em afraid of the live American." Smith

rose to his feet, towering over Lawrence like some primitive monolith. "Larry."

Lawrence stepped back, adjusting his hat lower over his bare head: "I hope your self-confidence will be borne out."

"Every superstitious native in California repeats this tale of the gold and how the padres cursed it. The way I see it, you gotta believe in the curse for it to take effect. You gotta believe your arms'll get chopped off and your guts will spill in the dirt and you'll drop a thousand feet to your death. You gotta believe those priests got any power at all."

"You don't?" Lawrence quivered, reacting to the vivid description.

"Nah. What kind of jellyfish would believe all that?"

"It's a stupid story. Even the part about the gold."

Smith remained unimpressed. "Maybe so, maybe not. I know for sure that quite a few people believe it. They even believe it's been found. The way I see it, all I have to do is follow them that believe it's been found."

"You don't know that my cousin and that man who calls himself her husband have found a treasure." Lawrence worked hard to whip up his scorn. "You don't know anything for sure."

"I know a lot of things you don't know. I know the truth of that slick deal you made in the cantina."

"What about it?" Lawrence asked defensively.

Smith chuckled. "That de Casillas knows how to part a fool from his money, don't he?"

Lawrence rubbed his sunburned nose. "That's not true. I still don't know that he took my money in bad faith."

"I don't know that, either." Smith sounded reflective. "De Casillas is trouble. I wish I could have another nice, long talk with him."

"You're in league with him? He's the mysterious man behind this silly quest?" Lawrence's voice rose on an incredulous note. "Someone hired you to help find the gold. That's what you said."

"Yes, when my boss paid me good money to follow de la Sola, I knew I was onto something." Smith grinned, admitting and denying nothing. "Taking money for watching your cousin Kathy was no strain on these eyeballs."

"Won't your boss be angry that you're following them without reporting in?"

"To hell with that. I'm doing the work. I'll keep all the beautiful cursed gold of the padres."

"You're going to cheat your boss?"

Smith put his face down even with Lawrence's and tapped Lawrence's chest with a greasy finger. "I'll keep the gold."

"Fine, fine." Lawrence pulled out a handkerchief once white and starched, now grimy and wrinkled, and waved it in the air. "I don't care about this fabled treasure, as long as I can have Katherine when you're done."

"Oh, yes, Larry." Smith polished his pistol with long, slow strokes. "You can have Katherine when I'm done."

"Will they leave a trail?" Katherine asked as she watched the vaqueros ride off.

"A trail even your cousin can follow," Damian assured her. "That should deceive whoever is waiting for us to lead them to the treasure." Watching the female servant dressed in one of Katherine's dresses and the Indian wearing his own hat and coat, he worried silently. Surely it would.

From inside the hacienda, the sound of voices rose. Nacia and Julio were fighting again, and this morning the Roderiguezes joined in. The battle continued without abatement until Damian and Katherine prepared to leave. Then their hosts stepped out.

On the veranda, Nacia stood with her chin jutting out, two bright spots of red in her cheeks. Her erect carriage rivaled her mother's, and her tiny figure quivered with an indomitable air that had been previously hidden.

Julio squinted against the morning sun, his face an odd mixture of excitement and mortification. He spoke quietly, as if loud noises were an agony for him.

From Señor and Señora Roderiguez Katherine expected a stiff reprimand; instead she got a bewildered dismissal. What their daughter had said to them, she didn't know, but they stood in magnificent disarray, looking as if somewhere, somehow, their correct world had gone awry.

Katherine thought, as she left the de Casillas home, that she'd love to blend into the walls and hear the controversy the rest of the day would bring.

But perhaps de Casillas thought the same thing about them.

The land of grass gave way as they rode north and rode higher. Gradually the mountains grew rockier, rougher, and the occasional oak gave way to woods of pine and scrub. Neither Damian nor Katherine fought against the silence between them. They rode through the overhanging trees, along a narrow trail that climbed up, until their hunger grew strong. They could put it off no longer; they would have to eat. Talk would be the inevitable result, and after last night, talk wasn't something either one of them sought.

"We'll stop here." Damian indicated the little clearing with his whip.

In the sunlight that filtered through the cover of pine trees, the carpet of fallen needles appeared to be gold. The scent of spice filled Katherine's nostrils as she lifted her head to gaze up through the branches towards the cloudless sky. "Lovely."

He dismounted and unhooked the dinner basket. "The de Casillas cook packed a heavy meal. I hope she was happier this morning than the rest of that family."

"Why's that?"

"Because otherwise, we'll be poisoned."

She wasn't even moved to laugh. "Too true."

Damian relieved Confite of the saddlebags and loosened the flank cinch. Slapping Confite on the rump, Damian told him, "Go on. Graze to your heart's content."

Sliding down from the saddle before he could help her, Katherine led her mare to the grass. "Make sure you tie him," Damian ordered.

"Of course," she said coldly, looping her rein around a branch.

Strips of cold meat, cheese, tortillas, and fruit appeared from the basket, and a bottle of new red wine made from California grapes. The meal was quiet and polite, and for Katherine, uncomfortable. She wanted to say something to Damian; the words burned on her tongue. She didn't want to disturb their fragile truce, but she wouldn't rest until she'd told him. "Don Damian."

"_Si, mi mujer?_"

"Last night you compared me to Señora Roderiguez."

"Not in so many words," he protested. He sipped the wine from a wooden cup.

"That is what you meant. Perhaps I am so slow to insult that I need to be flayed with my deficiencies, but I understood that."

He hesitated, uncomfortable with her bluntness. "That is what I meant."

"Very well. I've taken your criticism under advisement. Now I'd like you to do the same."

"A wife doesn't criticize her husband."

"A man who doesn't wish to be criticized shouldn't marry," she answered, and with a flourish added, "My father used to say that." The quirk in his cheek told her he agreed, and she relaxed enough to state her case boldly. "You feel that I'm becoming a Señora Roderiguez. Very well, I'm afraid you're becoming an Uncle Rutherford."

His head came up; his smile disappeared.

"Not in terms of cruelty or lack of responsibility," she added. "In terms of your conviction that you're right about everything. Uncle Rutherford never allowed anyone in his home to disagree with him. He squashed all the initiative out of his children. He tried to squash it out of me."

"What has that to do with me?"

With a gentle tact she normally disdained, she laid one hand on his and stopped his determined drinking. "I am an American." When he would speak, she squeezed his fingers. "There's no room for discussion. I am an American. In your eyes, by your church, we're not yet married. Until I'm satisfied that you can accept me as I am, we will not be."

"What?" His roar shook the treetops, echoing down the mountain.

She bit her lip. She hadn't meant to say that. She hadn't meant to threaten him. She'd meant to approach him with the wile of a señorita, not charge him like a bull. But the damage was done, and she firmed her lips as she stared at him in challenge. "I said—"

"I heard you!" Rising to his feet, he dashed the contents of the cup against the rock beside him, splattering them both with wine. The crimson stain spread on his white shirt; she wiped the liquid off her face.

Staring at the raging hidalgo, she pulled the restraining scarf off her head and scrubbed absently at the wet spot on the sleeve of her riding costume. "It's not so difficult to understand. I just want you to change—"

"Myself." He tapped his chest with his forefinger. "You want me to change the man you married."

"Just what do you want? Who do you want me to be? Not myself. You don't want me to be Katherine Anne. You want me to be some mythical woman who transforms her heart into that of a Californian while retaining the outward appearance of an American. That *is* what you want, isn't it?"

"No," he denied, but he faltered just a little.

"Is Señora Roderiguez right? Is it my blond hair that makes me the wife of your choice?"

"Of course not." He sounded more confident now.

"Then what is it about me that you want? You don't want me to be an American. You don't want me to think for myself. You don't want me to criticize you. What is it you want? Why did you marry me?"

As if he saw her for the first time, he gazed at her with his heart in his eyes. Something about the way he stood, the way he stared, made her breath quicken. He wanted to say something, something that would change her, something that she'd never thought of before. Concentrating on her with all his might, he knelt in front of her, knees to knees. He wiped a drop of wine from her jacket. He caught at her hands; she awkwardly dropped the scarf into her lap. His intensity made her shy, and she looked down at the wadded material and wondered, in a distracted way, why she'd gripped it so tight.

"Catriona," he began, and took a breath. "Katherine Anne—"

She looked up, and as if he couldn't resist, he leaned toward her, his eyes melting her tension. Her own eyes fluttered closed; her lips parted in anticipation.

A rustle behind Damian, a hollow crack of a gun butt against his skull, and he pitched forward onto her chest. Confused, she scrambled to catch him, but his head struck her breastbone. She struggled against his dead weight, seeking the source of his unconsciousness and finding it as she looked up—up at Mr. Emerson Smith and the pistol he held in his hand.

Chapter 19

Damian wasn't dead. He couldn't be dead. He'd been alive when they left him. Katherine clenched her teeth against the shudder that racked her and urged her horse up the ever-rising trail behind Emerson Smith. Damian wasn't dead, for he'd moaned and rolled beneath Smith's kicks. The skin on the back of his skull had been split open by Smith's gun butt. Dear God, Damian had been hurt so badly he never regained consciousness during Smith's search for the map.

That horrible map.

"Hey, Kathy, what do you suppose your lovey-dove has done with that map?" Smith drawled.

"I don't know," she answered, her voice dull with worry.

"Sure you do," he encouraged.

She raised her head and glared, jarred from her anxiety by his hearty indifference. "I don't know!"

"Well," he said, "we certainly searched for it. Remember?"

She didn't answer.

"Remember?" he insisted. "First we looked in the saddle-bags."

"Looted them," she muttered.

"Then we searched your lovey-dove. Searched all over his body and in his clothes, but that map wasn't there. Remember what we did then?"

She hung her head, embarrassed by the mere memory. From

the horse behind her, Lawrence called, "Leave her alone, Smith."

"Naw," Smith refused. "I was just getting to the best part of the memories. The part when we searched our little lawyer." He smacked his lips, and the moist sound made Katherine's stomach heave. "Too bad you were along, Larry. You're like the skeleton at the feast. It would have been a lot of fun to strip her and check her all over for the map. All my vaqueros were ready to see that. You could tell by those kissy noises they made."

"These vaqueros are scum," Larry said with disdain.

"Yes, but they work cheap and don't ask no questions." Smith turned and grinned at Lawrence, then at Katherine sandwiched between them. "Which is more than I can say for you, Larry."

"Is he paying you for this, Lawrence?" Katherine asked, feeling pain struggling to break her numb despair.

"No," Lawrence denied. "He thinks I ask too many questions."

"Only thing that ever shuts him up is a good snort of liquor." Smith grinned at her again, showing the red gums around his teeth. He turned to face the front again. "I still say we ought to stop and search our Miz Kathy right now. Yes sirree, she could be concealing that map on her body."

"You're worrying that map like a dog would worry a meaty bone," Lawrence accused. "You know that map went off with de la Sola's horse. That horse ran off even before you hit de la Sola with your gun butt."

"Yes. There's a good chance that map's on the horse," Smith admitted with sullen acceptance. "I sure would've liked a peek at it."

Katherine's relief was so thick she could almost taste it. Lawrence had distracted Smith, and he'd done it on purpose, she knew. Lawrence might be a worm, but he didn't want her to be used by Emerson Smith. She suspected Lawrence might turn into a reasonable human being, in thirty years or so.

Sickness washed over her again as she thought of Damian, his head bleeding into a little pool in her skirt. She hadn't fainted at the sight. In a futile effort to help Damian, she'd held onto all her senses. She answered Smith's questions, holding Damian's head protectively in her lap. She hadn't wanted to give him up. She hadn't wanted to let go of him, but when Smith threatened to shoot him . . . She felt so ill.

Her horse, thankfully, had been tied. Katherine had mounted in a hurry when threatened with a dual ride behind Mr. Smith. Five scruffy vaqueros grinned and shoved at the flash of ankle she revealed, but that was better than having one of them boost her up.

Now she watched the afternoon sun light the back of Mr. Smith's head. She stared at his long neck, at his ears that stuck out too far and the bald spot usually hidden with his height. A real hatred boiled up inside her. Thick and rich, she could taste it on her tongue. A year had passed since she'd felt this way, but she recognized it.

This hatred she'd felt for her Uncle Rutherford when he threatened her mother; this hatred she'd felt for Aunt Narcissa when she'd insinuated her father was a wastrel. It wasn't the hatred Katherine felt when someone hurt her, but the hatred she felt when someone hurt the one she loved.

That frightened her. Frightened her more than almost anything that had happened. Almost more than the chance that she would die before she saw Damian again. Almost more than the thought of Damian, lolling unconscious in the dirt.

In front of her, Mr. Smith interrupted her thoughts, pulling back her futile remorse. "Larry? I never asked why you wanted this woman back so badly. She seems like a real nuisance to me."

"Family duty," Lawrence said.

Pulling a handkerchief out of his back pocket, Mr. Smith blew his nose with distressing thoroughness. "Ah, Larry, surely that ain't a reason to come all this way when you could have stopped her at the boat in Boston."

Lawrence cleared his throat in sympathetic reaction. "We didn't realize how much we'd miss her."

Katherine saw Mr. Smith's shoulders heave. She guessed he was laughing. In a way, Smith reminded her of the Chamberlains, and she said, "They missed my labor. They missed the money I made for them."

"You shut up, Miz Kathy," Mr. Smith retorted. "Women should be seen and not heard."

"That'll be the day." Lawrence lowered his voice, but not enough. Both Katherine and Mr. Smith heard him say, "If we could have got her to shut up, her life with Father would have been so much easier."

Smith nodded. "That's women. They cut off their noses to spite their faces. They never know what's good for them."

With a bitter inflection, Katherine quoted, "Men have many faults; women only two. Everything they say, and everything they do."

"But I can cure you of that," Mr. Smith said softly.

She didn't know how to respond. She knew better than to respond. She hated to let him think that he'd cowed her—but he had. In a quick gesture for luck, she touched the cool metal of her watch in its pocket.

Satisfied, Mr. Smith called back to Lawrence, "This Miss Smart-Skirt said something about being a lawyer. Being a really good lawyer. Why, she bragged all over hell and California about it. A' course no one believed her. They all laughed at her and called her names, but with you showing up and wanting her back so bad, I can't help but wonder. . . ."

"She's knowledgeable about the law," Lawrence admitted. "She helped raise the family's fortunes."

"An' you want me to help you get her on a boat?"

"A ship. Yes. She finds you the treasure. You deliver her

aboard my ship bound for Boston. I get her, and she won't be able to tell anyone about your sudden acquisition of wealth."

"But I'm just a dang bit worried," Smith confessed. "What if she can't help find this treasure?"

"She says she saw the map," Lawrence reminded him.

"Yes, but the only reason she said it was to stop me from kicking that husband of hers right off the mountain. That's none too reliable a confession."

The scene rose too vividly before Katherine's eyes, and her own censure made her sway. She'd betrayed Damian's trust by cooperating, and she'd ridden away from her unconscious husband. Surely all would come right, but if it didn't—how could she live with the guilt? She clenched her hand around the pommel of the saddle. "It's what you wanted to hear."

"It had better be the truth, or these ghouls that guard the treasure will be the least of your problems."

A shiver snaked down her back. He hadn't turned, tried to look at her, or raised his voice. But there was something about Mr. Smith—the way he held his head, the flat toneless quality of his threat—that made her think of rape and murder. At the fiesta she'd wondered if he'd fled a warrant for his arrest. It seemed like years ago, so many things had happened, but surrounded by friends and laughter, it had been a distant worry. Today, in the wild, she marveled at her own naivete. "It's the truth, but my sense of distance is poor. The map pointed to the treasure and said, 'This ye will know by the signs.' "

"What signs?"

"I don't know. I don't know." She heard the shrill note in her voice, and she gulped her panic back. "Nobody knows, but the vaqueros are uneasy. If you keep talking about ghouls, you'll lose them."

"Yes, they're like everybody else in this godforsaken land. Scared of their shadow." He blew his nose again, but this time he didn't bother with the handkerchief.

"The de la Solas are a powerful family in California. Don

Lucian is my father-in-law and fond of me. Don Damian is my husband. He's resourceful and smart."

"If he ain't dead yet," Mr. Smith offered.

Her heart felt like a stone in her breast. She said in a rush, "He'll destroy you."

Mr. Smith whistled in one long expiration. "Whew, you got it bad."

"What?" she asked.

"What?" Lawrence asked.

"Can't you tell, Larry? She's in lu-ove." Mr. Smith gave it all the sweet and sticky accent of a prepubescent boy. "Kathy's in love with her greaser."

She hurled her denial like a bird tosses a snake. "No, I'm not."

Lawrence answered almost as quickly. "No, she's not."

"Oh, yes, Larry. That's why she up an' marries some guy who she's got nothing in common with, who doesn't even like her people."

"I'm not in love with him." She wished she could know what message he'd tried to give her before he was hit, but defiantly, she concluded, "But I think perhaps he has an affection for me. If you harm me in any way, he'll kill you."

"My golly, he's got you bamboozled," he marveled.

"You're a fool to have challenged Don Damian de la Sola." Her hands tightened on the reins.

He laughed rudely. "You're the fool. You're the fool if you think he'll have any interest in you after you've stayed overnight with me."

"He trusts me."

"I'm sure he does—a cold fish like you. But he can't trust me."

Her breath caught.

"Now, see here." Lawrence interrupted with his father's best bombast. "Now, see here, I agreed to this on the understanding Katherine wouldn't be harmed."

"Oh, I won't harm her." Mr. Smith sounded as innocent as a boy with a fishing pole hidden behind his back.

"Well," Lawrence said, "good."

"Impressive, Lawrence," Katherine murmured under her breath.

Mr. Smith added, "Anyway, your lovey-pie won't care if we're pure as two nuns. It still won't look good."

"Don Damian is my husband."

Now he twisted in his saddle, laughing out loud in short donkey brays. "You really are a fool. Haven't you noticed how he hates us Americans?"

She stiffened.

"Look at that expression on your face, like you bit into one of those sour, puny lemons they grow around here. So don't you know that greaser would do anything to protect his lands?"

"He wouldn't marry me to protect his lands."

"Didn't your cousin just say how conniving you are? And an American to boot. Marrying someone like that is a winning combination. He couldn't find that in a man."

She almost laughed at such twisted reasoning. Almost laughed, but it did make sense.

"Your wonderful Don Damian would do anything to keep his lands, even marry one of the hated Americans in hopes that such a marriage will legalize his good-for-nothing land grant. Not that that will help," he sneered. "Being married to an American woman won't save Damian's lands. If an American man wants to claim the property, the officials will look only at the name on the title."

"Yes." Lawrence Cyril Chamberlain sounded like a boy in a snit.

"He's just using you," Mr. Smith finished with a flourish.

"That's not true," she protested.

"You'll get the chance to find out. That General Castro is drafting a proclamation ordering all noncitizens out of California. If your Don Damian jumps at the chance to get rid of you, you'll know how he really feels."

"According to your theory, if he doesn't jump at the chance, I'll think he's using me to save his land."

"Yes." Mr. Smith sounded immeasurably cheered. "You can't win no matter what he does."

Damian woke, his fists rotating in useless combat. "Where am I?"

"With me."

Her voice sounded like mission bells, like the most soothing ministration of the angels. "Vietta!" He jerked his head toward her and groaned with the pain. Specks of red and yellow swam in front of his eyes.

"Lie back down," she urged. "Lie back in my lap."

"Where's Katherine? My God, where's Katherine?"

"I don't know. Lie down."

He found he had no choice. The pain in his head throbbed to the rhythm of his heartbeat; he had to swallow to keep down the contents of his stomach. He slipped backwards and clenched his teeth when the swelling on his skull met her lap. With tender fingers, he pressed the goose egg above his neck, wrapped in a clumsy bandage. *"Madre de Dios,* what happened?"

"Someone hit you. He kicked your ribs, too," she said helpfully. "You've got bruises all over your chest."

He plucked at his shirt, ragged and without buttons. "Smith."

"What?"

"Emerson Smith."

"Did you see him?"

"No, but it must have been Smith." His hands shook as he tucked the shirttails into his pants. "It must have been Smith. I've always had a gut feeling about him."

"You had an intuition?" The leg beneath him jumped a little. He narrowed his eyes against the light. "An intuition. Yes, an intuition about Smith. Just as I had an intuition about Julio de Casillas."

"You thought Julio hit you?"

"No, no. Not Julio. It couldn't have been Julio. Not Julio."

"Julio . . . I never thought about Julio." She patted Damian's shoulder to console him. "I'm sorry."

Not understanding the sympathy in her voice, he tensed in instinctive rejection of her words. "What do you mean?"

"I went by their hacienda on the way up here, and Julio had disappeared. Nacia was crying, of course. What does she ever do?"

"Damn!" he exclaimed. "After the time we had there, I had hoped she was done with that."

"Poor thing, she was all alone."

"Her parents had gone?"

"Oh, yes." She nodded vigorously.

"I would think they'd remain to point out the error of her ways," he said in disgust. "However, that doesn't mean Julio is the culprit. It just means he's off on another drunken spree."

"I saw a man up on the mountain. . . ." Rubbing her eyes as if to wipe away tears for the loss of her friend Julio, she added, "A man with that reddish blond hair. He was riding ahead, but as I sought to catch him he disappeared."

"This trail is narrow and steep, Vietta," he pointed out. "Where could he have gone?"

"I don't know. I don't know the area. Julio does."

Grieved, but not at all convinced, he sighed. "Which way do the tracks go from here?"

"Up." She pointed towards the top of the mountain.

"Is my horse gone?"

"Yes."

"Oh, God." He rolled over onto his stomach and buried his face in his hands. "Then he has the map. He knows where he's going." The darkness comforted his eyes; his elbows supported his head. The pain eased, and he could think. Cautiously, he raised his head and squinted up at Vietta—Vietta, that pale flower of Spanish culture. "What are *you* doing here?"

She ducked her head and pleated the material of her skirt to avoid looking into his eyes. "There were rumors flying around Monterey."

"What kind of rumors?" He was sorry for his sharpness when he saw the way she flushed. He put his hand over hers and gentled his voice. "Vietta, this is important. What do the rumors say?"

"That you have gone after the treasure of the padres and misfortune will follow you." She twisted her hands in her lap, then earnestly apologized, "I'm sorry, Damian, but I had to come. I was so worried."

He was struck by an odd kind of vertigo. Her colors reflected an exact opposite of Katherine—she seemed the exact opposite of Katherine. Her long, black hair was braided down her back. Her dark eyelashes and heavy brows ornamented her hazel eyes, making Katherine's sandy lashes and sea-green eyes seem almost tame. Her perfect, white complexion had tiny wrinkles around her mouth and eyes. It contrasted with Katherine's, with the faint gold and small dusting of freckles that enchanted him. Her riding habit and hat were a stylish red, not blue; the decorative braid on her jacket was silver, not gold.

His gaze settled on her throat. Her throat was bare, not wrapped in a scarf to hide a scar.

Nervously, Vietta touched her neck with her fingers. "Is something wrong?"

"No." He rubbed his eyes. "No, I'm just confused by this thump I received. How long was I out?"

"I've been here only a few moments," she answered. "I don't know with any certainty."

Crawling up on his hands and knees, he dropped his head and kept it down as he stood up on wobbly feet. He grabbed for a branch; she grabbed for him. "It's all right. I'm dizzy, but it's getting better." Squinting up at the sun, he estimated the time.

"They haven't been gone long. You'll be safe here. I'll take your horse—I *can* use your horse?"

"Do you think I'd let you go on your own?" she asked in a shocked little voice. "You'll need help. You'll need a backup. And I can shoot, remember? You and Julio taught me how."

He wavered, then strengthened with resolve. "No, I can't let you. You came all this way on a rumor. It would be a poor way to repay your kindness, to subject you to such violence."

"There are more than one of these villains who kidnapped your Katherine. How do you propose to unman all of them? You need me." She put her hand on his arm.

He looked down at her hand. "How do you know that? How do you know there was more than one man?"

She gestured. "Look about you. There are the marks of many horses in the dirt. Besides, Damian," she fluttered her lashes, "it would take more than one man to overpower you. You can't save Katherine without me."

"Katherine wouldn't want me to put you in danger."

"Katherine may be in pain; she may be dying. Or worse. At the fiesta, that Smith man would look at her and cold shivers ran up my spine." She shivered in emphasis now. "Even now, he might be ripping her clothes."

He made an odd noise, one he didn't anticipate and couldn't contain.

Sympathy shone from Vietta's pallid face. "Damian, we must save her."

"Come on, then."

The cry of a hunting owl roused Katherine from her uneasy slumber again. According to the old wives' tale, the owl boded ill with its call, prophesied death with its hoot, but Katherine didn't believe that. She just believed she would wring that bird's neck if it didn't stop waking her.

Every time she woke, she shivered on the cold ground and wished she dared ask for a cover. Her riding habit was velvet, yet she seemed bare against the elements. Every time she woke, she stared at Smith, at the huge log of a man who cuddled close to the fire. Every time she woke, she remembered his insulting invitation to join him. He'd laughed when she refused him, sure she would change her mind, sure she would suffer if she didn't.

Unwillingly, she cursed Damian for failing to rescue her.

It was stupid to assume he could rescue her when he might be still unconscious. When he might be dead, for all she knew. When she couldn't rescue herself. The vaqueros had hobbled her to a tree like a dog, laughing when she tried to push their hands away from her ankles. They wrapped her feet together, then attached the long length of rope around the trunk. They hadn't tied her hands, insultingly sure of the strength of their knots. She'd found, to her distress, they had been correct. She tugged at the rough hemp that bound her feet until her fingers bled, but she couldn't free herself.

The vaqueros had taunted her, too, with their own invitations to sleep among them. Lawrence told them to shut up. They'd howled at that, clutching their sides in blatant disrespect until a fog crept down the mountain and settled over the tiny camp. That cut their merriment like a knife.

At the first murmur of "*el padre*," Mr. Smith ordered quiet, but all his commands couldn't rebuff the damp blanket that muffled sound and brought an odd white light to the night.

Now, all because of that damned owl, she lay awake and huddled in a little ball. And she thought. She couldn't turn it off. The seeds of doubt had always been there; Smith had watered them carefully, and they'd sprouted into huge, strangling vines of suspicion.

Just before Damian had been hit, she had thought he'd been about to confide his tender feelings for her. Over the past few days, the realization had been growing on her that Damian had no real reason to marry her unless he had these tender feelings. Perhaps he even felt affection, although she'd felt like a fraud when she'd bragged about that to Mr. Smith. Furthermore, it had been dawning on her that she might in some way reciprocate those tender feelings. Even the affection.

Even if there were no tender feelings or affection, even though they'd fought and she'd been afraid, she'd thought that she was secure in Damian's regard.

Now Mr. Smith insinuated that she was in love with Damian, and Damian respected her not at all. Of course, she wasn't in love with Damian. Mr. Smith had been digging at her when he'd said that. But the other sounded so reasonable.

Where was Damian? Was he hurt badly, or had he taken this chance to get rid of her? Had he romanced her, married her to save his land, and found the sacrifice too much?

After her years with the Chamberlain family, she had sworn she'd never be used again by anyone. Yet she had never probed into Damian's real feelings for her as an American. She'd been afraid to. A coward. Did he secretly despise her? Even if he came for her now, would he cast her aside after her usefulness to him was done? Or would he keep her as a responsibility? Would keeping her as his wife be the debt he felt he must pay for her assistance?

Had she made a mistake?

Every time she awoke, she wandered the same tortuous path. Every time she awoke, she thought she'd never get to sleep. But when next she struggled to open her eyes, the light of the early sun had seeped into the fog and turned the white to gray. Katherine stared dully at the embers of the fire, then glanced around.

The blankets were gone.

So were the vaqueros.

She sat up with a bound, forgetting her tethered ankles.

They were gone. Not a trace remained.

Mr. Smith was gone, too. Only Lawrence still slumbered by the fire, his nose stuck into the air and a gurgling snore emitting from his open lips.

Where was everybody? She jerked at her bonds, as she had a hundred times, but now she experienced a new urgency. With only Lawrence there, she could escape. She had a chance. If only she could saw through the ropes.

With what?

She crawled around the base of the tree, looking for a rough stick, a sharp stone, a knife someone had dropped. She gave a triumphant laugh when she saw a two-foot-long, sturdy branch lying atop a pile of scrub. Stealthily she reached for it. It lay just beyond her grasp. She pulled at the rope. Closer. She stretched. Her fingertips touched it, but she couldn't clasp it. She pulled and stretched, but she couldn't quite get it.

She stopped, panting, glanced around—and there they were. She'd looked for escape, instead she'd found two feet. Two immense feet. Sitting back on her heels, she stared up toward the tombstone face she knew was hidden in the fog. There was no dignity in her position. There was no escape, no excuse for her flouting of his custody. She knew Mr. Smith well enough to know her tiny attempt would be cause for revenge; she had, perhaps, been set up.

"Well, Miz Kathy," he asked in hearty goodwill. "Where you going?"

"Around," she said acidly.

"I been around, too." He hitched up his pants, ran his palms down over his crotch.

Pretending she didn't see or understand, she asked, "What happened to your vaqueros?"

He snorted. "They ran away, the gutless sneaks."

"Smart boys," she approved. She scooted back just a little, and the feet moved forward.

"Why do you say that?"

"Didn't you hear the owl call last night? That's a sign of death."

"Yes. So's sleeping on the ground without a blanket, but you did it." He nudged at her anger. "You coulda slept with me. I'd have kept you warm."

Valiantly she plunged on, hoping to frighten the man, using

the only weapon she possessed. In a low, falsely soothing tone, she warned, "This fog's a bad omen, too. It came on so suddenly. It's so ominous. They say that's part of the curse."

"Ooh." He wiggled his fingers like ten worms. "That scares me. I bet pretty soon you're going to tell me about the girl with the green ribbon around her neck."

"I—" Confused, her tone returned to normal. "The green ribbon?"

"Yes, she never took it off. Her husband asked her why, so when she lay dying, she told him to untie it." His deep voice resonated with fear, suspicion, desperation. "And . . . her head fell off!" He shouted it; she jumped; he roared with laughter. "You are such a chump," he marveled. "Fell for the oldest one in the book."

She put her finger to her lower lip and pushed against it to still its trembling. Angry that he'd frightened her, angrier that she'd let him, she said, "You have a lot in common with those vaqueros."

"Yes? What?"

Scooting back a little more, she accused, "Only a gutless sneak would tie a woman to a tree."

One of those huge shoes stepped down firmly on the edge of her skirt. She tried to back up, but with her feet tied and the restraint of her clothing, her struggle was futile. His legs came down right on top of her thighs, crushing them into the dirt.

A huge hand grabbed her chin, jerking it up. She whimpered at the pain in her throat. He growled, "You're just as uppity as you ever were, girl, but there's no one to save you today."

"Lawrence," she called with a quaver. "Lawrence!"

"You calling Larry? Larry? Larry the wino?" His fingers inched down towards her throat, stroked it. "Shit, he drank enough last night to keep him out for days."

"Where did he find so much wine?" she asked, her tone an accusation.

"Golly, I don't know."

His feigned virtue made her grind her teeth, and she snapped, "Procurer!"

"Honey, that's the least of the names I been called." He pressed on her windpipe enough to cut off her air and bring her hands beating against him in a panic. "I been called 'thief' and 'coward' and 'murderer.' They're all true. Imagine that, all true."

He released her. She breathed in big gulps of air, air made putrid by his rotting teeth smiling too close to her face. Her fist shot out, but he grabbed her before she made contact with his Adam's apple. He'd caught on to her defense, and she was slowed by cold, exhaustion, and breathlessness.

"Still want to call your cousin?" he teased.

Her mind raced, but there was nothing. No flash of brilliance, no last-minute escape. That big, bony face came at hers with its lips puckered and all she could think of was revulsion and death. Left-handed, she hit at his eye, but her strength and aim was pitiful. She was afraid, and the shriek started at her toes. It came up, but when it hit her throat, pinched by his grip, she could only whisper, "Don Damian!"

"He's not here." He pushed her over on her back, and she fell in a flurry of raised skirts and cramped limbs. "He's never gonna be here, so you might as well do like all women do. You might as well lie back and enjoy it."

7 June, in the year of our Lord, 1777

A cave is the ideal place to hide the gold. A cave is
what God has given us. Tucked into the mountain and
almost impossible to detect, it shines with an inner light
that betrays God's pleasure in our undertaking. Inside, it
looks like a huge crack in the interior of the rock, and I
think perhaps that is its definition. It extends up and out
of sight, then down into the depths. A rock dropped down
into the chasm in the middle of the cavern falls for a long
time before a small sound of impact reveals the bottom.
Stone shelves jut out at intervals; the floor of the cave can
be no more than a huge shelf itself.

It is a gift from God. A gift!

Yet the women are frightened of this place, refusing to
enter.

Fray Lucio, also, turns his face from me and refuses my
commands.

He believes I have fallen from the grace of God.
Somewhere on this wretched journey, I have lost their
confidence. My orders and my pleas fall on deaf ears.

Tonight I have determined to do what I have been
resisting. I will spend the night in the cave and I will pray
to God, as Fray Pedro de Jesus tells me I must.

I will listen for the answer.

—from the diary of Fray Juan Estévan de Bautista

Chapter 20

He fell on her with all the weight and subtlety of an oak log. The breath whooshed out of her; her leg twisted painfully beneath her. His hands groped for her thigh, bared by her skirt. His palms were clammy as he grabbed her knees and tried to separate them; he cursed on a sour breath when he realized her ankles were still tied.

"The map," she croaked. "The treasure."

"You don't think I really brought you along because you said you'd seen the map?" He laughed, snorting in his amusement. "How gullible do you think I am? I can find that treasure using the clues these greasers are afraid to chase. I brought you along for the entertainment value. So entertain me."

He knocked her fists away from his face, striking one wrist hard enough to numb it. She tried to scream, rampaging against his ugly domination. Her flailing hand caught one ear and yanked, and he toppled off to the side. Roaring, he came up; her grip slipped. Blood dripped off his face and he slapped her, openhanded. Her head rang; she tasted salt. He ripped at her jacket, tearing the braid, catching her watch chain. He clawed at the buttons when they wouldn't snap off, cursing in language she'd never heard before.

Some detached portion of her mind thanked the seamstress who'd sewed for the rough outdoor life. That same portion noted she couldn't win this fight. She had experience with defeat. She'd lost time and again to her cousins, but she'd never lost with such a great penalty at the finish.

She hit Mr. Smith again. She ripped his face with her finger-nails again. She called again. "Lawrence!"

Her scarf dangled, and Mr. Smith caught the end. She caught a glimpse of blackened teeth when he grinned, then he jerked it tight. The pain of her scar was nothing compared to the lack of breath. She closed her eyes, fighting for strength, for the thin stream of air he allowed in. Through the explosions of light behind her eyes, she could hear him saying in a conversational tone, "Do you remember that I said I was a murderer? Well, Miz Kathy, this is how I did it. I choked her. She turned funny colors, just like you. She tried to talk, just like you, but I just did this." He tightened his grip.

Agony exploded in her throat. She writhed until her cogni-zance slipped.

The pressure relented, and she sucked in the damp air with-out being aware.

That flat voice droned, "Makes you a little more amenable to some fun. It worked with her, too."

She couldn't bring herself alive. She couldn't make her hands work, or her feet, or her eyes. All she could do was breathe. Her consciousness drifted when his hand fumbled with her shirt, and she breathed some more. Her eyes opened, then closed against the sight of him. She tried to turn away, and the pres-sure at her neck increased.

"Don't want too much piss and vinegar outta you. Don't like women who move much."

She went limp.

"Hey, now, don't overdo it."

He throttled her. She struggled.

"That's better," he soothed. "I like to see—"

She heard a whack right by her ear, a scream she didn't think was hers. The clamp on her throat released; his knee smacked her hip. He scrambled away, dragging his legs over her chest.

She thrust at him, but her hands met the air and fell to the ground, useless. She tried to make sense of the sounds that filled the clearing, but she couldn't do that, either.

She opened her eyes. She was blind.

No, it was the fog, thicker than ever, obscuring everything.

It was swallowing up Mr. Smith. She could hear him struggling, shouting to escape.

She had to do something. She had to pick herself up off this ground and get away. As her brain became clearer, she considered jumping up and running. But no, her feet were tied.

Sit up? Perhaps that was possible. By slow inches, she wiggled so her head rested against the trunk. She raised it, winced as her neck throbbed.

She screamed.

She thought about that. No, she hadn't screamed, but someone had. She smiled. It must have been Mr. Smith. Perhaps he was being chewed.

Up the tree trunk she crawled, halting when she half sat, half reclined. That was enough.

Mr. Smith's shrieks were music. She didn't worry about being eaten herself. *El padre*'s fog would be just. Abruptly, Mr. Smith and his yells faded. All the noise stopped. She was alone in the swirling grey.

She must have slept, because someone picked up her hand before she knew anyone was there.

"Catriona." He spoke sweet and low, like someone calling the dead.

Her eyes popped open. "Don Damian." Her lips formed the words.

He looked beautiful, with his hair dank and a scratch of blood on his cheek. He knelt beside her, her huge stick grasped in one of his bloody hands. The bark had been stripped from it in places; it was cracked down half its length, but she recognized its width. Damian was the mouth in the fog; the stick was the teeth. Damian was the one who'd made Mr. Smith go away.

She'd known it, but she was glad to see her stick had been the instrument of revenge.

"Catriona." His hand reached for her neck. She flinched; she couldn't help it, and his hand fell away.

Tears flooded her eyes, raced down her cheeks. She tried to cry silently, because the sobs hurt her throat and made her cry more. He reached for her as if she were a delicate flower, taking her into his arms.

Finding strength in the shelter of his body, she burrowed into his chest.

"You're safe now. There's nothing here to hurt you," he told her. "Smith is unconscious."

She touched the stick, touched her head in pantomimed query.

Understanding, his hand touched her hair. "No, that's not where I hit him. He might die from where I hit him. Most men would."

She couldn't stop her grin, but Damian winced with reflex male empathy. "I tied him just in case he didn't die. I tossed his gear into a creek. I didn't tie your worthless cousin, though." He tugged her jacket closed. "When he wakes from his drunken stupor, he'll run, and if I never see him again, it will be too soon. How could he drink himself senseless, when he should be protecting you?"

He glared at her fiercely, expecting an answer, but she just shrugged.

"Can you stand?"

She shook her head.

"I'm glad. I wanted to hold you." He pulled her closer, hugged her as if he would never let her go.

She was content to rest there, to let her mind clear. He had come barely in time. Wetting her lips with her tongue, she tried to talk and found a whisper. "Your head?"

"Hurt a bit."

She nodded, tried again. "Long wait."

"We would have been here sooner, but we got lost in the fog." He rubbed his head against her hair. "You knew I would come, didn't you?"

She hesitated. The doubts of the night scurried through her mind like unwelcome rats.

"Didn't you know I'd be here to rescue you?"

She hid in his arms.

"Catriona?" His voice warmed with concern mixed with indignation. "We've been up all night in the dark, trying to get to you. I walked so I wouldn't lose your trail, and I lost your trail, anyway. I've got a headache and I'm hungry because that bastard took my food and you didn't believe—"

Tugging at his jacket, she whispered, "Illogical."

"Who? You or me?" With gentle hands, he thrust her back against the tree trunk. Running his fingers through his hair, he closed his eyes as if he were hurting.

She touched his arm. "Sorry."

He looked at her. "I'm sorry, too. I thought that you would realize—"

She widened her eyes in question.

"Nothing." He turned away.

She understood that she'd hurt him. She wished she'd lied. She wished she could have told him she believed he'd be there whenever she needed him. Even now she was thankful he didn't know the extent of her doubts. She wondered if she'd ever have the nerve to tell him, to question him about his intentions, about his tender feelings. Twining her fingers in her lap, she discovered how deep her streak of moral cowardice extended.

"Vietta," he called into the fog. To Katherine, he said, "Vietta followed us from Monterey because of the rumors. She brought food and a horse. She agreed to back me up in case I couldn't handle it."

His voice failed, and Katherine looked up.

Like a phantom at the edge of vision, Vietta stood cloaked in fog. Her black hair faded into the dimness, her pallid skin glowed. Her scarlet riding costume attracted the eye, and the ornate silver decorations looked grey. Then Katherine realized why Damian no longer spoke, why he stared at Vietta with such intensity.

In one scarlet riding glove, she held a pistol pointed at Damian.

Damian's pistol.

"Vietta, put that thing down," he ordered. "What do you think you're doing?"

She said nothing, answering with a crooked smile.

He stepped towards her, his hand extended. "Vietta, I've taken care of Smith. Give me my revolver."

"Thank you, Damian, for getting rid of my mistakes. I should never have hired Smith, but life's full of poor choices and loathsome consequences." Sympathy dripped from her voice. "You've found that out."

"Vietta?" he said, puzzled.

She aimed the gun at his chest. "Let's go after my treasure, shall we?"

From her pocket, she lifted an object. Katherine's breath caught in her throat, held as tightly as if Smith still choked her. She lifted her hands in rejection, twisting away from the sight of the knife Vietta held. A knife whose handle was black, whose blade shone black, with a tip so sharp it could slit a man's throat—or a woman's. She wanted to speak, to warn Damian of his peril, but she could only moan, "No."

Damian couldn't understand Katherine's violent reaction, didn't understand anything right now. Why was Vietta smiling at his wife like that? Like a sorceress pleased to be recognized?

Why was Katherine contorted in a protective shell like a victim of torture forced to confront her executioner?

This was Vietta, his little friend, not some monster.

Katherine begged him to step back, using her damaged voice, and he waved a hand. "What? You believe her? She wouldn't hurt me."

"Don Damian," Katherine croaked. "The knife. That is the knife."

He stared at his wife, and she touched her throat.

"You better pay attention to your Catriona," Vietta warned. "She remembers that night in the boardinghouse."

He looked at Vietta again, then back at Katherine. She nodded urgently. "Vietta, where did you get that knife?" He sounded like a scolding father, but he couldn't help himself. This situation was ludicrous. How could Katherine believe Vietta was capable of such an act? How could Vietta threaten them with a gun in her steady hand?

"It's my knife." Vietta displayed no defiance, no guilt, only a warm delight in his skepticism. "Julio gave it to me."

"Julio." He stroked his mustache.

Vietta shook her head at him reprovingly. "Julio gave it to me years ago. Remember? When we were children, and the vaqueros taught you boys to use a knife, I cried because I didn't have one. Julio gave me this one. His vaqueros had made it for him of the black glass stone. He thought it wasn't as good as your steel blades." She flipped the knife, catching it in an efficient fighting hold. "I practiced just like you did, and I found this black stone blade is better than your steel blades. It can slice anything."

Sure he'd unraveled the puzzle, he suggested, "Julio's had it."

Her mouth puckered and she shook her head.

Incredulous, he stared at the knife, expecting to see incriminating blood dripping from it. That couldn't be the knife. "Have you lost it recently?"

"No."

This couldn't be the person. "A man attacked you," Damian said to Katherine.

Vietta laughed, low and rich, while Katherine denied it. "No, I never said a man attacked me. You assumed a man attacked me, and I was so confused and upset, I couldn't put my finger on the discrepancies I'd seen." Her tortured voice turned hoarse, dwindled to a whisper. She gulped in moist air before she could continue. "It's Vietta. Her voice, her height. They deceived me."

"Women don't kill people," Damian said in desperation, his confidence tumbling as his precepts shook.

"I never killed a person before I killed Tobias," Vietta reassured him. She glanced down at her hand with a sort of distaste. "It's not easy to kill a man. I planned carefully, but I hadn't realized how messy it would be."

"Messy?" Damian stared at this woman he thought he knew. It was as if she were evolving before his eyes: changing from a genteel lady to a freak who had no morals or sense of virtue. "You kill a man, and you call it 'messy'?"

"I attacked him from behind, jumped on his back. If my first stab hadn't hit that blood vessel, I would never have got him down." Like a matador recounting a difficult fight, she reminisced with the assurance of their avid interest. "Then I had to saw through his windpipe."

Katherine put her hand on her throat, as if the memory of Tobias's death and her own disfigurement were too close.

With a defensive edge in her voice, Vietta told Katherine, "I couldn't have him identify me in his death throes. I had to cut his throat."

Sickened, Damian asked, "Could he have identified you?"

"Oh, yes." She sounded as delighted as a girl with her first posy as she slipped the knife in her belt and patted it fondly. "He ripped the scarf off my face. I'll never forget that look on his face when he realized who it was." Confiding to Katherine, she said, "He never liked me, you know."

Turning his back on her with insulting deliberation, Damian scrubbed at his face with his hands. Right now, he understood the ancients' custom of tearing their clothes in the event of a death. Hearing this, he'd lost Tobias once more, and his soul wallowed in guilt. He'd argued with Tobias about this woman, refusing to see her evil, and Tobias was dead because of his willful blindness.

He'd lost Vietta, too, his memories of her destroyed forever. With her, he'd lost a piece of his youth, his trust—and he'd almost lost his Catriona. "Why would you have repeated your crime with Katherine? She knew nothing. She was a victim of Tobias's curiosity."

Vietta's voice lost her nostalgia and gained a defensive edge. "She was never in any danger. It's not that easy to kill someone with a knife to the throat, but I knew she'd be terrified after losing Tobias. It was just the best way to find out what I wanted to know."

Katherine stared, her eyes round.

"Oh, Katherine, would you stop holding your throat and whimpering like that?" Vietta said in disgust. "I told you, you weren't in danger. I could have cut on your throat for a long time before I killed you. Just stop whining. I never even would have killed Tobias if he hadn't taunted me."

Damian jumped, whirling around. "What?"

"Oh, Damian." Never removing her gaze from him, Vietta slid over to a boulder and perched on it. "Tobias knew what I wanted. He was no fool. Tobias showed an interest in the treasure, and he interested you in it, also. That's when I discovered my girlhood affection for you renewed. I knew if I just kept close to both of you, the gold would be mine."

"The treasure of the padres is nothing but a legend." He corrected himself. "We thought it was nothing but a legend."

"I always enjoyed reading."

Unable to follow her garbled logic and not caring, he knelt at Katherine's feet. Reaching for the rope the vaqueros had tied to bind her, he tugged and frowned. Looking down, he gave the knots his fullest attention, intent on loosening Katherine.

"Didn't I always enjoy reading?" Vietta insisted.

He nodded absently. Katherine had to be free, to run if possible, to flee this situation.

"My family's been in California longer than yours, and one of my ancestors left a diary. She had actually seen a chunk of the gold. She wondered what happened to it. She deduced its importance."

"Someone else saw the gold?" Katherine whispered.

Vietta's attention abruptly switched to Katherine. "You've seen the gold?"

Damian closed his eyes in brief exasperation. Katherine had given away information. Right now, he wanted to keep Vietta starved for information.

"You have," Vietta breathed. "How wonderful for you. No matter how carefully I've researched, no matter how thoroughly I've pursued my findings, I've never seen the gold at all. Was it beautiful?"

Katherine shook her head. "No."

"Did you find it in Tobias's possessions? Well, of course you did. You must have. Yet I searched his room, his trunk."

Unable to maintain eye contact, Katherine dropped her gaze, and Vietta crowed. "It *was* in his trunk! Now where—it wasn't one of those chunks of rock was it? It was, wasn't it? One of those rocks contained gold, didn't it?" Her laughter rang with a sleuth's excitement. "I held it in my hand and never realized. . . ."

"What would you have done if you realized?" Damian asked.

"There was nothing more I could have done. I couldn't find a clue as to the treasure's whereabouts, but I knew Tobias had been in these mountains. I followed him, you know, until he lost me. So after I killed him and Katherine disappeared, I came up here to search. That's when I fell. That's when I hurt my leg." Vietta's voice still rang with its deep, pleasant tone. No bitterness, no unhappiness tainted her voice; it seemed that for her, the gold was worth any sacrifice. "I would have been back for Katherine sooner, only the fall from the cliff hurt me badly." She rubbed her thigh in remembered pain, and the pistol sagged.

Damian leaped for her, and the pistol went off in Katherine's direction. Unable to help himself, he flung himself back at Katherine, seeking to give her his belated protection. In the tree trunk above her head, a hole smoked. He grabbed up his wife, holding her with his body between her and the gun.

Vietta held a pistol in each hand now. Her pistol had been discharged; Damian's shone clean and bright and deadly. "I'm not going to kill her. Do you think I'm a fool? I know you, Damian, better than you know yourself. You'll do anything to protect that woman."

"Why don't you let Katherine stay behind? She can hardly walk." Damian assisted his wife over stony ground, through the fog that defied the sun.

"Keeping your beloved Catriona in my gun sights is a guarantee for your good behavior." Vietta followed them, keeping her horse well back from Damian's grasping hands. Her pistol remained in a holster by her horse's neck. "I like guarantees."

Katherine stumbled, and he put his arm around her waist. She murmured, "Thank you," but he didn't dare look at her. She must hate him. He was the _patron_. He should know best, make the correct decisions, see the most clearly, and he'd gotten them into this damnable mess.

Now he wondered how he could have doubted the ferocity of the cultured California lady he grew up with. What an idiot he'd been. Driven by a curiosity he couldn't contain, he asked, "Was your love for me ever genuine?"

Katherine glanced at him, startled, but Vietta mocked him. "Are you talking to me, my hero? Your poor, lonely, scorned _friend_?"

"That is an answer in itself," he answered. She chuckled. The sound was so comforting, he couldn't believe her menace, yet she'd trained the pistol at Katherine.

"I did love you once. Who doesn't love you, Damian? You've got everything. You're handsome, charming, competent. Everything I'm not." She chuckled again. "Oh, and you're rich. How could I forget that most important thing? You're very, very rich."

He glanced around at the encircling cloud, depressed by his stupidity and the continuous gloom. "Yes, I'm rich."

"Tactful, too. When I was so young and silly with love, you tactfully turned me away. You were so kind."

"I was always kind to you."

"Yes, you were. You were kind when no one else was, because I wasn't privileged like you. Do you know, you were my inspiration to find the treasure?"

He lifted one foot, put it in front of the other. His head throbbed; he wanted to shout at her, but old habits kept him sane. "How could I be your inspiration to do this?"

"Because if I'd been rich, it wouldn't have mattered that I was charmless, homely, unaccomplished. We would have been betrothed."

He stopped, turned, and looked at her.

She faced him from atop her surefooted mare and used every inch of her height to impress him. "I was a proper lady years ago, but I've lived in genteel poverty for too long. I've been on the edges of society, taking the crumbs tossed to me and pretending I was grateful. I've listened to my father moan about his bad luck at cards, about how we'd be living on the rancho if he hadn't lost it. I've heard my mother sigh like a martyr while she dresses in secondhand silks. I've heard them nag me, tell me if I would only flirt like an idiot, I could get a rich husband and lift them out of their ghastly destitution." She stared at him with satisfaction as he stood in the middle of the trail. "You made a mistake when you refused to wed me because I was poor."

Deliberately, he pushed Katherine out of the way. "I would never have wed you." He gazed at Vietta, telling her the truth with his proud rejection.

Her breathing grew strong; her chest rose and fell. The pistol leveled on him. She was angry, as he hoped.

He continued, "Had I expressed the desire, my father wouldn't have let me. He never liked you. He compared you to a creature found beneath a rock."

From one inhalation to the next, she grew in stature, and grew, and grew. If she had been a dragon, Damian thought, she would be breathing fire. Her hands tightened on the reins; he prepared to leap out of the way.

Regaining control, she denied him. "No, Damian. I can't run you over. It would make as much sense to shoe a goose. I'd gain nothing. No, as long as I've got your darling wife as hostage, we'll continue as we are."

He was laid to rest in the lower chancel,
Barbara Allen all in the higher;
There grew up a rose from Barbara Allen's breast,
And from his a briar.

And they grew and they grew to the very church-top,
Until they could grow no higher,
And twisted and twined in a true lover's knot. . . .

Katherine held the watch in her hand, playing the wistful tune over and over. It comforted her and annoyed Vietta—a winning combination. Vietta had already ordered Katherine to stop it, but Katherine knew Vietta wouldn't shoot her for a song. The woman had proven herself greedy, not insane.

"I wish the fog would lift," Katherine said. She sat on a fallen log, her riding boots on a stump beside her. Her skirt was hitched up almost to her knees, her bare feet wiggled in the creek that trickled down the mountainside. She didn't care about modesty or propriety; for the first time in hours of walking, the blisters on her heels were numb. Purple bruises laced her legs and arms; she hadn't had the nerve to remove the scarf and check the damage done to her throat. Her complaint was husky. "This gray is so gloomy."

As if responding to her words, the sun stabbed through the cloud with one beam. Katherine blinked in the sudden brightness; every pine needle, every leaf was delineated in the sharp mountain air. Above her she could see blue sky. Wisps of fog streamed past, then closed in once more.

"A valiant try," Damian said. He shook the pebbles out of his boots and sighed. "Look at the holes in these socks. Leocadia will have a fit."

"Your socks! Never mind your socks. We're lost," Vietta nagged, a peevish edge to her voice. "I wish you hadn't lost the map."

"You didn't even know there was a map until I told you," Damian snapped back.

Damian and Vietta had been arguing for the past hour, ever since they'd come to the end of the trail and found no pot of gold awaiting them. They'd argued through the meal of tortillas and cold beans Katherine had demanded. They were stuck in this perilous little spot, held by Vietta's gun and stubbornness.

Katherine shrugged away their quarrel. Vietta's menace had been diffused as the hours wore on. She seemed nothing more than a spinster, frazzled with the plans gone awry. Right now it was easy to forget the gun she held so firmly, the knife tucked into her belt.

"Damian didn't lose the map," Katherine pointed out. "He hid it under the saddle blanket of a very intelligent horse and when that horse sensed danger, he left. I wish Damian and I had been so clever."

From their expressions, it was obvious the others failed to appreciate her logic.

Their only possible route was down the way they'd come. On one side, the ground dropped away, falling straight down to some pointed rocks. On the other side, the trail died in a sheer cliff that rose before and around them. Looking like large slices of bread dropped by a giant, slabs of rock decorated the perimeter of the cliff. Scrubby bushes grew among them. The little stream fell straight down that cliff and nourished the lone climbing rose that struggled in the rocky soil. The rose twined across the stones and around a few random sticks thrust into the ground. Carried on a moist breeze, the first pink blooms of summer filled the air with fragrance.

Katherine liked this place. All through the long, wearisome day, she'd longed for a spot to sit and rest. Here she had cold water to drink, a babbling stream for her feet, a pleasant smell, and an unhappy Vietta. What else could one ask? Inspired, she wound the watch's mechanism once more. "I love this ballad," she said. "I'm glad Tobias built it into the watch." She sang, "He was laid to rest in the lower chancel, Barbara Allen all in the higher—"

"Are you sure this is where we're supposed to be?" Vietta waved the pistol around.

"No, I'm not sure this is where we're supposed to be," Damian mimicked nastily. "Without the map, I can't be sure."

Katherine interrupted her tune. "At least Confite is safe."

Vietta snorted, moving restlessly on the stump where she sat. "That's a relief for me."

"Has the poor señorita got saddle sores?" Grinning offensively at her, Katherine sang, "There grew up a rose from Barbara Allen's breast, and from his a briar—" She faltered.

The map had said, *By these signs ye shall know it.*

A rose bush, lost in the wilderness, growing where no other rose bush could be seen. Growing against an impenetrable cliff where gold was supposed to be hidden.

Supporting herself with her hands, Vietta rose and stared at that valiant rose bush. "That's it." Vietta pointed with a shaking finger. "That's it."

Impatient with her, Damian ordered, "Don't be so dramatic."

"That's it." As if drawn by an irresistible force, she took a step toward the cliff. She stopped with a visible effort. "You go." She waved the gun at Damian. "And you." She waved it at Katherine.

Katherine knew what Vietta wanted. She comprehended the workings of Vietta's mind in the way she now comprehended the workings of Tobias's. The music of the watch wound down, tired with its efforts to make her understand. She slipped it into her watch pocket, lifted her feet from the water and dried them on her skirt. Thrusting her feet in her boots, wincing with the pain, she stalked towards the cliff. Damian was staring at the women as if they'd lost their minds, but he joined Katherine as she picked up the long, twining arms of the rose. She traced to the base of the plant, lifting them aside as best she could. There, beside the thorny bush, was a small hole in the wall with a clock face scratched in the stone below it.

"Tobias," Katherine whispered.

"*Madre de Dios*, you found it," Damian said in awe.

8 June, in the year of our Lord, 1777

In the darkness of the cave, in the deepest part of the night, I heard the voice of God. Fray Pedro de Jesus says the voice of God is the fount of love and kindness. I tell you here that God speaks in the tones of an avenger to one who has ignored Him. His patience with me is at an end. I trembled in the face of His terrible anger. Yet the dawn brought a relenting of His displeasure, and I crawled out of the cave tempered into a sword of God.

I assured the women of unending protection if they did as I ordered, and the voice of the Lord spoke through me, convincing them to work without a qualm. I assured Fray Lucio that he would not perish, and for the first time his paralyzing fear waned. The women labor with a will, singing the hymns I have taught them. Using the materials which abound in the area, we created a cradle for the gold, much like the manger that cherished the baby Jesus at His birth. Then the difficult work began.

I live with the Lord's assurance of the women's safety, and of Fray Lucio's. I shall ask for no more, nor expect it.

—from the diary of Fray Juan Estévan de Bautista

Chapter 21

Damian used his boot to scuff loose dirt over the clock face.

"What are you doing?" Vietta's shrill voice betrayed her worry and the end of her patience. "Let me see."

Shrugging, he stepped back. She saw only the hole, not the faint remains of Tobias's scratching. That was enough; her mouth dropped.

"Go in." She stood back from them, but for the first time today, the hand that held the gun shook.

"In that hole?" he asked incredulously. "I won't fit in there."

"Then dig it out. Tobias fit. You will, too. There's gold in there."

"Yes. Gold." He caressed the word.

Damian and Vietta moved with jerky anticipation. They trembled; they spoke too rapidly. The Spaniards' greed made them shine with a kind of light, and Katherine turned her eyes away. Watching them was like watching a starving man eat, and knowing that with incentive, she could be like them.

"I don't want to go in," she murmured.

"You're not going in," Vietta retorted.

Damian swung on her. "Of course Katherine's going in."

Vietta backed to the saddlebags that lay beside her horse. She opened the clasp, pulled a spade from a leather loop and tossed it to Damian.

He kicked at it with contempt as it skittered through the dirt beside him. "You came prepared for everything, didn't you? But Katherine must go in with me."

The revolver leveled on Katherine's chest. "No."

"Katherine and I belong together."

Vietta pursed her lips and shook her head. "I don't believe there's any way to escape from the cave, but you'll try to find one if I send the two of you in. This way, Damian, you'll look for the treasure and hurry about it."

"Let me go in," Katherine urged. "Don Damian can stay out here with you."

"No!" Vietta and Damian said simultaneously.

Startled to find themselves in accord, they glanced at each other.

Damian shook his head. "No, Catriona. According to the legends, there are traps inside set by the good fathers."

"Is that supposed to dissuade me?" Katherine asked.

"Remember this?" Vietta waggled the pistol. "This will dissuade you. I want you out here. Damian adores you, God knows why, and I can control him with the threat of your death. I don't know if you care enough about him not to escape if offered the chance."

Katherine sank down on a stump, feeling as if the breath had been knocked out of her. "I beg your pardon. What kind of person do you think I am?"

"You're an Americana." Vietta condemned her with the title.

Damian stripped off his jacket and picked up the shovel.

"Be careful not to stumble into the traps. Find the gold first." Like a draft of winter wind, a faint, chilly smile swept Vietta's face. "Don't come out without the treasure, or I'll shoot her."

Bending his back to the task, he enlarged the hole into the mountain.

"Don Damian," Katherine protested, but he didn't turn around. "You don't believe I'd leave you to your death."

"Of course not. You're too valiant for that. You'd come out fighting like a cougar." He glanced over his shoulder and smiled kindly at her. "This is easy digging. Someone has filled it in not long ago."

Katherine didn't like the way he dismissed her.

"How recently?" Vietta asked in alarm. "Within the week or so?"

Bits of stone fell, slowing his progress, but he steadily outstripped the miniature landslide. "I shouldn't think so. I imagine it was Tobias. But perhaps the gold has already been removed by some other treasure seeker."

She gripped the pistol tighter. "That would be too bad for you and for your lady."

Katherine clenched her teeth, frightened by the dangerous game they all played. "Don Damian, she has to kill us. If we find the gold, if we don't find the gold. She can't let us live to spread this tale around California."

He didn't turn around. "I know that."

"Then why are you doing what she says?" Desperation brought her hands together in a prayerful attitude.

"What's the alternative? Have her shoot you? Jump off the cliff?" He tossed the shovel aside. "I have to try to live, no matter how the odds run against me. The hole's big enough. Before I go in, Vietta, I want to kiss my wife."

"No." Vietta's voice rang flat and plain. "If your love is so undying and you believe in heaven, you'll meet there sooner or later. You can kiss then."

Leaning against the cliff, he looked at Katherine as if he would memorize her. "I hoped for something more physical, at least one more time."

"When you come out," Vietta promised.

He scowled. "If I still have all my parts after a brush with the good fathers."

Katherine thought he'd never looked more like a god or a young Caesar. The bandage on his head contrasted starkly with his tanned face, his midnight hair, the growth of beard on his face. His shirt had been white and crisp; now it was smeared with dirt and the brown stains of wine and blood. Buttons dangled; his hands were bruised. His breeches and boots showed the strength of their construction, enclosing him, clasping him as she longed to.

He had never looked better to her.

The words bubbled to lips before she thought. "Tobias will tell you if there's a trap."

Vietta asked snidely, "Oh, is he communicating with you now?"

Damian glanced down at the spot where the clock face had been, then back at Katherine. "Perhaps he is." He saluted her. "You are indeed everything I ever wanted in a wife." With a lopsided smile just for her, he disappeared into the hole in the wall.

Katherine stared after him, but he was gone. She checked her watch for the time. Five past twelve. She waited, checked it again. Five past twelve. She glanced overhead. That wasn't right; it was long past noon. She wound the clock mechanism, shook it, put it close to her ear and listened to it. The clear, steady ticking had stopped.

Frantically, she wound the music. The tinkling bells were silent. Tobias's watch was dead. Death was everywhere. Death lurked inside the cave; death lurked in the barrel of Vietta's gun.

Yet birds rustled in their nests, ignorant of the drama. Squirrels scurried in the underbrush. Fog clung close to the ground, parting only on the occasional command of the wind to reveal a flash of sunshine.

Hunched over like an old woman, she kept the watch in her hand, warming it with her body heat as if she could revive it. She treated it like some lucky charm that would shield her from harm. Perhaps it could be cleaned; perhaps it would run when the dirt and the sweat that clogged its works were removed. Perhaps.

The silence around her strengthened. Vietta said nothing,

moving restlessly back to the edge of the path like a person expecting an ambush. Katherine watched her, saw the occasional fearful glance. At first she thought Vietta worried about Damian leaping out of the cave, but no; Vietta's fear was directed at the cliff that twisted away from the cave entrance and plunged straight down from their feet.

Katherine asked, "Is this the cliff you fell off?"

Vietta jumped and the gun barrel wavered. "No. No, this isn't it."

"You mean you never got this close to the cave before?"

"No," she said, a clipped edge to her voice.

Standing, Katherine stretched and wandered with fake interest to the edge of the cliff. "Whoa, it's a long way down."

"Get away from there."

Katherine shrugged. "Maybe I'll fall off and you won't have to worry about pointing that gun at someone."

"I wouldn't wish that on my worst enemy," Vietta muttered.

"I suppose I qualify." Katherine scuffed her foot, kicked pebbles over the edge. "There's quite a view." She pointed off into the distance. "See? There's another cliff right across from here. Is that the cliff you fell off?"

"I don't know." With a rush of ferocity, Vietta said, "You don't know what it's like. Falling through the air, screaming all the way. The bushes slap you, the ground rushes up, one big stone waits to stab you."

Her voice thickened, quivered with intensity until Katherine could imagine the terror. She mocked that terror when she said lightly, "Look straight down there! Why, those rocks look like the inside of a cat's mouth."

"I'm not watching you."

Katherine checked. Vietta wasn't. She had her gaze fixed on a tree not far away, as if she could keep Katherine in her peripheral vision and that would be enough. Katherine moved a step closer to the cave. "Those rocks look like sharp, jagged teeth.

Imagine how much that would hurt if you fell on them." She took another step.

"You'd better stop that," Vietta said in a fierce decree.

"What? I'm just telling you about the view, since you're too cowardly to look yourself."

"I can see you moving toward the cave."

"Were you wearing petticoats when you went over the edge?" Katherine chatted. "I bet if you hadn't been wearing petticoats, you would have been broken up even more. Were there a lot of broken bones?" Katherine saw the way Vietta was sweating in the cool of the shifting fog currents, the way she shuddered in periodic tremors.

Vietta's belligerence grew as her authority shrunk. "I'm going to kill you. I want to kill you. I hate you, with your golden hair and your green eyes and your funny accent. It's going to be fun to kill you. It was fun just cutting your throat a little and seeing you faint like I'd really hurt you."

"Vietta, there's something behind you."

Laughing harshly, Vietta took a step forward. "How foolish do you think I am? You think you can scare me with your talk of falling and cliffs. Yet, when I talk about slitting your throat—"

"Vietta." Something moved over Vietta's shoulder. Katherine squinted, trying to identify it through the restless fog and the shadowy trees. When she saw him, her gasp of horror warned Vietta, but too late.

Vietta swung the pistol as Smith's fist descended.

With a yip of fear, Katherine dove for the cave. "Don Damian," she shouted. Waterfalls of dirt cascaded onto her as she wiggled through the compact opening. Standing, she smacked her head on the rocky wall between her and the outside world, then she stumbled forward to maintain her balance. Her knees met a higher level of the floor; she pitched forward, catching herself with her hands and knees. "Don Damian," she whispered, her voice disappearing as the dust worked on her throat. She wiped at her face with her arm and ground sand into her eyes. She trembled in fear: afraid, alone, tears of pain trickling from under her lids. Where was Don Damian?

Where was Smith?

A noise close to the wall had her scrambling away in a crawl. A large shape swooped on her; crazed, she fended it off with flailing arms.

"Catriona." Damian snatched her to him, rendering her defense ineffectual. "Are you hurt? What happened?"

She hugged him, babbling, "I'm fine. Smith's here."

"*Madre de Dios.* Has Vietta still got the gun?"

"I don't know. I ran in here. What have you found?"

"Not a way out." He dragged her against the wall, back into the shadows. "There's no way out."

"Traps?" She stumbled on the rocky floor, slipped as her feet went out from under her. He grabbed at her; she put her hand down to catch herself. Her hand squished into a wet, mossy spot and slithered away; he seized her when she would have landed in an ungainly sprawl.

"Careful, it's slick." He stopped their forward rush and pressed her against the wall. "If you listen, you'll hear water dripping. Stop here. Here, at least, I know the floor won't collapse."

"Smith?" she whispered.

"Where will we run?" he demanded.

She sagged against the rough rock. This was, indeed, a cave, and a very large one. A soft gray light smudged the outlines of the cavern and its contents. The walls around her curved off into the mountain; beyond that her perception faded. The ceiling, too, extended out of sight. The floor around her looked quite solid, almost flat, and in spots, faintly glistening. Listening intently, she could hear the drip of water and the rush of the wind through unseen vents, carrying the scent of pine.

"It's dark," she said.

"It's the fog," he answered. "If the sun were out, we could see. If the sun were out, they could see us."

She strained her eyes upward. "This isn't just a cave. It looks like a giant crack in the solid rock. I can't see the ceiling, but I can see . . . it looks like . . ."

He stared up. "Yes. Beams."

"Like someone built a kind of open support across the roof. Why would they do that?"

"To prevent a cave-in."

"Oh." Sitting down, she tucked her feet beneath her and rubbed her stinging palms. Grit packed beneath her fingernails, ground in her teeth and sifted from her hair. How she hated the feel of dry dust. It made her shudder, made her long for a bath. Made her realize how foolish she was to worry about cleanliness when death stalked her from all directions. "Everything looks fine. It seems so odd that this place would have such a reputation when—" there was something beside her, and she squinted as she turned her head "—this place would have such a reputation when we haven't seen—" She made an ugly noise. A fellow treasure seeker sat beside her. He stared out of empty sockets, a pile of bones and clothing.

Damian knelt beside her and pulled her away with his hands on her shoulders. Her knees shook as she nestled into his chest. "How long do you suppose he's been there?"

"There's only bones and a few shreds of clothing left, so it's been a very long time." Stroking her back, he clasped her as close as he could. "I should have warned you, but . . . right now, it doesn't seem important to me. I aged twenty years, wondering what was happening to you, trying to find a way out."

She hugged him back, remnants of her panic lending strength to her grip. "Can't we move to a different place?"

"We're hard to see, and I figure that if this character has been in this spot for so long, we'll be safe." He amended it. "Or as safe as we can be."

She curled closer to him, "Did you find any more clocks?"

"Oh, yes. The place is riddled with them, but in this light they're hard to see. I found one almost too late."

"Don Damian?" She ran her hands over him, looking for injuries.

"I'm fine. Only . . . it's a long way down if you take a wrong step. There's a pit over there. I can't get over it or around it." He nodded toward the other side of the cave. "There are some well-camouflaged holes in the floor. It makes me wonder about this whole place."

"What do you suppose happened to them?" she asked, verbalizing the question that vibrated between them.

"Smith and Vietta? Maybe they killed each other."

The silence grew too big, the corpse too present. She asked, "Did you find your treasure?"

"It's not my treasure. And no, I didn't find it."

She looked at him. He was a blur seen from behind her tears. "I feel so helpless. There must be a sensible way out of this, but I just keep wondering if we'll become just another part of this legend."

His palm, rough and scraped and dirty, cupped her cheek. "No. One way or the other, we'll be the end of the legend."

In the dimness of the cave, they stared at each other. It seemed to Katherine she could hear his thoughts, his feelings. It seemed they were communicating on a level above the ordinary. Her weariness, her fright dropped away. If they had this, how could anyone defeat them?

Far above them, outside in the open air, the cloud that surrounded the mountain whipped away like a tablecloth beneath the hand of a magician. Better than torches, better than candles, the sun beamed through the hidden crevices, filling the room with light. It bounced off the shiny wet spots, it created shadows.

"Your hair looks like gold," Damian murmured.

Katherine didn't answer, speechless from amazement. Her shaking hands pushed him around; she croaked, "Look. Don Damian, look."

He followed her pointing finger and rose, transfixed. His

hands hung open at his sides. His torn shirt showed his strong throat and the emotion he swallowed. He looked like a man seeing a vision of heaven.

A sunbeam shone directly on a pillar in the middle of the room, close against the pit. There on a shelf rested a cradle heaped with gold. Huge nuggets of gold and chased golden cups, holy vessels, sacred bowls.

The treasure of the padres.

The cold, hard stone floor made Katherine shift. Tugging at his pant leg like a child seeking attention, she questioned, "Don Damian?"

He never moved. The sun illuminated his face, lending him a perfection that awed her, then angered her. How dared he lust for that gold when so many men had died for it, so much evil had been done for it? How dared he ignore their peril when every move they made, every word they said, weighed in the balance of their survival?

As he gazed with rapture at the gold, she gazed with fury at him. An impulse grew in her, and grew and grew, until she couldn't contain it any longer. Leaning close to his thigh, she bit into the muscle above his knee.

He whirled and leaped back. "What do you think you're doing?"

With elaborate care, she checked her teeth. "Seeing if you loosened any." He exuded menace as he stared down at her. She'd distracted him, yes, but at what price?

With elaborate calm, he ordered, "Don't you ever do that again. Men have divorced their wives for less."

"I think I don't want a man whose interest in gold surpasses his interest in life itself."

He glanced up at the treasure and it trapped his gaze, holding him for a long minute before he shouted towards the ceiling, "I'm not interested in the gold."

Was he speaking to her? She wasn't sure.

Thrusting his hands in his hair, he held his head as if it

ached. "The gold is fascinating. It catches my eye, it holds my attention, but nothing fascinates me like you do." He dropped his hands and stared at her. "Nothing's going to separate us. Not the gold, not your stubborn pride."

"Do *I* fascinate you?" Lacing her fingers, she wrapped them around her knee to still their nervous activity. "Or is it my legal training?"

"What?"

Katherine hurriedly asked, "Would you marry me if I weren't an American and a lawyer?"

His exasperation found vent in a sigh. "What nonsense is this? Only yesterday, you were convinced I *resisted* marriage because you were an American. Now you believe I married you *because* you are an American?"

Picking her words with care, she said, "It has been pointed out to me that you could reserve my legal expertise and my nationality against the day when the Americans take over."

A tremendous crash from the wall turned their heads. A chunk of the rock that separated them from the outdoors collapsed into the hole. Dust and sunlight billowed in, and inside, everything quivered. Damian grabbed her, dragging her against the wall.

Before the dust had even settled, Vietta stepped through a vertical break, coughing and complaining. A hand containing a gun followed her, and Katherine recognized both the gun—it was Damian's repeater—and the hand. It was Mr. Smith's.

"No," Katherine breathed. The near rape, put from her mind by other matters, had affected her more than she realized. Just the sight of the tall man shrugging his way through the wall brought a sick jolt to her system. The cave, previously so large, shrank around her. Stifled, she tried to disappear into the stone and she grasped Damian with all her fingers.

Beside her, he grunted as if he were in pain. "He won't touch you."

He pried her hands off his arm. Blood welled up from ten

little crescents in his skin, and she felt an abstract sorrow for hurting him so. But she couldn't think beyond her terror.

Like a wolf smelling fear, Smith saw her before he saw anything else. "Well, this ain't such a bad cave. I can't imagine what everyone's been bellyaching for. It's big and open. Don't see no traps, and the decorations," he insulted her with his gaze, "are right pleasant to the eye."

"What good does it do you to leer at a woman?" Damian asked. "After the way I hit you?"

Smith answered too quickly. "Takes more than a little pain to stop me."

"I should have killed you when I had the chance," Damian said.

"I would have done it if I'd been you. You go get me all unconscious and tied, and you could have shot me where I lay and nobody woulda cared, and you didn't. Don't understand that."

Speaking in a mumble, Vietta accused, "He's too soft."

Katherine shuddered at the sheer ruthlessness. "Some people would characterize the inability to kill a man in cold blood as a strength."

A new lisp characterized Vietta's speech. "Look where it's gotten us."

Some of Vietta's teeth were missing, Katherine realized, broken out, no doubt, by the same fist that had blackened her eyes and bruised her jaw. "Don Damian and I are in no worse condition. It's you who hired Smith to work for you." Katherine's courage returned as she spoke. "It's you who has brought this disaster on yourself, and you've managed to drag Don Damian and me down also. Don't ask for my pity."

"Saucy little thing, ain't she, de la Sola?" Smith tucked one thumb into his belt and rocked on his heels. "No wonder you like her so much. But I did you a big favor. A big favor. She was expecting happily ever after and all that rot, and I told her the facts."

Katherine cringed under his hearty manner.

"The facts?" Damian asked, cold, uninterested.

"Sure. I told her how you married her just to make sure you can keep ahold of your land when California becomes an American possession."

"Shut up," she said, wringing her fingers.

Without removing his attention from Smith, Damian took her hands and separated them. Holding them, one in each of his, he encouraged, "Go on."

"Told her you'd get rid of her once she served her purpose." He stabbed a finger towards Damian. "But you know, I was thinking. I bet this marriage of yours might not even be legal when the United States takes over. I bet you won't even have to divorce her."

Damian turned Katherine to face him, and she clenched her teeth together. "You believe every word this maggot says, and you won't believe me?"

"Don Damian—"

"If I were going to bind myself in an unhappy marriage, my dear, I would do it for money. It's the best cushion against the future, and I've had offers to do just that."

He blazed with anger, and the previous emotion between them was nothing compared to his bitter disappointment in her. The words were inadequate, but she had to say them. "I'm sorry."

"Hey!" Smith shouted. "Damn it, bitch, get away."

Katherine jumped, but it wasn't her he spoke to. The treasure had shone too brightly for Vietta to ignore it, and she had edged closer and closer. Smith's vendetta against Damian and Katherine interested her not at all. No one person interested Vietta like the cold metal that glinted above their heads. Now she climbed the pillar, finding the toeholds and finger grips that carried her to her goal. Not the threat of the pit beside her, not the danger of the heights, not the pain of her thigh, could dissuade her from her goal. Only a few more steps, only a few more. The sunlight glinted off Vietta's black hair as she reached and strained, grasping the top of the ledge. She almost had it.

Smith lifted the revolver. "Get away from there." Without waiting to see if she obeyed, he aimed.

Without a sound, Damian dove for him. The pistol went flying; Damian flew after it.

Smith shrieked, his attention still fixed on Vietta, and he grabbed her foot from below. "Get away from that. Don't you touch it." He jerked and she slipped, caught herself, dragged herself up. "Get away."

She leaped up and seized the wooden container. Smith leaped after her. Hanging on both her legs, he shook her. Gold showered around them, littering the floor, then the whole box tipped and lurched. It fell with a smack that shook the floor. Gold nuggets, worked vessels, chunks of quartz scattered, skidding over the rocks.

"Hot damn!" Smith jumped down after it, salivating like a wolf chasing a tender child.

Vietta shrieked in fury, then in pain. She couldn't keep a toehold with her damaged leg; Smith's handling had rendered her helpless. Katherine ran toward her, but Vietta slipped, clutched, lost her grip and fell, tumbling to the middle of the cave. The floor broke beneath her. Gravel poured down into the abyss. She screamed, reaching out with flailing arms. She caught at the edge; Katherine caught at her. She pulled at Vietta, dragging her back up on the solid rock.

Vietta sputtered and groaned, resting on the ground.

Katherine stepped away. She leaned her hands against her knees, gasped, tried to pull in enough air.

"Katherine," Vietta whispered, raising herself. "Katherine, thank you." She smiled, showing newly broken teeth. "You fool." She shoved at Katherine, and while Katherine was still off balance, tumbled her into the pit.

15 June, in the year of our Lord, 1777

Fray Lucio sits in the sun and shivers with the cold. He seeks to help by keeping a constant lookout, and I encourage him. Feeble though he is, he wishes to assist in any way possible. I suspect it is to hurry our work here so he can return to the mission and civilization, but I have learned to leave judgment to He who is the governor of all things.

The women work with a will, and I work at their sides, performing tasks I previously considered the province of animals and peasants. My body is strong and hearty. I can lift and carry heavy objects unfit for the weaker gender. Cutting logs, hewing stone, installing the snares to reform the greedy, I take pride in the toil and in my sagacity.

This work which I envisioned in the darkness of the night takes too many days. I fear the noise will bring our pursuers before we have finished. I begin to sense the need to hurry our labors. Every night I pray, every night I listen, and every day I wake with renewed urgency. My premonition of disaster is at odds with the assurance of my God that all will be well, but the Lord is silent on this point. No doubt my understanding of God's plan is so infinitesimal that I am presumptuous in seeking reassurance. Indeed, the mystery of the ages has been the difference between God's definition of grace and man's.

Nevertheless, I hurry.

—from the diary of Fray Juan Estévan de Bautista

Chapter 22

Katherine grabbed the jagged ledge as she went over. Her fingers burned as they slipped on the gravel, and her feet dangled in midair. The air that rushed up smelled like a grave. She jerked when the pistol discharged above her. "Please, God, not Don Damian," she said, gritting her teeth, struggling to get her elbow up. She succeeded, only to have it shoved down again. Above her, Vietta peered down, smiling. Katherine's strength gave way; she hung with her arms extended.

It was night below, but a diffused light around showed her a sheer drop of rock in front of her. She could reach it with her toe extended, but why? Desperately, she glanced around. A few feet away, carved into the rock, was another drawing, another smiling clock. Its hands pointed down. Cursing Tobias's quixotic sense of humor, she realized she would have to move over and let go . . . and hope she landed on something without breaking her bones.

To advance, she would have to move hand over hand, and her mind refused to envision it. Yet she didn't have time to debate with her fear. Impatient to finish, Vietta was staggering to her feet. With the sole of her shoe she ground Katherine's fingers into the crumbling rock.

Katherine wanted to tell her how thin the shelf was, how only an idiot would stand there. But Katherine couldn't free the words from her throat. She could only move her hand to the left when Vietta struck sharply with her heel. Emboldened, Katherine moved the other hand. The rock disintegrated beneath her fingers as she moved hand over hand. Vietta's trampling feet followed with a vengeance.

Katherine wished Vietta's destruction would come with the collapse of the floor beneath her feet, and at the same time prayed that it would not. Tumbling to her death with her enemy was death nevertheless.

The clock was right in front of her, pointing straight down. All she had to do was loosen her fingers . . . loosen her fingers. For some reason, it was important she prove her faith in Tobias by loosening her fingers before Vietta's painful assault forced her to.

Taking a breath, she swung forward and jumped.

She landed almost before she started falling. She tasted blood in her mouth; she'd bitten her tongue. Her spine ached; she'd sat down hard. Crouching down, clutching the rock, she shook with a belated palsy of fear.

She was alive.

Glancing down, the dark rushed up at her, and she bit off a shriek.

A roar from above answered her. Damian called, "Catriona," and his anguish lured the tears from her eyes to splash on the stone at her feet. But at least he was still alive.

She retreated. Her back found the wall; she leaned against it, seeking security in its cool, solid strength. Clearing her eyes, she lowered her gaze. Dizziness assaulted her, turned her stomach, made her break out in a sweat.

She rested on a narrow shelf that jutted from the stone supporting the floor above. Around her, there was nothing. Just a bottomless chasm in endless space. She closed her eyes. She opened them, stared straight ahead, and concentrated. There had to be a way off of this shelf. Tobias had been down here. Tobias had gotten out. There had to be a way off of here. Of course, Tobias would have brought a rope.

A flash from above attracted her attention, and she froze. Vietta's head and two hands, outlined against the light from above, sent Katherine burrowing back. The shadow hid Vietta's expression, but not the searching sweeps of her head as she searched for evidence of Katherine's death.

Katherine didn't blink, didn't breathe, didn't think. A small laugh from above signaled Vietta's satisfaction, and Katherine held herself still until Vietta disappeared. She could hear grunts and cries from above. With her back hard against the chill wall, she fought to stand up. Betrayed by the seemingly solid rock, her head, then her shoulders slipped backwards. Where was the cliff? How could it disappear into a void?

Yet here she was, wedged into a crevasse. She twisted, and her hand met nothing. There should be stone, but it was empty. She squinted at the wall in the twilight. A hole, the darkest part of the already charcoal night, led off into the rock. With both hands, she probed the narrow passage, but she couldn't find the back of it. She pushed her head in; black assaulted her. Her eyes strained against the gloom, and she shut them. She twisted until her shoulders could fit, wiggled until her hips jammed at the entrance, wiggled some more. Her knees, her feet followed, and the burrow widened and lowered.

Her own stupidity stopped her. Where was she going? Into the bowels of the earth? Perhaps Tobias had escaped this way; perhaps not. What if she took the wrong turn? Would she wander until she died?

She tried to look back at the opening, but she couldn't turn enough to do that. This reminded her of a tomb, chill and silent. Would she be buried alive? This was a stupid place to die, and she was afraid. Her trembling made her slip on the damp stone. A drip of water from above made her jump and knock her head; she slithered backwards.

The fetid air moved; a breeze, light and unexplained, touched her cheek. She halted, experienced a tiny surge of courage; remembered her mission and what the stakes were. Somewhere in the cave above her, three people fought, all at odds with each other, and only one could win.

Damian had to win. She would make him win. She would prove herself to him and explain everything.

Thrusting out her hands, she groped forward. The tunnel dropped at first, frightening her again. Then it rose, a tiny passage leading almost straight upward. It twisted to the side. Where was she going? Oh, God, what would she find when she got there?

The tube that contained her lifted again, throwing her equilibrium off until she found handholds and toeholds. She climbed until she wondered why she didn't break through the floor, then she blinked. Was that the light? Staring up, she blinked again. It was. It was light, subdued, perhaps, but after the night in this tunnel, it looked like the blazing sun. Encouraged, she struggled on—and touched something. Something soft. Shuddering, she recoiled, wiping her palm on her skirt.

She could barely see it, a something on the shelf she must use to climb further. What was it? A piece of rotting flesh? A long-forgotten trap? Could she stand to touch it again?

Yet it rested on the one place she must use to climb farther. She had to go on, and she reached out again. A leatherbound book fit into the palm of her hand. Puzzled, she held it, but a sound made her lift her head.

In the tunnel, a low whistling swept her ears, and she obeyed the command of the wind. "Hurry."

His eye was swollen closed, his nose was bloodied, yet Damian lowered his head and drove it into Emerson Smith's belly. The big man went down, and Damian slumped.

Katherine was dead.

Katherine was dead, and nothing mattered. Nothing but making sure that neither one of these animals—not Smith, not Vietta—escaped the consequences of their villainy. If he could just get his hands on his gun. . . .

It had been all he could do to stay out of Smith's grasp. Smith's reach was long; his fingers were like tentacles. His fight-

ing expertise bespoke the streets, and Damian's training with
the vaqueros had been barely enough. Now, Smith writhed on
the ground. If Damian could just get his hands on the gun, the
contest could be his. He would have won the battle, and lost
everything.

If he could just get his hands on his gun; but the gun had
been kicked all over the uneven floor. Vietta scuttled past on
her hands and knees. Damian grinned and stalked toward her.
Her knife rattled to the floor, loud in the cave.

She ignored it. She sought the gun. He would have it first.

Like a wounded rattlesnake striking, Smith grabbed Damian's
ankle. Smith jerked; Damian kicked with his other leg, using his
boot heel to smash Smith's face. Smith's neck snapped back,
and Damian scrambled away.

He couldn't let Smith catch him, for those long arms gave
Smith an advantage Damian couldn't counter. Yet Smith
leaped, tackling Damian and rolling all the way over. The pit
yawned beside them; Damian felt its breath, knew its terror. He
was trapped, Smith on his chest, death beside him. Smith
reached for Damian's throat.

Damian understood Katherine's agony, now. Smith throttled
him, silent, intent, working to finish the job and be done.
Damian struggled, twisting, seeing colors explode and the floor
lift like ripples under his gaze. A shiny object caught his eye.

Vietta's knife.

He clawed for it. Smith pulled him back. He reached again,
and beneath his cheek in a flat paving stone set into the floor,
he saw a clock.

A clock that had the face of death.

He knocked Smith's hands away, rolled and groped desperately. He sought a fingerhold, an edge to lift. His fingernails
scraped in a bone-chilling shriek. There was nothing, and Smith
had him again. In frustration, his fingers closed around a large,
cold rock, a heavy rock. A gold nugget.

Strike Smith? That made sense.

Strike the clock in the floor?

How stupid.

Lifting the chunk of gold, he smashed the clock with all his might. Startled, Smith leaned back and laughed. "You are soft," he shouted. "Soft and stupid, and you're going to die for it."

Above his head, Damian saw the beams move. "Am I?" He pointed up, and the triumph in his face brought Smith scrambling to his feet—right into the path of an oak log, swinging in a wide arc from the ceiling.

It rammed Smith in the chest, lifting him off Damian. The force of it carried him over the pit, slipping down as he clawed frantically at the wood, then back, until his long, dangling legs smacked against the rim. He hung for a moment, an expression of terror and surprise on his face.

He fell, screaming, all the way down.

The log completed its huge arc, its pivot point above Damian. It swung, creaking, and he stirred uneasily. Above him, he saw more movement, as if the whole structure had been unbalanced.

He rolled, snatching up the knife and scrambling for the edge of the cave, for the spot where the dried body slumped in safety. End first, the oak log punched down, crushing away the rock where he had lain. The floor broke off like a piece of hard candy, collapsing into the pit. The beams above groaned in protest; the abyss gobbled the ground around it in mighty chomps.

Damian measured the distance between him and the outside, but the tumult died. Pebbles and sand still slithered down, but for the moment the cave was secure. For the moment, he could seek his revenge.

"Vietta," he called, levering himself up.

Out of the shadows she stepped. "Yes, Damian?"

She held his pistol pointed at him. He had known she would. They'd performed this scene before, but this time there would be a different ending. "Are you going to shoot me, Vietta?"

"Yes." Her lovely voice crooned the word, and she seemed to

take pleasure in the thought. "I want the gold. That's all I want, and I'm going to have it."

The fading sunlight hardly touched him. "You've wanted it for a long time, but it's not real. It's just a rock, like every other rock in this cavern."

"It's not a rock," she declared. "It's gold, and it's real. I've never had it, and I'm going to have it now."

"Love is real, Vietta," he mocked, "and you've never had it."

"What do you mean?"

"What will you do with the gold? Buy yourself friends? Buy yourself a lover? Buy yourself parents who care about you? Why, all of Alta California waits somewhere down the mountain, prepared to kill you for your precious gold. What makes you think you can keep the gold, when you can't even find one person to be your friend?"

"You bastard." Her voice cracked with strain. "When I have the gold, everyone will love me."

His laughter swelled from his toes, from his chest, up through his throat to a full-bodied merriment.

"Everyone. Everyone." She backed from him, her eyes glowing hot. "Everyone." She cocked the pistol, but still he laughed, watching her.

"No one will ever love you with the intensity that I've loved Katherine." His amusement stopped, cut from him with a stab of pain. "You murdered my Katherine."

Vietta fired. A muffled pop, a puff of smoke, and she screeched, her hand burned by the misfire.

From above them, Katherine screamed, "No!"

"Katherine?" Damian leaped for her as she struggled out of the dark opening above their heads. Vietta screeched again, shaking her hand, and he halted, remembering their peril, recalling his need to live.

She raised the gun while Katherine called, "Vietta, no, listen to me."

Vietta didn't listen, didn't even hear. She stared at Damian, muttering, not seeing anything but him and his threat to her plan.

Katherine jumped from her perch. She landed with a thump, and Vietta swung toward her. Surprise, horror, stupefaction shook Vietta. She ran forward, her arm outstretched and the gun pointed at Katherine's head. "You're dead. You're—" She stepped in a wet spot, slipped and twisted; the rock beneath the two women broke with a crack. Damian grabbed for Katherine and threw her behind him. The gun discharged loudly, cleanly. Vietta plunged—into nothing.

She fell in an eerie silence.

Katherine dragged at Damian. She felt him falter as they scrambled backward away from the widening hole. They halted, panting, against the wall. "She missed me," Katherine said. "Look, she missed me."

"I'm looking." Tears swam in his eyes. "You look wonderful."

Her own tears sprang up to join his. "Don Damian, dear Don Damian." She grabbed him, hugged him with all her might.

He groaned.

"Don Damian?" Stepping back, she stared at her hands. They were covered with blood. Memory came in a wash. What would she see when she looked up? Would she see Tobias, dying while she struggled helplessly to save him? Or would she see Damian, dying? "Don Damian?" Her voice quavered in panic.

"Stop it." He grasped her arm and shook it. "I need you, Katherine. There's only you, and you've got to help me."

Encouraged, she peeked at him. He looked even paler than she felt. Red stained the shirt over his ribs, and she could see where the material had been ripped away by the bullet's blast.

His pleasure in the sight of her had faded, replaced by the torment of a man in pain. "I can't make it without help. You'll have to bandage me."

"Yes." Her faint answer disgusted her, and she strengthened her voice. "Yes. I'll help you." With her hand under his arm, she helped him to sit. "Here, right by our friend."

Chuckling at her feeble attempt at humor, he seated himself beside the corpse. "He's more congenial than our other companions have been."

Wetting her lips with her tongue, she lifted her skirt and took a grip on her cotton petticoats. "Petticoats are a woman's disposable garment. I was taught at my mother's knee to tear them in an emergency."

"I'm grateful to your mother." He caught her waist as she ripped the material into strips. "I'm grateful to her for more than one reason."

She never paused, but she put her emotions into the prosaic sentence. "You are a very nice man."

"I was wondering when you'd realize it."

"But your complacency doesn't bear looking into." She monitored him with a hand on his forehead. It felt clammy, at odds with his humor. Taking his hand from her waist, she kissed it surreptitiously and put it in his lap. Ripping at his shirt, she bared his side. She wouldn't faint. She was too sensible to faint. But oh, how could the human body look so much like butchered beef?

"Katherine, what do you have in your pocket?" He tapped the watch pocket at her waist, bulging with the book she'd found.

Distracted, as he'd meant her to be, she lied, "It's Tobias's watch." Shaking out the piece of petticoat, she made a pad and pressed it against him.

Head thrown back, he clenched his teeth as she wrapped the long strips around his chest, securing the flesh and stopping the flow of blood with the pressure. As she tied him, he asked, "Really? It didn't feel like the watch." A large slab of rock fell off into the pit.

"Do you want to discuss it now?"

"Not now." He took her arm and let her pull him up. "Now we should leave, before the sun sets and leaves us here in darkness."

"Yes." They stepped towards the opening, and Katherine tripped on a stone. It rolled ahead of them like a siren, luring them on. The faint light of the setting sun turned the gold to liquid and added tints of red. She picked it up and held it out to him. The nugget was rounded and heavy, and it glowed with all the beauty that tempted men to murder and steal.

He took it, smoothed the surface with his finger. "So many deaths. The padres, first. The vaqueros of long ago, Smith, Vietta, even Tobias. So much pain, all for this accursed gold."

Uncertain of his mood and his thoughts, she asked, "Will you take the treasure with you?"

His crooked smile grew, became wicked and passionate.

In the twilight and the silence she could hear bits of rock crumble away, falling into the abyss. She stirred, anxious about the way his gaze lingered on her face as if he would memorize it for eternity.

He said, "The treasure? It's my treasure. I'll take it." Carefully, he pulled a knife from his belt.

Her gaze fixed on it; she croaked, "Where did you get that?"

"Vietta dropped it." He flipped the knife and caught the handle, and Katherine couldn't tear her eyes from its razor edge.

He murmured, "I've got to get rid of this."

"Yes," she agreed faintly.

With all his strength, he threw the knife—and the gold—into the chasm and turned back to her. "Hurry, my treasure. Let's go while we can."

Love broke over her like an avalanche, burying her in it, buoying her up in it, carrying her along. All the emotion she had suppressed, misunderstood, pretended away overwhelmed her now, and she stepped close to him. "Don Damian, you warm me, excite me, anger me, create a rejoicing in me that I couldn't recognize or put name to." She waved her arm, encompassing the cavern. "In this room, I have seen—" A glimmer on the other side of the chasm distracted her, and she stared into the shadows. There was nothing there, and she continued, "I have seen . . . what is that?" She pointed. "It looks like a—"

"_Madre de Dios,_" he muttered.

"A ghost," she whispered, lowering her arm.

A wisp of fog wavered across the pit. To Katherine's shocked gaze, there seemed to be a figure inside it, struggling to get out. As they watched, the mist resolved itself into a man's figure— the figure of a cowled priest. One diaphanous arm lifted a lighted candlestick.

Katherine found herself outside the cave, clutching Damian's hand, staring at the mountain. "What was that?" she breathed.

The rock on the outside of the mountain cracked and rumbled in reply. Before their eyes, a landslide obliterated the entrance and the rosebush that marked it, while a groan of agony swept from the cavern. A ground tremor rattled their feet, and the precipice where Katherine had frightened Vietta crumbled.

The whinny of a horse cut the air and they whirled to see Vietta's mount struggling as the rocks around it, the tree it was tethered to, the very earth beneath its feet fell away. "No," Damian shouted, lunging at the animal, but Katherine went after him, grasping his coat and pulling him back. In horror, they stared as the horse went down and realized the ground was eroding toward them.

Somehow their feet found the path. Tripped by tree roots, slapped by branches, they descended the mountain. The journey that had taken so long in the morning now flew as they raced away from the cave, the gold, the death. Katherine didn't want to stop. A stitch pulled in her side; the blisters on her feet were bleeding, but the survival instinct urged her on.

Someone—something—pursued them.

At last, Damian pulled her to a halt. She tugged at him, but he shook his head. "I can't run anymore. We're away. Nothing can hurt us now."

She flung out a hand behind her. "What about that?"

He didn't look. "There's nothing there."

"No?" She turned around. "What do you call it?"

"It's fog," he replied shortly.

"Just fog," she agreed. She stared into the white blanket creeping down the hill at their heels. "A sensible woman would realize her fears were just the result of the coming night and the strain of so many harrowing experiences, and she wouldn't imagine ridiculous things when it's just fog."

Something in her face brought Damian spinning to face the fog.

In the midst burned a small flame, like the light from a candlestick. A tremor shook her, like the one in the ground above, but this tremor came from within.

Beside her, a similar tremor shook Damian, but it was stronger, deeper. In a hoarse voice, he told her, "I see nothing wrong with panic."

Inappropriately, she laughed, teetering on the fine edge of hysteria. Whirling to escape, she said, "Don Damian, we're going to be fine."

He didn't move. He stumbled heavily, falling on his knees, and for the first time in their agitated flight, she remembered. He'd been shot. He'd been shot and beaten, and he'd run for miles.

She could appreciate the training he'd received while working with the bulls, the training he'd received from the vaqueros. She could appreciate the jolt that fear had dealt them. For those reasons only had Damian kept pace with her. "Let me help you," she urged. In the waning sunlight, she could see the agony of his one open eye, the pain that clamped his jaw. She knelt beside him, put her arm around him, and the unnatural heat of his body transferred to hers. He was ill and hurt. The mantle of leadership passed into her hands without a word spoken.

"You can do it." She encouraged him with soft sounds as he lifted himself to his feet. His whole body shook under the strain he put on it. He progressed like an old man stricken with rheumatism.

The last light of the sun left them, and Katherine monitored their path with care. The foothills rolled away from them endlessly. The scent of pine should have been a pleasure; the cooling evening breeze should have refreshed them. Instead the tree tops blocked the evening stars that shone, and the wind racked Damian with periodic spasms.

He needed rest. They needed to stop.

But inexorably, the fog followed them, always just at their heels.

The owls hooted, and she remembered the predictions of death she'd used to scare Mr. Smith. She hadn't scared him, but he was dead, anyway. She clasped Damian tighter, willing her strength into him.

They'd gone only a short distance when Damian stopped and sagged against a tree. "I can't go on."

She didn't argue with him. She'd realized for the past hour they couldn't flee from these mountains tonight. "Can you stand alone?" she asked him. "I'll build you a bed from some branches and keep you off the cold ground."

He chuckled, and it sounded more like a cough. "How will you cut them? We've got no supplies. No food, no blankets, certainly no knife." His head drooped against his chest. "Aren't you sorry I gave up my cigars? At least then I'd be carrying a lucifer to light a fire."

"Please, Don Damian." Catching two of the lowest branches in her hands and swinging on them, she broke them off. "I feel guilty about this already. Don't reproach me for your cigars, too."

"Guilty?" Shaking his head, he admonished, "Don't feel guilty, no matter what happens. I'm so proud of you. . . ." He sighed. "I can't stand up anymore."

She rushed for him, but he'd used the last of his energy. He collapsed into a limp pile of flesh.

Her terrified breath cut the silence. Was this it, then? Had she lost another husband to the curse of the padres? More important, had she lost the man she loved? Afraid to touch him, to discover the truth, she pressed his throat. The thump of his heart beat into her fingers. "He's alive," she whispered.

Like a squirrel preparing for winter, she scurried to stack her branches beside him, tucking them beneath his body and rolling him on top of them. Using her primitive technique, she broke more branches and piled them on top of him, covering it all with the tattered remains of her riding jacket.

She sat down and stared at Damian, then at the fog that tiptoed toward her. The fog would kill him. The damp would take this man, leaving her only an empty body, and she couldn't live if Damian died. In a fury, she rose to her feet and stalked to the edge of the fog. Focusing on the wisp of flame that flickered in its midst, she shouted, "We didn't steal any of your gold, so you can't steal my husband. Leave us alone!"

Like a long, low cry of the wind, she heard, "Katherine?"

She stepped back from the fog.

"Damian? Katherine?"

She glanced wildly at Damian, wondering if he would have to answer the entity in the fog. He didn't move.

"Katherine?"

It sounded nearer, and reluctantly she called back, "Yes?"

"Katherine!"

"Yes?"

"Keep calling, *amiga*, keep calling." The ghostly voice sounded frantic, not at all ephemeral, and rather unceremonious. "I'm almost there."

"I know," she moaned, staring into the fog. A clatter of hooves on stone made her think of a hearse, and she swayed. "You can't have him."

"Katherine? Are you ill?"

Hands grasped her shoulders and turned her around. A haggard face floated before her eyes. "Julio," she whispered, and fainted without another sound.

17 June, in the year of our Lord, 1777

I hurt my leg. One of the logs we used to prepare the cave fell from the ceiling and crushed my knee. The bone protrudes from the open wound. I cannot walk. The agony is such that I cannot be moved. God does not hear my pleas for succor or death.

Is this another punishment for my arrogance? For all the times I cared for my fellow man in my infirmary and told them to stifle their cries and seek relief in prayer? Is this a punishment for my pride in my body's usefulness, in my labor? Will I have nothing left when this is done?

—from the diary of Fray Juan Estévan de Bautista

Chapter 23

"Until I arrived in California, I never fainted at the sight of blood."

"So you've said." Julio puffed on the twigs, kindling them with the fire he'd set.

"I was always calm and practical and—"

"Sensible?" he supplied the word with an irony lost to Katherine.

"Indeed. Sensible. In Boston, I could have handled a day like this with a modicum of dignity." She leaned close to the fire pit, catching the warmth with her outstretched hands.

A handful of branches and moss caught as he laid them around the flame. "In Boston, you would never have had a day like this."

"True," she said thoughtfully. "Today, I've been hit and dropped into a pit and shot at and almost been—almost suffered bodily harm."

His razor glance passed over her, exposing more nerve endings, but she couldn't stop making excuses. "And bandaged Don Damian."

"Most women would be hysterical." He added, "Most men, too."

"I've been tripping over gold and outrunning an avalanche."

"And talking to the fog," he said. "Let's not forget that."

"I wasn't talking to the fog." She was talking to what was inside the fog. But she didn't say that. The fog was gone, retreating up the hill as if it knew they were vanquished. There was too much of this day she didn't believe, too much she didn't want to expose to Julio's keen intelligence. Leaning over, she tucked the blankets tightly around Damian's shoulders. "How did you come when we needed you?"

"When Damian's horse arrives at my stable, saddled, demanding entrance, I worry. When I find a crumbling map beneath the saddle blanket and my vaqueros tell me of a parade of criminals across my land and up the mountain, I panic." He poked the fire, adding more wood, bringing it to a healthy flame. "Damian would never 'lose' Confite, so that means there was more trouble than he could handle. Also—" he grinned at her "—we had an unusual visitor."

She raised a puzzled brow at his jocularity. "Oh?"

"A balding Americano, dressed in a ragged outfit, staggered off the mountain."

Light dawned. "Lawrence."

"Yes, your cousin." His sympathy was palpable. "We dressed him and fed him, gave him a horse and sent him on his way."

"Thank you."

"He got lost and ended up back at the hacienda."

She shut her eyes in embarrassment.

"We sent a guide with him, with orders to take him to Monterey."

Her thank you this time was heartfelt.

He grimaced ruefully. "Thank you, indeed. He took the best mount in our stable."

"What?" Katherine cried. "Why did you give him a good horse? He can hardly sit a broken-down nag."

"I owed him."

Katherine pulled a face of disbelief. "You owed him what?"

Julio examined his fingernails. "Money."

"Money?" she asked incredulously.

"Quite a bit of money." He looked into her eyes. "I took his money with the understanding I would help him get you on a ship to Boston."

"You're joking."

He shook his head.

"You're mad."

"Not at all. He made it clear to all of Monterey that he'd gladly pay to have you back. Sooner or later, someone would have taken his money in good faith. I had hoped I was giving you time to escape and breaking his pocketbook."

"Julio, you have no morals." She chuckled in appalled amusement.

Acting as if she'd complimented him, he agreed, "No, I don't, do I? But I don't know if I helped matters any."

"Perhaps you gave us the time we needed to escape from Monterey, and it's hardly your fault that my bumbling cousin stumbled onto one of the worst villains in California." Dropping her head into her palm, she laughed again. "Poor Lawrence."

"Relatives are a burden. It warms my heart to find that others carry this burden, too." He looked thoughtful. "I guess I'd forgotten that."

"What did Doña Maria Ygnacia say when you told her you suspected foul play? Good riddance to the trollop who tried to steal her husband?"

The name of Maria Ygnacia transformed Julio, and the sweetest smile Katherine could imagine lifted his mouth. "Nacia knew the truth of our kiss."

Katherine turned cold green eyes on him, and he shifted uncomfortably. "All right," he allowed. "My kiss. Nacia always knew I was at fault, but she's a woman in love. She wanted to blame anyone but me."

"You created that scene on purpose," she accused.

"And accomplished all my goals." He caught her outstretched hand and kissed the back of her smoky fingers. "I owe you, Doña Katherina. My in-laws are gone, sent away by their daughter. Nacia and I understand each other now. That is why, when I showed her Confite, she packed my saddlebags and put me on my horse with an admonition not to return without you. One of my best vaqueros came with me, and when you fainted he went for Nacia immediately." He nodded down the hill. "She's following with the vaqueros in a wagon, and bringing a mattress, blankets, a ten-course meal and medicines for everything."

"He'll need it." She stroked Damian's sweeping eyebrows. The fever burned her hand, and she winced. "He's getting worse. Are you sure he'll be all right?"

"No hay que achicarse! Keep your chin up. Damian has the constitution of a horse. One little gunshot and a brisk run down the hill isn't going to hurt him."

He didn't look at her when he spoke, and she didn't press him. Right now she needed the reassurance, halting and unsure though it was. "Doña Maria Ygnacia isn't still angry with me?"

"Nor with me, but if you call her by that name, she's likely to snap your head off."

Taking a cloth from the saddlebag, she dipped it in the bowl of water Julio had fetched her and bathed Damian's forehead. "I can't imagine Nacia snapping."

"I couldn't imagine her telling her parents that they would do well to visit elsewhere, either, but that's what she did." He wiggled like a puppy.

"What did Señora Roderiguez say to that?"

Lifting his chest, raising his chin, he converted himself into Nacia's mother. Imitating her slow, precise, aristocratic speech pattern, he said, " 'Maria Ygnacia will come to her senses soon.' "

"And Nacia said?"

He became his own irritating, elated self. "That she had already come to her senses. That nothing she did would ever please them, so she would please the one who matters to her."

"Who's that?" She laughed at his crestfallen pout. "Oh, it's you, is it?"

Tapping his chest, he said, "Only me."

She combed her fingers through Damian's hair in the eternal gesture of a sweetheart. "I wish I had seen it. I can't imagine Nacia doing such a thing."

"I assure you it's true. Nacia is . . . transformed."

"What brought this transformation?"

"I believe you did."

Startled, she watched him in the firelight. "You tease me."

"You've shown us more in the short time we've known you than all the aristocracy of California ever could."

She shook her head.

"You have," he insisted. "Nacia has always been a good, obedient daughter to those people. She had her own way once in her life, when she married me. "I knew that inside her lived the stubborn, determined woman who stood up to her parents and declared she loved me. But since our wedding day, she has devoted herself to proving to her parents she loved them. I had lost her."

"You had lost her, or she'd lost you?"

"Ah." He poked the fire with a stick and ignored her. "Nacia sent a bag of food. Are you hungry?"

Katherine snatched her hands away from Damian and put them in fists at her waist. "You waited this long to ask?"

He fetched a leather bag. "I thought you'd say if you were hungry."

Katherine ripped it away from him, painfully aware of the need that clawed at her belly. "Is there anything we could feed Don Damian, do you think? He feels so limp." Her hands went back to Damian, kneading his shoulder.

"Some beef broth." He recovered the bag and pulled something out. "Eat this while I heat it." He handed her a rolled tortilla.

"I ate once today, a meager meal. Look at this. Nacia sent her cheese-filled tortillas. I'm in heaven. Mmm." She chewed and closed her eyes in ecstasy. "It's marvelous, but it must have gotten gritty in the bag."

"More likely from your hands."

Katherine looked down at her filthy fingers.

"The creek is just across the path." He pointed the way. "Take your time. I'll try to feed your husband."

Katherine didn't take the time to wash as thoroughly as she would have liked, curbed by the memory of Damian, lying there so slack and hot. With a clean face and hands, she returned to the fire. Julio had built it up again, creating a roaring blaze that shot sparks up above the treetops. The smell of soup and meat blended with the smoke, and Damian leaned against Julio's shoulder to sip broth from a cup.

She bounded forward. "Is he awake?"

Damian whispered, "My Catriona."

Kneeling beside the bed of boughs, she stared into his beloved face. "You must get well."

"Yes." As if the words and the effort of eating were too much for him, he drooped, sliding sideways.

She caught him in her arms. Putting down the cup, Julio helped her make him comfortable. "I would like it better," he said, "if he were tossing and complaining. This stillness worries me." Seeing her stricken face, he added, "Of course, I'm no doctor. When Nacia gets here, she'll help him."

The blankets twisted in her hands.

"Better tuck him in," Julio advised. "You have meat cooking on the fire, and you were asking about Nacia and me. I was going to tell you."

She stared at him blindly, not understanding a word.

"I've been fornicating with every loose woman in California in hopes of fathering a child."

She blinked. His bluntness penetrated her stupor. "I—what?"

He seemed pleased that his shock tactics worked. "Nacia and I have been married for years. We have no children."

"No." Katherine wrapped a blanket close around Damian and bent her head, listening.

"Nacia was a maiden when I married her. It's nothing, this producing of children. The lowest gorrón drops his seed and children spring up, unwanted. Yet we didn't have any." He sighed. "I realized that, despite my youthful debaucheries, *I* had no children."

"Most men consider that a fortunate circumstance."

"Such bitterness," he chided, and she remembered what an acute man he was. "There are rumors you've had a bastard child."

"You joke," she said horrified.

"There are always unkind people, and the Americans who come here frequently aren't of the best caliber." He flipped the beef on the fire. A pot steamed on a rock close beside the flame, and he dipped out a bowl and passed it to her. "Not every moment of your existence has been lived under their watchful eyes, and there's speculation."

Not even horror could obscure her appetite, and she savored the spicy beans. "No wonder Señora Roderiguez considered me unsuitable for Damian."

He grinned at such blunt speaking, but he let her distract him. "I tried to keep my experiments quiet, but there's no way a man like me—a bastard, a bad seed—could keep the gossip from spreading. As it spread, and none of the women conceived, I became careless." His lids drooped as he remembered. "Even . . . reckless."

"Julio, you almost killed your marriage for male pride," she reproved.

"No," he denied. "I didn't mind that I couldn't father a child."

She pulled a disbelieving face.

"Well, only a little." He made a so-so motion with his hand. "At one time, I cared too much, but I have become resigned to my unfruitful state. But I did know how Nacia wanted children. She talked about them, longed for them, planned for them."

Incredulous, she asked, "How would producing a baby elsewhere help your marriage?"

"If I could have fathered a child with another woman, Nacia and I would have had hope for a baby of our own. Or perhaps, if Nacia had never conceived, my consort would have been amenable to letting us raise the little one." He shrugged sheepishly. "Stupid, I suppose, but I had to know if there was hope. I was afraid Nacia would leave me."

"Where do you think she would go? Back to live with her parents?"

Her scorn faded beneath his sad dignity. "When she chose, Nacia had a way of leaving me even when we were in the same room. I didn't want the dutiful wife. I wanted Nacia's heart and soul, forever."

Indignant for Nacia, she said, "So you did everything in your power to drive her away."

"Just because spiteful people call me a bastard doesn't mean it isn't true."

"A masterful justification."

He continued hastily, "Nevertheless, you're right. I couldn't stand to see Nacia so unhappy. I didn't stop trying to prove my manhood with every whore down the coast, but I couldn't stand Nacia's unhappiness and the way she supported me against every attack. I made plans to convince her to stay with me."

"As if she needed persuasion," she scoffed.

A smarmy expression of satisfaction softened his face. "She is wonderful, isn't she?"

She enjoyed seeing the cynical Julio moved to adoration by his own wife. "Very."

"I thought to persuade Nacia with my own land. I thought if we could go and build our own house, one that wasn't part of her inheritance, perhaps she could forgive me for depriving her of children. So I played a game of cards with the governor, and won a grant of land in the Sacramento Valley. Hmm, the food's ready." He cut chunks off the beef and handed her his knife, threaded with beef.

The odor of the meat made her mouth water; her first greedy taste burned her tongue. "So why did you kiss me? Why did you fight with Damian? It seems you had destiny in your command."

Rubbing his face, he left a streak of charcoal on his nose. "One day I was in the Sacramento Valley, working like a dog, when I thought—what is Nacia doing while I break my back building a rancho?"

"Pining for you?"

"That didn't occur to me." With wry self-mockery, he said, "I just knew how hurt she'd been about my women. What if she took a leaf out of my book and took a lover? Or several lovers?"

"Nacia wouldn't want revenge."

"No, I know that now. I knew that then, too, but if it was so clear to me that I was without seed, it could be clear to her, too. She did want a child, and she could have one with another man. I told myself it wouldn't matter. If she had a child, I would raise it as my own."

"Noble."

Solemn, he said, "I *would* raise it as my own. I'm the last man to cavil about a child's background. It was the thought of Nacia beneath another man's hands that drove me to drink."

"Literally."

"Yes, and when I'm drinking, I see things with a warped logic. Damian had loved Nacia before I had. He would be her choice to become the father of her child." He handed her a rag. "Damian had everything. He'd always had everything. Anyone else would have killed me for insulting him as I did."

She wiped her hands and handed his knife back. "A healthy dose of cowardice, too. You're a sensible man."

"A high compliment coming from you, indeed."

"Didn't it occur to you it could be Nacia's fault that you had no children? That you'd simply been unlucky in your timing and your choice of women?"

"I wish that were the truth, but I'm afraid it's not. Nacia's parents had nagged us to produce an heir, not unfairly, I thought, and we tried. And tried and tried." He closed his eyes in retrospection. "We've been making regular and passionate attempts our whole married life. Do you understand what I mean?"

"Yes, I understand what you mean," she snapped.

"It's hard to know," he drawled. "You lack the sensuality and emotional good sense our women have."

She turned her face away from the firelight, afraid her own sensuous memories would show in her face.

The sly, amused voice of her companion proved she hadn't concealed her expression. "I have always thought you considered Californio men to be useless. Perhaps Damian has proved we are good at something?"

"You're a pig, Julio." She wet the rag again and laid it on Damian's brow. "What good will such knowledge do me, if fate takes him from me? I'd be better if I'd never met him and lived in ignorance all my life."

He leaned over her and knocked her hand away from Damian. "Never say that. To live without ever having loved? Without the pain and the effort and the kind of physical pleasure that brings tears of delight to your eyes?"

"I was happy before."

"You were not even living before," he said. "Katherine, listen to me. We're alike, you and I. We're the outcasts. I'm Spanish, I'm Californio, I'm a man, but none of that cancels the fact that I'm a bastard, and there's no way to change that." He waited.

She waited. She didn't want to ask, but he wouldn't continue until she signified her curiosity, so she answered with a grudging, "I agree."

"You're an Americana. You're educated, you're cultured, you're a lady, but none of that cancels the fact you're an Americana. More than that, I think, you've been an outcast your whole life, simply because of the mean-spiritedness of your family."

"Yes."

"We're both married to people who are the epitome of California society, and we will never, ever, measure up to that society's expectations of a mate for Nacia, a mate for Damian."

"True."

A little smile quirked his mouth at her monosyllabic answers, but they satisfied him. "No matter what we do, no matter how properly we act, for the whole rest of our lives we will hear the occasional hiss of a narrow-minded person. Nacia doesn't care what they say about me. She never did. Only I care."

"You're a good man," she offered.

"I know. But still I hurt when they whisper 'bastard' just loud enough so I can hear. Only with Nacia, I forget the hurt." He tapped his chest above his heart. "Damian loves you."

"He hates Americans."

"But he loves *you*. I've known Damian my whole life. He'll grow with California, adjust to the invasion. The only thing that would ever harm him is if you don't trust him enough to give him a chance."

She stared at him, unmoved by his vehemence.

"Katherine. My mother-in-law married at thirteen. She hasn't changed an opinion or shared an emotion in all that time. Nacia was sixteen when she married me, yet she could teach her mother everything about life, about kindness, about joy. Nacia makes me whole. I make Nacia whole." His palms joined, fingers twining. "If Nacia vanished from this earth at this moment, I would still be more than I was before. Has Damian taught you nothing?"

She looked down at her own hands as they stroked Damian's head. She thought about the things that Damian had taught her. About passion, and tenderness. About the impatience of a man ignored, and his sweet revenge. About adventure and trea-sure—real treasure, the kind she'd seen in his eyes.

Whatever she had been shifted. A new person emerged, forged of the old Katherine and the strands of Damian.

Like a newborn, angry at being thrust from the safety of her previous being, she cried through the long night until she slept, exhausted, at Damian's side.

"What will she do when he dies?" Nacia whispered, her gaze resting on the two still figures in the sickroom.

"I don't think it has even occurred to her," Julio answered solemnly. "She's kept him alive this last week with her sheer strength of will."

"The fever burns him and I can't stand to watch her hover over him." She touched his hand. "Night after night, she stays and strokes him with cool cloths and talks to him. She naps only for a few morning hours, when his fever's down. This is the first time I've seen her asleep at night."

"Poor woman. She's exhausted." Julio held the door for his wife as they looked in on the sickroom. "If anyone can save him, just from pure determination, it's Doña Catriona."

Nacia acknowledged the use of Katherine's pet name with the scrape of her fingernails lightly across his stubbled chin. "You admire her?"

He caught her hand and kissed the palm. "Almost more than any other woman in the world. Almost."

She leaned against him and his arm went around her, their own love all the sweeter as they realized how near the long parting was for their friends. Quietly they crept away, leaving Katherine in the big easy chair they'd placed for her comfort.

One candle burned low at Katherine's elbow. Her unresisting mind had at last sunk into the slumber she so desperately needed. Exhaustion had worn her down like the drip of water on cave rock. Sleep nourished her like sunshine on a mountain evergreen.

And like a journey she couldn't resist, she followed the sunshine up the mountain and into the cave. She sought something, although she didn't know what. There was something in that cave to help her, to help Damian, and she sought it with dream recklessness.

Baffled, she turned and looked down the mountain and she could see all the way to Julio's house.

That something was in the room with Damian.

Abruptly, she was back in the chair, pressed against the cushions and staring towards the bed. *He* was there, leaning over Damian. She'd never seen him as more than a fog, or a diaphanous form seeking human shape, but she recognized him. Tall and powerful, he exuded the kind of aura only men with a mission displayed. Clad in a brown wool cowl pulled close around his face, he laid a hand on Damian's chest.

Stiff with dread, she tried to move. She tried to speak.

She was paralyzed. That's because I'm asleep, she told herself with dream logic. I can't move because I'm asleep, and that cowled figure isn't really here.

But he looked so real. She had to help Damian.

When she heard the deep and painful breaths that shook Damian's chest, it released her paralysis. Leaping to her feet, she screamed, "Leave him alone. He's mine."

That woke her. That released her from the nightmare, only she was standing up and her eyes were open.

She could still see him. The priest. The priest from the cave. He looked up at her, and deep inside the cowl she saw the gleam of two eyes. He lifted the candle he held and cast a light on her and on Damian.

Then he disappeared.

She blinked, but the candle left a little blot on her vision, sensitized by the darkness.

Julio and Nacia burst through the door with three servants on their heels. "What happened?" Julio shouted.

On the bed, Damian jumped and groaned, and Julio ran to his side.

Nacia grabbed Katherine's arm and shook it. "What's wrong? Why did you shout?"

Still caught by the dream, Katherine asked, "Did you see him?"

"See him?" Nacia's hair swirled around her shoulders as she glanced around. Her eyes fixed on the bed. "He's there. Damian's there. See?"

Crouched over the still figure, Julio muttered, "Hail Mary, full of grace."

In a tremulous voice, Nacia asked, "Have we lost him?"

Julio lifted his head, strong emotion twisting his features. "The fever has left him. He'll live."

Nacia ran to the bedside and laid her hands flat on Damian's face. "It's a miracle. A miracle. Katherina!" Sharply, she scrutinized the stunned woman by the armchair and bounded over to her. "Come here. Feel him. He's going to be all right." Dragging Katherine by the arm, Nacia thrust Julio aside and placed one of Katherine's palms on each of Damian's cheeks.

"He's going to be all right," Katherine repeated. Joy burgeoned in her, pushing aside the fog of sleep and the magic of the dream. Looking at Julio and Nacia and their stunned, blissful smiles, she laughed a little and stroked the beloved, bearded face.

"You did it," Julio told her. "You pulled him through, with your prayers and your attention."

"Maybe." She nodded, her eyes unfocused once more. "Maybe my prayers did bring that priest to save him."

"What priest?" Julio asked. "There hasn't been a priest in the room."

"Later," Nacia interrupted him. Hurrying to the window, she scolded, "Why did you open this? The draft is too much for a sick man."

Chapter 24

"You're enjoying this, aren't you?" Julio asked as he walked along the path beside Damian.

"Whatever do you mean?" Damian asked right back.

"This." Julio waved his hand. "Being carried home to Rancho Donoso on a sumptuous litter by four vaqueros. Having your father ride back and forth to check on your progress. Having Fray Pedro de Jesus leave San Juan Bautista and go to your home to perform the wedding ceremony. Having Katherine hover over you like a brooding hen."

"Especially having Katherine hover." Damian grinned, relaxed in the sunshine.

"How do you feel?"

"I enjoy having Julio hover, too." Damian gave a crack of laughter at his friend's grimace. He pressed his side with his palm. "I feel tired and sore." He looked sideways at Julio and caught Julio looking sideways at him.

"Two months is a very long recovery for someone of your robust health."

"You're a suspicious soul."

"Suspicious? Suspicious isn't the right word." Julio tapped his lip. "Incredulous is a better word. Disbelieving. Skeptical."

"What would make you—" Damian hesitated "—skeptical?"

"Many things can make a man skeptical. Things as simple as walking past the window of the sickroom and seeing the invalid trotting across the room. Things like watching him stretch and turn."

"Julio—"

"Things like standing out there and feeling like a fool."

"Now Julio—"

"What in the hell have you been hoaxing us for?"

"Shh." Damian glanced at the vaqueros that carried his litter and ordered, "You never heard this." Their smiles flashed in reply. "I have my reasons for playing the convalescent. For one thing, it's kept Katherine close."

"Oh, it's done that," Julio snapped. "The girl is pale from lack of sun."

"I know and I'm sorry, but I'm not in any condition to go chasing after her should she decide to travel to snowy Boston or sunny Los Angeles."

Julio grunted.

"For another thing, I recovered so rapidly that I felt a fraud. I can't remember when I've felt so good."

"Surely an exaggeration."

Damian rolled his neck on the pillows. "A little achy, perhaps, but good. Katherine and I aren't as fortunate as Nacia and you. There are still things that need to be settled between us. With Katherine, I prefer to have the upper hand. The element of surprise."

"All right," Julio said, the grudge fading from his voice. "That's what I thought. My first instinct was to come in and punch you in the nose, but I decided I'd done enough of that."

Damian covered his nose with one protective hand. "Please, no. I couldn't take any more weeks of recuperation."

"Amen to that," Julio agreed fervently. "You're a dreadful invalid."

"Yes, well . . . at last I've been cured of my craving for cigars."

"Totally cured?" Julio started laughing at the irony that slanted Damian's mouth.

"I came too close to smelling the fires of hell to wish for a flaming leaf in my mouth."

Julio laughed until the ladies turned around and smiled at the sound of mirth, until the vaqueros joined in out of sympathy.

Damian punched Julio's arm. "If I don't get a chance later, I want to thank you."

Julio waved a dismissing hand. "Think nothing of it. I liked it when you were cranky and lucid."

"As a contrast to unconscious? I'm flattered. But Julio, I will not allow you to deflect my gratitude. Katherine told me about your rescue that night and Nacia's efforts the next morning to revive me."

"It was all Katherine," Julio answered. "I've never seen anyone so determined."

"She's lost weight."

"She would hardly eat. I tell you the truth, Damian, Nacia and I had given up on you. That last night when you were so sick, I didn't expect you to see the morning. When Katherine screamed—"

"She screamed?"

"I don't know that I should tell even yet. It was odd." Julio observed his friend. Damian smiled at him reassuringly, and he confided, "She screamed, 'Get out.' When Nacia and I ran into the room, she was staring at you as if she were insane. The window was open. Your fever had broken."

"It's very confusing," Damian murmured. "And probably meant to stay that way."

"Look." Julio put his hand on Damian's shoulder. "There's the hacienda."

"Rancho Donoso." Damian told the vaqueros, "Stop and let me look."

Before them, the Salinas Valley rolled out, fertile and green with the flush of June. The hacienda stood decorated with the colorful banners of his homecoming. The servants waved white handkerchiefs from the porch. It had been over two months since he'd ridden away from it. More than once he'd thought he would never see it again.

"I must be weaker than I thought," he murmured, wiping away the salt water he found on his cheeks.

Propped up on the bed pillows like an Arabian potentate, Damian complained, "I could have washed away on a river of tears."

Katherine smiled as she progressed around the attic bedroom, settling her belongings once more.

"Everybody—the servants, my father, Nacia—wept and wailed as if I *had* died," he said.

Wrapped in one of her secret little silences, Katherine glanced at him. Since the morning he'd awakened in the de Casillas bedroom, she'd been restrained and quiet. Nacia told him about Katherine's devotion, and he'd put her peculiar quiet down to weariness. Now he wondered.

Using his querulous invalid voice, he demanded, "Come here."

On a cloud of powder and soap, she came to the bedside. Her hands smoothed his brow. He didn't even think she knew she had done it, but it gave him hope. "Lie down on the bed with me."

"What?"

"Come on, come on." He waved his hand at her. "You rode half the morning. You were in charge of getting me carried up the stairs. You bathed me and put me in my nightshirt. You got rid of the soggy servants. Take off your shoes and lie down. You're tired."

She stared at him as if he'd gone mad.

"Don't you think I can tell if you're tired? Take off the dress, too. I need a nap. So do you."

"You'd sleep better alone," she said gently.

"That just proves you're not always right. Turn around and

let me unbutton you." He shoved at her. "What happened to your riding habit?"

"My riding habit?" She sounded amazed, and she turned obediently. "What riding habit?"

"The royal blue one. The one you wore to become a heroine."

"It's in a bag somewhere." She shrugged under his hands. "I thought I'd burn it after I showed it to your father."

"The state of it should shock him. The next riding habit he gives you will be made of iron." He patted the bare skin above her chemise. "Don't burn it. I'll save it to show our grandchildren, to prove what an extraordinary woman their *abuela* is."

She didn't say a word about that. She dragged the new dress off her shoulders and kicked off her shoes. He examined her remaining clothes. The chemise, the corset, the petticoats, the stockings. "You'll never be comfortable in all that." He snagged his fingers in her corset strings as she tried to move away. "I'll loosen your corset, you put on your nightgown."

"Don Damian, it's just after noon."

"What better time to take a siesta? If it were nightfall, we'd be going to sleep. Hurry up. I'm getting cranky."

Turning, she watched him thoughtfully. "You do a lot of that when you don't get your own way."

He widened his eyes.

Removing her nightgown from a chest of drawers, she moved behind the screen and he heaved a silent sigh of relief. Katherine was too clever. Now that her shock and distress had eased, he had to move fast. Settling himself on the pillows in an artistic pose of suffering, he closed his eyes and waited.

In his mind, he imagined her every move.

She was taking off her clothes and hanging them neatly on the pegs. She was donning the soft cotton gown, her arms outstretched as she put first one, then the other in the long sleeves. It slithered around her breasts, her waist, her legs. . . .

He clenched his fists, fighting down a groan. Playing sick was more difficult than he'd thought.

She was fastening the long row of buttons from the floor-length hem to the collar; she was walking to the bed, lifting the sheet, snuggling close to him. She should be with him by now. She'd had sufficient time to change. Hearing the soft rustle as she moved past him, his suspicions crystalized into certainty and he barked, "Get in here." Opening his eyes, he lifted the covers. "Get in. You don't need to sleep in a chair anymore."

Her guilty look betrayed her. He tried to appear both stern and irascible, and apparently he succeeded. With suitable meekness, she climbed into bed, making soft noises about not hurting him.

He tried to avoid looking at her, all prim in her nightgown. For a man who'd faced death not two months before, the sight of her proved magnificently invigorating. He didn't want her to know yet. He'd been languishing in a mixture of infirmity and desire for too long to spoil his plan at this late date. She tucked her feet inside the gown to keep from touching his bare legs, and he ordered, "Lie here on my shoulder, where I can hold you."

"Your wound—"

"That's true." Stroking his chin, he suggested, "Climb over me and sleep against the wall."

"If you need something—"

"I won't."

Her shift over the top of him wasn't nearly as tidy as she would have liked. He could tell by the squeak of dismay when her knee touched down between his legs, by the way she gathered the sheet close to her neck. He gathered her against him in a grasp that belied his supposed weakness, but he was past the point of caution. "Your hair's all fastened up." Attacking her pins, he pulled them out with ungentle hands.

"Ouch. That hurts." She swatted at him. "I'll have a mess. It's still damp from my bath."

"So?" He dropped the handful of hairpins beside the bed. "Mine's still damp from my bath, too, but I'm not complaining."

"It'll take me forever to comb it out."

"Go to sleep. You'll need it." He wondered if the threat had carried too plainly into his voice, but he didn't move again, seeking slumber greedily as a bolster against later weariness.

As the afternoon reached its zenith, that moment when the sun shone brightest before it began to dip towards evening, his inner clock woke him. His fingers prickled; Katherine still slept, tucked onto his shoulder. He liked it; he absorbed the closeness, satisfied with it for the moment. That moment wouldn't last long, he knew, but he'd learned to treasure every bit of happiness as it came his way. Flexing his hand to bring the circulation back, he eased her head onto the pillows and faced her.

As she had predicted, her hair was a mess. An erotic, tousled mess.

He loved it. He loved her.

There was unfinished business in this bedroom. Not merely the unfinished physical business, but the unfound solutions to their disagreements. Damian was a wiser man than he'd been before; where before he'd made love to Katherine to stir her desire and satisfy his own, now he made love to Katherine to bind her to him. With this woman, he needed every advantage, no matter how unfair. A little smile crept over his face.

If he found rapture in this curbing, so much the better.

Like thieves, his fingers wisked down her buttons and stole her covering. The buttons close to her feet proved to be the most difficult; his eyes were occupied by the glories above, and he fumbled. This wasn't the return of his illness, only proof that his memory could never replace the reality of Katherine.

The bruises and scrapes of their adventure had healed. Only here, on her knee, and there, on her ankle, were faint pink reminders of pain. The skin of her fingertips were no longer ragged from her struggle with rock and rope, but callouses still marred her palms. He kissed each mark in homage.

Damn, the woman had long legs. Muscular, too. The type that could wrap themselves around a man and never let him go.

Once, he'd promised her heaven.

From her ankle, his hand skidded to her thigh, then her waist. Strands of her long, blond hair tangled around her hip; he pushed them aside. He dipped his tongue in her navel, and the act that it symbolized crystalized in his mind.

He whispered soft curse words against her skin as he fought to maintain his sense of balance. He'd schemed for this moment. He'd imagined every variation possible. But in every version, Katherine had been mindless with pleasure. Mindless, overcome, and less than her sensible self. In no version had he had to fight for his own control, but he should have suspected it. Had there ever been a time when he hadn't desired her? Perhaps before he'd known her—even then he'd known she was out there, somewhere.

Mindless? He could make her mindless, but was she ready for novelty? Waves of temptation swept him. His lids drooped as he remembered her surprise in her own erotic savagery. The pleasure he found in her overwhelmed him, and deliberately he followed her lure. His freshly shaved cheek glided down.

He explored every curve of her, relished every flavor, used all his skill to arouse her fledgling hunger. This was Katherine.

Rising to rest on the pillows close against her, he smoothed the ridge of her nose, the ridge of her eyebrows. He waited until she opened her eyes.

"You are the most magnificent woman in the world." He said it as if he meant it.

"I don't feel like that," she whispered. "I can't imagine why you would think so."

"That's not the right answer," he reproved. "You're to tell me I'm the most magnificent *man* in the world."

"You're the most magnificent man in the world," she repeated obediently.

"Who would the most magnificent man in the world pick as his mate?"

Eventually she suggested, "The most magnificent woman in the world?"

"That's correct, _mi vida_. Now close your eyes and let me kiss you."

It was easy to let her eyes glide shut, easy to let him sample her mouth.

"You're mine." He held her head in his hands. "Forever mine."

She didn't answer, only stared at him with her heart in her eyes.

Still, the unspoken feelings of her heart weren't enough for him. His hands dropped away and he sighed.

"This is too much for you," she said, struggling from her lethargy.

He couldn't allow that. Wetting his finger in his mouth, he smoothed the rim of ear. "Such erotic little shells," he murmured. "You like that, don't you?"

She shuddered at the chill his touch created, her breasts tightening. Her gaze dropped to her chest; she seemed to be aware of her near nudity for the first time. Tweaking her buttons back into their holes, she scolded, "You must go back to sleep."

"Sleep?" His laugher hiccuped from him. "I'm afraid that's quite impossible." He took her hand and wrapped it around him. She jumped as if she'd been burned, stammering, "Oh."

"Oh?" he teased, all confidence and amusement. "Is that the best you can do? What about, 'let me help you take care of that'? Or 'lie still, darling, and I'll do the work'?"

"You're in no condition to do anything." Caution and curiosity fought a battle; curiosity won. "What do you mean, I can do the work?"

He settled himself against the pillows, trying to look tired, but not too tired. Ill, but not too ill. "I need support for my head," he complained.

Leaning over him, she adjusted the pillows. Her breasts, barely covered, swung against his chest. He wanted to cup one in his hand, but instead, he asked, "Could you help me take off my nightshirt?"

She sat back a little, but he kept his gaze fixed on her lips. "I feel like half a man. I have this—" she wrestled him a little when he brought her hand to him again, but he won the skirmish "—but I can't do what my body wants me to. If you could help me . . ."

A frown puckered her forehead.

"Only if you still feel like it," he added faintly. Would she take the bait? The bait of pleasure for his sake? His backup plans were endless, but the longer they waited, the stronger she would be. He wanted to exhaust her with passion, relax her with love.

She helped him to sit up, lifted his nightshirt over his head. "I'll do whatever you want."

Absently, her hands stroked him and he braced himself against his surge. If she'd looked into his face at that moment, she'd have known . . . but she didn't.

She stared out the window as if she could distance herself from her act. "It's just I've never done anything like this before."

"Your buttons are crooked."

"What?" Her gaze flew back to his.

Sweeping her conservative neckline, the tip of his finger just brushing her skin, he repeated, "Your buttons. They aren't in the right buttonholes."

She didn't want to change them. He could see that. But her clumsy fingers unbuttoned the buttons—all the buttons. She glanced at him when they were open, and he shook his head. "What do you mean?" she asked.

"You know what I mean." His hands met hers. "There can be nothing between us. There's no shame in this. We're married."

"Not according to the Church."

"Even if we never go before a priest and speak our holy vows, we will be married. Even if we'd never stood before the *alcalde* and repeated our civil vows, we would be married. Our marriage is of two souls, two bodies." With a gentle care, he eased her towards him. "Watch. Watch as we fit together."

Her nipples touched first, nestling into the hair that covered his muscles. Her breasts flattened. Their two bodies connected as they pressed together, from the stitching of his bandage to their bare stomachs, their bare chests.

His hand cupped her face, lifted it to his. Their lips almost touched; their eyes locked. "*Por favor, mi mujer.* I die for you." He pushed her nightgown off her shoulders; she let it drop off her hands.

"Tell me if I hurt you," she whispered.

"Tell me if I excite you," he whispered back. "Tell me of every feeling. I want to hear."

Tanned skin and light skin. Tough muscles and soft curves. The contrasts occupied her as he moved surely to his goal.

All her shyness melted in the heat of the afternoon, the heat of his gaze, the heat of his enthusiasm. "I've never seen another woman as wonderful as you. I've never felt a woman . . ." He closed his eyes as if her ecstasy was his.

She put one palm flat on his stomach.

He opened his eyes and stared into hers. "Who taught you to tease?"

She tried to speak, but she could only whisper. "You did."

"It's all right, then." He halted, the effort of coherence too much for him. "I've never felt a woman as wonderful as you. Did I say that already?"

"You tried." She moved closer to him. "Oh, Damian, I wish I knew what to do, how to please you."

"I'm losing my eloquence." His laughter rippled, hoarse and

deep. "I'm losing my mind. I want to feel you in another way. Please, Katherine."

He brought her close, and her hands grasped his shoulders for support. Deftly, he caught one breast in his mouth. She waited for directions, waited in suspense, and he murmured against her skin, "Surprise me."

Chapter 25

Katherine tucked her cheek tighter into the curve of Damian's shoulder and stared out the window.

This was Damian, the man she loved. That would never change, could never change. But that rush of euphoria she'd experienced up on the mountain had changed. Now when she thought of loving him, a pain sank its claws into her.

Any other woman would have understood her emotion sooner; her own good sense had denied her that knowledge. Good sense said that two such unlikely people could never form a functioning union. Good sense was undoubtedly wrong.

She loved him. He loved her. Life was perfect. Except for the fear that tightened in her belly whenever she remembered how fever and infection had overwhelmed his defenses. Death would put no better mask on him than it had on Tobias or on her mother.

She'd loved them, too. Tobias she'd loved with the whole-hearted gratitude of a prison escapee for her partner in crime. Her mother she'd loved with the devotion of a daughter. They were both dead, and when they'd gone they'd ripped her soul into bits. She'd put herself together again, but her soul wasn't whole. Some parts of her soul she'd never found again. Some parts wouldn't fit back in.

Now she loved a man who had the ability to destroy her. Julio was right, she knew. Everything he'd said on the mountain was right. She was better for having Damian. Still she held a tiny shield between them, protecting herself just in case . . . just in case he fell from his horse or was killed by a lightning bolt or caught pneumonia or . . . died of old age at her side.

"Katherine." His voice was a bass rumble under her ear. "For a woman who's clinging to me in a most intimate manner, you're remarkably stiff."

"Am I hurting your side?" she asked, but she didn't stir.

"Not at all. It's almost healed, which is more than I can say for us." He rolled over and she rolled with him, landing on her back on the sheets, the pillows skittering away.

Like a procrastinating child, she stayed close to him, hoping to avoid the confrontation she knew was coming. He peeled her away, forcing her head back with his hands on her hair. "Katherine, do you really believe that I would marry you for what you can do for me? I can say with all honesty that such mercenary scheming never crossed my mind."

His eyes pierced hers and she blinked away the shame that rose in her. "I should never have believed Smith. That was foolish of me, and I can only offer my agitated state of mind as an excuse."

"Are you sure he didn't echo your own suspicions?" he asked shrewdly.

She stirred against him, and he flung a leg across her to keep her in place. "The heart of the matter," he marveled.

"I could never understand why you wanted to marry me." Her hands clenched in fists at his shoulders. "When Smith said you'd married me because I could help you keep your land, it seemed such a good idea, so sensible."

"Was perhaps something you wanted to believe? You have let your family have too much influence over you. You believe them when they say you have no worth."

"I don't!" She bit her lip. Her very vehemence betrayed her.

"Yet any man would be privileged to marry you. Why do you think I laid claim to you so quickly?"

"You said it was to protect me from harm," she pointed out.

He shifted under the prod of culpability. "That's true, but not entirely. If I hadn't, every other hidalgo in California would have been around you." His indignation at the thought showed in the flare of his nostrils, the straightening of his shoulders. "I have saved myself many duels."

"That's sensible," she approved.

She was laughing at him. A self-conscious smile crooked his mouth, and he pinched her ear lightly. "You'd do well with a little conceit—but not too much."

"No, Don Damian."

He sobered at her words. "I have tried to show you, with words and with my body, how I love you. Now I need to know. Do you love me?"

She wanted to say so. She wanted to. But her lips wouldn't form the words. It would be too real if she admitted it. Perhaps the gods would hear and snatch him from her. Tremulously, she smiled at him. "Do you think we could host a fiesta? We could reaffirm our vows."

"Our vows?"

"Our wedding vows. In front of Mr. Larkin."

"Larkin? Why?"

"He's the American consul, you know. And we could invite *Alcalde* Diaz to officiate, too. Fray Pedro's already coming, as quickly as he can move, he said. That will make our marriage official in the United States, in California, and in the Catholic Church." Encouraged by the grin that threatened to break over his face, she blurted, "No one would dare dispute it then, would they, Don Damian?"

He stroked the line of her chin with his thumbs. "No, *mi amor, mi vida*. No one would dare dispute it then."

Damian was a man who appreciated respect. He appreciated the old ways and the use of honorary titles. Yet as he worked his way through the throng of wedding guests, he wondered when

Katherine would dare to call him Damian. Not *Don* Damian. Just Damian.

Probably about the same time she gave him a real answer to his question. He'd tried to be satisfied with her unspoken affection. She was from Boston. Perhaps she couldn't say what was in her heart. Perhaps she would never say what was in her heart. He'd never realized what an unabashed sentimentalist he was until he'd been blessed with a decorous wife.

Julio caught him as he walked past, mingling with the people who stood in clumps among the trees. "We can't wait much longer to begin the ceremony, or all your wedding guests will be fighting."

"I know. Have you seen Mariano yet?"

"No." Julio raised his voice above the noise. "None of the Vallejos are here, and I've never seen such a crowd as this. All the talk is about Castro, Frémont, and the Americans. There are more rumors than limbs on a tree."

"I know," Damian repeated. "It's been a mere four months since my fiesta. We're here at Rancho Donoso, in the same place with the same people, yet it seems our world has changed."

"Not all the same people are here," Julio said.

"Who? Oh, you mean Smith. We won't miss him."

"And Vietta and her parents. They're still in mourning for their heroic daughter who tried to save you and Doña Katherina and tumbled to her death. That was a kind thing you did, Damian."

"There's nothing to be gained by exposing the truth. Let the poor girl rest at last." He didn't want to talk about Vietta. He didn't want to remember Vietta, or the treasure, or the cave. Inside him, he was a brew of frustration, worry, and just plain fear. It was bad enough that the Vallejos hadn't arrived. That meant something awful had happened in the unstable world of California politics.

On top of that, he was getting married.

Somehow, sweeping Katherine off her feet and in front of the *alcalde* hadn't been nearly so nerve-racking.

Nothing had ever been so nerve-racking. A million preparations hadn't distracted him from the fact that Katherine was becoming his official wife. His greatest ambition would be attained. He stared at the hacienda. Inside, he knew, the women milled around, preparing the bride with their female rites and their womanly warnings. He wished this wedding were over, that Katherine were back in his bed where she belonged.

If only the guests behaved. If only no one threw up, or fainted, or cried so loudly he couldn't hear the vows. If only Fray Pedro de Jesus refrained from admonishing him in front of the crowd and his guests.

If only Katherine didn't change her mind.

He wiped his palms on his jacket. "Have you seen Señor Larkin, yet?"

"No, he's not here," Julio denied.

"Let's wait a little longer." Damian wondered if he were stalling for the Vallejos or Señor Larkin or for fear of the wedding ceremony.

His guests were indeed drinking. The talk was loud and ugly in places. In other places, groups huddled in hushed, serious discussion.

His father stopped him as he paced past the quiet ranchers. "These gentlemen say Castro's on the move."

"Against whom?" Damian asked sarcastically. "Is he going south to fight Pio Pico or north to fight Frémont?"

A ripple of laughter stirred the group. Don Lucian said, "It is indeed a question. Does General Castro consider the Mexican governor in Los Angeles a greater threat than the Americans?"

"I don't know," a young man said, "but the Americans say Castro is stirring up the Indians in the Sacramento Valley."

"Isn't that asking for trouble?" Damian asked. "Do the Indians care whether it's a Californio or an Americano scalp they take?"

The ranchers nodded agreement.

"There aren't many Californios in the valley," one offered.

"Cold comfort for the one who loses his scalp."

Don Lucian slapped his son on the shoulder, and Damian moved on to the boisterous group.

Rico grabbed him by the arm. "Have you heard? Frémont's on the move. The Americans in the Sacramento Valley are gathering."

"Not surprising, if they've heard that General Castro is raising the Indians against them," Damian answered.

"That's just a rumor," Rico said with scorn. "The truth is that some Americans stole a herd of horses that were being transported for Castro."

"Stole them?" Damian was stunned. "What do you mean?"

"I mean that Zeke Merritt led a bunch of wild Americans on a thieving spree," Rico insisted.

"Zeke Merritt? That explains a lot. Zeke Merritt hates Mexicans, and he's a man to hold a grudge. I'm not surprised to hear that Merritt's behind the trouble. Let's hope he stops with the horses."

"We'll see." Alejandro snorted.

"Yes, we'll see." It was Hadrian, coming from the stables, sweating and smelling of horse and looking not at all like a wedding guest. "I've just come from Sonoma, and by the saints, you'll never believe this."

"What?" the group asked in unison.

"Some Americans—the ones who stole the horses—they captured Sonoma, taking Mariano Vallejo prisoner."

A silence fell over the brash group, a silence that grew and overlapped into the other groups. Whispers ran through the crowd; everyone pressed closer.

"What have they done with Mariano?" Rico asked in alarm.

"Drunk him under the table, for one thing." Hadrian lifted his hand and dropped it. "I rode in the day after it happened, or I would be a prisoner, too. I heard all about it from one of the residents of Sonoma, you understand, but I believe *Alcalde* Berreyesa is a reputable source of information."

Don Lucian struggled into the center of the men. "The *alcalde* is not hurt?"

"No one was hurt! The Americans just rode into Sonoma early one morning and took the post. Not a shot was fired."

Rico stammered, "How?"

"They rode in the back way," Hadrian explained. "No one was on lookout at Sonoma. What for? There's no war, and except for Mariano's home, it's not a rich place. There aren't even many guns."

"You said they took Mariano prisoner?" Damian reminded him. "Why him? Why Mariano? He's said that we must throw off Mexican domination. He has spoken out for annexation to the United States."

"Why any of this? They rode him away along with another seventeen citizens to Sutter at Nueva Helvetia. They tried to make it look official by drawing up documents of surrender, and they put up a flag."

"They're experts at putting up the American flag, aren't they?" Damian asked in exasperation.

"Oh, it's not an American flag," Hadrian corrected. "It's a flag they made themselves."

Damian cocked a brow at the undercurrent of amusement in Hadrian's voice.

Hadrian smothered a grin. "I saw it. The raiders call themselves the *Osos*—the Bears. So they got this white cloth, put a red stripe and a star on it. Someone drew a grizzly bear. He was not an artist." Hadrian chuckled, rubbing his side with his palm as if he had a stitch.

"No?" Damian encouraged.

"It looks like a pig." The crowd tittered, and Hadrian laughed out loud. "They wrote 'California Republic' on it and spelled 'Republic' wrong. They had to change it." He laughed some more. The crowd's hilarity died, but Hadrian's merriment grew all out of proportion. "I had to slip into Sonoma like a thief and leave like a hunted man because I held a gun. What has California come to?" His laughter stopped, cut by pain. "What has my home become?"

Damian wrapped both arms around him in a restraining hug, and Hadrian dropped his hands onto Damian's shoulder. Slumping against his friend, Hadrian mumbled, "Have I lost my home?"

Turning him away from the sympathetic faces, Damian asked, "How long have you been riding?"

"Forever, I think."

Damian signaled Julio. Julio stepped to Hadrian's other side and lifted an arm to his own shoulders. The three of them headed toward the hacienda.

"I rode to warn you not to marry your Katherine," Hadrian mumbled. "She's an American, and they're going to strip us of everything we own."

"Perhaps they are, but it was too late for me long ago."

Hadrian lifted his bleary eyes to the hacienda. "You say you fell in love with her on first sight, but that's no basis for a marriage. You have to have things in common. You have to have a common heritage."

Hadrian was tired, collapsing now that he'd delivered his message, and Damian gripped his temper. "I did fall in _love_ at first sight, but I fell in _like_ when I got to know her. We have many things in common, if not our heritage. For one thing, we both care for our friends, Hadrian, and you need to sleep."

"You're diluting your good Spanish blood with the blood of an enemy."

"So our sons will be leaders of a new part of the United States. Our daughters, too, for they'll be Katherine's daughters." Damian urged him up the stairs to the veranda.

"Katherine isn't part of a conspiracy," Julio added.

"No?" Hadrian asked groggily.

Damian said, "She's part of my fate."

The threesome stepped over the threshold and into the feminine world of wedding preparations. A few screams, a few scoldings followed them as they weaved towards the stairway. Damian ignored them. "Katherine is your friend, Hadrian. You know she is."

"Yes." The admission was dragged from the honest Hadrian.

"Most of the Americans are our friends." Julio sounded firm, like a man trying to convince himself.

Damian nodded. "The ones who aren't, the ones who have just arrived and make no attempt to honor our ways, Hadrian, those you should warn me against."

"Consider yourself warned." Hadrian lifted his legs as if each step were too high. Reaching the top, he twisted his hands against the newel post.

He didn't see Katherine, peeking out of Damian's upstairs study, but Damian did. He promptly forgot the American problem, Hadrian's exhaustion, his own distress. Enthralled, he stared at the golden woman beneath the mantilla. As Doña Xaviera had predicted, Katherine's creamy skin glowed beneath the black lace. The women had loosened her hair; it matched the silk of her dress in texture and color. Her smile was both enticing and shy, and she shone with the beauty of a bride—his bride.

He stepped toward her; she reached out her hand.

A ringed, beefy hand slapped onto her wrist, and Doña Xaviera's bulk placed itself between them. "This is not acceptable."

Julio gave a bark of laughter at Damian's frustration.

Damian complained, "First we send out the invitations, then we slave like animals getting the fiesta ready. I've hardly seen her for a week."

"Another few hours won't hurt." Doña Xaviera pushed the resisting Katherine back inside the room. "What you mean is, you haven't slept with her for a week. What your father permitted was scandalous."

"We were married," Damian insisted, disgruntled with the way everyone ignored the civil ceremony.

"Not in the Church!" Doña Xaviera shook her finger at him. "She is still Mrs. Maxwell."

"Katherine says she is Señora de la Sola." He leaned toward Doña Xaviera. "*You* tell her she isn't!"

Doña Xaviera backed up and her little grin popped out. "Not I."

Oblivious to the little scene, Hadrian said loudly, discordantly, "Damian, do you know what Mariano Vallejo said to his wife when the Americans marched him off to their prison? Do you know what he said?"

Damian glanced at the open door and sighed.

"He said, '*Quien llama el toro aguanta la cornada.*' "

From inside the study, Damian heard Katherine's voice translate the phrase into English. " 'He who calls the bull must endure the goring.' " She asked someone inside the room, "What have the Americans done now?"

Doña Xaviera shut the door, but Damian had no great faith that even that great woman could keep Katherine restrained within.

Loosening the bow that strangled him, Damian wondered desperately if the wedding ceremony he'd been afraid of would ever have a chance to begin. The American consul and his wife had arrived, but that hadn't freed them to start the wedding. It had created another barrier as the hidalgos crowded around Larkin and demanded explanations. The discussions had taken over the whole day, and the fiesta spirit was subdued as the men fretted.

Tactfully, Don Lucian tried to frame the question on all of their minds without insulting his friend Larkin's nationality or honesty. "The Americanos have different traditions than we do. Not long ago, a group of them insinuated they could take my property by staying on it. Squatting, they called it."

Alejandro blurted, "Will the American government respect our land grants?"

Larkin tapped his fingers on the desk where he sat. "I believe so."

"Pardon me, Señor Larkin, if I lack confidence in this assurance." Damian shook his head. "We have heard that Americanos stole two hundred horses, that they imprisoned one of our prominent citizens and confiscated his property. These are not actions designed to make us feel secure."

A feminine voice broke through the babble that followed his comments. "Don Damian is right, Mr. Larkin." Katherine stepped into the library, glorious in her wedding finery. The shocked men cleared a path for her, a path that led straight to Damian and Larkin. "What are the Americans thinking about? Is this all the work of Mr. Frémont?"

Larkin answered her with ease. "I don't think so, Mrs. Maxwell."

"Señora de la Sola," she corrected.

"Has the wedding already taken place?" Larkin asked. "I thought I was here to officiate."

"You're to officiate at our second wedding."

"Of course." Larkin nodded, calm and precise. "As far as I'm able to ascertain, Mr. Frémont had nothing to do with the regrettable incident at Sonoma, but I fear I recognize his method of planning."

"None at all?" Damian asked bitterly, remembering the aborted battle at Gavilán.

"He plans, but recklessly and with no dependence on his informants. He's made no attempt to contact me."

"*Will* the American government respect these land grants?" Katherine demanded, her mobile mouth serious. "Except for your own conduct, I've seen nothing to admire in American handling of California. Let me speak bluntly, Mr. Larkin. Will a Spanish name on the title put the de la Sola possessions in jeopardy?"

Larkin hesitated.

"Would an American name be more likely to secure the lands?"

"That is a possibility," Larkin allowed.

Katherine turned to Damian and Don Lucian. "I have an alternative. Put your family lands into my name."

An excited babble broke out. "That's foolish," Ricky protested. "You're a woman."

Katherine turned clear green eyes on him. "I'm an American citizen. Throughout the American West, women own property. With the legal and economic training I've had, and the considerable monetary backing of the de la Solas, only an idiot would try to take these lands away from *me*. What do you think, Mr. Larkin?"

Larkin rubbed his bewhiskered cheeks. "Well, it is a solution to a tricky situation. Mind you, I don't know if it would work, but I believe it's a good idea."

As one, the room turned and stared at the de la Sola men. Don Lucian nodded, but Damian stood frozen in place. He felt again as he had after he'd been shot. His skin felt stiff and pale, his eyes wide and staring.

This was his family's lands they discussed so casually. *His* family's lands. How could they suggest such a thing? How could his father stand there and indicate agreement?

His Californio lands.

They would be Katherine's lands. Seventy-five years of masculine Californio pride would be ground into dust. What kind of man would he be, living on his wife's charity? He would owe her everything.

Katherine was a strong-minded woman. She had indicated that she believed a woman could survive and thrive without the care of a man. Could he trust this American woman to marry him and not destroy his dignity by reminding him how much he owed her? He didn't know another woman he could trust so far.

His gaze was caught by a glow in the room. It was Katherine.

Golden hair, golden dress, golden woman. His treasure. In a rush he remembered her pride. She'd agreed to marry him, regardless of Smith's insinuations, accepting that he wouldn't take advantage of her.

How could he give her less trust than she'd given him?

"Draw up the papers," he told Larkin. "My wife's going to become a landowner today."

Señora Katherine Anne Chamberlain Maxwell, soon to be the newest rancher in California, clung to her father-in-law's arm and laughed at the good-natured teasing. She'd never seen a wedding procession as informal as this one. Don Lucian followed a circuitous route to the guests who ranged all over the yard. No one was solemn. The men predicted Damian's subjugation at the least, the fall of civilization at the most. The women asked her if she would charge her husband rent, or kick him out during a fight. They seemed to relish it all, using the occasion to jab their husbands.

She didn't answer. Her attention was fixed on the bower under the trees. There Damian, Fray Pedro, Mr. Larkin and *Alcalde* Diaz waited. That was where she wanted to be. She wanted to speak her vows, to tell Damian how she felt about him, to make love with him. Like a veil lifting, she could see into the future. See the years of sleeping together, serving each other, adapting to each other until they were the one entity the romantics spoke of.

She knew what it would cost him to sign his lands over to her. He was a hidalgo, a Spaniard, a man, and he trusted her with everything that was his. Once he'd made the decision to deed her the lands, his main concern had been the speed with which the papers could be drawn up. They were ready, waiting in the study for their signatures, but right now Damian wanted to get married.

She wanted it, too.

Each moment she waited stretched her temper. This delay

had gone on long enough. Deciding her geniality had been extended beyond its limits, she tugged at Don Lucian, subtly at first, then with greater energy. "Come on," she demanded, "or I'll go by myself."

"She's giving the orders even before the ownership has been transferred," Ricky teased. "Watch yourself, Don Lucian. Soon you'll be serving her dinner, dressed in an apron."

"It would be an honor," Don Lucian said with gallant good nature. He raised his eyebrows significantly as he stumbled sideways under her propulsion. "I have to go now."

They stepped out, moving in the direct line that she set. When she heard the galloping hooves and the shout, "Katherine," she only increased her speed.

"Katherine!"

She swung around. Lawrence Cyril Chamberlain brought his prancing horse to a halt only a few feet from her and dismounted in a tumbling haste. "Am I in time?"

"You're in time to see me wed." Her chill should have warned him.

"Katherine, you can't do this."

She wanted to shout at him, but instead she stared at Lawrence. His colorful clothes no longer matched, as if he'd mixed the remnants of his Boston wardrobe with apparel bought in California. His tall hat and red toupee had disappeared. His nose had been broken, its elegant hook knocked sideways. Worst of all, he was sunburned, his fair skin peeling in flakes. Benignly, she asked, "Who do you think's going to stop me?"

Lawrence blinked. "Why, I am."

Still in a voice of rationality and moderation, she asked, "Do you think you can follow me around, badger me, kidnap me, and still influence me to return to Boston?"

Desperately ignoring the interested group that surrounded him, he heaved a shaky sigh. "Can't you see this is no place for a gently bred woman? Look at what it's done to me."

She pressed her lips together to curb her smile. "It's done nothing like that to me."

"Yes, well . . . you do look appallingly healthy." Glancing around, he took her arm and tried to lead her away. "I didn't want to tell you before, but Father said to promise you anything if you would return. Please, Katherine, we would treat you like a queen. I guarantee it."

She shook her head. "Lawrence . . ."

"Don't say no. Please come. You must know I can't return until I bring you. Don't you feel sorry for me?"

"I always have, but I still won't come back."

He glared, but it had no effect. The Californios pressed closer, and he whispered, "This isn't your home. These aren't your people."

"Lawrence . . ."

As the pity in her voice deepened, his own voice rose. "They're all mean and horrible."

The sympathy she felt for Lawrence melted, and she warned, "Lawrence."

He didn't read her correctly, too agitated by their audience and his own looming failure. "They're crude and ignorant, with their horses and their misplaced arrogance. They're—" he waved his arms, searching in the air for the right word "—they're barbarians."

She took the tattered remains of his cravat in her hand. With a slow and steady pressure, she pulled him down to her eye level. "Barbarians are people who exploit their helpless relatives. California is my home. Californios are my clan. And Don Damian de la Sola is my love. You can go back to Boston and tell my uncle and aunt I'm never coming back. Or stay here, if you're too afraid of your parents, but stay away from me."

Warm arms caught her from behind and spun her. Damian laughed down at her, bright with joy. "You love me."

"Of course." The pleasure in his face brought tears to her eyes. "Didn't you know it?"

"Yes." He lifted her and swung her in a circle until all the blood rushed to her head and her laughter joined his. "Yes, I always knew it."

She'd said it at last. She loved him, and as loudly as she was shouting, there wasn't anyone who didn't know.

Putting her down, he invited, "Let's go get married."

She tucked her hand in his. "Let's go get married."

30 June, in the year of our Lord, 1777

I am sending the others away. I am sending this diary to Fray Pedro de Jesus. I am sending Fray Lucio back to the mission.

He will arrive, I know it. That is God's plan for him.

For me? God's plan is more complex, more circuitous. I will stay here in this cave until I die. My leg is gangrenous. I, of all people, recognize the signs. There is no doubt. The poison pumps through my system and an odor grows from the ulcer where the muscle and bone are clearly visible.

Yet even now, in my defeat, my trampled pride stirs. What other person would be strong enough to bear what I must bear? Whom God loves, He chastises. Light a candle for my soul, little brother, for I'll long be in Purgatory for my sins.

Would that I had a chance to redeem them.

Thus ends the first attempt to convert the Indians of the interior. I fear no other expedition will be sent unless my brothers return and retrieve the gold the Indians brought us. Greed is an evil that can be turned to good; when we bring the treasure forth from its resting place, we will surely be allowed to return and continue God's work. I wait for that day. I will always wait for that day.

—*from the diary of Fray Juan Estévan de Bautista*

Chapter 26

As Katherine crossed the porch, she heard Fray Pedro de Jesus call, "My daughter."

He sat in the cool shadow in a chair with a footstool. A plate of food sat untouched at his elbow.

She sank down on the stool beside his feet. "Yes, Padre?"

Adjusting his spectacles over his ears, he said, "My daughter, I found more joy in the ceremony I just performed than in any other in my long life."

She smiled. "I told you we would wed as soon as we could."

"So you did." He chuckled. "So you did. But I sent you to a place that many men have found a tomb, and I didn't know if you would be able to marry. I prayed for you and for Damian after you left me, knowing that if you died, you would die in a state of grace, yet not wanting the blossom of your love cut down in its youth."

Leaning forward, she wrapped him in her arms. "Thank you, Padre."

His wrinkled head dropped onto her shoulder, and she realized how much he'd pushed himself to leave San Juan Bautista to marry them.

His body was bony beneath the cassock and he shook with a fine tremor. "I knew my prayers had been answered when God spoke in my ear. He told me that . . . Fray Juan Estévan had been redeemed and laid to rest. Is that true?"

She stared at the old man, at his big brown eyes, so sad and wise. "I believe it is."

"Bless you." He squeezed her hand hard and sat back. A tear trickled down his cheek. "All these years, I have been lighting candles for my brother, hoping he would see his way."

She handed him her handkerchief, and he snuffled into it. "Your brother?"

"My brother in Christ," he clarified.

"I couldn't help but wonder . . . you seemed to understand this long-dead man. He came to you after his death. And coincidentally, you both came from Majorca." She watched him, a half smile on her face. "He was your brother in truth, wasn't he?"

The old man fumbled, coughing. "When we take our vows, we renounce the world. Everyone becomes our brother." He peeked at her and sighed. "You appear to be unconvinced. Very well. Yes, Fray Juan Estévan was my brother."

"You don't resemble each other at all," she said, remembering the spirit in the sickroom. "Except for the light in your eyes."

He leaned forward, his gaze sharp. "Have you seen him?"

Biting her lip, Katherine wished she had never mentioned her suspicions, but nothing could get past Fray Pedro. He'd had too many years of reading faces.

"I see you have."

She leaned forward and whispered, "I used to be plagued with nightmares. Nightmares filled with blood and death and corpses of those I love. I haven't had a nightmare since I saw him."

Beaming as if she'd given the ultimate praise, he said, "He wasn't a bad man, you know. Only proud."

"Did you say he was a curandero?" she asked thoughtfully.

Fray Pedro nodded. "Yes, indeed."

She kissed his hand and rose. "Light a candle of thanksgiving, Padre. Fray Juan Estévan de Bautista is indeed at rest."

Greeting the guests as she entered the hacienda, she climbed the stairs to her room and shut the door behind her. She reached under the bed and pulled out the cowhide bag Julio had brought up onto the mountainside. Holding it with care, she entered the attic and found Tobias's trunk. She knelt beside it. Pulling the leather strapping loose, flipping the latches, she opened it.

Inside were the rocks Tobias had saved, the newspapers, his watch-working instruments. She touched them all with tender hands. Reaching inside the bag, she pulled out the intricate silver watch she'd worn as a memory of him. One last time, she wound it up. Still it wouldn't work, and so without accompaniment she sang,

"He was laid to rest in the lower chancel,
Barbara Allen all in the higher;
There grew up a rose from Barbara Allen's breast,
And from his a briar. . . ."

She shut the watch. Wrapping it carefully in the papers, she nestled it in the toolbox.

From the bag she next pulled out a tattered brown book. She wiped the dirt from it and opened it. The scrawl of a man long dead met her eyes. As she leafed through the fragile pages, she saw that some of the entries were written with ink, some with a native substitute, but all were signed with the slashing signature —*Fray Juan Estévan de Bautista.*

"Katherine?"

She heard Damian summon her from the bedroom, and she hurried to place the diary beside the watch. She shut the chest, locked it, called, "I'll be right out." Maybe someday one of her granddaughters would find the trunk and all its booty. She didn't begrudge that unknown girl the adventures that would result, but her own adventure had just begun.

In the attic room, she found Damian frowning over the

burned mark on the window sill. "We'll have to have this sanded and painted."

She touched the rough black his cigar had left that night he'd come to her. Mixed in her mind was the stench of smoldering paint, the amber glow of Damian's naked body, the emotions he made her feel that night, his demands for honesty. That night was the end of her old life, the beginning of her new life. That night marked her reawakening, with its pains and confusions and sweet, sensuous joys.

Watching her finger as it stroked the scorched line of his last cigar, she said, "I think I'd like to leave it here."

His hand closed over the top of hers. "We'll see it every night before we go to bed." She gazed up at him. "Our children will ask us about it every time they look out the window."

"Will they?"

"If we're to use this as our bedroom." He grinned into her eyes.

"Are we?"

"I think so."

"Yes. For the time we are here, we'll use this as our bedroom." Her own smile blossomed. "That's why I had your clothing moved up here earlier today."

He caught her around the waist and pulled her against him. "What will we tell our children when they ask?"

Hooking his arm around her neck, he said sternly, "We'll lie."

Laughing, she leaned into his chest. "I've been thinking. Do you think we could go to live in your home in the Sacramento Valley?"

"Hmm." He leaned over her neck and breathed deeply. "You smell wonderful."

"It's close to Nueva Helvetia, you said, and that will protect against any Indian attack."

He nibbled her skin and whispered close against her ear, "They're a danger, but yes, Sutter's presence would probably protect us."

His hand pressed her hips up to his, and she squirmed against him. "We'd never have to be bothered by gold again." Her voice dropped as her control slipped.

"God, no. Never again." Damian leaned back and smiled at her, tugging at the comb that held her hair. "All the gold I want is right here. Our treasure is our lands and our heritages."

Daringly, she added, "And each other."

He caught her mouth in an approving kiss. His palm no longer burned through her skirt with its hard pressure; now her body fought to get closer to him, fought the restraint of her petticoats and moved against his hips. Right now, the press of his body against hers filled her with a pleasure only equalled by the press of his lips against hers. He lifted her in his arms, carried her to the bed. "My wife," he said hoarsely.

She threw her arms around his neck and pulled him down with her as he laid her on the mattress. "Yes, and Damian?"

"Hmm?" As her use of his first name, and only his first name, penetrated his lustful daze, he jerked his gaze to hers. "What did you call me?"

How foolish to feel shy now. So much had happened between them; they'd faced so much together. Yet, the words wouldn't come. She couldn't maintain her smile; it kept slipping away beneath his serious mien. He waited; she cleared her throat. "Damian?" she squeaked. "Damian."

"*Al fin!*" he sighed.

"At last?"

In his characteristic gesture, he stroked his mustache. "Does this mean I have at last reached a plateau above the one occupied by your hero, John Charles Frémont?"

She pushed his hand away and ran her fingers along the trimmed edge at his upper lip. "There's room for only one hero in my life."

"And who might that be?" He chased her fingers with a kiss.

"The man who thought I was worth more than treasure and gave his childhood dreams to keep me safe."

"I'll always keep you safe," he vowed. His fervency that brought tears to her eyes, and his light touch along the scar at her throat contrasted with the weight of his body on hers. "I have you now, and God willing, I'll keep you. Pray that you never want out of our marriage, for I have wed you in a ceremony blessed by every agency in California and heaven."

"Damian." She savored the word, like a new flavor on her tongue. "Damian, surely California and heaven are synonymous."